My Bonsai Tribe

My Bonsai Tribe

A Novel Set in the Philippines

DOROTEA F. ROMERO

ISBN-13: 978-1505219470
ISBN-10: 1505219477

Cover: Emile Sanchez

For my children and grandchildren -

I took many roads trying to find myself...

But I wasn't there on any of them
Except on that one path that led to you.

CONTENTS

PART I

1959 – 1973

CHAPTER 1

"You're kidding," I said, grabbing the doll. "And Elsie is my doll!"

Chona yanked the doll back, laid its back on the floor and jiggled its legs. "Her legs up in the air, shaking like so."

"Why did she do that?"

"And then Daddy put the Johnson's Baby Powder tin beside the oil lamp. Then he crawled back inside the mosquito net."

"But why?" I said

"It made it darker, but I saw him get on top of her," my sister said, picking the grime from her toenails. "Here, smell this. Yum-yum, like *chicharon.*"

Expecting the aroma of crispy pork rind, I sniffed her finger. "Yikes!" I said, crinkling my nose and pulling away. "That smells like stale rice!"

She giggled and pushed her finger closer to my face. "I'm telling you," she said. "I saw..."

"Whaat? I don't know what you're saying."

"You were fast asleep," she said.

"You're a liar!" I said, picked up Elsie and dashed out of the room. Chona chased me and I ran faster.

3

Halfway down the stairs, I fell five or six steps to the concrete floor. I lay there stunned and then started screaming. Mommy came rushing, picked me up and carried me to the sofa. "What happened, *anak ko*?" she said. "Where does it hurt?"

My upper cheek hurt and I could feel warm liquid on my lips. I pointed to my cheek and touched my lips. When I saw blood on my hands, I screamed harder. Mommy cradled me in her arms and wiped my hands. "Don't touch it, okay? It will be fine. Now just sit here and I'll be back."

She left me for a few moments and when she came back, she brought *tawwa* leaves that she had pounded into a balm. It hurt when she applied the cool mush on my cheek. "Just a bruise here, it will be okay," she said. "I can't use this on your lip. Let's just leave it alone. It's only a small cut."

I couldn't stop crying.

A few nights later, I snuggled under my mother's armpit and rubbed her hard, swollen belly. "Mommy," I said, "how will the baby come out?" She was lying on her back on the reed mat on the floor, between my older sister Chona and me.

"Something will open up right here," she said, pointing below her belly button. "Then the doctor will take the baby out."

I rubbed her stomach some more and then slid my hand up and under her neckline where it felt soft and warm. When I found one of her nipples, I twisted it between my thumb and first finger.

"Don't hurt me now, *anak ko*," Mommy said. "And remember, when I start nursing the baby, you'll have to stop doing that."

"Yes, you'll be a big sister," Chona said. "You're not a baby – you're five."

"But, Mommy," I said, "Will I still be your *anak*?"

Mommy stroked my hair and said, "Of course, you'll always be my child. Both of you."

"When's the baby coming out?"

"August," Chona said. "Two months from now. Will you take

him to Daniw with you?"

"No," Mommy said. "I'll be here to nurse the baby for three months. Then I'll go back to teach in Daniw. Wait..." She got up to tuck in a corner of the mosquito net under the mat and pulled my cotton blanket up to my chest. It was newly starched, and it felt rough and itchy and smelled of the sun. My pillow also smelled of the sun tonight; my mother had washed the pillowcases and sunned the pillows on a tin sheet. I liked my blanket and pillow better when they weren't fresh; they felt cozier. And I couldn't wait for the baby to come out so Mommy's belly would be softer for snuggling again.

"I'll be here every weekend though, just like now," Mommy said, patting my thigh. "When you were a baby, I took you to Daniw with me, but you got sick there when the village kids had the measles. I don't want that to happen to the new baby."

"What's measles?" I said.

"Why not teach at Central?" Chona said. "Close to our house, just like Auntie Celina."

"Sshh... sleep now..."

My town Montaña, close to the northern tip of the Philippines, is ringed by rice paddies against the foot of the blue Cordillera Mountains. We lived near the edge of the main village, a grid of five paved streets and seven dirt roads, in a house that belonged to my grandmother. The two-storey house sat on the front end of a large property along Rizal Street, one of the paved streets, and looked like many of the other houses in town: dark hardwood, tin roofing and window shutters of etched glass.

I shared an upstairs bedroom with Chona and Manang Zenay, a cousin who lived with us and did most of the chores. Her father, Mommy's older brother, was a farmer who raised his big family in a faraway village. I had to address her as *manang*, the Ilocano word for big sister, because she was family and already in college. No one slept on the small iron bed by a window. We all slept on a mat on the floor, under a big mosquito net hung on nails on the bare walls. I woke up to the cocks' crows and the flutter of their wings, as they flew down from their roosts in the mango trees, and to the grating sound of Manang Zenay's broomstick as she swept the leaves from the yard.

In my town, and all of Ilocos Norte province, you were considered lazy if you were still asleep by sunrise. This day, as usual, I got up last and called Manang Zenay upstairs. She came up, broom and coconut husk in hand, and took down the mosquito net while I folded my blanket. We stacked the blankets, pillows and net on the tall open shelf in the corner, next to Mommy's dresser. My cousin rolled up the big mat, tucked it behind the shelf and started sweeping the floor.

"Manang," I said. "You just did that last evening, why are you doing it again?"

"Look at the dust that's settled overnight," she said. She swept to the door, then walked to the far corner of the room and set her coconut husk like a dome on the hardwood floor. I had watched my uncle fashion the floor scrubber out of a fresh coconut. He had cut the coconut crosswise with a saw, saved the juice and the flesh to make into candy, and sun-dried the two half-shells with the husks intact. Then with a hammer, he chipped off a bit of the shell at the rim to make sure that when the shell was used as a brush, only its husk touched the floor.

Taking off her rubber slippers and with her right foot, Manang Zenay pushed the coconut dome down against the floor, her leg going forward and back, forward and back. One foot inched sideways, while she scrubbed with the other leg. Her arms swayed as she did this, as if she was doing a dance. The floor shone when she was finished. I didn't like it when she scrubbed too much, because I'd slipped a few times before. Daddy had said it wasn't the floor but that I should've walked carefully.

The chore of putting away my pillow and blanket done with, I climbed the iron bed, the metal mosquito-net rods rattling with each move I made. Kneeling, I rested my forearms on the rough windowsill. The sun was just creeping up from behind Pecho, the nearest among the layers of mountains to the east. Pecho was dark green but the mountains behind it were blue. Daddy said it was so named because it was shaped like a woman's breast. Bands of orange and yellow framed the peaks, and the sky grew paler as the sun rose. When the glare became too much, I looked down to the yard below. Manang Zenay had made a bonfire out of the dead leaves. I hated the smell of smoke, but they said it made for more fruit on the betel nut palms, the coconut, cacao, pomegranate, mango, *chico*, and avocado trees. I worried about what the smoke did to all the pretty flowers, though – the oleander and bougainvillea in pink and white, the plumerias up on the trees, and the thorny *escarlatina* with the tiny red flowers, standing guard atop the gateposts.

Besides the hissing of the bonfire, I could hear the neighbors sweeping their yards and chickens cackling. Finally, I heard the sound I was eager for – the baker's son's shrill call of *"Pan de sal!"* as he walked around town with a wicker basket of fresh, hot buns on his shoulder. When I saw Mommy go out the gate, I got off my perch. Downstairs, I leapt over the sunbeams on the red-and-green concrete floor, rushed out to the front porch and ran the short gravel path to the gate. "Wait until we get inside," my mother said when I tried to grab one of the mouth-watering buns.

"Mommy," I said, thinking of the blue can of cheddar that Daddy had brought home from Manila the week before, "I want it with Kraft."

"The cheese is gone, my child," she said. "We only have Star margarine today."

I loved it when Mommy was home, like today. She always spread margarine on my *pan de sal* and made me hot chocolate.

After lunch, Mommy had Chona and me take a nap on the living room floor. My grandmother, whom we simply called *Lola* – the Ilocano word for grandma – crocheted in her rocking chair at our feet, a warm breeze ruffling her sleeves. When I awoke, Auntie Celina lay on the sofa reading *Women's Magazine*, her head on

Ninang Florie's lap. Ninang Florie was my godmother, so I called her *ninang*. She was also the town's doctor. Ninang stroked Auntie Celina's hair, and both of them giggled. I ran to the porch hoping to find Chona playing with our cousins who lived next door. I saw only Ninang Florie's jeep parked on the gravel path. Chona wasn't there.

"Auntie, where's Chona?" I said.

"Your mother's getting her ready," Auntie Celina said. "She's coming with us to your *ninang's* house." Ninang's house was in the capital town Laoag, but she slept in Auntie Celina's room during the week. Manang Zenay said Auntie Celina and Ninang Florie were each other's darlings.

I thought, Again? Ninang said they needed a child of their own, so they often borrowed my sister on Saturdays. Chona always came back with stories of new places she'd seen and delicious foods they'd eaten. I wished to see those places, too, and taste all that food, but they never took me along, and Mommy said she didn't have the money for those things.

After the three left, Mommy went to water the plants. The pigs grunted in the backyard, and I knew that Lola was approaching the sty with a pail of fodder. Daddy wasn't there; Mommy said he was out with his friends. Feeling left out, I ran upstairs into Auntie Celina's room, climbed her bed and jumped over and over. Then I got off and tried to lift the straw mattress. It was heavier than I'd thought. I pushed, and it moved a little. I pushed harder. Climbed the bed and pushed until the mattress fell off, knocking down a framed picture on the night table – Auntie Celina and Ninang Florie on a horse by the river, Ninang in *toreador* pants, holding the reins behind my smiling aunt.

When Mommy discovered the mess, she called me and said, "What a temper you have, child. Help me put these back so I won't tell your father."

I said I was sorry, but Daddy came home before we could put the room back in place. "What's this?" he said. "You had a tantrum again?"

I went behind Mommy and clung to her skirt. She was picking up the picture frame. She started to say something but Dad took me by the arm to the other room. Picking up his leather slipper, he said, "How many times do I have to tell you not to touch your aunt's things?"

I shut my eyes tight, knowing what was coming. Once the slipper hit my butt, I started to bawl.

"No crying! Do you hear?"

I didn't know how to not cry and kept bawling. Afraid of another whack, I tried hard to keep any sound from coming out of my mouth. When I was down to sobs, Daddy pulled me onto his lap and had me kiss his cheek, and then the other. "Good girl," he said. "Good girl."

I was happy to have my parents all to myself to cuddle up to that night. Daddy hugged me from behind, which was wonderful, because he felt more cushiony than Mommy. I fell asleep with my mother's nipple between my fingers. The next morning, Mommy roused me. "Church bells. Get up."

After mass, I went with my mother to market in Laoag and tried to keep up with her brisk waddle. I helped her find firm melons with coarse, webbed skin, but because she told me not to touch the meat, I just waited for her to haggle for a long time with the vendors. Before we headed home, she bought me a box of raisins saying it was all mine, no need to share with Chona. Because Mommy's cooking tasted better than Manang Zenay's, I loved Sunday lunch the best. Pork *adobo*, liver *higado* and rice fried in the drippings. Sweet, finely shredded cabbage sautéed in a lot of lard. Crushed melons with milk and sugar for dessert.

Auntie Celina brought Chona home for lunch but had her eat at their table. In that house, we had two dining tables. "Simpler to have two pots," Daddy said. Lola cooked the other pot – for Auntie Celina, Ninang Florie and herself. When Chona saw that we had melons, she crossed over to our table. I stuck my tongue out at her when Daddy gave me his share.

After the meal, Chona didn't want to play with me so I sat at the dining table with crayons and a coloring book. Manang Zenay went to the backyard, gathered Mommy's clothes from the clothesline and ironed them. Mommy packed a box with some of the *adobo* and *higado* and then put her clothes in a bag.

"Mommy, don't go," I said.

"*Anak ko*," she said and carried me in her arms. "I have to earn money to buy us food."

I tugged at her round earring. She had dusted herself with baby powder and some of it had gotten stuck in her ear and on the edges of her little nose. She smelled fresh. "You have too much powder," I said.

"I'll be back again Friday night," she said, kissing me then putting me down. Rubbing the trace of red lipstick on my cheek, she told me it was a long walk to Daniw, and her group didn't want to be caught on the road by nightfall. That the river was swift and swollen from the rains, and since there was no bridge, it was not easy to cross the water.

After Daddy left with my mother to carry her things and help her across the river, I went upstairs to her dresser and played with her pink crystal powder case. A fawn stood on its lid that I called Bambi. I lifted Bambi carefully and sniffed inside the smell of my mother.

Chona had just started Grade One that year. I was left alone with Lola during the day. Daddy was teaching at a college in Laoag and Manang Zenay was at school. Auntie Celina and Ninang Florie were also at work. Lola taught me how to read, and I loved the comics section of the local weekly magazine *Bannawag*. A while later, I went on to the no-picture stories. Or else, I kept to my coloring books.

A few weeks later, I awoke to footsteps in my parents' bedroom. Muffled voices in the dark. I got up and walked out the door. Daddy was in the hallway, pumping the Coleman kerosene lamp to life. "Go back to sleep," he said. "Your mom's having the baby now."

I wanted to go to my parents' room but lay back down on the mat as Daddy had told me. I heard Ninang Florie's voice, Lola's too, as well as Auntie Celina's. When I got up in the morning, Daddy was snoring next to me. My parents' door was closed.

Down in the kitchen, Chona was sipping hot cocoa before a plateful of *pan de sal*. Manang Zenay asked me what I wanted. "What's that bad smell?" I said.

"Oh, that's your baby brother's *kadkadua*," Manang Zenay said.

"I have a baby brother?" I said and smiled. I had secretly wished for one.

"Yes," she said. "Your dad is overjoyed. He'll name him Francis."

"Francis... can I go and see him?"

"No, Mommy is tired," Chona said. "The baby is asleep, too. Later."

I wrinkled my nose and said, "What's *kadkadua*?"

Manang Zenay said, "The chunk of flesh that comes out after the baby. It's attached to the baby's belly button."

"Hmm," I said. "Can I see it?"

"In the backyard pit," Chona said, grinning. "Barbecue."

"We'll bury it after it burns," my cousin said.

"I hate the smell," I said but ran outside to the pit. The *kadkadua* looked like the slabs of pig flesh that they'd roasted in the pit after slaughtering one of Lola's pigs at Christmas. Only it was thicker, and it really smelled bad.

Francis's skin was brown, the color of ripe tamarinds. He had chubby cheeks, wide eyes, and no hair. A big dimple appeared in the middle of his left cheek when he cooed and grimaced. I watched Mommy clean the lump on his belly button and give him a quick bath in a basin on the dining table. I asked her if I was also born in her bed and if I also had a *kadkadua*.

"Yes, of course," she said, "but I had a harder time. You were a bigger baby. I had pains for ten hours, longer than with Francis. When at last you came out, the cord was wrapped around your neck. You had swallowed and inhaled a lot of mucus, and no matter how hard your Ninang Florie slapped your butt, you refused to cry."

"Why did she want to make me cry?" I said.

"So you'd breathe in some air. Your *ninang* had nothing in her bag to take out the mucus, so she sucked your nose with her mouth."

"Yucky."

"Don't say that. Most women are helped only by a midwife. Be thankful your *ninang* is a doctor. You could have died."

I was happy to have Mommy home each day, even if she was busy with the baby. I stayed close to her, watching her fasten the diapers with big safety pins, massage the baby's legs so he'd not grow up bow-legged, give him her breasts and lull him to sleep. When Francis napped, Mommy sometimes read me English fairy tales from comic books that Daddy had brought home from trips to Manila, and then we'd nap together. She ate a lot of stewed *marunggay*, dark green leaves that she said made for more milk at her breasts. Also clams and chicken soup. She always gave me a chicken thigh. At night, she cuddled me on the mat – her belly soft as a pillow once more – and left to be with Francis in her bed only after I fell asleep.

One hot Sunday, Chona and I were at the backyard well splashing water on each other, while Manang Zenay kept watch over us with Francis in her arms. I saw my mother come out of the storage shed with a box. I left Chona and dried off. Mommy was packing some leftovers in the box.

"Why, Mommy?" I said.

"I have to go back to Daniw, *anak ko*," she said.

"No!"

I sat there watching her every move. When her teacher friends arrived to fetch her, she picked me up and squeezed me tight. Then Chona and Francis. I started to cry. Mommy cried, too.

Chona and I stood at the door and watched Daddy, Mommy and her friends walk out the gate. Once their backs disappeared at the bend, I ran up to Auntie Celina's room and struggled to overturn her mattress.

CHAPTER 2

When Daddy took the lid off his rectangular tin of Colonial pomade, the smell hurt my nose. With his black Ace comb, he scooped out some of the green goo and slathered it on his straight, black hair, making it slick and shiny. Then he combed his hair backwards, stroke after stroke. When every strand was in place, his face looked like a roundish heart – wide forehead, jagged eyebrows, slight smile – and I thought he looked like a movie star. I wanted to touch his hair to see if it was sticky, like the way I wanted to know if Mommy's curls felt soft, but I didn't because Lola said it was not respectful for a child to touch a grown-up's head.

"I'm going to Manila, *anak ko*," he said.

"Will you bring home some *sangkis*?" I said, thinking of the sweet, juicy fruit with *Sunkist* stamped on its orange skin that weren't in the local stores. My mouth watered.

"Sure." He brushed his brown and white leather shoes and his gray suitcase.

"Daddy, when are you coming back?"

"I'll be on the de Leon on Saturday. Your mom will be home Friday."

It was only Tuesday. Good, I thought, many days without a scolding.

The de Leon was the one bus in Montaña that ran the overnight trip to and from Manila. It left town on alternate days and picked up passengers from their homes. When the bus came by to pick up Daddy, he made Chona and me promise to be good girls.

The farmers who worked the rice fields close to our house were on their way home now, in mud-caked bare feet, their water buffaloes trailing them. I envied their children who walked through the fields without soiling their feet by balancing on the *tambak* – little walls of earth that divided the land into square paddies. I was tempted to go and try to do it myself, even if Daddy didn't allow us to go there, saying the place was full of worms and bugs. He was gone anyway, but I wanted to be a good girl, so I didn't.

When I woke up Saturday morning, everyone was gathered around Daddy in the living room. They were fussing over a black-and-yellow plastic box on the coffee table. Daddy held something black that looked like a thin dinner plate and laid it on the center of the box.

"What's that?" I said.

"It's a phonograph, my little girl," he said and flicked a switch. The disk spun slowly.

"Like a jukebox?" I said, my eyes wide.

"Chiribiribin…," a woman's high-pitched voice rose from the record. Daddy led Mommy to the middle of the living room. While our parents danced, Chona and I watched the record spin. Manang Zenay, with Francis on her lap, went through the stack of records on the table. My jaw dropped when I saw one labeled *Mother Goose Nursery Rhymes*.

"Daddy," I said, "can we try this please?"

Sing a Song of Sixpence, Baa Baa Black Sheep. I also found a record with *Cinderella* on one side and *Jack and the Beanstalk* on the other. Although the English words sounded different from the way I heard my parents say them, I was thrilled to listen.

For mass the next day, Mommy dressed Chona and me alike – red dresses, socks and hair bows. On the walk home, a lady said behind us, "Are they twins?"

Mommy turned and said, "No, they're a year apart."

When Chona and I also turned, the lady said, "Oh yes, this one's so pretty, looks like you." She pinched my sister's cheek, then she looked at me and said, "And this one looks like her father."

I didn't like what the lady said. I wanted to be pretty, too, to look like Mommy. I started walking faster. Mommy called out my name, but I kept walking. After a block, I looked back and saw Mommy chatting with the lady. I ran the two more blocks home. When I walked in the door, I kissed Lola's hand and Daddy's cheek. He asked where Mommy was, and I told him she was right behind me.

"When will you learn to listen?" he said and reached for his leather slipper. I trembled as I waited for the slipper to hit my butt. He did it swiftly. It hurt, but I didn't cry.

"That should remind you that it's not safe to walk alone. And your *lola* tells me that when I was away, you stole fruit from her cacao tree. Is that the right thing to do?"

"No, Daddy." I closed my eyes and my fists.

Another hit.

"Let me see," he said and peeled down my underpants. "Does it hurt?"

And then I cried. Ate breakfast silently. Upstairs I read my *Ten Commandments* book: "Honor thy father and thy mother." Mommy said that it was a bad child who did not obey her parents. Ashamed of doing something bad right after mass, I tried to be good the rest of the morning. I followed my mother around, knowing that after lunch, she was going to leave again.

"Mommy, why can't I go to school?" I said.

"You're too young," Chona said. "When you're seven like me, you'll be in school."

The two schools in Montaña started at Grade One, no kindergarten. The following school year, Mommy told me I was going to Holy Ghost in Laoag, where they had kindergarten. Daddy drove me to school in his army-type jeep. The school was much bigger than Chona's school – two stories and L-shaped, with the nuns living at one end. It had many more pupils, too, all the way up to high school. I had the most fun answering the teacher's arithmetic flash cards, usually coming up with the right answer before the other girls. Daddy drilled me this way at home, too, but without cards.

After class one afternoon, I waited for my father at the usual spot by the school gate. Other girls' parents came to fetch them one by one. When there were just a few girls left, my palms began to sweat. Then I was all alone. To my right, the giant doors of Saint William's Cathedral were shut. I faced a wide square and imagined shadows creeping out of the brick belfry up ahead. Very soon, it would be dark. I remembered the stories about headless nuns that roamed the school grounds at night and didn't dare look behind me.

I ran through my head what Daddy had told me to do if I needed to leave the school alone: "Hail a buggy and ask the coachman to take you to Texicano Hotel. Your Ninang Florie's house is right next door, to the west." I felt for the coins in my pocket. I had ten centavos, just enough for the ride. A buggy came by, but I didn't flag it down. Over and over, the clop-clop of horses' hooves came near and then faded out, but I just stood there.

Daddy finally came, got out of his jeep and took my hand. "I was playing *mah jong* with my friends and lost track of the time," he said. "Were you scared?"

Abogado Blas, Daddy's lawyer friend, was in the front seat. He smiled and gently helped me onto the back seat where I cried without making a sound.

"Don't cry now," Daddy said. "You're my brave little girl." I felt good when he said I was brave, not like Chona who was afraid of the dark and ghosts and many other things, so I stopped crying. Daddy and Abogado Blas talked about the town mayor and laughed a lot. We passed a few busy streets and then turned north on the road to Montaña. The sun had just set, and the trees along the gravel road looked like shadows of tall men marching by. When we got by the cemetery at the edge of Montaña, I closed my eyes. I only opened them again when Daddy said we were home.

After a few more weeks in Holy Ghost, Mommy told me that I was moving to Central School, six blocks from home. "Why not Gabaldon?" I said. Chona went to Gabaldon; it was only a block away.

"You're only six," she said. "Your Auntie Celina is the principal at Central, and she's allowing you into Grade One."

The thick walls of the two-storey Central School reminded me of church. The window sills were so wide, I imagined lying there to take a nap. The first few weeks, I walked with Auntie Celina to and from school. She told me which houses had dogs lurking in their yards, and to beware rabid ones; if they bit me, I could die. After that, my parents allowed me to walk home alone.

I liked Central School more than Holy Ghost. I loved my teacher Mrs. Pacis. When she had to leave the room, she gave me her pointing stick, and I drilled my classmates on the day's reading or arithmetic on the board. The stick was not just for pointing; it was also for spanking pupils who gave the wrong answers or who were noisy, so I felt big holding it in my hand.

One day, Mrs. Pacis gave us a test. I needed to go to the washroom, but I didn't go because I wanted to finish the test. Next thing I knew, I had peed in my pants.

"Daniela peed on the floor!" yelled Felipe from behind me.

Mrs. Pacis approached, and I waited for her to spank me. "Are you finished?" she said.

"Yes, ma'am," I said and handed her my test paper.

"Get your things, my child, and go home." She walked me out the door.

I was glad she hadn't hit me but felt ashamed as I wobbled on my way. A block from home, a barking dog sniffed my behind. I ran, trying to keep my feet from slipping on my wet rubber flip-flops. The dog barked louder and chased me. I ran even faster and thankfully reached home before the dog caught up with me.

Daddy got home before supper and took me in his lap. "Your Auntie Celina says you wet your pants in school," he said.

I looked at the scuffs on the floor and at his slippers.

"It's okay," he said. "She also says you're the brightest in class. Now that's my girl. You do take after me. See, we not only look alike, we're both smart, too."

Seeing that he wasn't angry, I said, "Daddy, a dog chased me home."

"Remember what I told you?" he said. "First, don't look the dog in the eye. What else?"

I remembered. "Don't run. Pick up a stone to hurl at the dog."

He squeezed me and kissed my cheeks. I didn't want him to stop.

CHAPTER 3

I was up before light that Easter morning, eager to put on my first long dress to be one of the angels for the *alleluia*. Chona was excited, too, although this was her second time. Mommy pinned in our hair coronets of flowers that held a short veil and handed each of us a basket of fragrant pink and white plumeria petals.

My new shoes hurt, but I tried to walk to church in small steps, so I didn't ruin my long organdie dress. When we reached the churchyard, a small crowd had gathered, and several "angels" were already on the makeshift balcony, boys and girls all in white. Mommy helped Chona and me up the shaky ladder.

"Regina Coeli," the lead angel sang to violins. He was a bigger kid, a boy of eight. The rest of us chorused, *"Alleluia, al-le-e-eluia."* Before long, statues of Jesus and Mother Mary came from either side of the stage on the ground below us, propped on men's shoulders. When they finally met in the middle, the lead angel stooped to lift Mother Mary's black veil. She looked beautiful in her blue dress, and I threw all my petals in her direction.

"You two were the prettiest angels up there," Mommy said afterward.

It was the middle of summer. Chona was playing with Francis on the floor while I read *Bannawag* at the dining table. Manang Zenay ironed clothes close by. Daddy was feeding the chickens in the backyard.

"Look what I've got," Mommy said, wobbling in. She was going to have another baby soon. She had brought pictures from the photo studio: one of Mommy pinning a ribbon on Chona's dress for finishing second in her class; one of Daddy, Mommy and me with a ribbon for being the best in my Grade One class; and one of me in my white organdie dress, kneeling down, palms together, praying to Jesus.

"My darling girls," Mommy said to Chona and me. "See how good you are in school. And you know," she said, looking at me, "you're moving to Gabaldon next year."

"*Yehey*," I said. "I'll walk with Chona."

"Look how pretty you are here," Mommy said, pointing at my angel pose.

Manang Zenay chuckled. "Not like her face at Leila's birthday," she said. "She looks like a dumb bully in that picture."

"Don't tease her now," Mommy said. "She's pretty, too."

I ran upstairs and looked for my photo album. I knew exactly where that stupid picture was, on the third page. I had posed with a group of kids at a cousin's birthday party, all of us arranged like a set of bowling pins, the taller kids in back. I was alone in front and center, the smallest, Chona behind me, smiling and pretty as usual. My eyes were half shut, my mouth in a big pout, my hair cropped close to my scalp. I tore off the page and ran downstairs.

"Why is my hair like this?" I asked my mother.

"You had head lice, *anak ko*," she said.

Yanking the picture off its photo corners, I ripped it in two and threw it out the window. Mommy went out the back door and picked up the picture pieces. I walked all the way to the cluster of banana trees in the far corner of the yard, into the outhouse. After a few moments, Daddy knocked on the door. "Come out," he said. "Why are you hiding in there?"

I came out and exhaled. "They're teasing me, Daddy."

He took me inside the house. "Nobody teases my girl," he said to all the others. "She's the best, the brightest."

Mommy was taping the photo together. I sat next to her and glowered at Manang Zenay.

I was happy to move to Gabaldon for Grade Two the following year. In the mornings, after doing my cleaning chores at home, I ran to school to play with my friends long before the teachers arrived. We used pebbles for jackstones and blew on rubber bands on the pavement. If I puffed at my rubber band and it landed atop someone else's, I won both. We went to class with grime under our fingernails and multi-colored rubber bands on our wrists. If we played hopscotch or jumped hurdles under the hot sun, we'd all be sticky by the time the bell rang.

Mom didn't leave for Daniw and soon after school opened, she had another baby boy. They named him Lorenzo, after Daddy, and nicknamed him Sonny. Manang Zenay's younger sister, Manang Aning, moved in with us to be Sonny's nanny.

In the middle of the year, my teacher sent me to Grade Three, to Chona's class. My new classmates gave me questioning looks, obviously wondering what a Grade Two pupil was doing in their class. My only friend was Chona. When school ended in March, I was at the top of the class. Macario, the boy at the top before I came, ended up second. My sister was third. I felt proud of myself. Chona said nothing, but I felt a little sorry for her.

Toward the end of Grade Four, Daddy coached me for a declamation contest. He had me memorize *Jack and the Beanstalk* from the vinyl record. I hated how he kept me for hours, making me imitate the voices and the accents in the record.

The day before the contest, I was trying to perfect the giant's voice when I felt an itch all over my body. 'Fee-fi-foh-faahm," I

22

boomed and then stooped to scratch my legs. "I smell the blood of an Englishmehn!"

"What is it?" Daddy sounded annoyed.

"Itchy, Daddy" I said, but he didn't let me go, because I still didn't sound enough like the giant.

At the contest, I tried not to scratch while reciting my piece. I won, and Daddy said over and over that I had made him very proud. I felt very proud as well.

When we got home, I ran a fever so high that even Lola's usual fix of a vinegar-dipped towel on my forehead didn't help. "It's the chicken pox," Ninang Florie said.

Mommy wasn't home, as usual. I stayed in bed and threw up a lot. Daddy bought me *sangkís* in Laoag and gave me the new *Bannawag* before he even read it.

I was still in bed when Mommy came home for the summer. I told her she couldn't be away again, ever.

CHAPTER 4

"I saw it again," Chona said.

"Saw what?"

"Legs up in the air," she said. "Same thing as before."

"What do you mean, before?" I scratched the chicken pox scab on my left cheek.

"Long ago, dummy. Didn't I tell you? You always sleep like a dead dog. The baby powder tin was beside the oil lamp. Daddy went on top of her."

She had indeed told me the same thing when we were younger, but I had thought then that she was just joking. "Why do you love to tell that joke?" I said.

"I'm not kidding!" She glared at me.

We usually slept on the floor together: Chona, Daddy, Francis and me. Mommy slept in the next room with baby Sonny. Lola and our cousins Zenay and Aning slept in another room, and Auntie Celina and Ninang Florie in the fourth room.

"No. She sleeps in the other room," I said.

"Up in the air," said Chona, "her legs shaking."

I sucked the scab stuck under my fingernail, along with a bit of blood. "You're a liar."

"Wipe your nasty cheek."

"I'll tell Mommy…"

"Don't you dare!"

I was nine years old that summer, and my sister eleven. We mostly played at home because Daddy seldom allowed us to go outside the fenced yard. This particular morning, Chona and I were playing an alphabet game in our parents' bed. At her turn, she stalled at the letter Q.

I said, "Why so slow when the game is freestyle?" Meaning we could name any word in Ilocano, Tagalog, or English. She shot me her look of death and declared the game over. And then she raised her legs, mimicking what she saw Manang Zenay do the night before. With Daddy. The baby powder tin to dim the light from the oil lamp.

I glanced at the hallway where the oil lamp sat on a small table. Besides subduing our night monsters, the faint flicker kept us from tripping on the chamber pot. I had once tipped the potty over, even with the lighted lamp, and the night's collective pee went drip-dripping between the wooden floor slabs, straight to the oleanders in a vase on the coffee table downstairs. Manang Zenay's face was dark with anger when Mommy roused her to help mop up the mess.

School had ended the week before. With shriveled chicken pox blisters, I had gone up on stage as the top fourth grade pupil. Daddy pinned the red ribbon on the blue lace dress that Mommy had stayed up nights to sew – a special dress, unlike the school playsuits that she made out of colorful chicken feed sacks from Daddy's backyard poultry. For the third year in a row, I put a big smile on my father's face and felt very important.

Mommy was away. She had just left for Manila to continue working on her master's degree, Sonny and Manang Aning with her.

The next day, Chona and I wanted to play Cinderella using our mother's wedding shoes. Mommy moved those shoes each time

25

she noticed that we had touched them, and they became harder to find. As we rummaged through her closet, we stumbled upon our past letters to Santa Claus.

"Maybe there's no Santa," Chona said.

"But we got everything we wrote him for," I said.

"Of course, dummy," she said. "Mommy asked the postmaster for the letters. And then she read them and bought the presents herself."

"But you shouldn't read other people's letters."

Chona rolled her eyes.

"But mommies and daddies don't lie," I said, looking at our parents' wedding picture on the wall. Mommy in a white princess dress, a long veil over her black curls, her eyes looking like cashews with her tender smile. Daddy in a white suit and black bowtie, plump cheekbones high, his watchful eyes looking straight at me.

I sulked. A few minutes later, when I got lonely, I asked my sister what we should do next.

"Nothing," she replied. I understood that if we told our parents about the letters, Daddy would give us a good spanking for going through Mommy's closet without permission.

Today, no Santa. Yesterday, a very strange story. I insisted we tell Mommy. My sister said no, and we fought about it many times.

A few days later, I said to Chona, "Tell me more about what you saw. Her legs were shaking, you said?"

"Yes, yes," she said, annoyed. "She was giggling softly. What else do you want to know?"

"What was Daddy saying?"

"Nothing... just breathing hard."

"I don't like that," I said, although I didn't know why. "What was funny? What was she giggling about?"

My sister had no answer to that. Whatever it was, Daddy couldn't have made a mistake, for he had always said he knew best. Maybe it was Manang Zenay's fault. "I don't like it," I said. "I don't like her."

The following weeks, Daddy had the kitchen redone. Lola and Manang Zenay did the cooking in a backyard open fire, shielded from the breeze by a tin sheet. One late morning, while I was tossing lumps of rice to the grinning monkey up the mango tree, a delicious smell drifted from the cooking pit a few yards away. I left the monkey and followed the tangy smell. Fried chicken – another poor hen that refused to lay eggs. I bent forward, drooling over the soy-saucy sizzle, and lost my balance. Next thing I knew, the women were peeling me off the scorching tin sheet. I felt like screaming, but I didn't. Daddy hated screaming, saying it was only for the uneducated. I froze for a while and then allowed myself several quiet sobs.

One side of my left forearm, from the elbow to the back of the hand, was a big, ugly, throbbing blister. When Daddy arrived from work, he yelled at everyone: me, for barging into forbidden territory, and the grownups for letting me. After a few moments, he sat me on his lap and inspected my arm.

"Does it hurt, *anak ko*?" he said.

I bawled with all my might.

I needed help to bathe, to change clothes, to dress the yellow-fatty burn, and who else would help me but Manang Zenay? In the bathroom one day, I sat naked on a wooden stool while Manang Zenay drew water from the well. She came in with a tin pail, her big breasts and hips bulging under her chicken-feed-sack dress. "Let's wash your hair first," she said, stooping to push my head down. "Hold your arm up."

I held up my left arm and trembled when my cousin poured cold water on my bowed head. The water splashed on her long, dark legs and bare feet, washing out some of the dirt on them but not the black stuff under her toenails. "Why do your legs look whitish like that?" I said. "Do you rub powder on them to hide your dark skin?"

"I'm not hiding my dark skin," she said, rubbing my hair with a bar of Camay. "It's just dry, because I use Perla."

Mommy didn't allow everyone to use the Camay bath soap, saying it was too expensive, so my cousins used the laundry bar Perla for bathing. And like Lola, they washed their hair with rice straw ashes dissolved in water and later coated them with coconut oil. When Manang Zenay was done with my hair, she started to scrub my body. I looked up to her face and said, "Why does your nose flare like that?"

"We poor people are ugly people," she said, scrubbing me harder, making me cringe. When she dried me with a towel, I wanted to bite her hand, to kick her, anything. But my tall, homely cousin now looked taller. Homelier, too.

"*Natangsit ka unay*," Daddy said one day. "Don't be haughty, especially to helpers."

"Yes, Daddy," I said. Figuring that Manang Zenay must have told Daddy that I'd been mean to her, I hated her even more. I itched to know what she and my dad were doing. And why. But I didn't know who to ask. Confined indoors, I kept to the few books I owned. In three days, I had memorized them all and became bored. I wrote Mommy about the burn and asked her to buy the scar ointment that wasn't in the local drugstores. And to please come home. Chona didn't show interest in finding out more about what Daddy was doing with our cousin that night and chose to play on the porch with her best friend Jenny. I turned to an English dictionary, the only book in the house that promised relief from boredom.

English being my third language, I was clumsy with the big dictionary. After many dead-end attempts, I tried the word *female*. I got a jumble of weird words – *vagina, uterus, ovaries* – that led me to the words *male, scrotum, penis*. I looked them all up and became even more puzzled.

A week of flipping through the dictionary and I finally got it. Like when two dogs' butts get stuck to each other? Which Lola says is bad to watch? People do that? What for?

And then I remembered Jenny describing pictures from her brother's medical book. I went to her house and asked to see it.

There it was, the picture of a baby's head coming out from between the mother's legs.

I tried to keep awake the following nights to see for myself if Daddy and Manang Zenay would do it again. But even with my stinging, weeping burn, I always slept like a corpse.

I figured that this was a bad thing for my mother and was eager to tell her, so she'd send Manang Zenay home to her parents. Again, Chona serenely gave me her look of death, saying if I knew what was good for me, I'd better keep quiet.

After what seemed like five hundred days, Mommy did come home, with some treats and the scar ointment.

"Now, *balasang ko*," she said after toweling my hair, "what do you fancy for lunch?"

Whenever she called me her young lady, I felt like cuddling up. She felt soft and warm when I pressed my face in her chest. Wanting to tell her what I'd heard, I looked up at her beautiful face, her small nose that did not flare, her kind eyes.

"I'm sorry, Mommy," I said. "When you were gone I played with your wedding shoes."

CHAPTER 5

I helped Mommy unpack her suitcase and saw she had some scrapbooks, projects from her Manila summer school, different crochet, embroidery and sewing stitches, and recipes she had created, all neatly laid out. She said she'd teach me how to do all of them. And did I know that when school opened in two weeks, she'd be teaching at my school? How wonderful.

In another week, my burn had become a scar and I was allowed to play outside again, even in the irrigation ditch that ran alongside our street that was shallow in the summer. One afternoon, Chona, our cousin Grace, and I sat on the loamy bottom of the ditch to pick shells, the water just covering our bottoms and legs. I was peeling a snail off a stone when three bicycles came along and then stopped right above us. It was Felipe and two other boys from my Grade One class. "Daniela," Felipe said, grinning. "Look this way and show me your pretty face." He was the one who told Mrs. Pacis I had peed in class. The other boys snickered.

"What pretty face?" I said. In a flash, I got up on my feet and propelled myself up and out of the ditch, grabbed a rubber flip-flop that I had left on the road and smacked it on Felipe's forehead. His face reddened. The other boys sped away, but Felipe glared at me for a few more moments before he followed them.

I went inside the house. "Mommy," I said. "Can I learn to ride a bike?"

"Your father says no," she said. "It's not safe for little girls like you."

"But even the smaller kids know how," I said, thinking of chasing Felipe on a bicycle if he ever came to bug me again. "I'm nine."

"What did I just say?"

I did not insist. Instead, I helped babysit Sonny, singing him to sleep on the hammock in the back porch. Some grownup always looked after him, but because he was cuddly, I'd ask to hold him. He was chubby, with two slits for eyes, his skin fairer than mine, much like Chona's and Daddy's.

"Can you watch Sonny while I gather the laundry?" Manang Aning said one afternoon.

"If you get us some green mangoes afterwards," I said. Manang Aning was more fun than Manang Zenay. I liked her wide, smiling eyes and the big dimples on her cheeks. She played hopscotch with us when Daddy was not around. She also loved to climb trees to pick fruit, especially green mangoes, even if Lola said they should be left on the tree to ripen. We'd dip the mangoes in salted vinegar and eat them in a hurry while Lola was busy with her pigs.

"Yes, I'll do that," she said and went to the clotheslines while Sonny toddled alone on his bamboo walker on the gravel path. The walker was an inverted cone with the pointed end cut off, the upper ring holding the baby up by the armpits like crutches. The hula-hoop ring at the bottom got caught on a stone, and the walker tipped over. When I picked Sonny up, his mouth was all blood.

Daddy didn't spank me for this; Manang Aning got most of the reprimand. But after that, I left the babysitting to the grownups and set my eyes on learning to ride a bike instead. Chona also wanted to learn, and when I suggested that we ask our cousin Sam to teach us, we agreed to do it without asking for our parents' permission.

Sam taught Chona and me how to ride a bike in the school grounds. It was summer, so we had the place to ourselves. That week, we'd tell Mommy we were going to play, and she'd say okay but to return before Daddy got home. Sam's father's bike was too big for us, but I was determined to learn. Chona and I wobbled and fell a lot, but pretty soon we were brave enough to set off without Sam's guiding hands. One day, however, I sped a little too fast and crashed the bike onto a gutter. It took Sam and Chona a while to pull me out from under the bike. I didn't know it would be that heavy. Its spokes were bent, but Sam fixed them; I was glad the mirror didn't break. I limped home with a skinned knee and bruises on my legs and arms.

"Daddy, I hurt myself," I said when he got home, knowing this was the easier way out, that if I didn't tell him, he'd know anyway and give me double the spanking for not telling.

"What did you do? Your legs are a mess. Look at Chona's legs – no scars."

I couldn't tell him about the bike, so I said, "Hopscotch, Daddy."

"When will you learn to be careful?" he said and gave me one big whack on the butt.

When school opened in June, I was excited to have my mother as my home economics and music teacher. She taught our class things I'd watched her do at home: sew, embroider, crochet, and cook simple meals. At home, I didn't study much, except for English composition. By the light of an oil lamp, after I struggled to write a few sentences, Mommy suggested ways to make them better.

The school principal always came to the playground while I was up on the monkey bars or in the corkwood tree. "Can't you see the trash lying around?" she'd say. "Suppose you get off and pick it up instead?" I hated her, but I obeyed without whining. I tended my own vegetable plot in the school backyard. Whenever there was a construction project in the school that needed a concrete foundation, the principal sent us to the riverbank four blocks down the road. We each had to bring one cantaloupe-size rock and made two or three trips. Afterward, the teachers gave us a snack of bulgur and powdered milk that came in *UN Feeding Program* cartons.

I was the best in everything – reading, arithmetic, writing, too. Even good manners and right conduct. When it was my team's turn to clean the classroom after school, I gave the boys the harder chores like scrubbing the floor and reaching for the cobwebs in the ceiling. If I didn't find the floor shiny enough, I whacked their thighs with a broom until they did it just so.

On Mommy's birthday, Daddy arrived home in the middle of a downpour with a foot-powered Singer sewing machine and a pair of Wiss Inlaid tailor's shears. My mother's eyes shone as Daddy set up the machine. Chona and I sneaked outside and frolicked in the rain, and for once, Daddy didn't scold us afterward.

I loved to watch Mommy work with her new machine. A measuring tape slung on her neck, she drew the pattern on thin brown paper with a square orange chalk called Dixon, then spooled the bobbin with thread and ran the fabric fast through the machine. I took Elsie, the doll I shared with Chona, and asked Mommy to help me make her a dress from the cloth scraps. "Be careful," she said, "or you'll get your fingers caught." I did try to be careful, but the needle ran straight through my middle fingernail. Mommy dabbed Merthiolate on the wound, blowing on it as I whimpered, and wrapped it with a Curitas.

"Mommy," I said. "When you were in Manila, Chona and I found our letters to Santa in your closet."

She laughed and said, "So you know. But you must not tell your kid brothers or spoil the fun for them."

"I won't," I said. I was tempted to tell her about Daddy and Manang Zenay, too, but quickly changed my mind.

By the end of the school year, I had become better at sewing. On Good Friday, Mommy convinced me to cut and sew myself a dress, which would be a good-luck dress if I finished it within the day. It was a sleeveless shift of pink cotton sprinkled with white flowers, my pick from Daddy's poultry feed sacks. My kid brother Francis picked up the cloth scraps and wore them as a veil, singing and dancing around me while I sewed. At five, he had a solid singing voice and very graceful moves. "You'd be pretty as a girl," I said. "Even be prettier than Chona." He spun around me, wide, bright eyes shining, his dimple sinking deep into his cheek.

"Take that thing off," Mommy said. Francis obeyed and went to play jackstones with Chona.

My parents talked a lot about a new boarding high school in Manila, the Philippine Science High School. It screened the country's brightest sixth graders and offered scholarships to the top one hundred fifty. High school normally ran for four years, but this new school had more things to teach these gifted children, and they needed five years to do that.

"You'll wear your good-luck dress to the exam," Mommy said to me and then looked at Chona. "You've mostly been playing outside; you don't care about sewing, so you don't have a good-luck dress."

Chona shrugged.

"They have to be ready with their English," Daddy said. He had heard that the exam was heavy on math and English. I knew he was happy with my math. He went to the storage room, brought out some *Reader's Digest* magazines and made us study *It Pays to Increase Your Word Power*. Some evenings, he would pick up one or two of the magazines and drill Chona and me on the strange, difficult words. I enjoyed it more than my sister did.

After Chona and I took the exam, our parents asked us how it went.

"Hard," Chona said with a resigned look.

"The math was okay," I said. "The vocabulary was hard. And there was a lot of *artek, bortek, cortek* that was easy. I wonder why they even asked those questions."

"What do you mean, *artek bortek*?" Daddy said.

"If all *arteks* are *borteks* and some *borteks* are *corteks*, then all *arteks* are *corteks*," I said.

"I see," Daddy said. "Careful with those – they can be tricky."

I forgot about the exam afterward. School was about to end, and I was eager to earn academic medals and to be the youngest-ever pupil in town, at eleven, to finish grade school. As expected, I was class valedictorian and my sister ranked fifth, making our parents very proud.

It was summer once more. My friends and I were having a contest that day, to see who could make the mud pie that most closely resembled cow dung. I was armed with a stick and an empty sardine can. I dug out soil from the roadside and got excited with my big mound of earth. Sardine can in hand, I crawled to the edge of the ditch, bent down to scoop out some water and fell, badly scraping my arms and knees. Of course, I got a spanking from Daddy, but this time it was on my palm. A hard blow, though.

"Look," he said, "you're eleven. This should be the last time I spank you." I sniffled. "From now on you should behave yourself out of shame, not fear," he said.

A few weeks later, Daddy brought home a copy of *The Sunday Times* that had my name among those admitted to the Philippine Science High School. There was one other pupil from Montaña on the list, and it wasn't my sister. I felt like the smartest kid in the world and didn't care that Chona didn't make it.

"You and I are going to Manila!" Daddy said, while Mom beamed. "I'd like you to become a doctor," he said.

My name carved on a wooden plate, DR. DANIELA BENITO – PHYSICIAN, nailed to our gate post? Just like Ninang's? It looked good to me, very good.

CHAPTER 6

On the day Daddy and I were to travel to Manila, I felt sick, thinking of how it would be after he left me alone. "It's raining," I said. "Can we go tomorrow instead?"

We took the bus the next day, leaving at dusk and reaching Manila at dawn. Although Daddy had taken me to the big city once before, when I was seven, I was again amazed at the streets that teemed with buses and taxis and beautiful cars, at the winking neon lights, at the store windows that held interesting things. The dormitory was on a street of big painted houses with pretty gardens. Very quiet. The dorm matron showed us to a room with two bunks. I picked a top one as Mommy had told me to, to keep other girls from messing it up.

"You're going to be fine, *balasang ko*," Daddy said, hugging me, kissing me on both cheeks. "Your roommates will come in soon."

"Please tell Mommy to write," I said. "When are you coming back?"

"Won't be long," he said. "I'm back in two weeks."

My father walked away, and I felt like a big hand was squeezing my head and my chest. I returned to my room, unpacked and put away my things and made my bed. A bell rang; the matron peered in to say it meant suppertime.

In the dining room, I found about ten girls lining up with army-style trays. Shredded banana shoots and flowers? Lola fed this stuff to the pigs back home. I pushed it down anyway, because it was a sin to waste food. I didn't say much and just smiled at the other girls.

Alone in the dark room that night, I felt uneasy lying close to the ceiling, even if the *kapok* cotton mattress was softer than my straw one at home. I got up and looked out the screened and barred window, feeling like I needed air, thinking of our wide, airy windows back home. Then I heard footsteps from the street, people's voices, a humming from somewhere. I closed the window and turned the light on, lay back down, pulled my blanket over my head, and started to sweat. I barely slept.

After breakfast, the matron walked us girls to church ten minutes away. Then more girls arrived. After supper, the matron gathered us for a meeting: dorm rules, meal times, curfew. She asked each of us to say our name and home province. Then the girls clustered according to their native dialects, and the place hummed with strange words and accents: Tagalog, Ilonggo, Cebuano. I was happy to find a handful of girls who also spoke my native Ilocano. We proudly called ourselves Marcos's Angels, referring to Ferdinand Marcos, a brilliant Ilocano senator who was running for president, promising the people that the nation could be great again.

On Monday, I walked the few blocks to school, in the rain, with my Ilocano friends – Nancy and four others. My white socks squished inside my new leather shoes. I hated how those shoes pinched my toes. Back home, rain or shine, I scooted to school in my rubber flip-flops and play clothes. Why did I have to wear shoes? Because this was the big city? But the school itself was not much to look at: a run-down, two-storey wooden box with creaking floors, a leaking roof and muddy grounds, in the middle of a barren block along Elliptical Road.

There were twenty-four girls and boys in my class. A lanky young man wearing square eyeglasses and flat-top hair walked in and introduced himself as Mr. Fernando, our homeroom advisor. "Okay," he said, "let's start from the front row. Tell us your name, where you're from, and anything interesting about you."

"I'm Federico, from UP Elementary," the first boy said in English. "I'm an only child. I love theater and was part of my school's debating team."

"My name is Alice, from St. Scholastica. I've been studying ballet and gymnastics since I was five." She sat down very gracefully.

I knew that Ilocano would no longer be the medium of instruction. It was now English, of which I had very little. When I heard these city kids speak, I began to feel very shy. Should I tell them about my mud pies?

"Very good," Mr. Fernando said. "Next!"

I stood up, muttered my name and quickly sat down.

I had even less Filipino. When the staid Filipino language teacher called on me, I froze. I didn't have the courage to say I didn't understand the question. And I knew that even if I did, I wasn't sure I'd be able to answer it in correct Filipino.

Mr. Fernando was back with us in the afternoon, this time to teach math. I was the best in math in my grade school, although we called it arithmetic. This should be okay. The teacher talked about sets and subsets and drew circles on the board. He called his sketches Venn diagrams. "A union B intersection C is this shaded area here," he said.

This is math? Where are the numbers?

Mr. Fernando had numbers all right. "How do you write four base ten in the binary system?" he said.

"Sir, one zero zero," Virgilio said.

"Good. Any questions?"

Where's my mommy?

English class came next. Mrs. Vea had a slight smile on her face. She looked older than my mother, her skin fairer, her slender body frail. She told us to buy a small notebook that we'd call our Scribble Notebook, and to write something in it as often as we could, anything at all. She'd collect the notebooks every Friday and return them on Monday.

Study time was after supper. The dining tables became study tables, and we had until ten p.m. to do our homework. Afterward, lights out and then silence. I didn't know how to do half of my homework and was too shy to ask my three roommates for help. I just kept wondering what they'd had for dinner at home.

I cried myself to sleep that night. And the next night. And the next. I had nightmares and sleepwalked. I was eleven years old, four-foot-seven, weighed eighty pounds. Most of the students were bigger, older and wiser at twelve or thirteen. Who cared about becoming a doctor? All I wanted was to go home.

"Class," Mr. San Luis said, "each of you bring a frog to dissect tomorrow. It you can catch a toad, the better."

I had seen giant toads after rainy nights, squashed flat on the road to school. Back home, fried frog's legs were a treat, but I had nothing to do with catching or skinning them. I had also played with tadpoles, but I stayed away from ugly toads. How was I to catch one?

After supper at the dorm, I set out with a bunch of girls to track the croaking sounds in the vacant lots nearby. I was terrified, imagining that there might be snakes lurking in the muddy brush. It took a while, but we managed to trap enough frogs in the empty ice cream cans we had brought along – and, thank God, no snakes. At lab the next day, I was amazed to see my frog's heart continue to beat after I sliced its chest open, and I forgot the previous evening's scary hunting trip. The following week, when we were required to bring frogs again, I was eager to go with my friends to catch more.

When I had the flu, the dorm matron kept me in a sick room. I cried into my chicken soup. Feeling better on Sunday, I went to church and fainted at mass. A good-hearted couple took me back to the dorm in their car. I looked hard at their faces, wishing they'd turn into my parents' faces.

I wrote in my Scribble Notebook about how homesick I was. Mrs. Vea returned it with kind comments and suggested I read to fight the loneliness. I tried to do so, but it didn't come easily. Writing was more comforting, and it soon became one of my favorite things.

My parents took turns visiting. Mom collected science project specimens from Montaña, dried and mounted them – butterflies, dragonflies, beetles, rare medicinal plants – and brought them to me ready to turn in to Mr. San Luis. She took me shopping. I didn't mind that we spent a lot of time in her sister's cramped house. She brought me old issues of *Bannawag* and letters from Chona, Francis and Sonny. She cried a lot, saying it was a big sacrifice to send me to the special school, and I cried a lot, too.

Each time he took me out for fun, Dad taught me how to work the big-city public transport system that included buses, jeepneys, taxis and horse-drawn buggies. We went sightseeing on a double-decker bus along Manila Bay, strolled in Luneta Park, and always – always – had a big Chinese lunch at Panciteria Wa Nam.

One weekend with Dad, I cried my eyes out watching the movie *All Mine to Give*, where six children are orphaned and the oldest, who is twelve years old, has to give away his siblings to different families in order for them to survive. When Dad took me back to my dorm, I wrapped my arms around his thick waist. "Take me home, Daddy," I said.

"*Balasang ko*," he said, stroking my hair. "You know you have to stay."

"I can't," I said, "too tough."

He rubbed my back and then cupped my face with both hands.

I squeezed him tighter and cried on his shirt. After a while, he took a ten-peso bill from his pocket and put it in my hand. "Here," he said. "Extra. Buy yourself anything you want. I have to catch my bus, child." He turned to leave, pulled out his handkerchief and wiped his eyes. I ran to my room, skipped supper, and cried all evening.

Ten pesos could buy many things, like a nice pair of shoes and two dresses, but I wasn't interested in those. If I added two pesos, it could pay for a taxi and bus ride all the way to Montaña. But I was afraid to do that, so I stayed and tried my best to learn at school.

On Dad's next visit, he took me to his sister's house for the weekend, as usual. "Give me your notebooks," he said, "I'll hypnotize you."

I handed him my notebooks and showed him the week's work. He had me recline on the sofa and told me to gaze at his pointer and middle fingers right above me. "You're becoming sleepy," he said, reading from a small book. "Your eyelids are getting heavy."

I awoke to Dad's voice counting down to one. "There," he said, "I read all your lessons to you while you slept." He gave me back my notebooks, and a chart he'd worked out of the best times to study each day, Mondays 4:11 to 5:38 a.m., Tuesdays 8:24 to 9:36 p.m., and so on.

Back at the dorm, I closely followed the schedule, but it didn't help.

I went to my first dance in the special dress that Mom had sewn – pink cotton with puffed sleeves and shirred skirt. I wore my party shoes, black patent with a buckle. They had folded up the partitions between the classrooms, turning the place into a big dance hall. I had never danced with a boy before; all I knew were the folk dances we did in Montaña. Mr. Fernando was walking about, telling the boys to get up and ask the girls to dance. Many of the girls had been asked and were dancing while I sat there

41

watching. It looked easy enough, just step to the beat, ¾ time like Mom had taught at music class in grade school. But what if no one asked me? When they played *Blue Danube*, I saw my classmate Eddie run and hug one of the partition posts. Mr. Fernando peeled him off the post and led him by the hand toward me. Standing up, I could see the top of Eddie's head. I put my left hand on his right shoulder and held his left hand. My eyes on other girls' feet, I tried to do as they did, dragging tiny Eddie along. I found that it was actually fun, but Eddie looked like he was going to cry.

I also found physical education exhilarating, especially a game invented by our teacher that she called merry mix-up. It was played like basketball, except that instead of a basket, we had a goalie whose task was to jump and catch a throw. I was the goalie for my class. I loved doing it and, short as I was, managed to do good. After the intramurals, I got an award for being the school's best goalie. My two minutes of fame that entire year.

But mostly I longed for home, especially when I wasn't well. Like when lesions appeared on my arms and the school doctor gave me a bag of crystals called potassium permanganate. "Dissolve a spoonful of this in a basin of warm water," he said, "and soak your arms in it for five minutes every day."

When I mixed the chemical with water, it turned purple. I soaked my arms in the solution each day, but the lesions chose to stay. I went to school in uniforms with faint purple stains, feeling like a leper.

"Goodness," Mom said when she came to visit. "All that takes is Pfizer ointment." In four days the lesions were gone.

Daddy came to fetch me home for Christmas. When the bus reached our province at dawn, I saw banners gushing over Marcos, the province's son who had just won as the country's president.

In Montaña, everything was smaller than I remembered. My grade school, the streets, the church, the town square, and the houses all seemed to have shrunk. But after a few days, they felt the same as before.

I had missed two of the nine dawn masses leading to Christmas, and I was eager to walk to church again in the cool breeze under the stars, never mind if the priest loved to give long homilies to a yawning congregation. On the way home from mass on December 24, I could hear the chilling screams of Mom's pig being slaughtered by the men, and the fainter pounding of pestle on wooden mortar by the women helpers as they made sticky rice flour for *tupig*, the Ilocano Christmas rice cake. I was home! As usual, the men took home parts of the pig as their compensation for work done, and my family kept the rest for *adobo*, *higado*, and barbecue. The *tupig*-making took all day. I helped in mixing the flour with coconut milk, molasses and shaved coconut, and in kneading the dough before wrapping handfuls of it in banana leaves. With Sonny in my arms, I watched the women roast the raw *tupig* over coals in a pit dug into the ground and drooled as the sweet smell wafted in the air.

I was thrilled to see familiar faces again, especially my parents and siblings. My kid brothers loved the small toys I had brought them. But I'd missed Chona the most. She and I spent hours giggling and exchanging stories about our new friends and new schools. She had gone to Holy Ghost Academy in Laoag. After reading my Scribble Notebook, she said she was lucky she didn't have to be away from home.

The two-week holiday whizzed by, and then I had to pack my bag which made me very sad. While Dad was fixing his hair, Mom and Chona made some egg sandwiches for the trip. Mom always made sure Dad and I carried some food, saying the eateries where the bus stopped for supper weren't sanitary.

"I wonder when it'll be my turn to need sandwiches," Chona said. Although she said it in her usual tender manner, I knew she was jealous of me. I didn't know what to say to make her feel better, so I just thanked her for the sandwiches.

My marks were pitiful the first year. This was the only high school in the country that kicked students out who didn't make the minimum grade. At least my grades made the cut.

Back in Montaña for the first summer, Auntie Celina told me how, as a young boy, Marcos read his lessons even before school opened, and that I could be like him if I worked as hard. But I simply wanted to enjoy my vacation, so I went about playing and chatting with my old friends.

I noticed that Dad was sometimes away all night. One morning, he came home on his bicycle, with a smirk on his oily face, his hair tousled. He called each of us and said, "I'm going to bed. Nobody make any noise. Understood?"

Without washing up or eating breakfast, he went upstairs. After he had shut his bedroom door, Manang Aning said he'd surely lost at *mah jong*. I followed her to the backyard well where she was doing laundry. She had a pile of soapy clothes in a pail and a basin filled with water. Sitting on a footstool, she picked up two pillowcases from the pail, laid them on the big flat rock next to her and began beating them with her *palek*, a thick wooden paddle a bit longer than a ping-pong one.

"What do you mean?" I said. "Is that where he was all night?"

"Of course," she said, scooping some water onto the pillowcases and turning them over. "Didn't you see your mom fret when his friend Blas came to pick him up yesterday afternoon? Your father didn't even stay for supper. That man Blas makes him do all sorts of foolish things."

"What foolish things? Abogado Blas is a respected lawyer," I said, surprised at my cousin's irreverence. In our town, we addressed all educated men by their profession – *Doctora, Maestro, Abogado, Apo Mayor* or Lord Mayor, *Apo Padi* or Lord Priest.

"It's hard to say much," she said and sniffed. "You know your dad's temper."

"Are you crying?"

She pounded harder at the pillowcases. "No, I have a cold."

"Does he do this often?" I said. "I mean, stay up all night to

44

play?" I thought of the day Dad came for me at Holy Ghost after everyone else had left, remembering how frightened I was when he'd come with Abogado Blas and told me they'd been playing *mah jong*.

"Never quits when he's down."

I tried to avoid Dad after he spent the night gambling. But sometimes, he surprised us by buying ice cream and treats and didn't mind so much that we were noisy while he slept. I loved it when he did this, especially because Mom was such a tightwad.

I didn't read any academic books during the summer as Auntie Celina had suggested. But when I went back to Manila the second year, I promised myself to do much better. I didn't want to shame my parents with my dismissal, even if I'd have loved to stay home. This year we had biology, and Mrs. Reyes was wonderful. She took us to a lagoon to collect plankton, much easier than catching frogs. We studied droplets of the lagoon water under a microscope. Hairy volvox, slimy hydra, cross-eyed planaria. She taught us how to catch *Aedes aegypti* mosquitoes without hurting them, sort them into male and female, and clip their antennae to mount on slides. I got a kick out of watching *Drosophila* fruit flies multiply into colonies and keeping track of who begot whom and what eye color their offspring had. I loved this stuff and my teacher. The boys drove her to tears, but she gave me high marks and was very kind to me.

I'm going to be a doctor, I told myself. A good one. And realizing that I was merely average in this pool of eggheads, I worked harder.

After I'd been two years in the big city, my parents came to visit less often. I didn't mind, because I had learned to go downtown with my friends to shop and go to the movies. Even though I was a year or two younger, only fourteen, I tagged along when they went to see *The Graduate*. I was eager to see why some movies were only for adults and felt greatly rewarded with the shocking thrill of the scenes where Mrs. Robinson seduces the young, wide-eyed Benjamin.

We had school and dorm parties, doing the jerk, the bugaloo and the bye-bye to Beatles songs. I danced in my favorite party get-up: a red pair of Ban-Lon bell bottom knit pants, a Vonnel pink-and-white sleeveless knit top, and flat sandals.

We were asked to choose between French and German; whatever we picked, we were going to learn for the next three years. I randomly picked French.

Mr. Estanislao walked in the door – bald head tilted up, plump chest out, shoulders subtly swaying, left eye twitching behind black horn-rimmed glasses. His voice boomed when he gave the French equivalents of our names. "Steve, you'd be Etienne. Daniela, you'd be Danielle. Santiago, you'd be Jacques, but why is your face so ugly?"

I was surprised to hear that we also needed to know if a noun was male or female; I thought this skill applied only to Mrs. Reyes's mosquitoes and flies. Mr. Estanislao didn't forgive missing *circonflexes* and *cedilles*, or *accents graves* that should've been *aigus*. When he taught us how to sing *La Marseillaise*, I understood why the newspapers called him the country's greatest baritone. Although he was known for his blunt remarks, he never spoke an unkind word to me, and at the end of the course, he gave me a perfect mark.

My math teacher in third year was Mrs. Ejercito. She waddled into the room, her eyeglasses hanging around her neck, books and chalk box in hand. Before starting the class, she pulled down the parts of her skirt that had slid up above her hips. "Daniela, to the blackboard," she yelled. Only Monsieur Estanislao's voice out-boomed hers.

I walked to the board and wrote my solution to the calculus problem.

"Absolutely wrong!"

At lunch, Nancy who had been in the classroom next to mine

said, "So Ejercito gave it to you today."

"You mean you heard her insult me?" I said. "How far can her voice reach?"

At the end of the third year, my report card glowed.

"No boys," Dad said. "Finish school first." But I had a big, secret crush on Billy, the cutest boy in school. He was seventeen, three years older. He wasn't that tall, maybe three inches taller than my five-foot-two, and he had his straight black hair cropped short for the required military training. His buckteeth protruded less than mine. While my class waited outside the physics lab for the next period, I kept my eyes peeled for his class to file out of the room. It killed me that he usually walked out looking down, even if he was chatting or laughing with a friend, because then I couldn't see his dancing eyes and caught only the mole high up on his left cheek.

After watching *Romeo and Juliet*, I fantasized that Len Whiting was in love with me. That I had Olivia Hussey's cleavage. I played over in my mind Dustin Hoffman's eyes popping out as Mrs. Robinson raised her black-stockinged legs.

Then Billy asked me to be his date at his military training graduation dance. I was delighted and proud that the campus heartthrob, my heartthrob, should pick me. By then, I'd grown my hair to look like Olivia's, and when Billy and I danced, I could see Len and Olivia tenderly making love. At the end of the evening, Billy gave me his cap and pin. I couldn't contain my joy, but I didn't tell anyone about it – except Chona, when I got home for the third summer.

"Look," I said, "he gave me these." I wore the cap on my head and showed her the pin.

"Good for you," she said, took the pin and examined it. "Oh, did you know that Manang Aning ran away two months ago? She'd always said Jacinto wasn't her boyfriend, and then she ran away with him."

"Huh? But she's here now..."

"Daddy went to bring her back. There was nothing she could do."

"She's pretty, smiling eyes and dimples. Not surprised that boys should easily notice her. But I'm glad she's back. I hope Zenay runs away instead. But maybe no one will want her."

"Stop that," Chona said.

I rolled my eyes, faced the mirror and tilted Billy's cap to the left. "You should try catching frogs."

"Icky!"

I looked out the window to Mount Pecho. "No, sister dear," I said, "it's fun. You can turn them into princes."

CHAPTER 7

When the metal rods holding the mosquito net over our bed rattled around midnight, I thought it was another earthquake.

"Do you two hear me?" It was Dad's voice. The bed didn't stop shaking, and I clung to Chona. She pulled the sheet over our heads.

"I don't care what you know or what you heard. If word of this reaches your mother," Dad said, "I'll break your bones." He shook our bed again and walked out of our room.

"It's your fault," Chona whispered.

"Why?" I pulled the sheet lower, gasped for air and wiped the sweat on my forehead.

"Because you've been mean to her, and she surely told Dad."

"Zenay?" I said. "I'll send that pug-nose to hell." It had been nine years since Chona saw our father in bed with our cousin.

Chona sighed. "But you've gone too far by telling her you know her secret."

"Why don't you care that they're cheating on Mom?"

"Yeah, smarty-pants," she said. "You're away at your uppity boarding school while I'm stuck with them all year."

The following morning, Dad acted as though nothing had happened the night before and left for school where he taught summer courses. Mom went shopping in Laoag. Zenay prepared the day's food and did the laundry.

"What to do now?" I said to Chona.

"Can't you see we have no choice?" she said.

"Coward," I said. "I know what to do. Come." She followed me to the bathroom where I picked up Zenay's toothbrush and brushed my toenails with it.

"You're so mean," Chona said.

"Oh yeah? Look at this." I dipped the toothbrush in the little puddle around the floor drain and returned it to the counter. "I'm telling Mom. Wait and see."

But I didn't. I couldn't, with Daddy's threat pulling me back.

Back at school and in junior year, a new boy showered a lot of attention on me, walking me home to the dorm most afternoons and staying a bit to chat. David had his curly hair cropped short, thanks to military training, but he looked cute anyway. Billy was still the handsomest boy in school, but I didn't fancy him that much anymore after seeing him spending time with another girl. When David asked to escort me to the prom, I quickly agreed.

For prom night, I went with Nancy and Trina to the parlour to have our hair done, mine with a tiny bun on top and some strands falling down my shoulders. We put eyeliner on each other's eyelids and tried each other's lipsticks. I splashed on plenty of Johnson's Baby Cologne and wore a pink chiffon tent with a beaded mock turtleneck. Then I carefully put on my only pair of nylons, slipped into my white pumps and fidgeted until David came to pick me up. He was in his shiny black suit and tie, a refreshing change from his sweaty basketball shorts and jerseys.

"You look great," David said. "I bet you're going to win."

"No way," I said. "Tomboys can't win."

"The class picked you, meaning we think you're pretty." That night, there was going to be a contest for prom queen among six girls: five winsome girls – and me.

Round tables were set in the hotel ballroom in the shape of a horseshoe, their white linen skirts almost touching the floor. Pink and blue balloons bobbed from the chairs. A disco strobe ball glinted above the bare center of the floor.

"Any table you like," a waiter said. We chose an empty one so I could save seats for Nancy and Trina. The stage was at the far end of the ballroom – *Prom Night '69* in big silver-foil letters pinned on the maroon velvet backdrop, with a huge, ornately-carved rosewood chair in the middle. At the foot of the stage, the band was testing their instruments. Then I saw the long table next to the band, with nine or ten seats.

"That many judges?" I said in the midst of the screeching static. "Makes me nervous." I squirmed at the glare of the lights, wishing they'd turn them all down and put the strobe to work.

"You'll be okay," David said. "We'll be okay."

The judges sat at one side of the long table, Pepsis in front of them, and the program began. David held my hand chest-high and led me in front of the long table and then along the inner edge of the horseshoe. I walked pigeon-toed, grinning nervously, fighting the urge to look down. When all of us six girls and escorts had paraded around the hall, we stood in a line facing the judges to answer their questions. Then, mercifully, they sent us back to our seats and dinner was served.

I was shoving a piece of cream puff in my mouth when they called out my name. "Prom Queen … Daniela!"

Can't be, I thought. Before I could say anything, David had taken my hand. As he walked me up to the stage, I still had a nervous grin, but I didn't feel plain any more. They put a tiara of fresh *sampaguita* flowers on my head and gave me a nicely-wrapped present. I sat on my throne on stage for awhile, David standing beside me. The air was full of his musky Brut cologne and sweet *sampaguita* fragrance.

"Let's get some air," David said later, panting after a bugaloo.

As we crossed the hallway, the elevator opened, and I caught sight of Trina and her escort smooching inside. God, I thought, what a daring girl. David and I went out to the balcony, leaned against the railing and watched the traffic on the street five floors below.

"Nice, cool breeze," David said. He inhaled long and deep and came closer. "I love you, Daniela."

"You're kidding," I said.

"I mean it." He took my hand. His hands were clammy, shaking.

Other boys had written me those words, but this was the first time I'd actually heard them. I felt tingly and said, "I like you, but my dad will kill me if I have a boyfriend. I have to finish school first."

"I can wait," David said. "I will wait."

We danced until the small hours to the Beatles, Santana, the Lettermen. The band played *Put Your Head on My Shoulder,* and David held me closer. I had to be on guard with a gentle push, to keep him from embracing me tightly. I wanted everything to be proper. In the cab to my dorm, I let him hold my hand. But I didn't let him kiss me goodnight.

Back in my room, I opened the prom queen present – a bottle of Chantilly perfume. Sweet, a bit heady. I dabbed some of it on my wrist, feeling like a grown-up lady, with David's 'I love you' echoing in my ears, lulling me to sleep.

When I returned home for the summer, I met my new baby sister, six-week old Marya, for the first time. My family had also moved to a new house just behind Lola's. There were three bedrooms: one for my two brothers and Zenay, another one for Mom, Marya, Chona and me, and the third for Dad.

"Why does Dad have his own room?" I asked Mom.

"*Anak ko unay,*" she said, "that's how he wants it."

Mom knew my heart melted when she called me her precious child, and that it also ended the conversation. I stepped out and found Chona in the back porch. Zenay was hanging laundry on the clothesline between two mango trees. "You think they're still at it?" I said, nodding toward Zenay.

"You bet," Chona said. "My friend even saw her and Dad at the *ilot*'s place last month."

"Why would Dad go to an *ilot*?" I said. He always took us to a real doctor, not the village quack. "You don't mean... Did you tell Mom?"

"No way."

Zenay finished her chore and went to the kitchen. I walked to the clothesline, yanked off her Sunday dress and held it up with both hands. "Why, two of me can fit in this enormous thing," I said and dropped the dress to the gritty ground. When Zenay came back a while later and noticed the dress, she quietly picked it up and rinsed it in a tub.

"You should use clothespins," I said. "Hey, why did Dad take you to the *ilot*?"

"Nothing," Zenay said.

"Nothing your face. What was wrong with you?"

"We just took a friend who was sick," she said and walked away.

"Sick friend, your ass," I muttered. "How can Dad prefer that dark tub of lard to Mom?"

"Makes you wonder," Chona said.

"He takes his beautiful wife to the town *fiesta*, the two of them dressed to the nines and dancing cheek to cheek. Gets her pregnant, again and again, but plays around like this," I said. "See, who can tell? It's all very neat, man and mistress don't have to go out on trysts, everything is contained in this house. How disgusting. Let's tell Mom."

"You want broken bones?"

"One day," I said. "I just will."

"Well, show me how daring you are. And what would Mom do, do a Nana Gening?"

Nana Gening was Mom's older cousin, a feisty woman whose husband was known to run around quite a lot. "What about her?"

Chona laughed. "So she heard about the latest mistress and one day, at the marketplace, she challenged her to a fight. 'Come, you bitch,' she'd said. 'Come and I'll pluck all of your pubic hair out!'"

"Can you imagine Mom doing that?" I said, imitating Nana Gening's shrill voice and flailing scrawny arms. We both knew it would be beneath our mother to do that.

David and I hung out together a lot during senior year. In the months leading to our high school graduation, there was an increasing number of student protests against the Marcos government. The economy was in decline and the Vietnam War was in full swing. Philippine soldiers were fighting with the Americans against the Communists in Vietnam, and the activists wanted this to stop. One of the rallies ended with the police using tear gas and automatic rifles, the students hitting back with Molotov cocktails. Four students died, and many were wounded. While most of the activists were from the universities, our high school was becoming involved in the protests. Because we were students at the nation's honors high school, which was funded by the taxpayers, most of us felt responsible for speaking up for the larger community. Some who secretly joined the protesting organizations were expelled from the school when they were found out. I didn't join, and neither did David.

After high school, David and I went to the University of the Philippines. UP was the country's best university, also the heart of student unrest. We were classmates once more. He had a scholarship in engineering. I had three scholarship offers, but none of them was for medical school, so I decided to pick one in math. We were a bit bored with the freshman courses, because we'd already taken them in high school. There were more interesting things to do, like joining rallies in the streets of Manila, or attending teach-ins conducted by the student protesters, where my ideal image of the great Marcos, now in his second term as president, gradually got eroded. Or bowling.

We skipped classes one day to go bowling with some of our new friends, including Jinky and her cousin Angelo. Jinky had said that Angelo had a crush on me, and what a pity that I was David's girl. I didn't tell her that I was intrigued by Angelo's piercing dark eyes, and that when I sat behind him in class, I wanted to rumple his straight hair from his bangs all the way down to his nape.

After the game, David walked me to my dorm as usual. We sat on our favorite couch in the big reception hall. "Let's do our algebra assignment," he said, his lean, brown arm brushing mine.

I said, "I'm tired," crossed my arms and slid farther from him.

"Okay," he said. "Would you like to go get some rest then?"

"Don't come and see me again," I said.

"What?"

"I mean stop being my shadow."

"But ..."

"I need space."

"No fair," David said. His sleepy fawn eyes drooped even more; his short curls clung to temples that glistened with sweat. "At least give me a reason."

I stared at the flowers on the coffee table and didn't speak. He fiddled with his books. We sat there until the dorm matron came to us. "It's five to eight," she said. "Your curfew, remember?" The regular curfew was nine o'clock, but my father had told the matron that *my* curfew would be eight o'clock.

"Look," I said to David, "you have to go."

"Is it Angelo?" he said.

"No."

"You're being immature."

"Who cares?" I said. I didn't want to hurt him by admitting it was Angelo, but who was he to stop me from getting what I wanted? And I was sixteen, how could I be immature?

The next few days, when David sat next to me in class and tried to start a conversation, I refused to talk. Two weeks later, he left a brown envelope on my seat and sat at the far end of the room. Inside the envelope were all the little things I had given him – photos, pins, notes. He ignored me after that. I was surprised by how much it hurt, but I didn't dare approach him because in those days, nice girls never did the chasing.

After that, David didn't bowl with us. I often saw him in the school building lobby, painting slogans on canvas streamers. *Marcos: Hitler, Dictator, Puppet! Down with Imperialist America!* He never looked my way.

Then Angelo asked me to help him with his math, and I was disappointed. Although I still liked his hair and the look in his eyes, I wanted someone smarter than I, not one who couldn't even handle basic algebra.

I approached Dennis, David's best friend from our high school. I wanted to tell him I wouldn't mind seeing David again, but I couldn't get myself to say it, quickly reverting to my default mode of clamming up for fear of being shamed or rejected. "Is he well?" I said. "I've seen less of him in class lately."

Dennis laughed. "I'll do my cry-ing in the rain…," he sang with eyes closed, his hands strumming a shadow guitar.

He's hurting? Should I go after him? A decent girl doesn't that. No, I can't.

Course-work got harder the next semester. Since I was still on a scholarship, I needed to maintain a minimum grade. I couldn't afford to skip classes, but the world outside demanded more attention. As I went to more teach-ins, I was convinced that the apparent corruption of Marcos and his men and the rising prices were good reasons to protest. The leaders, some of them friends from high school, read from a little red book they called their bible and spoke of national democracy.

One afternoon, a bunch of activists walked the corridors shouting "Boycott, boycott!" on megaphones. Meaning, get out of the classroom and join us in the rally. By now, this was happening once or twice a month. Together with most of the class, I walked out and boarded one of the buses that took us to a meeting point with protesters from other parts of the city. From there, we were to march to Mendiola, the bridge closest to the barbed wire surrounding the presidential palace.

It was the biggest rally I had attended. Standing on top of an old van, the student leaders gave impassioned talks. The crowd jeered when people impersonated Marcos and Nixon and cheered when their effigies went up in flames. Then we started to march, singing the Filipino adaptation of *L'Internationale* with raised fists. I thought this must be how it felt being part of a revolutionary phalanx. Noble. Invincible. With many of my friends around, I also felt I was on a picnic.

A booming crackle like a giant firecracker stunned the crowd. Silence. Then another loud bang and still a few more. Panic in people's faces.

"Let's go," I yelled to my friends, shaking. We ran from the sound of the shots. Other people ran behind us, the crowd like a colony of ants whose hill had just been tipped over. We kept on running for several blocks until we reached a street that looked normal and hopped on a bus, panting. It was a Friday, so instead of going back to the dorm, I went to my uncle's house for the weekend.

"Big rally this afternoon, huh," my uncle said over dinner. "Those are Communist groups recruiting innocent students. Out to overthrow the government."

"No," I said, "they can't be Communists." He's got to be kidding, I thought. Protesting was what the smartest students did. The protest fever started by students had spread, and some teachers and even beauty queens were now marching in the streets.

"Of course they won't tell you they're Communists," he said. "The devil seduces by appearing as a dashing gentleman. Then they'll turn us into another Vietnam."

I thought of the comment my teacher had scribbled on my essay: *Be sure you don't confuse the terms democracy and national democracy; the latter refers to Communism.* And the little red book. Although I had not read one, I'd heard that it contained Chairman Mao's teachings. China's Mao Tse Tung. I stopped arguing with my uncle, but I thought, so what if we adopt Mao's ideas? What's wrong with applying some of his concepts if they could improve the common man's lot? Besides, Marcos can't shoot us all down simply because we don't agree with him.

"Look, you're on TV!" my uncle cried. "Marching in Mendiola. Wait 'til your father hears about this."

Some TV camera had caught me. Let my father break my bones, I almost said, but I was thankful that we had no TV back home.

"Oh God," he said. "You know that boy?"

I looked at the TV. They were showing footage of two newspaper-covered bodies sprawled on the pavement. Their heads had been hit by Molotov cocktails hurled from a tall building. One of them was Kiko, a boy from my high school. I felt like throwing up.

A month later, students occupied the UP campus and barricaded the roads, to protest an oil price increase. There were, of course, no classes. One professor who was refused entry by the students fired at the barricade, hitting Johnny, another friend from high school, in the stomach. Johnny died two days before I turned seventeen. I didn't go to his funeral because I wanted to remember him singing and dancing on top of the lab table before the physics teacher came in. At least that's what I told my friends. But actually I was afraid of the government spies who were expected to be there, pretending to be press people, taking photos, building up dossiers of the defiant students.

I went to more student demonstrations with Trina and other friends, but we stayed on the fringes. David was on the front lines. He was now one of the leaders of *Kabataang Makabayan*, the most radical activist group on campus. The slogans became bolder. *Rebolusyon! Freedom from the Dictator!* He barely went to class anymore. Trina told me that he'd lost his scholarship and that he was dating someone else.

"She looks a bit like you," Trina said. "*Chinita* eyes. Except you're taller."

Must be the petite girl I usually saw beside him in the rallies, I thought.

Most nights, I dreamed of Johnny, feebly joking in a hospital gown. Of Kiko, with a bloody newspaper around his head. The faces of David and his petite *chinita* refused to stop marching through my brain. And I knew that I didn't know anything anymore.

It was a relief to be back in my sleepy hometown the next summer, far from the chaos in Manila.

"This is the best stew, Zenay," my father said. "Stop fiddling and come eat with us."

Zenay walked to the table, dragging her slippers. Why couldn't this hideous monster walk properly? Of course, because she was too heavy.

"I made it extra-nice, Uncle. Like poppy," she said, beaming.

Dad and Zenay chuckled. No one else got the joke, and it wasn't the first time this had happened. Chona kicked my feet under the table.

"I asked her to cook it, Daniela's favorite," Mom said, smiling at me. I glared at her, wishing she'd stop looking so stupid.

"Smart wife I've got here," Dad said.

Zenay took the seat beside me, her sweaty knee touching mine. She was wearing one of her house dresses, a knee-length duster that looked more to me like a maternity tent dress, and when she sat down, it rose halfway up her thighs. Without stopping to eat, I pushed back her knee with mine. She didn't look at me, but she moved her chair slightly away and started to eat. I itched to kick her feet – hard – but decided just to go for the delicious stew.

"So, Daniela, the papers say your university is a nest of activists," Dad said.

"Yes, Dad," I said.

"Don't join those rallies. Just finish your studies. You can't lose your scholarship."

"Yes, Dad." I thought: I'm not as dumb as that ugly woman of yours who has taken the civil service exam twice and flunked both times. By now, Zenay had finished college and was teaching grade school at a faraway village, just like Mom when I was small, and had been struggling to pass the government exam that would improve her chances of landing a job nearer to home. She'd be home on weekends and this time was back for the summer.

"And no boyfriends," Mom said.

"Yes, Mom."

Chona and I went to many dance parties, subject to Dad's midnight curfew. Because we whined about having nothing to wear, Mom tried to keep up with our frenzy by sewing outfits for us. One afternoon, Mom was seated on the floor at the foot of her sewing machine, drawing a pattern.

"*Yehey*, my dress," I said.

"Come help," she said. I brought a pillow to sit on. I held the fabric, and she started to cut. "You seem to have a lot of catching up to do with Chona, chattering away late at night. Any boyfriends?"

"None," I said.

"Sure? You can tell me, I'm your mother."

"Mom, uh," I said. "I've wanted to… tell you something else."

"Yes?"

"Nothing," I said, and then I took a deep breath. "Many, many years now, actually."

"Tell me."

"Did you know about Dad and Zenay?"

"What do you mean?"

"They're cheating on you."

She didn't look up from the fabric she was cutting. I saw her sharp shears go off the orange lines she had just neatly drawn. "Chona is too scared to talk," I said, my eyes feeling hot. I let go of the fabric and dug my fists into the pillow. "She saw them long ago. Dad said not to tell you."

My mother stopped cutting and looked away. I sat there and didn't move.

"*Balasang ko*," she finally said and looked at me with the saddest eyes I had ever seen. "A woman knows. A woman's heart knows."

"You've known? Then why don't you throw her out? Or him? Them both!"

"What will people say?"

I stood and looked out the wide open window. There was not a breeze, not even a hot one. The mango and banana trees baked stiff in the sun under a pale blue cloudless sky. My mother sobbed. Sweat trickled from my brow down the sides of my nose, mingling with my tears and snot.

"Why is it always about what people will say?" I said.

"Big scandal. I can't bring up my children in scandal," Mom said. "I'd rather die."

I knew what she meant. In our little town, a human being's most valuable possession was his good name, his dignity. The smallest hint of shame devalued that one treasure, and there was no way you could take it back. There were those who defied this unwritten rule, like Auntie Celina and Ninang Florie who openly lived together, but they were different. Unlike my mother, they didn't go to church.

61

Whose dignity was Mommy safeguarding, though? Her husband's, certainly. But maybe her own, too, for a woman whose husband strayed was regarded by the community as inadequate and had no choice but to take the blame for the infidelity. And woe to the children of a broken family, for they will forever carry the label of being defective, like items rejected from a factory run.

Damn dignity, if in its name my mother refuses to stand up for me, for my siblings, for herself. Damn her, too.

Mom had not moved from where she first sat. I tiptoed around her sewing things and left the room. After I closed the door, I could still hear her sobs.

I stepped out the gate. In the late afternoon sun, the tar was soft under my rubber flip-flops. The farmers were calling it a day in the golden rice fields, loading sheaves onto carts, shirts drenched with sweat, sickles hanging on their waists. Dad had forbidden me to go to the fields, but I headed for a *tambak*, half-hoping that he'd see me walking there. But the chest-high rice blades and the grains looked itchy so I turned back to the road, to the hedges of wild *tawwa* whose leaves my mother used to pound into a balm to soothe my bruises. I picked a stalk. With my fingernails I carefully slit it lengthwise in the middle, rubbed the torn ends together and slowly pulled them apart, making a diamond. Then I blew through the film of syrupy sap caught in the middle.

I stood on the dusty road and blew bubbles this way until dusk.

CHAPTER 8

Back at university the following term, I went bowling with my roommates Nancy and Trina and Lyn one humid afternoon. After I hit a strike and returned to my seat, Eric was there, walking toward me, a big smile on his face. He was one of the two guys in my math majors' class, the one who looked arrogant. As he came near, I realized that his gait gave him that cocky air – straight and tall like a seasoned soldier, in a crisp pair of khakis and yellow polo shirt.

"Hi, Daniela," he said, "didn't know you were a hustler here." This was my first time seeing him up close. The tiny spirals of hair crawling down his forehead reminded me of my notebook's spine. Black, springy curls on a fair-skinned *mestizo* was an unusual combination. Cute, actually, and with that fetching smile, he looked confident more than arrogant.

"Oh no, I'm not," I said. His wide, dark eyes drew my gaze, and I felt conscious of my chinky eyes.

"May I?" he said and sat on the blue plastic bench behind the scoring table. He patted the spot next to him so I sat there, eyes cast down. His spotless black leather shoes made me feel like I should've scrubbed my white sneakers more. Since I couldn't afford to rent bowling shoes, I sprinkled talc on my rubber soles to make them slide on the floor the way bowling shoes do.

"I'm no hustler," I said. "I win a Coke when I beat the girls, but that's about it." I tried not to stare at his long, curly lashes. I'd have needed a lot of mascara to make mine look that long. A tingle ran up my chest as I looked straight ahead. At the far end of my lane, a pair of hands picked up the bowling pins I had just struck down and arranged them back in a triangle. Then two bare brown legs in sneakers disappeared behind the pins, and the balls rattled on the conveyor back to our side, clanging to a stop. Lyn and Trina took the balls and aimed. Nancy sat at the scoring table.

"I was playing billiards and saw you hit three strikes in a row," Eric said. I creased my brows, trying to make out what he was saying amidst the rattle in the lanes and tinny strains of *Betcha By Golly Wow* on the juke box. He slid closer to me and said, "Thought I'd say hi."

I smiled and covered my mouth with my hand, an instinct to hide my buckteeth. I felt self-conscious with him so close and turned my gaze toward the billiard hall. It was up on the mezzanine behind us, like a balcony from where you could see the bowling lanes. The late afternoon sun streamed through the open side windows. It was almost twilight, but they hadn't turned on the lights.

Eric moved even closer. "These lanes are so uneven, your ball skips its way to the pins." His hands motioned like they were dribbling a tiny ball. "Amazing how you can hit strikes like that." His fingers were long and slender, nails neatly trimmed. I was impressed to see this kind of meticulousness in a guy. David's hands had always been clean but didn't have that manicured look. I looked away, trying to follow my friends' play. Lyn's ball felled nine pins. Trina stomped her feet hard on the floor, hoping that her hundred-sixty-or-so pounds might topple her three remaining pins.

"You're awfully quiet in class," Eric said. His rich, deep voice, like a grown man's, tickled me inside. "I thought you were a snob."

64

"*Yehey!*" Trina yelled and did a little jig. Only two pins were left standing.

"Oh, Trina," I said. "You're a big cheat." I stood to play my turn and asked Eric, "Wanna roll a couple balls?"

"No, no," he said, looking into my eyes. "I came to watch you."

My legs wobbled as I walked off, feeling his eyes following me. My ball first looked like it might hit a strike, but it later veered too much to the left. The rest of my throws were all so-so. After my set, Eric handed me a bottle of Coke. "For your perfect form," he said. "Join me for a sandwich?"

The girls gathered their things. "See you later," Trina said, winking at me. Then they all left. I picked up my bag and walked beside Eric to the cafeteria. His arm brushed against my shoulder, and I shivered. The Stylistics were still on the juke box, this time crooning about feeling brand new. After Eric bought two hotdogs and another Coke, we sat at a table.

"I have to be back at my dorm by eight," I said. "Curfew is nine, but my dad told the dorm that mine should be eight." I bit into my hotdog. Catsup ran down my chin. He took out a white handkerchief from his pants pocket.

"Why?" he said and wiped the goo from my face.

What was that scent? Not quite like David's spicy Brut that had made me want to drown in his chest, but masculine, grassy, powdery – I could bury my face all day in that hanky. I took a deep breath and said, "My father's just old-fashioned."

"No problem, I'll take you home before then." He ran his thumb on my chin as though to check for more catsup, then put the hanky back in his pocket.

My knees trembled. "I shouldn't stay long. Homework."

"I know, that slave-driver Serrana. Then there's math club. I see you're applying, too."

"Should've known how much work it takes."

"What do you say we work as a team?" he said.

Back in the dorm, I could smell marijuana in the hallway leading to our room. Trina and Lyn were smoking pot as usual.

"Man, come join us for once, will you?" Lyn said.

"No, thanks," I said. I wasn't going to try that stuff and risk ruining my brain.

"Let's talk about the new groovy boy."

"His name's Eric," I said, giggling. "My damn knees turned to jelly."

"And David?" Trina said. "Tell me again why you dumped David."

I sighed. "That was dumb. I wanted to give Angelo a chance after learning he liked me. Angelo's eyes, they killed me."

Lyn lay down in her bed, propped her legs up on the wall and laughed hysterically. Trina turned to me, her eyes glassy. "Why do we always prefer good-looking boys?"

"No other way," I said. "I want them handsome. And smart, okay? So I'll have beautiful and brilliant children. But it turns out Angelo gets lost in Grade One algebra. What a turn-off. Trina, listen to me. I want my gentle and patient David back."

"Does he know that?" Trina said. Lyn had stopped laughing and snored gently. Trina took a last puff and put out the stub. She sprayed the room with air freshener and lay in her bed.

"Nice girls can't do the chasing," I said.

"Oh, crap. It's the seventies, prudie."

"I'm just being proper. If he really loves me, he'll come back."

"Only in the movies, honey. You're just scared of your dad."

"That, too. No boyfriends, you're only seventeen, finish school first, blah blah blah." I waited for a reply but Trina was already asleep.

I lay awake long after the lights were out. The smell of freshly-cut grass from the lawn outside our window replaced the last wisps of marijuana, while the crickets in the acacias sounded like they, too, were having a good trip. What was Eric doing with me? David would just have offered me a hanky, knowing I didn't allow any touching. Eric didn't even ask. Wasn't that sweet? Had I ever met such a gentleman? But then David had always let me have my way. Why was he such a coward and hadn't asked me to take him back? Why couldn't he be like Eric and be firm and take charge? Maybe he didn't care about me that much. If at all.

The next Sunday, Eric came to my dorm. I could smell his cologne as I walked toward him sitting on a couch in the crowded reception hall. He looked smart in a striped pair of black slacks and a tangerine short-sleeved dress shirt. "For you," he said, handing me three red roses.

"Oh, thanks," I said and thought of the roses that David had given me. I still had all of them, dried and pressed in a scrapbook. The bunch of girls watching TV in the corner burst into laughter. I sat next to Eric, my cheeks feeling hot.

"And these," he said. Chocolates. He opened the box, picked one and put it in my mouth. "My favorite. Caramel."

I would have preferred to eat that big piece of candy in two or three bites, but it was already in my mouth, so I slowly worked my teeth into the sticky chunk. Eric's eyes were on my lips as I did this, looking eager for praise. With my mouth still full, I said, "I love caramel." Actually, I liked nuts-and-raisins more.

He took my hand in both of his. Hey, stupid girl, I thought. People will talk. But his touch sent tingles over my body, and I couldn't get myself to pull away. "Let's go to mass," he said, gently stroking the back of my hand.

"I've already gone to church, early this morning," I said.

"My grandpa is dying."

He looked crushed, so I said yes.

On Thursday, Eric didn't come to school. He phoned me to say his grandpa had died.

"Come with me," he said Friday afternoon after class. "I'd like you to meet my family."

"I'm shy," I said, wondering if they would like me. Was he serious about me? We took a crowded bus and were both sticky with sweat when we got to Loyola Memorial. His arm was around my shoulders as we entered the room where his grandpa's body lay. All at once, about fifty sets of eyes were on me. "This is my *lola*," Eric said. "And these are my parents. My friend Daniela."

"Hello, ma'am, sir," I nodded, unsure whether to offer a hand.

"Nice of you to come," his grandma said and embraced me. His parents did the same. I wanted to push them back because I was afraid I smelled sweaty. His mother went to the inner room and returned with orange juice and cookies.

The next day, Eric picked me up for the funeral with his family in a station wagon, which I had not expected. They greeted me warmly. After the burial, I joined them for a reception at their home and stayed there the rest of the day.

The following week, we were back to our hectic schedule with the math club. Eric wasn't his usual perky self. He didn't talk much, just held me a lot. I hadn't experienced death in my family, but I imagined how painful it must be, so I tried my best to be sympathetic.

Wednesday after class, we tutored math in one of the dorms, a good way to earn math club merit points. It was after sundown when we finished, but Eric didn't feel like going home yet. We walked under the canopy of ancient acacia trees in the University Oval, the loveliest road on campus. I thought of David – where was my David? David often took me there for strolls, but by day. I refused to go there after dark when all those lush, giant trees became spooky, and he never insisted. But this time, it felt safe with Eric's arm on my shoulders and mine wrapped around his waist, even if I was unnerved that his waistline seemed smaller than mine. We circled the deserted library, stopped at the bottom of the great steps, sat down and cuddled.

"Daniela, I love you," he said.

I broke into a cold sweat. Then he kissed me. He kissed my mouth, and I didn't know what to do.

"I love you," he said again. "Do you love me, too?"

"I wouldn't be out alone with you if I didn't," was all I managed to say.

CHAPTER 9

Eric and I were in the classroom, waiting for the instructor to come in, when Nancy appeared at the door, signaling me over. I left my seat to chat with her for a while and returned when I saw the instructor approaching.

"Why'd you do that?" Eric said.

"Do what?"

"Go out and chat."

Was he serious? I looked at him and said nothing. He grabbed my right hand with his left and stroked it. The lecture started, and Eric took out his notebook. When I pulled my hand away so I could also take down notes, he took my left hand instead. The girl next to me kept glancing in our direction so I tried to pull my hand away again, but Eric clasped it tight.

After class, he put his arm around my shoulders and said, "Let's go to my discussion group." We headed toward the grassy expanse that was the Sunken Garden, the inner part of the acacia-lined University Oval that was sinking by a few millimeters each year and where activist students usually held discussion groups.

"What org?" I said.

"Samahang Radikal. Fairly new, not as aggressive as KM, but as you can tell from the name, quite radical, too."

The KM, or Kabataang Makabayan, was the most radical organization on campus, the farthest to the left, and David was now one of its leaders. Since Johnny and Kiko died, I had become cautious about committing to any organization, choosing to be in the blur at the tail of rallies, ready to run back if there was any trouble at the front. I thought of David and how brave of him to dare to lead. Me, I joined marches, raised my fist and chanted, "*Makibaka, huwag matakot!*" meaning "Fight on, fear not," but deep inside, I was afraid for my life.

The Samahang Radikal discussion group was just starting. A willowy, long-haired girl in a micro-mini skirt sat on the grass, in the middle of a loose circle of five people. Her name was Marla, a political science major. I left my clogs and books on the grass behind the circle. When I knelt down to sit, I could see Marla's undies, and because my own skirt was also short, I tried to sit carefully. The only other girl in the group was in ragged jeans.

They all spoke forcefully about the recent bombing of the opposition Liberal Party's campaign rally at Plaza Miranda, in the heart of Manila. Nine people had been killed and scores wounded, including most of the party's senatorial candidates for the upcoming elections. President Marcos had blamed the Communists and suspended *habeas corpus*. The public largely believed that Marcos had ordered the bombing, as well as other recent bombings in public places, and by suspending *habeas corpus*, he had gone a step closer to declaring martial law. He could now have anybody arrested and detained indefinitely; in fact, he had started doing this with some radical activists. I agreed with the points raised but kept my mouth shut.

The group also encouraged Eric to join the activist party's line-up for the upcoming UP Student Council elections. Eric said he'd think the matter over. The opposing party was led by a charming guy rumoured to be an illegitimate son of Marcos by an Ilocana. As they discussed strategies to beat the other party, the topic was brought up of Marcos's philandering. Apart from the Ilocana, there was a famous singer that Imelda was supposed to have confronted. But the most sensational one was two years ago, involving an American actress named Dovie Beams who had been in the Philippines making a movie about Marcos. One day, she called a press conference. Before local and foreign media, she played a cassette tape of what she said was her 'Fred' in her bed – lovemaking moans, whispers, a man reciting a poem then pleading for oral sex, the same man singing the Ilocano love song that was known to all as Marcos's favorite song. People who had heard it claimed it was unmistakably Marcos's voice, but, not surprisingly, Ferdinand Marcos denied that he was Fred. Soon, Dovie's name appeared on many placards to taunt the president. Some UP students had gotten hold of the recording and aired it, looped, on the university radio station for several days before soldiers were sent to stop them. I regretted not having heard it, for it would have been fun. For many months, we never tired of hearing and telling Dovie stories, including ones about how the affair had driven Marcos's wife Imelda to a nervous breakdown.

The sun was setting behind the lush acacias when the session ended. They'd made a plan on where to meet the next day for a rally around Malacañang Palace. "I'm scared," I told Eric. "My friends have died in these rallies."

"All the more reason you should go," he said.

"I'll think about it," I said, gathered my books and walked toward the road to my dorm.

"No," he said, gently pulling my arm. "You're not going home yet."

Our arms around each other's waists, we walked behind the library building. He picked a spot close to a hedge, sat me down and started kissing me. Then he gently pushed me until my back was on the grass, and he was on top of me, caressing my neck and shoulders. I wanted to push him away, but I tingled all over, so I kissed him back.

"*Uuuy!*" The male voice was followed by a giggle. Then two

voices chuckled. A rustle. Eric got up and looked around. I also rose and saw the outline of two teenage boys running from the bushes toward the road.

"Great show," one of them said.

"More, more," the other taunted.

Without saying a word, Eric and I gathered our books, walked to my dorm and said good-bye. That night, I couldn't concentrate on my schoolwork. I was puzzled with what was happening, why I had no power to resist Eric's advances.

Anxious about what my parents would say if they found out I was seeing someone, I decided to write and tell them about Eric. Mommy wrote back to say that since I had decided against their wishes, they could only hope now that I didn't marry soon.

"Less than twenty pesos, you say?" I told Trina, admiring her new Happy Feet clogs. "I'd have loved to go shopping with you,"

"Look who's talking," she said. "You're always anchored to that groovy boyfriend of yours. No one can get close enough to say hi to you anymore."

"C'mon, Trina," I said. "You know how it is to fall in love, don't you?"

"Really none of my business," she said, shrugging her shoulders, "but Vivian next door says she won't be surprised if you get pregnant. Maybe you already are."

Trina had a point. Eric had begun to consume me, and we could hardly bear to part at the end of each day. I almost didn't see my old friends anymore. I swallowed hard and walked to the mirror. Stared at my face, then started rubbing rouge on my cheeks. "Vivian can try wearing a bra… or stop necking with blind dates. And leave me alone," I said, trying to sound like I wasn't hurt. I splashed on some Johnson's Baby Cologne, grabbed my purse and walked downstairs to the reception hall where Eric was waiting. We got in a cab and went off to his frat's party.

The boys were friendly. Marla, the girl from the meeting, was there, her skirt shorter than mine. She curled her arm around Eric's waist and put her head on his shoulder.

"You've met Marla, of course," Eric said, his arm around her shoulders. "She's like a true sister to me."

Sister? "Hi," I said, my temples throbbing. "Nice to see you again… Marla."

I danced with Eric and some of his frat brothers, and tried to be friendly to Marla, too. And whenever Eric talked about her afterward, usually glowingly, I pretended that I also liked her, for what straight-thinking student wouldn't admire a brave, brilliant, beautiful activist? But I not only disliked Marla, I hated her for having that unnamable hold on my boyfriend.

In the summer, from the moment Chona and I got on the bus for Montaña, I missed Eric. Chona had started college in Manila the year before and was renting a room at an aunt's house, so we now traveled together to and from Manila. For me, the most exciting thing about Montaña was our baby sister Marya, who had just turned three. When we got home, we found Marya running around in the yard, our cousin Rosita – Zenay and Aning's sister – trailing her.

Mom said that a few weeks earlier, Aning had run away again, this time with a man named Manuel. Once more, Dad went to get her, but she refused to leave Manuel, saying they had gotten married on the day she disappeared. My parents then arranged for Rosita, who was in her early teens and in high school, to live with them and be Marya's nanny. Rosita looked a bit like Aning – dark brown skin, round face, curly hair – but without the smile in her eyes. She spoke abruptly, as though always angry, which greatly annoyed me.

The next day, I was helping Mom fix lunch when I overheard Dad reprimanding Rosita in the backyard. She talked back in a rather defiant tone. I was surprised that in return, Dad was silent. "She sounds arrogant," I told Mom.

"Yes," she said, "she's quite young. How's your boyfriend?"

"He's okay," I said. "Very nice to me."

"You have to finish school," she said. "I'm afraid you'll get married before then."

"I'm just dating. Who gets married at eighteen?"

"Look," she said, "when you say yes to a man who courts you, it means you've already decided that he's a suitable husband, no?"

"Yes, Mom," I said. "I'm sure Eric will make a good husband. But not just yet."

She gave a heavy sigh. "You also know, unless I didn't teach you well, that a woman who loses her virginity before marriage loses all honor, no?"

"I know, mother dear. Don't worry about me. I'm a good girl. And Eric is a well-behaved guy, very religious if you care to know. He went to grade and high schools in Don Bosco and had wanted to enter the seminary and become a priest, but his father didn't allow him. He wanted his son to go to the Philippine Military Academy, but Eric didn't want to. As a compromise, he went to UP."

"Good," Mom said.

We shredded cabbage and peeled carrots silently for a few moments. Then I said, "Dad plays *mah jong* quite a lot, I noticed."

Mom wiped the sweat off her brow with the back of her hand, then began to chop with slightly heavier strokes. "It's more of always than a lot," she said. "Remember his jeep? He lost that at *mah jong*. It's that friend of his, Abogado Blas. Bad influence."

"Huh?" I put my knife down and looked at her. "I thought he'd sold the jeep to do some home improvement. Why do you let him?"

"You can never change a man, *balasang ko*," she said and stopped chopping. "That's why I fear for you."

"Fear not, Mother," I said. "I've got Eric around my little finger."

Abogado Blas and Dad had been friends since I was small. Two smart men, one a lawyer, the other a professor. Like Dad, the lawyer was married to a grade school teacher. He had six daughters and a very effeminate son. Talk was that he was keeping a mistress in the next town. "You mean Dad and Abogado Blas cover up for each other?" I said.

My mother shrugged.

There were no phones in all of Montaña, so Eric and I had promised each other to write as often as possible. That night I took out the box of perfumed aqua blue linen stationery I had bought in Manila and began to write. *I'm having fun with my baby sister, but I miss you already. My mother is afraid we're getting married soon. I think she's over-reacting. But I sorely miss you. I can't imagine going for eight weeks this way, I just might die...*

Five days later, I got a letter in the mail. It wasn't a reply to mine, but one Eric had written the day after I left. *I miss you. My father always manages to say what an idiot I am for rejecting the scholarship at the military academy. Says he's at least glad he didn't allow me to enter the seminary to become a useless priest, but how many more dumb choices was I going to make? I don't need all this. Criticism, criticism. When are you back?*

To pass the time between letters, I enrolled for the summer in a computer programming course in Laoag. I came home from school one day and found Mom chatting with a woman at the gate. Francis was on the couch, shivering under a sheet.

"I... I mm...might die," he said, wheezing.

"Your asthma again?" I said.

"Is th...there no cure to this?" In frustration, he tapped hard on his lap with each word that refused to come out.

Francis had just finished grade school. He was very bright, but because his asthma had forced him to stay home a lot, he finished only second in his graduating class. Three years ago, he'd developed a stutter, which we at home had been patient with, but other kids teased him. I sat by his side rubbing his back and said, "You won't die." Just then, Mom came in the door.

"Lorenzo!" she yelled. "Where's that boy? Come over here!"

When Sonny showed up, Mom said, "That was Alex's mother. What did you do to him? How many more parents will come to me complaining that you've beaten up their sons?"

Sonny looked down and said, "I punched him a few times to shake off his fat."

"God, when will you stop? That boy is much bigger than you." Alex was fat and tall and thirteen, Francis's age. Sonny was eleven.

"I can't let him do that to Francis," Sonny said.

"Do what?" Mom said.

"He imitates the way Francis speaks and says he's a sissy. Our grownup cousins, they also tease Francis. If only they weren't so big…"

"Stop it," Mom said, "and just pray your dad doesn't hear about this."

But Dad had heard. When he came home, he took Sonny aside and talked to him. At supper, Francis was able to come to the table to eat with us. Dad told him he had better stop being a sissy.

I wanted to surprise Eric with a slender body when I saw him again, so I went on a serious diet, eating mostly vegetables and very little rice. Mom said I was too young to be dieting. I suspected that she was also hurt that I didn't gobble up the foods she had cooked, knowing they were my favorites, but I went on dieting anyway and lost a few pounds. I sewed myself dresses, some new and some recycled from my cousin's hand-me-downs. Mini skirts, hot pants, muumuus. Tired of my waist-long hair, I had it cut to shoulder-length. Painted the nails on my fingers and toes. I thought I looked great and was excited to show Eric my new look.

"Why'd you cut your hair?" Eric said when I saw him again in June. "I like it long." He caressed my hands. "And I like these without polish." He said nothing about my body and the yellow mini skirt I was wearing. What a letdown. But at least he was happy to see me again.

This school year, I moved in with Chona at my aunt's home,

because I hated the way people gossiped about me in the dorm. Besides, Auntie Nelda's house was in the same district where Eric lived, and it would be nice for us to commute together to school. Every morning, I waited for him at a corner, and we took the jeepney to school together. We attended classes, ate lunch and studied in the library together. He took me home, and if we got there early enough, we might join Auntie Nelda's family in praying the evening rosary. Eric usually stayed for supper.

"You're a different person with Eric," my cousin Janet said. We were seated on her bed talking about boys – Janet, Chona and me.

"What?" I said.

"All coy," she said.

"And you clutch his thigh while watching TV, and go like this," Chona said, putting her head on Janet's shoulder. "Like you're afraid he might vanish, like a bubble."

They both chuckled. I rose and headed for the door. "Whatever happened to the tomboy?" Janet yelled behind me.

A big typhoon ravaged Manila in July, its floods leaving deep potholes and mud on the asphalt roads, its winds bringing down power lines and roofs and billboards. The best side of typhoons: school would be closed for a day or two, and Eric and I could hang out. When he called me at my aunt's place, I expected him to say we were going to the movies.

"I'll pick you up in an hour," he said, his voice grave. "We're going to Saint Luke's."

"Why?"

"Aunt Emilia has cancer."

I didn't know what to say, so I just said yes and got dressed. I had met his aunt when I went to his grandpa's funeral the year before. She had given Eric a jade ring as a birthday present and in turn, Eric had given it to me, saying it was one of the most precious things he owned – not only for its material value, but because it came from his favorite aunt. I had to wrap some Scotch tape around the band so it wouldn't slip off my finger.

Aunt Emilia reclined in her hospital bed with tubes in her nose and one arm. Eric and I kissed her on the forehead. "How sweet of you to come," she said.

"Get well soon," I said.

She told Eric there was cake and Coke in the fridge and invited us to play Scrabble with her. "What's this?" she asked, patting a deep red mark on Eric's neck. "Does it hurt?"

God, I thought, that's called a hickey, Aunt Emilia. I tried to suppress a smile and stared at the dextrose dripping slowly from its upside-down bottle to the tube that ran to her arm.

"Oh, this," Eric said, stroking his neck. "Cockroach bite; it'll be fine."

I thought we'd visit for a couple of hours and then go somewhere fun, but I was wrong. We stayed there in the hospital until dark. Did the same thing the next day. And because school was closed for almost a week from the big typhoon, we visited Aunt Emilia as many days.

The next few months, Eric and I spent most of our free time with Aunt Emilia, in hospital or at home. I counted eighteen people living in their home: eight siblings, parents, grandma, aunts, cousins, plus maids. One muggy Saturday, when we arrived at the five-bedroom split-level bungalow, Eric's parents and a maid were in the kitchen. Aunt Emilia was in her room with a couple of friends.

"Take off your shoes and get comfortable in these," his grandma said, handing me a pair of house slippers. I thanked her, did as she said and sat on the couch to watch TV with Eric. Another one of his aunts gave me a pillow and told me to relax and recline. Although I felt a bit uneasy with this kind of attention, I found these old ladies quite charming.

The dining table couldn't hold everyone, so the younger ones ate in front of the TV. Eric's father kept piling food on my plate and asking how I liked his cooking. The meal was delicious, a feast by my standards: *callos* – tripe and sausage with chickpeas – *chop*

79

suey, beef steak. They teased Eric and me. His sisters said he had never gone to any parties in high school, especially because Don Bosco was a boys' school. That he had always been so shy with girls, they couldn't imagine what he did to win me.

Although I found the atmosphere in that home refreshing, I wanted to see the movie *The Godfather* with Eric that day. After lunch, we said good-bye to his family. "Watch his back to make sure it doesn't get soaked in sweat," his mother said to me. "He might catch a cold."

I thought, what the hell? But I simply said, "Yes, ma'am," so we could quickly leave. Did she also want me to promise not to give her little boy a hickey?

"Don't you believe my sisters," Eric said. "I had a girlfriend before you – pretty and chic." He pulled out a photo from his pocket: a girl in a short tent dress that showed long, smooth legs, her hair in an updo, big eyes lined in black. A shorter, fuller version of Twiggy the model. A true-blue peaches-and-cream *mestiza*.

I fell silent. But then he took me in his arms and kissed me, just like nothing was the matter. I kissed him back and was careful not to give him a hickey – where it showed.

CHAPTER 10

September 23, 1972 was just another Saturday morning. When I got up around six, I flicked the bathroom light switch, but the light didn't go on. I found Auntie Nelda in the kitchen mumbling about how she couldn't boil water for coffee, that she should've bought a gas range instead of an electric one. Because short power blackouts were not unusual, we expected the lights to be back soon. She slipped out the front door and came back after a few minutes.

"The streets are deserted," she said. "No cars, no jeepneys. The corner store doesn't have fresh bread because the delivery van hasn't come. Something's terribly wrong."

I looked out the window and saw what she meant. It was eerily quiet. Public transport strikes were common because of the rising oil prices, but the bus and jeepney operators usually announced their intentions. And how come there weren't even any pedestrians on the street? I picked up the phone to call Eric, to say maybe Marcos had finally declared martial law. The phone was dead.

Auntie Nelda took out her battery-powered transistor radio to listen to the news and got nothing but static. When the rest of the family was up, we ate sardines and crackers and talked in whispers of the rumours of the past month: that Marcos had ordered the frequent bombings in the city, claiming the Communists were set for a violent take-over of the country, all to justify martial law. That he was actually doing this to keep himself in power because by law, he was no longer allowed to run for a third term. He even had his opponents bombed at Plaza Miranda.

At mid-morning, we heard a cackling voice from a megaphone and went to the front porch. A truckload of armed soldiers slowly drove by, the voice telling people to wait for a TV-radio broadcast and to stay indoors, because they were ready to shoot anyone roaming the streets.

I tried to keep busy, but nothing worked. Once electric power was back, sometime in the afternoon, we all waited for the announcement on TV. All we had was static for a couple more hours, before Marcos's grim face finally appeared on the screen. He sat at his desk and told the nation that he had declared martial law to avert a Communist take-over. That he had suspended the Constitution as well as Congress, Senate, and the judicial system. That the government had taken over all TV, radio, newspaper, and communication networks, as well as all electricity and gas sources. That all schools were closed. And that he had signed this into law on September 21.

We had been under martial law for two days and nobody knew? How devious.

Then Press Secretary Kit Tatad began to read the law verbatim. His face was stern, and a few times through the lengthy text of Presidential Proclamation 1081, he bent to scratch his leg without stopping the reading. He read on and on and on, to rub in that Marcos was now the law.

Eric came to see me the next day, looking sullen. He and other activists had recently been elected to the UP Student Council. Certain that the military had a dossier on them all, he was afraid they'd pick him up anytime. He said the streets were still desolate, although public transport had been restored. There was now an evening curfew, so he didn't stay long.

Not sure what to expect outside, I chose to stay home for a few days. There were only two TV channels working, and most of the broadcast was about the New Society, as Marcos called it. They all said that ordinary citizens had no more reason to fear, because the streets had been rid of the violence that had become commonplace in the past months. There was one newspaper left running, and it contained only praise for the new order of things.

Eric came to visit every few days and told me that he had been going to underground meetings of the Samahang Radikal. When I demanded to know where, he said it was safer for us both if he didn't tell me. Each time he came, he brought news that this or that oppositionist – student leader, journalist, politician, labor leader – was either detained or missing. That some of our friends had been 'invited to headquarters' by the military and never returned home. At that point, I knew that I didn't want to be identified with the Movement. "You can't fight something that's bigger than you and me and the whole country," I said. But he kept going to the meetings.

One day, Eric's mother phoned me. "Is he with you?" she said. I could hear the anxiety in her voice. "He hasn't been home for two days."

"No, ma'am," I said, "but he called yesterday to say he was at a friend's house."

"Which friend?"

"He refused to say."

I heard a heavy sigh. "Please tell him to call me if you hear from him again."

When I saw Eric again, after two more days, he invited me to his house for lunch. After the meal, his mother took me aside and said, "His father is worried. He'd rather see Eric get married than put himself into danger with his activism. He might stop all this nonsense once he has a family to worry about."

I told her I was afraid, too, but didn't comment about getting married. I was only eighteen, and so was Eric. I wanted to finish my degree and get a job before planning on marriage.

School opened again after six weeks. The first day I got there, the hallways no longer buzzed with students painting protest placards. I didn't see any small groups huddling on the grass nor crowds listening to teach-ins on the great steps. With all student organizations banned, the atmosphere was now supposedly set for unfettered academic study. I heard more stories about students who had been detained or – worse – simply disappeared. Some, including good friends from my high school, had literally gone to the mountains to join the Communist New People's Army. Some new faces took their place on campus: muscular guys with crew cuts, wearing jeans, T-shirts and sunglasses. They walked around with books and clutch bags in their arms. Sometimes a couple of them came to class and pretended to listen to the lecture and take down notes.

I didn't see David around for a few days, and I suspected that he might have gone to the mountains, too. One day, I saw his best friend Dennis as I walked out of my classroom. Eric wasn't in my class, so I was alone. I took Dennis aside, opened my notebook and said, "Can you help me with this?" Then I looked around us. When I was sure none of the crewcuts were nearby, I whispered, "Why do they carry clutch bags?"

"What good is a soldier without his gun?" he said.

"Of course… How's David?"

Dennis shook his head and said, "He's in a military stockade, I don't know which one. They picked him up last month."

"Oh," I said and felt like my chest might burst. I returned the notebook to my bag, clasped the railing and looked down at the acacia tops being tossed by the rain along the Oval. "And his girlfriend? She was quite active, too, no?"

"You mean Betsy?"

"That her name?"

"Betsy's no longer his girlfriend," Dennis said. My heart stopped. David is available? Then he continued, "They got married in the Movement shortly before Martial Law."

I knew about marriage in the Movement; they had their own laws and their own officials. When I first heard about it, I thought it was a strange concept. Now that it concerned David, it was more than strange. It felt like the summer I was nine, when I learned about my father's affair and I burned my left forearm and my mother was away.

"You okay?" Dennis nudged my arm. "No worries, he's strong. He'll be fine."

Once I managed to exhale, I thanked him and walked away.

One Sunday a few weeks later, Eric took me to his home to visit with Aunt Emilia. After a big lunch, most of us sat at the living room to watch TV. I dozed off after a while. His grandma tapped my shoulder and said, "You better go take a nap in one of the bedrooms."

I looked at her and smiled. "I'm okay here, ma'am," I said. She seemed to be telling me to walk into any room of my choice, but except for Aunt Emilia's room, I'd never gone into any of the bedrooms, and I wasn't about to do that. But Eric took my hand and said, "Come with me." A little groggy, I stood and followed him.

His bedroom was a tiny box that held a small bed, a wooden wardrobe, a chair and a desk on which books and papers were neatly arranged. On one side of the desk, next to a mug full of pens, sat a green glass bottle shaped like a station wagon. I said, "How cute, what is it?"

"Wild Country After-Shave," he said.

"So this is the scent you wear," I said and opened the bottle to take a sniff.

"Don't sniff that," he said, took the bottle from me and put it on the desk. "Just sniff me." He lay me down on the bed. The springs creaked. I giggled.

"Is this a trampoline?" I said.

Eric got up, locked the door and then lay beside me, kissing and caressing me. After a few more squeaks of the bedsprings, he pulled out a huge towel from his wardrobe and spread it on the floor beside the bed.

I wasn't able to take my nap. How could I... after I'd been made love to for the very first time? At first, I felt shy and self-conscious, especially with Eric's family just a few feet away, but I had no power to protest.

Over the next few months, Eric became more solicitous and tender, and I was drawn to him even more. When I turned nineteen, we went to the university chapel, silently prayed and sat in a back pew for a while. Then he handed me a gift-wrapped box. "Happy birthday, love of my life," he said. "Open it."

I carefully untied the dainty pink bow and peeled off the wrapper. Inside the box was a bottle of *eau de cologne* labeled *Calèche*. I unscrewed the ball-shaped top and out wafted the most sophisticated scent I'd ever smelled – very feminine. "I love it, very subtle and sweet," I said. "How did you pick this? Looks and smells very expensive."

"Don't ask," he said and put his hand in his pocket. "But be warned that if you wear it constantly, I'll make love to you just as often." Inside his fist was another present, a small one that had a Ding Velayo gift tag.

"How could you afford anything from Ding Velayo?" I said, knowing that the store was one of the finest jewelers in the country.

"You ask too many questions," he said. "Just look."

I ripped the paper, opened the box and found a ring – a white gold band with a crumpled, matted look. Simple but elegant. *Eric* was engraved inside. I remembered the silver ID bracelet that David had given me for my sixteenth birthday; he'd had my name engraved on the face, and his name on the reverse. I loved that bracelet. It seemed so long ago.

"It's a wedding band," Eric said. He held my hand tight and held up both our hands toward the altar. "I mean I'd like to take you there. All we need is a date on that ring."

I felt relieved, because I had worried that he might drop me after we'd had sex. Then I'd end up disgraced, and what other man would have me? At the same time, I knew that we were not ready to get married. "We're still in school," I said. "We can't afford to live alone yet."

"We'll manage," he said. "Just wear this ring."

PART II

1973 – 1992

CHAPTER 11

Aunt Emilia's cancer had spread despite the chemotherapy. The month after my nineteenth birthday, she died. She was only a little past forty. I had never seen Eric so broken; he was sullen for weeks. School had just closed for the summer, but seeing Eric this way, I didn't want to go home to Montaña just yet. I told my parents I needed a few days to put some of my school records in order and then I'd go home. I offered to give back to Eric the jade ring from Aunt Emilia. When his face lit up, I peeled off the tape and put the ring on his finger.

The next day, Eric called to say, "I'm picking you up in half an hour. Bring an extra shirt, but don't be obvious about it." I wondered what he was up to but also liked surprises, so without any more thought, I did as he said and got dressed.

Eric asked the cab driver if he knew of any clean motels. "Sure," the man said and drove toward the south side of the city, into a maze of narrow streets lined with high walls and closed gates and signs like SHORT TIME (3 HRS): 30 PESOS. Some went as low as fifteen pesos, the equivalent of two dollars, for three midday hours. This part of town was where prostitutes practiced their trade and where lovers went for sex. I squirmed and clung to Eric's arm, torn between hiding my face lest someone recognize me and surveying the gaudy signs.

"We don't want the cheapest one," Eric told the driver.

The cab stopped at a gate, a guard quickly flung it open and said, "Number eight." Along a semi-circular driveway lined with doors, door number eight slid open and the taxi drove in.

"Go up those stairs," the cabbie said after taking the money.

The staircase led to a small, spare room. The sheets and towels could've used some bleach; I tried to convince myself they were clean. I despised women who went to motels and asked myself why I was now in one. Before any reply came, Eric had undressed me.

We made love and napped, made love and napped. At dusk, we were starved and ordered room service. The food came through a tiny window by the door. Apart from the gate guard, I hadn't seen the face of any of the motel staff, and was happy that they hadn't seen ours either.

The whole idea, Eric had said for weeks, was to leave our parents no choice but to allow us to marry. My parents were the special target – they couldn't possibly allow their daughter to lose her honor, her priceless dignity. We needed their consent because we were both only nineteen. I'd always said my father would kill me and that we should wait. But there I was, in that shady place, holed up for the night. By midnight, I knew that Chona and Auntie Nelda would be worried that I wasn't home. I tried not to think of what Dad would do and say if and when he found out.

We meant to stay only until mid-morning to cover one day's rent, but we overslept. In the afternoon, when the bill came through the tiny window, we pooled our money but it wasn't enough, especially because we had to save some for the cab ride out. Eric left his watch and jade ring behind and was told he could go back for them once he had the cash.

I fidgeted in the taxi all the way to Eric's house. His grandma wailed when she saw us. They'd gone to the police to report us missing, and his parents looked more relieved than angry. When Eric took me to Auntie Nelda's, she, of course, reprimanded me.

Chona just cried and said she'd had the fright of her life, thinking I'd been in an accident.

That night, I wrote my parents a difficult letter to say Eric and I wanted to get married.

Two weeks later, I traveled with Eric and his father to Montaña, so they could formally ask my parents for my hand in marriage. "The kids," Eric's father said, "they want to settle down."

Dad simply looked at him, then turned to me. "What have your mother and I done to deserve this?" he said.

I broke down and cried. "I'm very sorry, Daddy," I said.

"Sir," Eric said. "I love your daughter. More than anything."

"Can you look after, protect her, the way I have?" Dad said. "*Balasang ko*, you'll be eating your tears." He wiped his eyes with his hand.

"But we can't undo what has happened," Eric's father said. "We know that they still have to finish school and find jobs. They can stay with us in the meantime. I have a big household, but Daniela is welcome in my family."

"How will you finish school when the babies start coming?" Mom said, sobbing. "Nineteen is too young to become a mother."

Although he was not sobbing, I had never seen Dad shed so many tears. It broke my heart to see my parents this way, and I was tempted to back out. But what if I lost Eric?

We wanted to get married before school opened in five weeks – in front of a judge in our Sunday best, because it was all our savings could afford.

"No," Mom said. "Since you insist on marrying, you have to do it before God."

"We can't afford it," I said.

"It doesn't have to be lavish," Mom said. "Make it simple. But you need to have the standard bridal trousseau. Happens only once, you can't miss out. I'll do the sewing."

"I'll help them out,"Eric's father said.

Two a.m. I tossed and turned on a mat on the floor next to my parents, Chona and Marya in Auntie Nelda's house. My bridal trousseau was all laid out on the small bed: white brocade gown, empire cut, long-sleeved, beaded bodice and cuffs; white cotton gloves; a frilled heart-shaped pillow holding two white gold wedding bands; thirteen coins for the dowry; white roses tied together by a satin ribbon; and a long, two-tier tulle veil gathered by a faux-pearl tiara.

Mom made sure she lay next to me. She put her arm around me, softly crying. I wanted to cuddle up like I did long ago, hug her and say I was sorry. Instead, I kept my eyes shut and didn't move. After a long while, she turned, put her arm around Dad and started snoring gently. It was weird to see Mom and Dad this way; I wondered when they had last slept together. Auntie Celina and Ninang Florie were a happier couple than my poor parents; ever since I could remember, they'd always been openly affectionate to each other and didn't mind that people gossiped about their relationship.

I forced myself to just look ahead. I wasn't excited to live with Eric's family in that crowded house, but I couldn't wait to have sex on demand. I thought it'd be nice to go somewhere for a few nights after the wedding, instead of holing up in Eric's tiny room. But, of course, we didn't have the money. Besides, we had to be back in school the following Monday.

I dozed off for about an hour before it was time to get dressed for the seven a.m. ceremony. I sat at the dresser and Mom fixed my hair. Chona took pictures with an instamatic camera. Marya started bugging Mom to help her into her flower-girl dress, so Mom asked Chona to help me instead.

Chona quickly finished her own make-up then started doing mine. "I wish Francis and Sonny were here," I said. My parents had left them behind to save on the cost of travel and the reception.

"I know," she said. "We should be complete as a family."

"I hope Sonny will protect Francis when people taunt him. Rosita won't rescue Francis. Zenay would, but never that arrogant

Rosita. Sure, Zenay has always treated Francis like a favorite son, but Mom should throw her out."

"Get over it. Mom seems at peace with her; why rock the boat?" she said and began to hum *Here Comes the Bride*.

"Stop, you make me nervous. Tell me, when are you dumping that boyfriend of yours?"

"Are you crazy?" she said. "He's sweet, my hero. This eyeshadow dark enough?"

"What's sweet about always being stoned?"

"He'll change," she said. "I'm going to love him into coming around."

"You better. I'll do the same. You know that girl Marla, and whatever her name is, Eric's *mestiza* ex-girlfriend? Twiggy. I'm going to make him stop flirting with those skinny, bare-legged creatures."

"Okay, let's get you into this dress now. Let's see how it looks on you."

"I hope it fits," I said. Mom hadn't allowed me to try the dress on, saying it meant bad luck. Although I thought it was pure nonsense, I didn't want to displease her more than I already had, so I didn't argue. "What if it makes me look fat?"

Chona helped me into the long dress, pulled it up from the bottom. We both gasped after she zipped it up.

"You look ravishing," she said. "Beautiful!"

The dress fit perfectly. "Nice! What about these gloves?" I said. "Won't I look silly in them?"

"Sshh... sit down," she said. I sat and she carefully pinned the headpiece in my hair. It sat snugly along my hairline to show off my Cher-long hair. The top tier of the veil over my face made me look like an untouched maiden. "Okay. Stay still," Chona said. "Let me get into my dress and we're all set." She walked out the door.

Alone in the room, I sprayed *Calèche* on my wrists, neck and veil, put on the gloves and looked at myself in the mirror once more. I still couldn't believe I could look so good – but I did. No wonder Mom insisted on dressing me as a real bride. I clutched my bouquet, turned to the right, to the left.

Would Eric think I looked beautiful?

Would my father?

Would David?

CHAPTER 12

The night of the wedding, Eric's parents invited mine over for supper at their house.

A green plastic tablecloth covered the table. There was a wooden bench on one side, mismatched chairs on the other. Ten of us sat at table; the rest ate and watched TV in the living room. Eric piled steamed rice and *ampalaya con carne* on my plate – beef strips and bitter gourd in oyster sauce. I got excited, remembering the lunches I'd had with Dad at Panciteria Wa Nam whenever he came to visit me at my boarding high school. There, I used to binge on *ampalaya con carne*. We ate a lot of bitter gourd back in Montaña, but it was never served at the dorms. Apart from Ilocanos, I didn't know many people who ate, much less loved, the bitter fruit or its shoots and seeds. I put a chunk of the translucent green gourd in my mouth. Crisp, watery, like cucumbers – but bitter. The oyster sauce gave it a tinge of sweetness. I let the piece linger in my mouth for a while. It was delicious, very close to Wa Nam's. Tasted like home.

"Tatay, this is excellent," I said to Eric's father, knowing he was the cook in the family. Eric and his siblings called their parents

Tatay and *Nanay*, the Filipino words for father and mother.

Tatay gave me a big smile and turned to my mother. "So, Marta, did I do justice to the Ilocano vegetable?"

"It's very good, sir," Mom said and smiled shyly. The two sets of parents were about the same age, in their late forties, but it was natural for my mother to politely address people she hardly knew.

"Please, Marta," Nanay said to Mom. "Don't be so formal."

"Try this, too," Tatay said and pushed the steaming bowl of *bulalo* soup toward me. Fleshy beef bones, Chinese cabbage, yams and plantains in clear broth, with a film of grease on top. "Give them some of the marrow," he said to Eric.

With a pair of tongs, Eric pulled out a big bone then tapped it on a plate until the marrow fell out. My mouth watered while he spooned the thumb-size yellow gel onto my plate. Then he shook off the marrow from another bone and offered it to my parents.

"Eat, eat," Nanay said.

And I ate and ate. I slowly savored the sweetish, fatty marrow, eating a little bit at a time with a spoonful of rice and vegetables. But throughout the meal, my parents were both reserved and quiet. I knew what they were thinking: Dad would've loved to gorge on the *bulalo* but didn't want to appear ill-bred; if she was the cook, Mom would not have squeezed out most of the gourd's bitter juice before tossing it in the pan.

"Be sure to help around the house," my mother said when I kissed her good-bye. Dad nodded in agreement.

"Yes," I said, but I thought: I know, I know. Why couldn't they trust me?

After seeing my parents off in a taxi, Eric and I retired to his room and made love with reckless abandon, forgetting how much the bedsprings squeaked, until we were half-dead with exhaustion. I woke up once, kissed Eric hard, he awoke and we made love and fell asleep again. I awoke once more in his arms and couldn't believe my good fortune of now having this gorgeous guy all to myself.

When I opened my eyes again, Eric was fast asleep. White stripes of sunlight punched through the jalousie windows. The smell of a lazy weekend breakfast wafted in – garlic fried rice and smoked fish. I could hear the sprinkling of water in the garden outside, ducks quacking, a bicycle honking, Eric's little sisters fighting over the comics section of the Sunday paper. From the living room TV, Popeye was yelling, "Well, blow me down!" and I imagined him and Bluto playing tug of war with the oh-so-elastic Olive Oyl.

Lying there, I noticed for the first time that two of the bedroom walls stopped about a foot short of the low ceiling. Meaning that our room was actually a semi-cubicle, sharing one concrete partition with Eric's parents next door and another with a narrow hallway. Across the hallway was a bathroom and a bedroom shared by Eric's three brothers.

I lay there wondering how I hadn't noticed the short walls before. Then I saw a curly head bob at the top of the hallway partition and recognized it as Chito's, Eric's ten-year-old brother. The head disappeared and I heard a thud, a crash that sounded like a wooden chair, some low giggles. Eric was sleeping so soundly this didn't wake him, so I just lay there quietly. When he awoke close to noon, I asked him to hurry so we could catch the noonday mass and said nothing about Chito.

We left his parents busy in the kitchen. When we returned, his mom told us to relax a bit, lunch would be ready shortly. Eric gave me a tour of the house, a split-level bungalow. Five small bedrooms, front porch, narrow garden in front, a carport that led to a small patio toward the back, four or five ducks in a pen, a mango tree and laundry tub in a far corner of the yard. Just like my first home in Montaña, the house belonged to his grandmother. Lola Bening welcomed anyone who needed a place to stay while visiting the city from their home province of Mindoro. That day, there were two distant cousins who had come to look for jobs in the city. Eric, me, and nineteen strangers. I felt like a welcome guest at a raucous party.

Lunch was another big fat meal. Afterward, Eric and I organized the bedroom to make room for my things and got ready to go back to school the next day. Eric was sorting stuff that he'd taken out of his wardrobe. I was unpacking my suitcase.

"Damn!" Tatay yelled from the bathroom across the hallway from our door. "I sent my boys to a technical school, and not one of them will fix a leaking faucet."

Eyes wide, I looked at Eric. Dad seldom yelled. When he was upset, he spoke in a low voice; the lower his voice, the more displeased he was.

"Don't mind him," Eric said.

"What do you mean?" I said.

"Haven't I told you how critical he is?" he said and smirked. "How he drives me nuts?"

"Maybe you should go and help him fix the faucet."

"Leave him alone; we're busy, right?"

Eric seemed unperturbed even as his father continued to yell, but I began to feel uneasy. And afraid.

When I woke up Monday morning, Nanay was fixing breakfast and ordering a maid to pack lunches for seven children: four in grade school, two in high school, and one in college. Another maid was busy helping the younger ones get dressed.

Eric and I sat down for breakfast. On the patio just outside the kitchen door, Tatay pressed a pair of pants and a shirt, a towel around his waist. At the kitchen sink, Nanay was squeezing toothpaste onto a toothbrush when a school bus honked at the gate. The two youngest girls rushed out. Toothbrush and lunchboxes in hand, Nanay ran to the gate and came back inside after the bus left.

"Here," she said and handed the toothbrush to her husband. Tatay took a glass of water and the toothbrush and went out the back door to the laundry tub. Nanay turned to me and said, "Put toothpaste on Eric's toothbrush, too, like what I did with your Tatay's."

I nodded, trying to conceal my mild shock, and did as I was told.

Sex was wonderful, greater than I'd ever imagined. It was all I lived for during those first days and nights. Eric wanted eight kids, just like in his family. And soon. Eight kids! Thankfully, Nanay took me to Doctor Edrosa, her obstetrician-gynecologist, and I asked to be put on contraceptive pills. Eric and I had one year left in school, and I wanted to graduate on time to show my parents that marriage wouldn't prevent me from getting a degree. A baby before then would set back my schedule. Besides, I wasn't excited about becoming a mother. How in the world would I know how to care for a baby?

In our room one afternoon, Eric and I heard a clatter at the jalousies. There again was Chito, trying to take a peek. Eric rose to close the windows, and Chito ran off. "Well," I said, "are you going to talk to him?"

He shrugged his shoulders and said, "He's just a kid."

I didn't pursue the subject, but the next weekend, I bought some heavy fabric and went to Auntie Nelda's to sew curtains for our windows. Not sheer, dainty window dressing, but floor-to-ceiling drapes. Of course, it also became hotter and darker but at least, for privacy, this was much better than the heckler-infested Sunken Garden at the university.

But it wasn't as simple as hanging a thick curtain. Sometimes, I'd catch his brother wearing my T-shirt or sleeping in our bed. And although Eric knew I didn't like the idea, he didn't do anything about it.

We had been married for a month when we went to a frat party one evening. I drank a little beer, half a bottle. After four bottles, Eric became noisy. I thought he'd had too much, but since drinking was supposed to be the macho thing to do, I let him go on. Besides, I knew that men didn't want their women to interfere when they were having fun. I sulked on a couch and didn't mingle, but during the cab ride home, I bitched about being left alone. When we got home, Eric showed me once more the picture of his old girlfriend, the Twiggy one.

"You're not really pretty," he said.

I creased my forehead and stared at the pretty face in the photo. "Why are you saying this?" I said, trying to look calm, but inside, I felt burning sensations gliding from my head, toes and fingertips and colliding in the middle of my chest.

"You should help in the kitchen," he said.

"I'm not a good cook," I said. "And I'm afraid of being yelled at."

"Tatay won't shout at you," he said. "It's just his nature to yell at anything. Don't take it personally."

I wasn't convinced but it made me feel a bit better. I was more disturbed by Twiggy. "What has that got to do with my being ugly?"I said and began to cry.

Eric said nothing more. Instead, he pressed me down on the bed and made love to me. Ravenously. I forgot all about Twiggy and the kitchen, and all was well again.

Afterwards, I forced myself to help in the kitchen every now and then. Everything had to be done with military precision: the string beans cut two inches long, all of them; the potatoes diced just so; the greens blanched exactly one minute. It didn't matter that Tatay always directed his criticisms to his wife or the maid or the *wok*; I felt nervous just the same. I'd always clammed up whenever Dad was displeased even if he seldom yelled. Now, with the yelling, I clammed up even more.

But the old ladies, Lola Bening and Aunt Pacita, were caring and gentle, smothering the children and me, Eric especially. When she was alive, Aunt Emilia was just as sweet.

After lunch one Sunday, Tatay told Eric to set up the *mah jong* table in the back patio. So that's how *mah jong* tiles looked: chunks of ivory a bit wider than piano keys but only a third as long, marked with Chinese characters. I'd never seen a tile up close until now, but I'd always known they clinked – I'd hear the sound whenever I passed by the *mah jong* house where Dad played in Montaña. Day or night, whenever I went by that house, there was that clinking and people crowding around tables in the carport. The sound had grated at my brain, especially if I knew that Dad was in that house gambling the night away.

Four players at table: Eric and his parents plus a neighbor. Eric had me to sit next to him so he could teach me how to play. I found it interesting, similar to poker. I watched for three hours, with Eric whispering to me what was going on with his hand. The play was quite even for a while, then Tatay went on a losing streak, mostly to Eric. Tatay cursed and banged his tiles on the table. When one tile went flying into the duck pen close by, the ducks quacked and scurried about.

My chest had started to pound, so I got up and went to the kitchen. Aunt Pacita was smearing guava jelly on a tray of *pan de sal*. "Don't mind him," she said, sensing my discomfiture. I helped her pour Coke into glasses and brought the tray to the *mah jong* table. Then I went to our room and started to do some schoolwork, but the clinking and the yelling disconcerted me, so I decided to read a Mills and Boon romance novel instead.

The heroine Lise likes that Conde Leandro, a Spanish nobleman, is the type that takes charge, although she's afraid he's too rich for her. Clink, clink. She closes her eyes and touches her lips, reliving the thrill she'd felt when he kissed her last night and thinking of how, when he squeezed her, she could feel his manhood coming to life. Clink. Curse. Clink.

Finally, I put the book down, curled up on my side with a pillow over my ear, closed my eyes and hoped to fall asleep. I couldn't.

Eric came to our room at dusk. I could hear his father in the kitchen, barking that no one in that big household cared if the sink was clogged.

"You're not yet dressed?" Eric said. "The last mass is in fifteen minutes."

"You must not play that much *mah jong*," I said.

"We're only playing for small change."

"I feel left out. Besides, *mah jong* ruined my father."

"See, I wiped everyone out," he said, emptying his pocket of coins. He started to count. "Big-time. Five pesos." I knew that five pesos – about one dollar – wasn't going to make us rich, that they were indeed just relaxing and not gambling. But still.

I hurriedly got dressed, and we went to mass. On the walk home, Eric said he didn't want to go to church anymore, that he couldn't stand how the priests spoke like they were the ultimate source of wisdom. I was puzzled but kept quiet. Wasn't it his burning ambition, just three or four years ago, to enter the seminary and become a priest?

When we got home, Eric began to do his homework. I tried to do likewise, but the tension in the room was palpable. "What's wrong?" I said.

He didn't reply. No matter what I said, he refused to speak. And then Aunt Pacita came knocking to say supper was ready. Eric didn't budge, so I also kept silent. We stayed inside, not talking, while the rest of the family had dinner. We worked away, not talking. Went to bed not talking. I woke up in the middle of the night and found Eric lying by the door. I woke him so I could go to the bathroom and asked him to go to the bed. He slid away from the door, but he stayed on the floor the rest of the night.

We went to school the next day, still not talking. In the evening, I asked him again what was wrong.

"I only wanted you to apologize," he said.

"I'm sorry," I said. "I'm sorry, whatever it was."

"What do you mean, whatever it was? You don't know what you did?"

I gave him a quizzical look.

"You might not have said a word," he continued, "but your

104

eyes can kill. Ever since we played *mah jong* yesterday, you've had that dark look on your face. You can't hide your anger."

I was quiet for a moment, thinking of what he'd said. Certainly, I was upset, but I didn't realize it showed. I apologized again, this time sincerely, and we made up.

I took Eric to Montaña for our first Christmas. Since Marcos's first term as president eight years earlier, the highways had greatly improved. He'd had a new expressway built and old roads widened and re-paved, from Manila all the way to my hometown. When the bus reached Ilocos Norte – Marcos's province as well as mine – Eric noticed that the roads were even better and newer. I'd always taken this for granted and didn't realize until then that Eric was right. The roads in my province were indeed wider and of better quality.

"That's not fair," he said. "You should come to Mindoro to see the terrible roads. What they call highways in those parts are dirt roads."

I had thought that whatever Marcos did in Ilocos Norte, he did for the rest of the country.

"The sunovabitch," Eric said. Although he seldom went to underground meetings any more, he was still passionately against Marcos. In contrast, I had taken a passive stance, seeing the futility of fighting the martial government. I now cared more about being a good wife and finishing school.

Eric was even more annoyed when he saw billboards praising Marcos all around the province. After declaring martial law, Marcos required that his photo be displayed prominently in all classrooms and public offices. In Manila, many resented the order but obeyed out of fear. Marcos's slogan was a neatly-coined Tagalog phrase about discipline being the key to progress, but it could very well have been, 'Do as I say, and no one gets hurt.' Penalties for disobedience ranged from manual labor at the military camps to imprisonment. Sometimes it was mysterious, and permanent, disappearance. However, in Ilocos Norte, the locals willingly obeyed, for they loved and were proud of their son, and it was clear that he loved them back.

"I can see how he's totally brainwashed the Ilocanos," Eric said. "Looks like no one here believes he is a murderer and a fraud."

He was referring to persistent rumours that Marcos – back when he was eighteen – had shot to death Julio Nalundasan, who had just won a seat in Congress over Marcos's father Mariano. As a law student at the University of the Philippines, Marcos had not only excelled in academics but also in sports and had become a sharpshooter on the college pistol team. He was jailed for Nalundasan's murder, and while in prison, he studied for the bar and wrote his appeal for a new trial. Later, he topped the bar with the highest-ever score on record. Five years after the murder, the Supreme Court reviewed and dismissed the case, and Marcos was free. Back in high school, I had seen a movie of Marcos's life that he'd used to campaign for his first term as president. In that movie, he is shown as a young lawyer defending himself in court with flawless, brilliant arguments. I believed Marcos might have killed Nalundasan, but most Ilocanos clung to the movie version as gospel truth.

"You're right," I said. "Just go easy on the topic while we're in Montaña. Especially with Dad and Auntie Celina. They're Marcos die-hards."

I was eager to be with my family again. They warmly welcomed Eric, and he got along well with everyone, but because he was new, I had to make him feel at home. Feeling self-conscious in front of him, I couldn't horse around with my siblings as much as before. Everything that was said in Ilocano I needed to translate into Tagalog for him, and sometimes it became awkward when my brothers told jokes that I thought best not to translate. Also, I wanted him to experience the things that made me happy as a child but oftentimes he didn't get it, like when I showed him how to make bubbles with *tawwa* and he wasn't impressed.

One day, as the sun was setting, Chona and I sat on the bridge across the irrigation ditch, right outside our gate. Eric was in the bathroom. Chona was strumming our old guitar, humming *Are You Lonesome Tonight?*

"Let's do Yvonne Elliman," I said, referring to the actress who played Mary Magdalene in the film *Jesus Christ Superstar*. I parted my waist-long hair dead center, spread it down my chest and put my hands together. "We need a little breeze to ruffle the hair," I said and closed my eyes.

"Forget the breeze," she said, for it was a hot and humid day. "Eyes, cheeks, hair – you look enough like Yvonne." She strummed the intro, and we both started to sing *I Don't Know How to Love Him*.

"Don't you just love that song and the movie?" I said when we had finished.

"Obviously," she said and waved to a friend passing by. "It's revolutionary, like *Hair. The Age of Aquarius*."

"This is the dawning of the age of weird," I said.

"What's weird?"

"That I can't spend more time with you, chattering away deep into the night, learning guitar pieces, singing together... I feel ancient."

"Well, you chose to marry, right?"

It had begun to grow dark. A farmer walked by with his water buffalo. Around a mango tree across the street, I saw five or ten tiny twinkles. Fireflies! I hadn't seen them in such a long time; never saw any in Manila. It felt like it was a hundred years ago when I left home for boarding school, a scared eleven-year-old. I realized it had taken me only eight years to move to the world of grown-ups and married people, one where I didn't quite feel at home.

"I guess I hurried to find myself a new home," I said, thinking of the years of moving from one dormitory to another. Seeing many more twinkles, a hundred or so, I rose and walked toward the mango tree. "Come, let's go and catch fireflies."

Back in Manila shortly after the Christmas holidays, I began to crave *cuchinta*, a jelly-like rice cake topped with fresh shaved coconut. Sometimes I'd wake up at three in the morning and imagine how the sticky cake would tickle my palate and how the slight sweetness would enhance the coconut flavor. I'd toss and turn in bed, salivating until morning. Getting up, I'd feel nauseated. Knowing women who had strange cravings after conception, I suspected I might be pregnant. After I'd been on the pill for six months, Doctor Edrosa told me to stop for a while to minimize its side effects and coached me on other birth control options.

The cravings persisted. Sometimes it was cantaloupes and green mangoes. Because I didn't want to be like some women I knew who took advantage of their pregnancy and pestered their husbands with unreasonable demands, I didn't ask Eric to produce them at odd hours. Doctor Edrosa ordered a frog test, which was what pregnancy tests were called in those days. Although by this time they'd stopped injecting frogs with a woman's urine to see if it produced eggs and had developed a method by test tube, the term stuck. I had to take the morning's first urine to a lab and wait about ten days for the results. The test wasn't that reliable, though, especially in the first two, three months of pregnancy.

Two weeks later, Eric was playing *mah jong* when I arrived home from Doctor Edrosa's clinic. The doctor had told me the test came back positive. I went to our room and sat there staring at the wall, anxious and confused. Eric came in. "Hi," I said. "Did you win?"

He frowned.

"I have news for you," I said.

"What?" he said without looking at me, arranging books on the desk.

"My frog produced eggs."

"What frog?"

"I'm... pregnant. We're going to have a baby!"

He quickly turned toward me, his face all lit up. "Are you sure?" he said, his big eyes even wider. I explained that it was too early to be sure, and that I needed to have another test in a month. He started to laugh. He hugged me tight, planted kisses all over my face, and then we both went into a laughing fit. After a few moments, he said, "You lie down, don't move," and left.

Half an hour later, he was back with a bag of *cuchinta* and green mangoes.

In spite of the odd fights, I felt loved and was glad to be married. Eric pushed me to study hard, reminding me that we were now a little family. And study very hard I did. When Eric and I received our bachelor's degrees in math from the University of the Philippines, I went up on stage three months pregnant. Eric graduated with honors. I missed the honors mark by a hair. If I hadn't spent so much time bowling and attending rallies in earlier years, I'd also have made it. Never mind. Seeing our parents' eyes gleaming, and thrilled by the thought of the little creature inside me, Eric and I felt bigger than the world.

CHAPTER 13

The summer after we graduated, Eric was accepted to teach math at UP. Since I was pregnant, I knew I wouldn't be able to find a job as easily, so I applied for, and got, a scholarship to do a master's in math.

Eric also started to work on a master's degree. We usually woke up to study at dawn, when the house was quiet. One night, at two a.m., we were doing our math problem sets at the dining table when we heard a scratchy sound coming from the living room. Eric got up and I followed him. Once he turned on the living room lights, we saw a hand trying to squeeze through a rip on the window screen, apparently to get to the front door knob two feet away and unlock it from the inside.

"*Hoy!*" Eric said. The hand withdrew, and then we heard footsteps down the porch and rustling in the garden. Our dog barked furiously and Eric's parents and a brother came out of their bedrooms. The three men rushed out the door. Nanay and I peered through the window, and seeing a small crowd on the street, we went outside, too.

All the dogs on the block were barking now. A handful of

neighbors had also joined the chase while about twenty of us stood on the street, waiting. Someone said he'd heard footsteps on his roof and guessed the thief wasn't alone. After fifteen minutes, the men were back.

"What happened?" said a neighbor.

"The *sanabagan* got away," Eric's father said. "He ran into the darkness in Escopa." Heads shook, tongues clucked. We all knew that Escopa was an impoverished section of town where people had to steal just to survive and the residents protected their own, and that if you were a regular person, you'd know better than to enter that territory.

"He sliced our window screen open and almost made it inside the house," Eric said.

"It must be an *aswang*," an elderly woman said, looking at me. "See, your wife's pregnant. The *aswang* is after the baby."

I certainly didn't believe in *aswangs*, and neither did Eric. Old folks said that these ghouls – the most feared among Philippine mythical creatures – lived among the population as normal people, but at night they detached their upper bodies, grew bat-like wings and flew around town looking for prey. That they fed on cadavers and human blood and regarded fetuses as a delicacy.

"Of course not," Eric said. "I saw the thief myself."

"You should hang bunches of garlic at your door," the woman said. "*Aswangs* fear garlic. Salt, too."

"A stingray's tail is best, if you can find one," the woman's teenage daughter said, glaring at me as though I was responsible for disturbing their sleep.

Knowing it was usually a futile exercise, no one called the police, and we all returned to our homes. "Maybe those two women are *aswangs* themselves," I told Eric, and we both went back to our books.

One night, after his family and I had had supper, Eric arrived with Manny and Jojo. He said they'd eaten and just needed to talk about

111

some fraternity matters. He sent a maid to buy some beer from the corner store and sat on the porch with his friends. I was fond of Manny and Jojo, they were like my big brothers; I chatted with them for a while and excused myself when they started drinking. Seven months pregnant, I told them I needed plenty of sleep. I curled up in bed with a romance paperback, anticipating the thrill of making love with Eric after he was pumped up with beer; it was a different kind of fun when he was 'sex-drunk.' I soon fell asleep. After two hours, I awoke to the sound of guffaws. With the bedroom jalousies wide open, I could hear the voices from the porch just a few feet away.

"You're surely keeping in top shape," Manny said. "You jog every day?"

"I try," Eric said.

"To keep those knees strong, huh?" Jojo said. Bottles clinking. Laughter.

"Right," Manny said. "When you were still dating, we'd squirm over how you were always all over her. By God."

Then the voices were muffled and mixed with chuckles. Jojo said something about getting pregnant. More laughter. Then Manny, sounding concerned: "But weren't you damn proud of your bright and pretty girl?" I heard Eric's voice but couldn't make out what he was saying.

"You need more beer, brother," said Jojo.

I was intrigued and a little upset that I couldn't hear everything clearly, but after a while decided to brush it all aside as booze-talk and tried to sleep. It was past midnight when Eric came into our room. He took off his clothes, plopped on the bed in his underpants and kissed me hard. I tried to kiss him back, but he reeked of alcohol, so I said I was sleepy and turned to face the wall. Then he turned his back to me and puked.

"Damn," I said and got up. Most of the vomit had splashed to the floor, some of it on his pillow and the edge of the bed. I held my breath and turned his face toward me, hoping to get him up, but he just snored.

The maids were fast asleep; I felt nauseated myself mopping the floor. I inserted a towel between Eric and the soiled mattress and then sponged him, wondering what part of my marriage vows this chore fell under and what God would do to me if I just wrung my husband's neck instead.

"You threw up on yourself last night," I said at breakfast.

He looked at me. "Sorry," he said and returned to his crossword.

I wanted him to say more to make me feel like he was truly sorry, but since he'd apologized, I shut up and didn't bring up the matter again.

Past midnight. Eric and I awoke to the sound of footsteps on the roof. When we went outside to check, most of the family was up. Neighbors were on the street, comparing notes. No one had seen the thief; the old woman insisted once more that it was an *aswang*. Soon after we'd gone back inside, Eric fell asleep. I tossed and turned, unable to find a comfortable position, sleeping fitfully, awaking to aches that seized all of my pelvic area.

I tried to wake Eric but he wouldn't budge, so I endured the pain as it came and went. At four a.m., I found Lola Bening in the kitchen and told her about my pains. She forced me to drink a tall glass of hot milk in which she'd dropped a raw egg. Then she took me out to the porch and had me go up and down the steps, saying it would speed up the labor. When Nanay awoke at six, she roused Eric to tell him it was time to take me to the hospital.

At the hospital, I followed an orderly down a hallway, feeling exposed, clutching the gown tight behind me. I saw Eric and his parents sitting on a bench at the far end of the hall. We entered a room that smelled of blood and alcohol. Two other women were in bed. The attendant helped me onto the bed closest to the door and then left the room.

The woman to my left growled. The other walked around the room, blood stains on the back of her gown, cursing. I lay there breathing heavily, staring at the clock. It was now close to eight o'clock. My stomach rumbled. I got up. The weight of the baby bore down on my pelvis much more heavily than an hour ago. I waddled to the door and peeked. I could see a nurses' station a few feet away and Eric down the long hallway, too far to hear me if I called out his name. I wished he'd look my way, but he was intent on reading a newspaper. His parents were chatting. A nurse came toward me and said, "What is it?"

"Can you please call my husband?" I said. "He's that guy in blue down the hall. I need something to eat."

"No, you can't eat."

So I weakly lay on my bed once more, anticipating the pains, then wishing them to stop. The woman to my left screamed for an hour before they took her away to the delivery room next door. "They all do that," the nurse said and smirked. "Curse their husbands, swear they won't do it again. Next thing you know, they're back here with a swollen tummy. That woman was here just last year."

The woman next door screeched. Reminded me of Dad's pig giving birth in the middle of the night, when Dad let Chona and me sit just outside the smelly sty and watch him catch the tiny bloody piglets with an old towel and then hand them to Zenay to wipe and line up on the floor. As the image gripped me with fear, I heard more wailing. And then silence.

My pains became excruciating, came more often, stayed longer each time. I began to wonder if my belly would burst. I forgot all about food and thought of how some women died in childbirth. After half an hour, a resident doctor came to examine me, a tiny lady, maybe a few years older than my twenty years. She tried to be gentle but I felt like her entire hand was inside me. It was horribly, horribly painful.

"Five cm," she said to the nurse beside her. Then they left.

After a few minutes, she came back, poked her hand inside me again.

"Six cm. Does this hurt?"

"Very much," I said.

"Some pain threshold you have," she said. "You should be screaming by now."

"It's uncouth," I muttered. And louder, "Where's Doctor Edrosa?"

"He's on his way," she said, peeled off her blood-stained gloves and walked away.

God, I thought, how many cm's will I have to go? Where's *my* doctor? Will I die?

Shortly after eleven, the resident came to examine me again and said it was time to move me to Delivery. I followed the nurse next door, doubling over with pain. A table with many attachments stood in the center. The nurse pulled out the step stool, helped me onto the table and supported my back as I lay down. Beneath the thin sheet, the steel was hard and cold. "Let's get your feet up here," the nurse said, guiding my legs to the stirrups on the side.

"I don't think I can do this," I said.

"It'll soon be over," she said, fastening my ankles to the stirrups, covering my lower body with a green sheet. "You'll be fine." She unlatched the lower part of the table and left me there on half a table, feeling suspended.

How can this be fine?

I stared at the lights above me, wondering how my eyes would stand the glare when they were turned on. Looked at the rolling tables with instruments, the oxygen tank in a corner, the tiny weighing scale on a steel counter. A few minutes later, I heard Doctor Edrosa's gentle voice. "How are you, my dear?"

I wanted to get up and cry in his arms and ask him what took him so long. "Doc, I'm scared," I said.

"Nothing you can't do," he said, holding my hand. "We're giving you anaesthesia on your lower body, okay?"

Although I felt much safer, I couldn't tell one pain from the other anymore. It felt like even the ends of my hair were in agony.

Voices urged me to push. Breathe, push, breathe, push. They said to push only when told. So push I did, on cue. Harder. Harder still. I'd never experienced pain so intense, and if the only way out was to push until my belly burst, I was going to do it.

After what seemed like an eternity of vain struggling, I felt an abrupt release.

"A boy!" Doctor Edrosa said. I exhaled heavily and gave a weak smile. I'd often wished I had a big brother; I really wanted a boy.

The doctor held the little thing upside down by the ankles and slapped his butt. The baby, all covered in blood, screamed. My mother had told me that I had refused to cry as a newborn; my nose and mouth had been filled with mucus that could've killed me if the doctor – my Ninang Florie – hadn't sucked the mucus out with her mouth.

The baby, my baby, screamed. He could breathe!

Doctor Edrosa put the infant on my belly. I tried to hold him, but I realized that my wrists were tied to the handlebars so all I could do was look. Then a nurse took him and laid him on the tiny weighing scale on the counter to my right, made some notes and began to clean him. The baby looked normal to me. But why was the head so long? Does he have ten fingers and toes, not eleven or nine? In my stupor, I didn't speak. My lower body was numb, but I could feel a dull tugging and dabbing around my pelvic area and heard the swoosh of liquid on some receptacle.

"There, there," the doctor said. "You're like brand new." I managed a weak smile.

After half an hour, the doctor and nurses walked out. Two attendants untied me from the bed and, with impressive skill, moved me to a stretcher and wheeled me out. In the hallway, Eric walked alongside us, stroking my hair. "We have a boy!" he said, the grin on his handsome face even wider than when I told him I was pregnant.

"Where is he?" I said. "Did you see him?"

"They took him to the nursery; I just caught a glimpse."

I felt too spent to say anything more.

In a room where my parents-in-law were waiting, the attendants moved me from the stretcher to the bed. A nurse came in, asked a few questions, made some notes and said it was time for me to rest and that, finally, I could eat as much as I wanted.

My belly felt light and hollow, cramping faintly. The voices faded and I fell asleep.

When I awoke, Eric's parents were gone. Eric sat on a chair by my bed, watching TV. "What time is it?" I said.

He got up and sat next to me. "Six p.m. You slept for four hours."

"My tummy feels hollow," I said, "I can't believe it's over. I can't feel my legs."

"Doctor Edrosa was here," he said, caressing my face and hair. "He says the anaesthesia will wear off shortly. The baby is fine, seven pounds four."

"God, it was horrible. The pain."

"I love you, okay?" he said and kissed my cheek.

"I love you, too," I said and pulled him closer. "Have you seen our baby? I'm afraid his head is too long."

"He looks red and squirmy. I couldn't see the rest of him; he was all bundled up in a blanket. I could only peek through a window."

"When can I see him?"

"Tomorrow, I'll take you down to the nursery. Tonight, you rest. Your meal is here," he said, pointing to a covered tray on the side table, "but I don't think you'll like it. Tell me what you want, anything. I'll go get it."

"Big, juicy *sangkis*."

A short while after Eric left, Chona arrived. "How did it go?" she said, sitting on the bed, smoothing the sheets.

"You can't imagine the pain," I said. "You usually have dysmenorrhea, no?"

"Really bad periods? Of course."

"Well, a hundred of those, let's say. Maybe a thousand. For nine, ten hours."

"Aw!" She furrowed her brows. "That's cruel."

"Makes you lose all your respect for yourself, the things they do to you. You feel like being prepped for slaughter. You know the poor pigs and chickens they kill at home? They didn't exactly douse me with boiling water to loosen my feathers, but they poured something cold down there and shaved it like it was nobody's business."

"Yikes!"

"They fastened my legs and wrists to the table. I felt like a slab of meat in the market, waiting for someone to come along and pinch me and ask, 'How much per kilo?' And all the while I wanted to go take a poop. I'm telling you, it's crazy."

She sat there, silent.

"And I'm bleeding a lot," I continued. "How's my baby? Have you seen him?"

"No," she said. "The nursery has visiting hours; too late."

"I have to see him," I said and put my hand on my empty belly. "I have to hold him."

"I can't get over it," she said, grinning. "The tomboy is now a mother – at twenty."

I tried to wiggle my toes but felt only faint tingles. "Are my legs still there?" I said.

She rubbed both of my legs, massaged my toes. "Of course, dummy."

"Where's Mommy?"

"She'll be here tomorrow."

"We're naming him Miguel."

In those three days in hospital, I received layer upon layer of love and attention – from Eric, his family, Chona and Mom. Dad and my other siblings sent their love. Doctor Edrosa assured me it was usual for a newborn's head to be elongated from having to squeeze through the birth canal and that it would normalize in a few days. The only thing missing was the baby in my arms. In those days, hospitals didn't allow newborns out of the nursery for fear of infection and fed them with infant formula, so I didn't get to hold Miguel until it was time for us to go home.

When I took the small bundle from the nurse, he was sound asleep, very light and looked utterly delicate. Tingles rushed all over my body. My breasts grew heavy and painful and then I felt something wet on my chest: my milk was dripping. Miguel smelled so sweet, I wanted to squeeze him tight but was afraid he'd get crushed. I ran my fingers through his hair which Mom said was quite thick for a newborn. Soft, black ringlets on a tiny, tiny head.

"Just like yours," I told Eric and began to tear up. He took the baby from me, his face glowing like I'd never seen before, and tenderly kissed the little red cheek. *This is what I signed up for when I said those vows.*

CHAPTER 14

When we got home from the hospital, everyone fussed over the sleeping baby. Once he opened his eyes and cried, Mom told me to give him my breast right away, because the first few days' milk contained antibodies, and showed me how to help Miguel latch on. He finally got it and began to suck. My nipple stung, like the many times Mom doused my scraped knee with Merthiolate not so long ago. I cringed, squeezed my eyes shut and could hear the baby's gulps. My other nipple dripped. After a minute, the burning in my breast subsided, and I began to feel a deep calm. I opened my eyes and saw Miguel's face looking content, his sucking and gulping more relaxed, a bit of thin milk seeping out of the corner of his mouth.

For the next two weeks, Mom stayed at Auntie Nelda's and came every day to help me give Miguel a bath, staying for a couple of hours. She warned me that nursing might get my nipples bleeding, but the important thing was to keep on going.

Miguel slept almost all day and was up most of the night. The older women said it was colic and told me to rub chamomile oil on the baby's stomach and wrap it with a binder every evening, but it didn't help. Miguel usually woke up needing a change. Change. Feed on my sore breasts. Pee. Change. Nap. Less than an hour later, repeat. Whenever I managed to sleep for four hours in twenty-four, I felt very lucky.

One night around two a.m., I had just gone to sleep when Miguel started screaming wildly. I changed him, picked him up and cuddled him. Although I'd just fed him half an hour earlier, his head fumbled for my breast so I nursed him again, struggling to keep my stinging eyes open. He quieted down, but after a while he stopped sucking and screamed again. When I tried to burp him, he threw up on my nightdress. I put him down to change him, but he screamed even harder. Both of us soaked in curdled milk, I picked him up once more and danced about, humming.

Rock-a-bye baby on the tree top. When the wind blows, my baby will stop. Sssh... sleep now, little boy. Stop. Please stop. God in heaven, where the hell is my mommy? Please make this baby stop, or I'll throw him out the window.

Miguel didn't stop. Eric finally got up, then Nanay, too. They took Miguel and changed him. I pulled out a fresh nightdress from the closet and went to the bathroom. Miguel stopped screaming and cooed. I started to cry.

I soon realized I had been much freer when I was pregnant. These days, the only time I had for myself was bathroom time. I longed to be able to go out again and see my friends, or go to the movies with Eric, or shop with Chona. I eagerly looked forward to going back to school when the second semester opened in a few weeks. But when that day came, I didn't want to leave Miguel with the teen-aged nanny we'd hired a couple of weeks earlier. What if he cried and wanted me? I knew Lola Bening and Aunt Pacita would be at home and would make sure Miguel was fine. But still.

Also, I had nothing to wear. Since I couldn't fit into my regular clothes, I wore one of my maternity dresses, convincing myself it didn't matter. When I arrived at the university and saw the girls in hipster jeans and tummy shirts, their cute bellybuttons peeking out, I felt like a frump and wanted to hide.

In class, I struggled to follow the math lecture while imagining what Miguel might be doing at home. In the second hour, my breasts ached; the milk seeped through my nursing pads all the way to my bodice. Mom had said that whenever a mother's milk dripped, it meant her baby was hungry. I'd trained the nanny to feed Miguel with infant formula from a bottle, but I felt queasy nonetheless.

I rushed home right after school. The moment I walked in the door and saw Miguel, my milk gushed out and dripped to my feet. The nanny said he'd been crying for a while. As soon as I held him, he stopped crying and, like a blind puppy, fumbled for my breast. When he gripped my little finger with his tiny hand and sucked eagerly, I forgot how ugly I felt.

One evening after supper, I joined the family watching TV in the living room. They were roaring over a basketball game, which I wasn't fond of, but I stayed just the same, with Miguel in my arms. After the game, we watched a feature about the reigning Miss Universe. When the pageant was held in Manila a few months before, the country went crazy over the contestants and gobbled up all available information about them. The Spanish beauty Amparo Muñoz had been a crowd favorite, also Eric's. Whenever he raved about her, I'd feel hurt, even if I knew she wasn't a real threat. This evening, here was the ravishing Amparo in a swimsuit parading across the TV screen, and Eric was taking it all in. "I ate a lot of noodles in Manila," Amparo was saying, "and gained ten pounds." Ten pounds? Where? I glanced at my belly bulging through my milk-and-pee-stained housedress, squeezed Miguel and kissed him.

They were now showing clips of the previous pageant. "Look at that," Eric said of the Folk Arts Theater where the pageant had been held. "Imelda's million-peso splurge."

"Good way to show our hospitality," Tatay said.

"Such frivolity in a poor country," Eric said. Imelda Marcos had the new amphitheater built in seventy-seven days specifically for the Miss Universe pageant, and had also started building a huge convention center and a hotel to host a forthcoming World Bank conference.

"The pageant made the world notice the Philippines," Tatay said.

"So they could see how we are a nation of cowards with no balls to stand up to a dictator? Look at America; they shamed Nixon into resigning," Eric said.

They argued on; I went to our room to rock Miguel to sleep. I was tucking him in when Eric came in. "What a lousy debater," he said. "Winning by yelling."

"Maybe you should just shut up," I said and lay down in bed.

"Forget him. Can we make love?" he said, pulling me closer to him.

One night, Miguel was edgy and hot to the touch. He breathed with a rattling sound in his chest. Worried, I barely slept. When we took him to a pediatrician in the morning, she said it was a virus and prescribed two medications: Tempra to bring down the fever and Phenobarbital to prevent seizures.

I read the literature on both drugs. Tempra was a pain-reliever and fever-reducer. That was fine, just what Miguel needed. Phenobarbital was a barbiturate. Knowing that barbiturates were on the list of dangerous drugs, I read the literature more thoroughly: A sedative, for the treatment of insomnia, the relief of anxiety or tension, and to control seizures. Okay. Could be habit-forming. Apart from a long list of when the drug should not be taken, the fine print carried a warning about the risk of overdosing. I thought of Marilyn Monroe: Barbiturates were what she'd overdosed on. Oh my.

I'd never heard Mom mention seizures. When my siblings and I had fevers back home, Mom and Lola put vinegar-soaked face cloths on our foreheads and wrapped us in blankets until we sweated the fever out. And it always worked. So, I hesitated to use the Phenobarb on Miguel, but Nanay insisted. It seemed to have helped, because Miguel began sleeping like an angel, and in a couple of days, he was well.

I always made sure that once I got home from school, I was the one who looked after Miguel, not the nanny. When Miguel had gone to sleep, I'd bring out my books to study, but before I was done, he'd be up again. I slept even less than the four hours a night that I'd managed to steal during his first few weeks. I lagged behind in the schoolwork, and the catching-up I needed to do was compounding by the day.

Eric was also in graduate school but didn't need as much studying as I did. He quickly absorbed abstract theories, as though he kept a library of math books in his head and all he had to do was pull out what he needed for the moment. How come I required a lot more time to figure out math? How come, even if I stayed up all night solving the absurd problems at the end of each chapter, I still blanked out at exam time? Because we were now following different tracks – I was in actuarial science, he in pure math – I couldn't ask him to help me out as often as before. So I pushed myself to work harder by sleeping even less. When I got married, I'd promised myself to show my parents that I could be a good wife, mother, and student all at the same time. I wasn't going to let anything stop me from getting the master's degree that Dad had always dreamed of for me. He even wanted a doctorate down the road, and I could give him that, too, could I not?

One Sunday afternoon shortly before Christmas, Eric was playing *mah jong* with his parents and a neighbor in the back patio. With Miguel feeding at my breast, I sat at our study desk in our bedroom and read an actuarial textbook, vainly trying to follow the derivation of some complex annuity formula.

When Miguel was finally sound asleep, I laid him in his crib. I tidied up the room a bit, took a quick shower, went back to my textbook and started over. I needed to understand all those formulas before I could begin with the problem set due the following day. The Jackson Five were singing *Santa Claus is Coming to Town* on the living room TV, and Eric's two kid sisters shrieked as they danced along. I began to hear a whizzing inside my head that felt like an electric current. Yeah, it's Christmas, but why don't I feel it? Who invented all this actuarial crap anyway? Why should I care about it? Okay now, what happens if compounding is weekly but payments are made monthly? I turned the page over, my fingers shaking. What is the future value of the annuity if compounding is continuous instead of weekly? With the buzz in my head intensifying, I was startled by a knock on the door.

"Come have a snack." It was Aunt Pacita.

I closed the book and went to the kitchen. Tatay and Eric were arguing over an upcoming referendum that was going to ask the nation for a yes-vote on whether martial law should continue. I sat at table with Aunt Pacita, poured myself a glass of Coke and buttered a *pan de sal*.

"You look haggard," she said. "Go take a nap while your baby is asleep."

"I have a ton of school work to do," I said.

"But your eyes are bloodshot. Go, even just fifteen minutes will help."

I ate the *pan de sal* and brought my glass of Coke to our room. I lay down on the bed with a baby care book, groaning from my aching back. What exactly is infant colic? Is it gas? I closed my eyes, but my ears kept on buzzing, and my entire body trembled. How about taking some of Miguel's sedative to quiet me down? It works for him, why not for me? I popped a pill in my mouth, downed it with Coke and went back to bed. I dozed off. Then I heard Miguel screaming.

I saw something moving in his crib. A baby who didn't look like Miguel fell to the floor. A dark figure stood next to the crib and then came at me. An old man with a long beard. He tugged at the chain in his hand, and a big black dog lunged from behind him. The dog ran toward the bed and leapt onto my chest. The baby kept on crying. I tried to get up but couldn't move with the weight of the big dog. I yelled with all my might, gasping for breath.

At last I opened my eyes and saw Aunt Pacita sitting on the bed beside me, my crying baby in her arms.

"You were moaning," she said, rubbing my back. "Must have had a bad dream." She rose to fetch a glass of water and handed it to me. "Drink this."

My heart thumping, I sipped the water, blinked and looked around. The alarm clock on the desk said it had only been five minutes since I'd gone to bed. There was neither a bearded man nor a dog, just the drapes moving slightly with a breeze.

My body shaking and my head buzzing, I took Miguel and went through the usual routine. The stupid math book sat on the desk, opened to the page I'd been stuck on for hours. Once more, I tried to read, but all the formulas looked like one big blur on the page, muddled by the yells and clinks and quacks from the back patio.

I called the nanny and asked her to take Miguel out for a walk. Back to my book, but nothing was making sense. I picked up the bottle of Phenobarbital. There were five pills left. Five pills. Maybe they'll do the trick, and I won't see the light of day again. Let's hope so.

I swallowed the five tiny pills with what was left of the Coke and lay face down on the bed.

CHAPTER 15

Miguel kicked and screamed and fell to the concrete floor. I heard his skull crack. Looking more menacing this time, the big black dog came at me and sat on my chest. I struggled to get up and looked for blood on the floor, but there was none. The old man stooped and picked up the fallen baby. The baby stopped crying, but his eyes were blank.

"Nooo!" I yelled and tried to push the dog away, but I was pinned down and couldn't move. "No! My baby!"

"Wake up, wake up!"

I opened my eyes and saw Eric beside me. "You're dreaming," he said.

"My baby," I said and clung to him, crying. "He broke his head."

He stroked my hair and said, "He's okay. Look, he's fine."

I sat up and looked around the room. It was dim, but with the streetlights streaming through the window, I could see Miguel fast asleep in his crib. "What time is it?" I said.

"Almost ten. We didn't wake you for dinner because you were sound asleep. Nanay left your portion in the fridge."

"Hold me please," I said, unable to stop sobbing. "I don't want dinner. Just hold me." I gripped his arms, buried my face in his chest, wishing my whole being was absorbed by his body. After a few moments, I realized that the Phenobarb hadn't killed me. I clung to Eric even tighter. "Do you love me?" I said.

"Of course I do," he said. I thought of telling him about the pills, but he kissed my mouth and started caressing me, so I said nothing and wildly kissed him back.

The following weeks, each time I looked at my helpless baby, I'd feel guilty that I'd tried to kill myself. I was grateful that the Phenobarb, being in baby-size doses, hadn't been strong enough to harm me, although I suspected it might have caused the nightmares. But the weird dreams and the sleep paralysis kept on happening, usually after I'd exhausted my brain over schoolwork without much sleep. The old ladies said that drinking a lot of water before bedtime made for more peaceful sleep, so I tried to remember to do that. The night terrors had me in a state of half-consciousness; I was aware that if only I could move a finger or a toe, I'd be fully awake, and the ordeal would be over. I continued to look after the colicky Miguel while wrestling with my schoolwork. When my mind or body refused to go on and the only logical thing to do was rest, I dreaded going to bed for fear of the nightmares.

One Saturday morning at Christmastime, I was at breakfast with Eric and his parents. Tatay was buried in the newspaper, his coffee half-finished. Nanay, Eric, and I were deboning salted dried fish with our fingers, dipping bits of it in a saucer of vinegar and eating them with garlic fried rice. I savored every bite, reminded of lazy breakfasts back in Montaña.

Looking at Tatay's newspaper, Nanay said, "So, Marcos is pushing through with that referendum. Is that all we do now, say yes?"

"Sure," Eric said, "to make puppets of everyone. To show the world how much we adore him."

Upon declaring martial law, Marcos had the constitution rewritten and in mid-1973 consulted with the people on whether or not they agreed to the changes. He got a ninety-percent yes-vote, which was hardly a surprise, because before that referendum, he had decreed that registered voters who didn't go to the polls faced a fine or six months in prison. This new constitution, among other changes, allowed Marcos to stay in power beyond his term, which, under the former constitution, should have expired in 1973.

Now, eighteen months later, Marcos wanted another referendum. The question this time was whether the nation approved of the way he'd been exercising his martial-law powers. From his jail cell, Ninoy Aquino, Marcos's most vocal pre-martial law critic, joined some opposition leaders and filed an objection to this new referendum with the Supreme Court. They lost because, of course, the justices were all Marcos appointees. When some Catholic bishops called a boycott of the referendum, Eric and I agreed that this was the way to go. For a few weeks, the holding of a referendum was not certain, and this day, the big news was that Marcos had at last decided to proceed with it in February.

"But look at Ninoy, ever daring," Nanay said. "Same with those bishops."

"Protesters, protesters!" Tatay snapped. "How do those people find time to protest? Can't they see it's useless?" He put down the newspaper and finished his coffee.

"Of course," Eric said. "Martial law is great. Remember how Marcos got a ninety percent vote on his new constitution? I bet next February's vote will turn out the same way."

I secretly cheered for the brave protesters but squirmed at the raised voices around me. Thankfully, Tatay stood up and left the table. Nanay followed him. I put the last bits of dried fish and fried rice in my mouth and licked my fingers. Eric sighed and rolled his eyes.

Early on referendum day, Eric's parents went to the polls. Eric and I didn't. In the afternoon, I left them playing *mah jong* and went to buy groceries. When I returned, the nanny and Miguel were at the gate. Miguel cooed to me and I picked him up. The nanny took the grocery bags and said, "Manang Daniela," her eyes wide and voice trembling. "Manong Eric had a fight with your Tatay."

I wondered what else was new with father and son being at odds and said, "What happened?"

"They were shouting at each other. Something about Marcos. The refrig... what's the word?"

"The referendum?"

"Yes, yes. Your Tatay almost threw a chair at Manong Eric."

Shocked, I tugged at her arm and said, "What? Why?" It had always been barbs and raised voices, never anything physical. "And then?"

"Your Nanay came between them, so they stopped. Manong Eric left soon after. He told me to ask you to call him at his uncle's house in Cubao."

"Where's Tatay?"

"Inside. Everyone's inside."

Oh God, I thought. I walked to the porch and slowly opened the front door to an empty living room. I found everyone seated at the dining table. "Come eat," Nanay said.

I gave Miguel to the nanny, kissed my in-laws' foreheads and quietly sat down. All through the meal, I looked down at my plate. No one spoke.

After supper, I called Eric at his uncle's house. "What happened?" I said.

"Long story," he said. "I'm not coming back."

"What?"

"I'd like you to pack my things, also yours and Miguel's. You must leave in the morning, before anyone else is up. Go to Auntie Nelda's."

"But..."

"Do as I say," he said and hung up. Just then, Tatay came to the living room to watch TV, so I decided not to dial again. I told the nanny to get packed and went to our room.

I debated with myself whether or not to speak to my in-laws, half-expecting Tatay to barge into the room and yell at me. He didn't. He watched TV with the family as usual, although he was very quiet. When they had all gone to bed, I started stuffing our possessions into two suitcases and several grocery bags. I slept fitfully and at daybreak, before anyone else was up, I took a cab with Miguel and the nanny and our things and asked the driver to take us to Auntie Nelda's, ten minutes away.

When Auntie Nelda opened the gate, she looked at the three of us and our luggage, her eyes widening. "What happened?" she said.

I had no choice but to tell the truth. "Auntie, Eric and his father had a fight. And, uh, can we stay here for a little while?"

"Of course, of course," she said, picking up a bag. "Come on in. Where's Eric? Why did they fight?"

"The referendum," I said.

"Ha!" Auntie Nelda said. "We all know it's just a show, but do we have a choice? Besides, Marcos isn't so bad; the streets are quieter now, see?"

Auntie Nelda got me and Miguel settled in my cousin's room. I waited until after breakfast to call Eric at his uncle's place. He arrived an hour later. "Thank you for taking my family in," he told Auntie Nelda. "I'm staying with my uncle until I find us a place."

After three weeks, we found a tiny apartment down the road from Auntie Nelda's. It was actually one big room with a makeshift cubicle to enclose a bed. Because we needed the bed and desk and other things we'd left in Eric's parents' house, we went there to tell them we were moving out. Eric's father just said okay. By then, the referendum results were out: eighty-eight percent yes-vote for continuing martial law in spite of boycotts.

The school year was finishing, and despite all the disruptions, I somehow managed to pass all my courses. When summer school began in early April, Eric taught at the university. To improve my chances for employment, I applied for a summer scholarship to study computer programming. It was tedious work handwriting programs, sending them to keypunching stations and big computers that we didn't even get to see, and later on receiving comments from the computer station on whether or not our programs worked. However, I didn't mind spending long nights on the sometimes fruitless exercise of debugging a program because I found it more stimulating than my actuarial books.

Eric earned seven hundred pesos a month from teaching summer school; I had no income. After we bought a Formica dining set and a one-burner stove, our savings were down to nothing. Now, we also had to put food on the table and pay rent. But even if all I had to cook was *galunggong* and *saluyot*, the poor man's fish and Ilocano greens, I was thrilled to finally be free.

Two days after we moved to the little apartment, Nanay and Aunt Pacita came to visit and handed me two warm Tupperware containers: beef steak in one, stewed pig knuckles and pigeon peas in the other – Eric's favorite dishes that only Tatay could cook perfectly. The tangy steam from the *kadyos* stew made me lick my lips. I wondered if Nanay thought we were starving. Or maybe she didn't believe I could cook at all? I thanked her anyhow.

"How's Miguel?" Aunt Pacita said.

"Fine," I said.

"The poor thing," Nanay said. "Just him and the nanny while you're gone."

I couldn't see what was so poor about that, so I said, "They're quite okay." And to ease her worry: "Auntie Nelda is just down the road, if we need help."

A few weeks later, Miguel had a fever. The doctor said it was viral and to just let the fever run its course. The next night, the fever returned, even higher this time. I stayed up most of the night watching his labored breathing. Skipping school the next day, I took him back to the doctor who said it was asthma.

"Oh my God," I said. "My brother suffers from bad bouts of

asthma." I recalled Francis having attacks as a young boy and asking if he would die.

"It's genetic," she said. "And I'm afraid that your baby has primary complex too."

"What's that?"

"The first stage of tuberculosis."

I stared at her while Miguel whimpered in my arms. "Didn't he have an anti-TB shot? I thought he'd had all the shots you recommended."

"We don't give BCG vaccines that early anymore. New studies tell us it's not that effective," she said, scribbling something on her prescription pad. "Give this to him daily for the next three months. Then we'll see."

The medication was very expensive; it broke our pocketbooks. But more than that, my heart broke to see my baby suffer.

Every now and then, Nanay sent us food. One day, Aunt Pacita came with Tatay's home-made corned beef. "You'd better come back home," she said.

"What for?" Eric said.

"You can't starve here," she said. "Don't do a Ninoy."

"We're fine, Aunt Pacita," Eric said. "We're not on a hunger strike." Ninoy Aquino had just started a hunger strike in jail, to protest the way Marcos was treating him and other political prisoners.

"I've trained him to eat *galunggong* and *saluyot*," I said, chuckling.

"And you need help with Miguel," Aunt Pacita said. "The poor baby."

I didn't know how Eric truly felt about the shabby meals I served, but I certainly didn't want to move back. Perhaps Miguel had picked up the TB bacteria from the big household, maybe from the maids and the frequent stream of visitors. Besides, this was the life I'd wanted from the start – to be queen of my own little world. It was tough, but I had no plans of turning back.

We kept looking for a more comfortable but affordable place. In two months, Auntie Nelda found one nearby. A bit too big for us, but because it was owned by one of my godmothers, we had it for a good price.

CHAPTER 16

The nanny was on the street with Miguel, chatting with the neighbor's maid. "Manang Daniela, here they come!" she yelled. I rushed out the door. Four men were walking down the middle of the narrow asphalt road toward us, each with a chair or table on his back.

"A bit embarrassing that they didn't come in a delivery truck," I told Eric. I had bought the rattan living room set from a roadside shop a few blocks away.

"It's okay," he said. "Who cares what the neighbors think? You've got a brilliant husband here, baby. Stick with me and we'll go places."

We settled on how to arrange the pieces of furniture. Then I picked up Miguel's ball from his crib. "I can actually practice here," I said and, in perfect bowling form, sent the ball rolling across the vinyl floor. It stopped under the wobbly table in the kitchen. "That would've made a strike," I said. "What do we do with all this space?"

"We'll work hard," Eric said. "It's going to be grand. After all, we're only twenty-one." He tried out the love seat, pulled me in and spooned me. We didn't have cushions, but it felt cozy even with the hard wicker against my side. I could hear the neighbor's radio. It was Minnie Riperton whose voice was everywhere in those days, screeching, "Lovin' you is easy 'cause you're beautiful..." I sang along; Eric hammed up the lalalalala.

I got up to fix lunch; Eric gobbled it up and said he was off to give an exam.

"It's Saturday," I said.

"Make-up exam," he said.

I took Miguel upstairs and cuddled him in bed. I rubbed his forehead lightly, amused at how quickly this trick lulled him to sleep. How nice of my husband to be working so hard, I thought. When I get up, I'll go and catch him at school. We'll eat at Ferino's and watch the movie *Jaws* that everyone's been raving about.

I left Miguel with the nanny and went to the university with Minnie's song stuck in my head. I had a key to Eric's faculty office, lalalalala. I let myself in. Not a soul. The school building was like a ghost town. Well, maybe he's left, I told myself.

He wasn't at home either. I played with Miguel, watched TV, and cooked pork *sinigang*. More TV. Around midnight, Eric came in.

"C'mon, I'm hungry," I said. "Fixed your favorite stew." He kissed my cheek and took his seat.

"I came to your office to ask you out," I said.

Silence.

"Poor baby, you look tired," I said, stroked his hair and then spooned some rice onto his plate.

He smoothed his place mat and pulled out a loose thread. Rolled it into a tiny ball. "You need to know," he said, his usually bright eyes cast down.

I raised my eyebrows and stared at his lips.

"Her name is Mingming," he said.

I felt like somebody had pounded an enormous gong inside my chest. Eric lit a cigarette and sucked deeply.

"Meaning?" I said. He had to be joking. But the pounding in my

136

chest had become frantic.

"I'm seeing her."

"What?" I said. "How? How is that? What's her real name? How old is she?" I tried to be businesslike.

"Romina. Seventeen, freshman."

"Romina what?"

"Bactol."

What an ugly name, I thought.

"Can't you leave me alone," he said, "wait until I get tired of her?"

My stomach turned. Eric's Marlboro burned itself out on the ashtray. He lit another one and went upstairs. The stew sat on the table, with clumps of lard floating like tiny rafts on the surface.

I lay on the hard rattan love seat, my gaze fixed on the house lizards chasing each other in a circle on the ceiling. Is that their mating dance? I lay there long after the lizards had latched on to each other and disappeared from view. What an ugly name.

Morning. Still lying on the love seat, I could hear my baby whimpering upstairs. The nanny came down with him but I couldn't figure out what he needed. The lizards were chasing each other again. The shrill lalalalala from the goddamned radio drove straight between my eyes and slithered down my chest to puncture the bag of tears that had ballooned around my heart through the night.

A week later, Eric came to bed smelling of beer. My body tingled when he groped me. I caressed his beautiful *mestizo* face, his afro, his lean body. And wept.

"Just a physical need," he said before dismounting.

"Fuck you!" I tried to slap him, but he caught my wrist.

"I never loved you."

I winced at his grip, now on both of my arms. "But you were the one who couldn't wait to get married."

"That?" Eric said. "I needed to get away from my exacting

father. And you make a good stand-in for my mother."

He lay back down. I thought I heard him saying something. Something about how he needed to be with her.

Back to the ceiling. Where are my lizards?

I went to Manny and Jojo, Eric's fraternity brothers. They already knew. "How long has it been?" I said.

"Tsk, tsk," Manny said, shaking his head, pity in his eyes.

"Please answer me," I said.

"Been a while," said Jojo. "We thought we could stop him."

"So that's what you were talking about that night on our porch when I was pregnant?" I felt betrayed even by them for not telling me earlier, but I quickly realized that it was Eric who was first their friend, not me.

"We'll watch out for what he does," Jojo was saying as I walked away.

I also told Eric's family, my friends, and Chona. I went to see a counselor who said love begets love, to keep on loving him.

"He needs shock treatment," the counselor said one day. "You have to leave him. Do it today."

I mustered all my courage to pack a suitcase and, as instructed, wrote a note to say that I and the baby were gone for good. My parents were an overnight bus ride away, and I wasn't sure I wanted them to know. Besides, I had to stay in Manila for school. With nowhere else to go, I ended up in my in-laws' house. Tatay fumed at Eric; everyone else was upset. They were all solicitous to Miguel and me, and I felt a little safer.

Sometimes, Nanay tried to make light of the situation, perhaps to make me feel better. She'd recount how Eric traced his roots to a nineteenth-century Spanish missionary friar who got a local woman pregnant. Not bad, because that's how they got their *mestizo* features. She'd enumerate other womanizing ancestors and say that her son had obviously been stamped with the same seal, but not to worry, he'd eventually come back.

"See, that's where the term 'missionary position' comes from," one of Eric's brothers would butt in. And then laughter.

I didn't find it funny. I cried for days on end. It helped that I didn't have to worry about what to cook and how to look after the baby, because I didn't have the energy for those. I tried to think, but all that tumbled in my mind were damning words blaming me. In Philippine culture, if the husband strays, it can only be because the wife isn't performing her duties well – in bed, the kitchen, housekeeping, husband care, baby care. I couldn't accept the way society condoned a husband's infidelity, explaining it away as a given. That men will always be men, and if a woman gave the faintest hint that she was available, it would be an insult to a man's machismo if he ignored the bait. So the wife took the blame, and to ease her pain, she needed to pass on the blame to someone else. Who else but the mistress, the whore, the family wrecker? After tossing all these confusing concepts around in my mind, I told myself I could, would, try harder to be a better wife, if only I was given another chance. Besides, I wanted to prove wrong my parents who'd predicted I'd be eating my tears. My friends, too, and the world in general. I needed to show them that this one teenage marriage was going to work.

And so I didn't write home to tell my parents. However, a week later, Mom came to visit. Chona must have told her I'd left Eric. "I went to your apartment and found only Eric there," she said. "I asked him where you were, and he just shrugged."

The creep, I thought. "And then what did he do?" I said.

"He excused himself, got dressed and left, saying he had a class," she said. "What happened, *balasang ko?*"

Amidst sobs, I told her what had happened, why I had left. "Mom, how did you do it with Dad? This is so hard."

"I didn't leave," she said.

"But the counselor says this should shock Eric into realizing he can't lose me and Miguel."

"Let's hope so," she said. "Let's pray so."

I fervently prayed novenas to San Jose, patron saint of

husbands and fathers. But there were no signs of Eric, not even a phone call. "He'd have figured out by now that you're here," Nanay said. "He should be here soon."

He wasn't, so I cried and prayed even more. Because I was under a scholarship I couldn't afford to lose, I dragged myself back to school even if my head was hollow. But I cried even in class, so I took a leave. I got a job at the Labor Ministry, to replace the scholarship money that was cut when I quit school. I cried there too, but the people were nice. They taught me to smoke. To drink. And not just beer, but Scotch on the rocks, in discos.

"I saw your picture in the Manila Hilton elevator," Tatay said over dinner.

"What picture?" I said.

"You know," he said with a smirk, "the hotel ad for their disco. You dancing with a big guy."

Dammit, I thought. I looked down at my plate and silently ate. That's Arthur, I almost said, the guy who gives me flowers.

Fridays after work, my girlfriends and I walked to the Santo Niño Cathedral to say our novenas. They said the Infant Jesus did miracles. And then, in our red and white office uniforms, black pumps and Farrah Fawcett hair, we met the office guys in the disco. Arthur was a labor attaché who wanted to take me away to New York, where he was based. He was too old and too fat, but it was great that he paid for my drinks.

The nanny stayed behind in our apartment to keep house for Eric and came to babysit during the day. She brought me scraps of Eric's writing that she found in the trash. Several pieces of paper that I put together like a jigsaw puzzle contained a poem about how wrong Nietzsche was about God being dead. The nanny also told me what time my husband got home at night, if he did at all. One day she said Eric had brought a group of guys over to drink. After they left, there was vomit all over the beds, the rattan love seat and chairs, and the bathroom.

"I've cleaned up some, Manang," the nanny said after three days, "but I can't stand doing it on my own."

"Tell him to fuckin' do it," I said.

But those sheets were all I had and I couldn't afford to throw them away. My mother never threw anything away; it was almost a crime to do so. So there I was, sitting on a footstool in the carport, near the faucet, scrubbing slimy sheets in a soapy tub with my bare hands. I could see they had hotdogs with the booze. I scrubbed and the nanny rinsed. Scrub. Rinse. My knuckles stung. I didn't know the men who had done this. They had left me no chance to hurl rocks at their faces if I met them on the street.

My mother-in-law believed that if we could get Mingming out of the way, Eric would quickly come back. So we went together to Mingming's UP dorm.

Mingming's hair was shiny black, parted in the middle, and ran down to her waist. She had clear olive skin, wide eyes, and hairy arms. Her red tank top hugged her slim torso and showed a bit of her tummy. She wore black plaid bellbottoms and wooden clogs, and sat on her hands in a chair across from me and Nanay, a coffee table between us. The dorm matron was at a nearby desk, glancing at us every now and then.

"You know that your boyfriend is married?" my mother-in-law said.

Mingming looked away. "I know," she said, "but he says it's fine."

"We have a baby," I said.

"He's very good to me," Mingming said. "Always waits outside my classroom."

I wanted to pull her hair, but I stopped myself since we had assured the dorm matron that we wouldn't make a scene. Nanay tried to make Mingming promise to stop seeing Eric, but seeing her stance, I knew it was pointless to do so.

A month after I left, Daddy arrived from Montaña, asking to talk to Eric and his parents. I didn't want to call Eric, because the counselor had said I shouldn't, so Nanay did.

On the appointed date, Eric arrived before my father. It was the first time we had met after I left. His hair had grown long, his curls crawling under his collar. He'd lost some weight, his jaw was tight and he wouldn't look into my eyes. I didn't know what to say or do. I wanted to hug him and ask him to come back to me, but I wasn't sure it was the right thing to do, so I waited for him to speak. "I'm sorry," he finally said.

I said nothing and wept.

When Dad arrived, we all sat in my in-laws' living room, Daddy on the chair closest to the door, Eric's parents on the couch next to Dad, and Eric and me next to each other opposite my father. On the coffee table sat a tray of Coke glasses and hot *pan de sal.*

"I've come to take my daughter back," Daddy almost whispered. He looked right at Eric who stared down at his own fingers.

No one dared speak. Not my parents-in-law, not Eric, not me. The ice cubes crackled away in the Coke glasses.

"It's only been two years," Daddy said, "since you said you'd take good care of her." He wiped a tear at the corner of his eye.

"Why don't you move back here and save the rent money?" Tatay said. "We'll help you make a fresh start."

"I apologize, sir," Eric said to Dad. "I will do better this time. We will start again."

I bawled no end. Eric, too. My hope rose of Miguel having a complete family for his first birthday just a week away.

Satisfied, Daddy went home to Montaña. Eric stayed the night. We made love and didn't talk about Mingming. Neither did I ask who had vomited on my sheets. Feeling his passion meeting mine, those things didn't matter at the moment.

Eric and I let the apartment go and moved back to his parents' house. Although I was aching to rant to make him understand how deeply he had hurt me, I hesitated to speak, for fear of sparking another fight and pushing him away. I interpreted his bitter weeping to mean remorse and convinced myself that that should be enough. He was back, we were a family once again, and that was the one important thing. Family. Weeks later, when a friend told me that Mingming's father had pulled her out of UP and taken her back to her home province, I felt relieved that the temptress was out of the way, making my job easier of keeping my man.

I tried my best to be nice to my husband, even if inside me, the heartache refused to heal and refused to heal. Would I ever be able to bring the old Eric back? Some days, I would pour it all out to Aunt Pacita, and she'd take me to the shrine of San Judas Tadeo to pray his novena. She said that when all else failed, San Judas Tadeo, the patron of desperate cases, was the one to run to. "San Judas will plead your case," Aunt Pacita said. "Don't give up. God will take away your pain."

"But Eric is becoming harder to reach," I said. "He's too cold and distant."

"Remember the saying," she said. "He's coming home to you, you should be grateful."

Aunt Pacita was echoing what the church – and society – expected of the Filipina wife: Don't complain, just be a good wife; it might take forever, but your husband will come around. She mentioned the case of a famous actress whose husband had many mistresses. They had been separated for almost thirty years, but he eventually returned to her when he was old and crippled. She graciously took him back and nursed him until he died.

Realizing that Aunt Pacita's support for me went only as far as the novenas, I let things go, even if I knew I wouldn't do as that actress did. I didn't want to settle for simply being the woman my husband came home to. I wanted love, the kind of love and devotion I was giving him, the kind he gave me at the start. I set myself apart from the less-educated Filipina, who would say, "*Ginamit ako*," when she meant she and her husband had had sex. Literally, it meant, "He used me." I found that repulsive. At the other end, there were a handful of women's libbers who impressed me as too extreme. I didn't want to do traditional manly tasks. I wanted to be a female who felt special. When we were first married, my husband and I had intelligent conversations and good sex. I didn't feel used then, I felt loved.

But that had changed, and just as Dad had known it would happen, I mostly kept to myself and ate my tears.

For over a year, there were good days and bad days, but mostly so-so days. The best day was when Miguel turned one, and we had a small party with the neighborhood kids. Otherwise, a good day might be when I got off the bus from work in the evening and found Eric and Miguel at the stop, waiting to walk me home. Or when we went out for pizza on a Sunday and then took Miguel to the kiddie carnival. Or when Eric and I had spontaneous, silent sex, even if only for two minutes.

Arthur continued to give me flowers. One day, I brought a bunch home, and when Nanay saw them, she smirked but said nothing. Saying nothing myself, I put the flowers in a vase on our bedroom desk. Eric came home drunk that night and didn't seem to take notice. The next day, I quietly threw the flowers in the trash. I didn't care a bit about Arthur, but because I loved the attention, I didn't tell him to stop sending me flowers. The next time, though, I left them at the office.

Eric kept on drinking. I kept on drinking, too. I came home past midnight most Fridays after an evening of dancing, drinking and smoking with my office friends. Eric usually came home later. The few times I arrived home after he did, I felt viciously triumphant.

I stopped keeping his closet in order and pressing his clothes. I let the washerwoman do the ironing and stopped doing over the parts where creases should or shouldn't be – collars, cuffs, pants. I ate supper with the family without him. When he came home late, I no longer asked him if he'd eaten; if he went to the kitchen looking for food, I left him alone instead of serving him his supper.

"Manang," the nanny whispered to me one day. "This afternoon when you were at work, I heard them talking about you."

"Who do you mean?"

"Just them," she said, shrugging her shoulders. "They say you don't behave like a wife. They mentioned some woman. What's her name again? Juanita?"

"Juanita who? What about her?"

"They say, look at Juanita, her husband beats her up, but she continues to serve him."

"Really?" I said. *"Putang-ina!"*

When I was nineteen and starry-eyed, I vowed to love, honor and obey my husband forever. And with the way we couldn't bear to be away from each other for even a day, I didn't imagine unfaithfulness ever entering the picture. But it did, and here I was, twenty-one, no longer as starry-eyed, but still determined to keep my vows. And to enable me to do that, I had to learn to forgive my husband for his infidelity. However, I drew the line at physical harm, telling myself that I would have to leave him if he ever laid a hand on me. So my blood boiled for a few weeks over what the nanny had told me. One day, I told myself that my in-laws could throw me out if they wished, but I wasn't going to take this sitting down. I asked to talk to them after Eric left on an errand. Taking a seat across from them at the dining table, I said, "Tay, Nay, I hope you don't take offense."

"We're listening," Tatay said.

"As you can see ..." I paused for a while to gather myself, "things are not good between your son and me. I've tried my best to make it work, in spite of the humiliation."

"You've been a good wife," Nanay said. "We know you're a good woman."

"Thank you. I am a decent woman, I assure you. I have done nothing to stain your son's name. Your good name. I'll do most anything to keep my marriage. But what I cannot do is be a slave. You probably expect me to serve him, kiss his feet, even as he strays, but I'm sorry to tell you, that's beyond what I'm capable of as a wife."

"We never said you should be a slave," Tatay said. Nanay was eerily quiet.

I didn't ask them who Juanita was, but I thought of Panyang, our washerwoman. At thirty-two, she had never gone beyond grade school, had seven kids and a drunk husband who beat her up if she didn't bring home enough money. Much earlier, when I had asked her why she wouldn't just leave her husband, she'd shrugged and said she had no choice but to endure her fate. I wanted to tell my in-laws that I wasn't like Panyang, but I just thanked them and ended the conversation.

It was now three months after Eric and I got back together. Most everyone said that time healed all wounds, and I wanted so much to believe them even if my pain remained. I realized that in order for my family to be restored, I needed to do my part in reconciling with Eric. I waited for a sincere apology from him, which I was ready to accept, but it didn't come. I sensed, however, that he wanted to make peace. On better days, he and I would talk. He wanted me to go back to school, so I left my job to resume my actuarial courses. I realized I could handle graduate-level math once again. It felt comforting to have my husband close by and to be back with the set of university friends that he and I shared.

One weekend, Inday invited us to her cottage by the lake in Los Baños town, at the foot of the mystic Mount Makiling. The men ran to the water as soon as we arrived. We women went to Inday's bedroom to try on each other's spare swimsuits. Everyone agreed that Amanda's white bikini looked great on me, so I ditched my blue one-piece, but before I could jump in the water, Eric told me to change. What a bummer, I thought, but maybe he cares? I put my one-piece back on, and after the swim, changed into my shorts and T-shirt.

After supper, the gang sat around the porch table with a pitcher of gin gimlet, three unopened gin bottles, a bottle of lime juice, Marlboros and one glass. *Tagay-tagay*: The glass is filled to the brim and goes around; at your turn you've got to guzzle the thing down.

No excuses.

Eric's one arm was around my shoulders, the other around Amanda's. He dragged us to the water to throw up. Asked Pepe to help Amanda back inside. Laid me down on a bamboo cot on the shore. Removed my wet sneakers. Licked my ears. Unzipped my fly.

"I love you," he mumbled. A wet, hot kiss on my mouth.

I rabidly kissed back.

CHAPTER 17

Before long, I was pregnant again.

Eric had just finished his master's in math, and one day, he came home with big news: a scholarship offer for a math doctorate at Monash University in Australia. "We're going to Australia!" he said, his eyes shining.

I had known about his application but refused to think of it. I didn't want us to move. I was afraid to give birth without Mom around, and afterwards to single-handedly look after a newborn and a toddler. "Are you sure?" I said.

"Dead sure, my love." He rubbed his palms together, then his thumbs against his fingertips. "My big dream within reach."

One of my graduate school teachers had recruited me to be his assistant actuary at a government agency. I had just started, and I loved the job; it was more challenging than my first one. The money was good, too. "You mean I'll have to give up my job? How much is your stipend? I don't suppose I can work there, can I? And who'll look after Miguel if I do?"

"No, you can't work there, because you'll be my dependent. They give a generous stipend. Look at Greg and Rod. They took their wives along, and they did okay."

"But... I'm afraid to give birth in that strange land, with no one to support me."

Eric said no more and let the scholarship offer go. He took a full-time job that paid a little better than teaching, as a financial planner at a government agency, but still kept a teaching load. He didn't want to stop teaching because he enjoyed it, and we could use the extra money. For his new job, he sometimes went to Davao on business and brought back luscious pomelos from the Dole plantation there.

Doctor Edrosa had died, so I went to a new doctor, Doctor Pineda. He told me to see him on the date he expected me to go into labor. Eric was in Davao, so I sent him a telegram to let him know. I didn't get a reply. I packed my bag and on the appointed date and went to the hospital with Aunt Pacita. After examining me, Doctor Pineda said it wasn't time and to return in two days. Happy with the two extra days to give Eric time to come home, I sent him another telegram. Still no reply.

Two days later, I was now truly in labor. After six hours, a resident told me the baby's heartbeat had slowed down.

Oh my God, will my baby die? Will I?

The pains intensified. Soon, Doctor Pineda loomed at my feet. I frantically did everything he said – push, breathe, big push, breathe.

I passed out and when I came to, I learned that the baby's umbilical cord had been wrapped around his neck – just like mine in my mother's womb – slowing his heartbeat. And worse, he had done a little somersault during labor so that his head wasn't directly aimed at the birth canal. But thank God, he made it out safely without the need for expensive surgery.

Chona stayed with me overnight. Eric came the next day, straight from the airport. He stood beside my bed with a long face, saying he had wanted a baby girl. After ten minutes, he left to pick up his share of a crateful of pomelos that he and Geraldine had brought.

Geraldine was someone he worked with, she of the long legs and creamy skin and fluttery eyes who spoke English with an American twang, her curly head tilted to one side. Of course...of course.

I turned to my side facing the wall. "I'm sleepy," I told Chona and let go of my tears.

We named the baby Mateo. When we took him home, Miguel went into crying fits and wet his pants. Whenever I was in the bathroom, he threw a tantrum by the door and stopped only when I came out. I tried to give him as much attention as I could, losing sleep if I had to.

Mateo was pretty much like Miguel, colicky. But because he was born smaller, I needed to handle him more carefully. Mom came to the city to help me out, and when she left for Montaña after two weeks, I felt forsaken.

By the time Mateo was a month old, Christmas was heavily in the air, but I didn't feel the usual excitement of the season. Instead, I often found myself in tears without knowing why. Chona came one day, bringing the dress I was to wear as matron of honor for her approaching wedding. Mom had sewn our dresses. Mine was a long dress in pink chiffon – delicate and flowing, except that I could hardly zip it up.

"I am a big blob of fat," I said, tearing up.

"What's wrong? You mourning for Ninoy?" Chona said. "Or Kumander Dante?"

"I wish I were," I said, struggling out of the dress. "At least it'd be clear what's making me weepy." After a long trial by a military court, Ninoy Aquino and a Communist leader had recently been sentenced to die by firing squad on charges of subversion. Like most people, I believed the trial was rigged. Then yet another referendum was coming up on whether people wanted martial law to continue. Although I was disgusted with the way Marcos got

150

back at his political enemies and manipulated everything, I had learned to live with it. What could I do to save Ninoy, or to influence the referendum results, when I couldn't even do a decent job of caring for a frail baby and a bad-tempered toddler? "I don't know," I continued. "Maybe I'm just exhausted. So, tell me about the wedding. You're so smitten with Rex, you scare me."

"He's not scary," Chona said. "He's nice to me."

"But he smokes pot, my dear sister. Or might be into drugs. What do you make of that?"

"He's going to be fine. And the wedding's in three weeks, everything's set. Do you expect me to change my mind now?"

It wasn't the first time I'd told her of my objection to Rex. Dad and Mom weren't happy with her choice either. I let out a long exhale and said, "You're much too good for him."

Around seven p.m., Eric got dressed for the company Christmas party and splashed on his green-station-wagon cologne. I was sitting on the bed nursing Mateo when a maid said someone was asking for Eric. I peeked through the jalousies and saw Geraldine standing at the gate while a taxi idled on. Eric pecked me on the cheek and rushed out. "Bye," he said. "We're off to pick up some other friends."

I joined the family for supper. After putting Miguel and Mateo to sleep, I lay in bed staring at the ceiling and the dancing shadows from the garden. The lights from the Christmas tree in the living room winked above our half-walls. I listened for vehicles approaching, only to hear them drive past. It was almost four a.m. when Eric arrived. I rose to open the front door. Smelling of beer, plenty of it, he headed straight for the bathroom.

"So," I said when he came to our room, "looks like you had a great time." My lower belly tightened and then sharp pain shot to my back. "Why didn't you just party all night?"

He said nothing. In a few moments he was asleep.

"Okay," I said, trying to ignore what felt like a car chase in my pelvis. "You look after the children. My turn to leave." I opened the door and walked out to the living room. Unlocked the front door and went to the porch. The crisp December breeze ruffled the palm leaves and my cotton nightdress. I grasped the iron railing and stood there shivering and crying, wishing I could simply vanish. A few minutes later, Eric came out and said, "What do you think you're doing?"

"I'm going away."

"Come back inside!" he said, pulling me by the arm.

My belly cramped like I was in labor once more. Feeling a gush, I ran to the bathroom. I was bleeding. I felt panic for a few moments, because my post-natal bleeding had stopped two weeks earlier. Then I thought: Well, some women die of hemorrhage after giving birth, maybe I'm meant to be one of them. Might be a neat way to vanish.

"I'm bleeding. I could die of this," I told Eric. "Are you happy now?"

He looked alarmed. "Please," he said and took me in his arms. "Please, let's go to bed."

I did not bleed to death. Neither did I say a word about Geraldine or my random crying fits. When the clock struck twelve on Christmas Eve, I had just finished nursing Mateo. I tucked him in his crib and joined the big household in kissing each other Merry Christmas. We all rushed through this exercise, eager to dig into the delectable dinner waiting at the table. Eric was kissing and hugging his parents, siblings, grandma, and Aunt Pacita. When he got to me, he said with a grin, "Merry Christmas."

"Don't I get a kiss?" I said.

He wrinkled his nose. "You look like crap," he said and walked to the table.

I looked down at my nightdress, damp with milk and baby drool. He was damn right. I went to our room and slipped into a fresh nightdress and joined the others at table, but no kiss came.

Another land mine planted in my heart.

I went back to work in mid-January and had the chance to talk to my girlfriends again. They thought I was too passive, that I should speak up and tell Eric what I was feeling. I had read about postnatal depression and told them that was probably what was wrong with me, and that it should be temporary.

"Where's all that devotion coming from?" Amanda said. "He's not being nice to you, in fact he's cruel at times."

"You'll understand when you get married," I said. "It's not a simple thing."

"Do you intend to be a Susan Roces?" she said, referring to a popular movie actress whose actor husband was widely known to be philandering but who had always stood by her man. "Or Imelda Marcos?"

"It could be worse," I said.

Even if I didn't get total sympathy, spending time with my friends lifted my mood. I didn't confront Eric about anything, afraid he might call me irrational. I focused on the bright side, like how he was becoming a good provider. For one, he bought a brand-new, apple green Corolla. To break in the car, we went to Montaña for Easter, along with the kids and the nanny. Eric drove the five hundred kilometers by himself. Euphoric with the new-found freedom of owning a vehicle, we stopped at beaches to wade and take pictures at places I'd always relished watching whenever the bus went by. Narrow roads that hugged cliffs and looked down at rocky shores. The boundless South China Sea, sometimes calm, sometimes angry, but always lovely.

Dad was thrilled, for one of his big dreams had been for me to own a car. Eric took everyone on joyrides around town and to the beach, and I was delighted to be able to put a smile on my parents' faces once more.

On the way back to Manila, we decided on impulse to take a side trip to the mountain city of Baguio. I had dreamed of visiting this popular summer spot since I was a child, but my family – ever on a tight budget – didn't go on outings any farther than twenty kilometers from home. This was my first trip to Baguio, and I was wide-eyed at the endless blue layers of the towering Cordillera Mountains, whose peaks were swallowed by the clouds. We only managed a quick look-see since we didn't have the money to stay the night in a hotel. I beamed as the car snaked on the zigzag Kennon Road that, until then, I had only seen in photos.

"Look, we're driving through a cloud," I said. Miguel bounced in his seat with delight.

"Wait, listen," Eric said, turning the car radio volume up.

The reporter was reading election results. Four months ago, around Christmas, Marcos had run a referendum to ask whether or not the people wanted martial law to continue. Eric and I went to the polls to vote 'No,' but, as expected, the official result was a landslide 'Yes.' Shortly after, Marcos declared that there'd be elections for representatives to the Batasang Pambansa, the parliament that was created after he amended the constitution. Ninoy Aquino ran from his prison cell, for although he'd been sentenced to die, he was still in jail. On a high school field trip, I'd seen him at work in the Senate: young, smart, articulate, daring, with an air that made you take him seriously. I had just voted for him.

The radio blared: Ninoy Aquino got zero votes in many places, among which was the precinct where we'd voted.

"Shit," Eric said. "They could've been less flagrant than that. What a stupid move."

CHAPTER 18

Miguel and I were tying balloons to chairs for Mateo's first birthday party, when a letter came in the mail from Mom. *Your Daddy was on his motorcycle four days ago when a dog chased him and he crashed. His head hit the pavement. He was rushed to the hospital in Bacarra. He has some broken ribs but he's home now.*

"Finish tying these," I said to Miguel, sat down and read the letter once more. Why didn't Dad wear a helmet? And those dogs on the streets, I always knew they were up to no good. Was there a lot of blood? I was doubly concerned, because for years, Dad had also been suffering from extremely high blood pressure.

There had been another letter just a couple of months before, about Dad's brother's death. Uncle Badong had drowned in Montaña's river that had become fierce with the monsoons. When he'd visited our house, I could hardly hear his voice, for he spoke very softly. Because he was a fisherman, Uncle Badong's skin was a very dark brown and wrinkly. Hard to tell they were brothers, because my father's skin was a lot fairer and soft and fleshy. I was sad to hear about this humble man's passing, especially because he had been the only member of Dad's family who lived in town.

A week later, yet another letter from Mom. Still recuperating at home from the motorcycle accident, Dad had received a devastating telegram: His oldest brother Ernesto had died alone in Davao and had been discovered only after a few days, when his house began to smell. When Daddy received the telegram, Uncle Ernesto had already been buried.

Dad had often talked about his Manong Ernesto, who was a full twenty years older, with deep respect. Being the youngest, Dad looked up to all of his siblings, but he had a special fondness for Uncle Ernesto, whom he regarded as a father because after their parents died, Uncle Ernesto and the older siblings supported Dad and sent him to college. Because I had never met Uncle Ernesto, I didn't feel a sense of personal loss, but I could only imagine how much his death broke Dad's heart.

Eric and I took the children to Montaña for Christmas, arriving there at suppertime. Chona, Francis and Sonny had arrived from Manila earlier. By this time, my two brothers were already in university at UP and shared an apartment with Chona and her husband. Dad sat on his favorite stool at the dining table in his pajamas, a bandage around his chest. Another bandage covered part of the back of his head. Although his face was still chubby, he looked haggard. I kissed him on the cheek, feeling sorry, not knowing what to say.

Daddy didn't eat with us. He said he was on a strict diet, and it was easier for him to eat his yogurt and vegetables if he didn't see us gorge on *adobo*, *pinakbet*, rice, and *tupig*.

Tired from the day-long drive, Eric and I and the two little boys went to bed upstairs after supper. In the middle of the night, I got up to go to the bathroom and saw Dad in the downstairs bedroom. The room smelled of alcohol. In the middle of the bare floor, Daddy sat asleep in a chair, his forehead resting on a pillow atop a high stool. Like a huge see-through tent, our largest mosquito net covered him and most of the floor. His breathing sounded uneven, labored.

"Mommy, you didn't tell me Dad slept sitting down?" I said in the morning.

"He's got stitches on the back of his head," she said.

"I thought he only had broken ribs," I said. "No helmet?"

"Nobody wears a helmet in these parts."

"What a shame. They should make it a law. He cannot lie down to rest his back then?"

"No," she said. "It's been more than a month. He's become a lot more irritable, so be patient with him... And remember he's counting the days." Mom's eyes watered.

"What days?" I said.

"When he realized that his two brothers had died within three months of each other, to the day, he began to fear that he'd die next..." Her voice trailed off.

"And then?"

"He's counted three months from your Uncle Ernesto's date of death, and ended up with a date around February."

"Mom, that's totally baseless," I said, although I shuddered at the thought.

"Help me pray."

Just then, Ramon walked in. "Ay, Ramon, come in," Mom said and led him to Dad's room. He was not a doctor, but most people in town went to him for sprains and broken bones.

I stayed in the kitchen but could hear what was going on in Dad's room. "Please inhale deeply, sir," Ramon said. In a few seconds I heard Dad's faint "*Annay!*" Dad had almost never said *ouch* before. How could a mere dog put my father down? Didn't he teach me as a kid to deal with them? For the next twenty minutes, I wanted to yell out each *annay* for him, wishing it would ease his pain.

Ramon came daily. Dad was indeed more edgy than usual, so I tried to keep a distance. Before supper on Christmas Day, he gathered all of his children in the dining room. He stood beside the china cabinet. I sat in front of him, Chona to my right. Francis and

Sonny huddled together on a bench. Mom sat by the window next to Marya.

"Listen, all of you," Dad said. Mom looked out the window. Dad put his hand on his bandaged chest and continued, "I'm not going to be around much longer."

I almost knew what he was going to say, but when I heard him say it, I felt the familiar big hand wring my head and chest, the same way it did after my father first left me alone in a dorm when I was eleven. It kept squeezing hard until my hands and feet and chest went cold.

No one spoke. No one moved except Daddy, who rubbed his eyes with his fingers. "Good for you, you are quite okay," he said, looking at Chona and me. "You already have jobs. How about these younger ones?" He pointed to Francis and Sonny. Then he gave a long, heavy sigh and said, "Marya, most of all, because she's only nine."

Silence. He took out a hanky. Wiped his eyes and blew his nose. "Promise me that you'll look after Francis and Sonny. They can get into all sorts of mischief in Manila. Make sure they finish college, so that they can in turn help Marya have a bright future. So I can die without feeling like a failure."

You can't die, I wanted to scream, but I just nodded and said, "Yes, Daddy," the words drowning in my throat. My siblings sniffled and mumbled their yeses. Mom just sat there, staring out the window, tears dripping down her cheeks. I had never seen my father's eyes so pained. I had never felt so helpless.

The next day, Eric and I had to return to our jobs and our city life. My head was hollow, and my heart flipped about on the endless road to Manila. While he drove, Eric held my left hand or else rubbed my thigh. "It's okay," he kept on saying. "It's going to be fine."

Three months later – not in February but in March – I was at work one bright Monday morning when my boss's secretary phoned me

158

at my desk.

"You have a long-distance call," she said. In those days, urgent messages were sent by telegram, and the more expensive long-distance phone call was reserved for extreme emergencies. I ran to my boss' office down the hall, knocking my thigh against a desk corner along the way.

"I want you to be strong," Auntie Celina said gently. My thigh throbbed, a chill washed over me, and my knees began to shake.

"I want you to be strong," she repeated. I clenched the phone. "Your father passed away last night." She was speaking in English, maybe reading a prepared message.

"*Apay*, Auntie," I muttered. "Why?" My eyes watered and in a second, teardrops dotted the secretary's desk.

"*Balasang ko*, he had a heart attack."

"When?"

"Last night. Around nine-thirty," she said softly. "He was in the hospital for a week. Please be strong." Then she said she needed to hang up.

Be strong? How?

I ran back to my desk and gathered my things. My officemates hugged and consoled me. By the time I was headed out the door, they had pooled some money that they handed me in an envelope.

"Take a taxi home," they said. "Use the rest for whatever else."

On the cab ride home, I recalled that while watching *Three's Company* the night before, I had suddenly felt sad. I couldn't understand why, because that TV show was always one big source of laughs for me. I had sat there watching a little longer, but the urge to cry was so intense that I went to bed before the end of the show. I'd slept fitfully. Now it clicked: the moment Dad died, my heart knew.

When I called Chona, she bawled. Auntie Celina had also called her but said Dad was fifty-fifty, obviously concerned my pregnant sister might not take it well. I told Chona that Eric would be driving the car, but there wasn't enough room for all of us because we were taking along the children and a nanny. She said she and

159

my brothers were taking the first bus home.

Eric and I managed to drive out with the boys early in the evening and reached Montaña at daybreak. When I saw the *atong* burning on the road outside our gate, I wanted to run away. This cannot be a dead man's house, I told myself; it can't be. Then I saw a handful of men playing cards on the patio and started to cry. To announce a death, Ilocanos keep a thick log smoldering in front of a deceased person's house until the day of the burial. During the wake in the house, the body is never left alone, and to keep the place awake at night, men come to gamble and donate a part of the purse to the family.

Once Eric had parked the car, he took Miguel by the hand. I gave Mateo to the nanny and ran past the gamblers to the front door. By the window – the window where Dad and Mom had sat crying when Eric asked them for my hand in marriage – instead of the two easy chairs, sat a coffin. And in place of Lola's crocheted curtains, a heavy purple drape hung on the windows. I saw Mom a few steps away, in a blue pantsuit, sitting on a chair's armrest, some old women around her. "Mommy!" I said, clinging to her. She sobbed in my arms. "Why didn't you tell me?" I said.

"I didn't want to worry you, *anak ko*," she said, sobbing even harder.

I approached the glass-covered coffin. There was Daddy, dressed in his favorite suit, his hair pomaded and combed just the way he liked it, looking like he was all set to take Mom dancing at the town *fiesta*. Hearing the shocking news and seeing the *atong* were big jabs thrust at my chest. But seeing my father, only fifty-four, all dapper but lying stiff inside a satin-lined box was the cruelest jab of all.

"Take care not to let your tears drop on the coffin, *balasang ko*," one of the women said. "So you don't weigh down your father's soul on its journey."

I nodded and turned to Mom. "What exactly happened?" I said.

"He had chest pains ten days ago so we took him to the hospital in Laoag. He was there for a week, but I didn't tell you because what could you do but worry? I was going to write you about it after he got well. They sent him home Sunday morning; he looked okay. I let him rest in bed. Half an hour after supper, he again complained of chest pains and sent Zenay to find a jeepney to take him back to the hospital. While waiting, he sat on Marya's bed and watched her sleeping. He sat there without taking his eyes off the little girl. I can't describe his face... When at last we reached the hospital, they helped him into a wheelchair. A moment later, he crumbled."

The wake lasted a week. Every day, we were busy welcoming visitors until late in the evening. I found the dawn hours a good time to have Dad to myself. One early morning, I stood by his coffin, stooped and pressed my chin on the glass right above his face – armed with a hanky to catch my tears – and silently talked to him. Is that a grimace, Dad, or a smile? Why did you leave? In three weeks, I'm marching up on stage to receive my master's degree; I did it for you, and you didn't even wait. You're so unfair. And who'll come and pick me up if my marriage cracks again?

After half an hour, my legs and chest were numb, so I straightened up to stretch and breathe. Zenay came and plopped into a chair close by. She was barefoot; her shift dress slid up to the middle of her thick thighs. "Uncle, why did you leave us?" she wailed. "Now who will tell us what to do?"

How unrefined. Mom cried a lot but never wailed. And why was this woman here, disturbing my quiet time with *my* Daddy? Zenay kept on bawling. "Uncle, we'll all be lost without you!"

I stared at her, from her oily nose down to her cracked heels, hoping my glare would make her shut up. But she was oblivious of me and wailed even louder. Why don't you have an ounce of shame in you? I wanted to yell. I wished to gag her with my hanky and drag her out by the neck. But I couldn't, I didn't. Not in front of my beloved father. I wasn't going to take away his honor. As a parting gift to him, I kept my dignity and left the room.

At the town hall, before the funeral mass, the town officials and the Northwestern faculty honored Daddy with gratitude and praise for his service to the community. His students and colleagues came to say how much they loved and respected him. The common village folk did the same. Because I was chosen to speak for the family, I stood there tall and strong in my black dress and veil, said a few words to thank the crowd and praise my father. Then I broke down. I was twenty-four, confused and afraid, angry and heartbroken. How could I say anything wise?

We walked the three kilometers to the cemetery, behind Dad's hearse. Mom was quite composed, silently crying, trying to comfort a shaken and bewildered Marya. Thankfully, Zenay behaved herself and did not wail. We older siblings stood at the edge of the deep hole, sobbing, comforting each other. When the casket was being lowered, Sonny screamed, "I'm going to behave myself, Daddy!"

That primal cry tore my insides into little shreds and made me weak in the knees. I needed to cling to Eric until the ceremony was over.

The elders clipped a lock of my father's hair and gave each of us children a small clump to keep. I put mine in a pouch and kept it in my jewelry box. That was the first time I had ever touched Daddy's hair. It was not as sticky as I'd thought.

Three weeks later, we joined Mom in Montaña for Easter.

Most of the graves in the cemetery were above-the-ground white tombs haphazardly scattered up a hill. Because Mom wanted Dad buried underground, his grave looked neater. A statue of the Crucified Christ stood at the grave's head, with Dad's tombstone at Christ's feet, between lilies that Mom had planted. The rest of the grave was enclosed by a low iron-and-concrete wall that you could sit on. Every afternoon, we walked together to the cemetery to light a candle, sit on the low wall, say a prayer and let Dad listen to the sound of our tears.

One night, I dreamed of Daddy's sister Teodora. She was one of the siblings who lived in Davao and whom I had never met. In the dream, she hovered above me while I lay in bed. I told Mom in the morning.

"How'd you know it was her?" she said.

"Well, funny things happen in dreams, right?" I said. "You just know."

We thought nothing more of it until later in the day when Mom received a telegram: Aunt Teodora had died of a heart attack, like Dad and Uncle Ernesto. This time, we were shocked more because the death had happened too soon, ruining the three-to-four month pattern we had begun to recognize. Again, the news came too late for anyone to go to the funeral. Maybe this was a good thing too, because we had no more money to buy an air ticket for any of us to travel to the funeral.

Four siblings gone in a span of barely nine months. Very eerie. But Eric was there, gathering me in his arms whenever I needed to sob until I ran out of breath.

The week after my family returned to Manila, we received news that Eric's Aunt Pacita had died of cancer in the States. She had gone to Philadelphia barely a year before, to be with siblings who had emigrated. Eric was, of course, devastated. My turn to let him cry in my arms. Or rather, cry with him, for among the old ladies in Eric's family, I felt closest to Aunt Pacita. When they brought her body back home, I got her the best bunch of roses that the last few pesos in my wallet could buy.

Five deaths?

But while the money was about gone, I had a glut of tears. Cried on Eric's chest until he ended up crying, too. On my graduation day, I tried to be cheerful, but when our little party was over, I let the tears out until my head throbbed in pain.

I had quit smoking when I became pregnant with Mateo, but

now was a good time to pick up the habit again. And furiously.

Mom wrote about how she'd anticipate Dad waiting for her at the curb when she got off the jeepney from Laoag, only to realize he was gone. About how Marya had become so insecure, she'd never let Mom out of her sight. How very little sleep she got and how money was tight. She had collected some insurance money from social security and from Daddy's employer – which helped – but what to do with Daddy's motorcycle mortgage? Might Eric and I be interested in buying it? Dad had a rifle and a revolver; Mom was keeping the revolver. Did we want his rifle? Realizing that I wasn't the only one grieving and life had to go on, I began to write Mom more often and offered to support my two brothers through college. Eric and I bought the motorcycle and took the rifle to have something to remember Daddy by, even if I was deathly afraid of guns.

CHAPTER 19

The year after Dad died, I went to UP one afternoon to submit my application for admission to the MBA program. When I'd finished, I dropped by the Math Department to say hi to my old friends and teachers; maybe if Eric was there, we could go home together in his car. His office door was locked, so I headed for the admin office. "Hi, Goyang," I said to the administrator. "Would you know where Eric is?"

She raised her eyebrows and said, "Did you come to check?"

"No. I just came to say hi."

"You don't know? Open your eyes and ears, poor dear."

"What don't I know?" I said, trying not to show my mounting anxiety. Goyang had a reputation as the juiciest gossip in the department and knew about the Mingming affair five years earlier. "At the math majors' party last week, they came and left together," she said. "I mean, Eric and one girl. They behaved very much like a couple through the evening. You know."

"I don't know, Goyang," I said. "Are you sure?" Eric had told me about that party but I didn't think much of it then. After all, student organizations sometimes invited faculty members to their parties. But now that Goyang had brought it up, I was surprised to realize I wasn't that shocked and began to feel ashamed.

"Suzie. Suzie Mata is the name. She's married, but the husband is in graduate school in the States."

I didn't bother waiting for Eric and went home alone. The kids were in bed when he arrived. I laid out his supper, but he said he'd eaten at a meeting. I confronted him about what Goyang had told me. This time, he looked me straight in the eye and flatly denied it.

"If you're truly innocent, let me talk to her," I said.

He creased his brows and looked away for a minute or so, then said, "I'll see what I can do."

Because he looked so confident in calling my dare, I wondered if I was the moronic one. I was tempted to take it all back and let the thing go.

Two weeks later, I sat smoking a Marlboro in Eric's office until he came in, a girl behind him. She looked a couple of years younger than my twenty-six, an inch shorter than my five-foot-three. Black wavy hair, square jaw. I thought her slightly flared nose didn't go well with her fair skin. Not someone I'd take a second look at, I told myself and smirked. Without asking her to sit, I said, "Okay." Took a puff, slowly blew the smoke out and rose from my chair. "I hear that you're going out with my husband."

Eric stood a few feet away, feet far apart, his arms behind him like a soldier awaiting orders.

"Don't mess with me," I said and pulled out a bottle of muriatic acid from my bag. This chemical was a cheap bathroom cleaning agent; it sizzled when poured on tiles, swallowing stubborn scum. I stretched out my hand to show her the label. "Don't mess with me or else this will sizzle on your face."

Suzie turned up her nose and glared at me. Because I really didn't mean to use it, I put the bottle down. I wasn't going to leave any physical marks on her and risk being sued and jailed. "I hear you're acting like a couple in front of everyone," I said.

"What's wrong with that?" she said, glowering.

My temples throbbing, I walked up to her, knocking down my chair. In one swift move, I snatched a bunch of her hair with my left hand and slapped her face with my right palm. Eric came between us. Suzie scrambled to get her balance, grabbed her purse that had fallen to the floor and headed for the door.

"Go to hell!" I said.

"See you there!" she said, slamming the door behind her.

"So!" I turned my rage to Eric. "Aren't you going to chase her?"

He just looked at me and put the chair back up.

"Don't you want to hold her and kiss the pain away?" I said, my heart pounding wildly. I gasped for air, then went on. "If you'd as much as made the mistake of stopping me, that'd be the end of us. Tell me, do you want to walk away now? Why don't we call this crappy marriage quits?"

"Let's go home," he said.

"Make sure you want to go home with me, not with her."

He didn't say anything more, picked up his things and mine, took my arm and led me to the car.

Over the next several days, I bitched endlessly. "Do you realize what you've done?" I said. "I've worked so hard to trust you again, because, believe me, it's the toughest thing to be betrayed. Imagine me running around with some guy. Being the Filipino macho man that you are, you'd probably kill me. Banish me at best, for dishonoring you. What gave you the exclusive right to demand faithfulness and to deny it to your partner? So, you stab my heart and I struggle to trust you once more. And just when a scar is finally forming, you decide to strike again – at exactly the same spot. You'd think it'd no longer hurt the second time, but no, it still hurts. It hurts twice as much. I should have given up on you when you first cheated on me."

"I did not do it," my husband said. "I'm sorry you feel hurt."

"How about 'I'm sorry I cheated on you again?'"

"I didn't cheat on you."

We had many versions of this conversation, each one ending with his firm denial. I ran to our common set of UP friends. Amanda and the other girls lent their usual listening ears and cursed with me. Although the men were not pleased with what Eric had done, they had a different approach. "Ha!" one of them said. "You've got a true-blue playboy in your hands, my friend. He seems to be learning well."

"But it's so unfair..." I said.

"One day," my friend said, "while his wife is away, a man lets his girlfriend in their house. The wife returns and catches the lovers in bed. 'Who is this girl?' the wife says.

'My cousin,' the husband says. 'She's in town for two days and asked to stay with us. She's in our bed to take a nap.'

'Why is she naked? Why are you naked?' the wife says.

'It's very hot, can't you see? Almost 40 degrees outside.'

'And why are you on top of her?'

'Oh, I was fixing the blinds when I tripped and fell on her.'"

Although I laughed hard at that one, I lamented how gravely sick our culture was. Staunch Catholic on the outside, cannibal on the inside. Was I alone in this battle to demand the truth?

At last, Eric begged for another chance. I gave in and forgave him, saying this was absolutely the last chance. I demanded that we live separately from his parents, expecting that this would force him into becoming a fully responsible man of the house.

When the school year ended a couple of weeks later, Eric tried to fix my heartache with lazy days soaking in the sun, sand and sea. He took the two little boys and me to his parents' home province of Mindoro. A long bus ride, then ferry, then a rickety bus on bumpy roads. When we at last we got there, the dust was caked on our clothes and bodies. The town is a narrow strip of land trapped between Mount Halcon on one side and the vast ocean on the other. Wild country compared to Ilocos: dusty, rugged roads, rice fields, coconut palms, fishing boats, and hot pink corals pulsing under a clear, blue sea. We had no agenda for a full two weeks but to visit with Eric's relatives, stuff ourselves with the feasts they laid before us, go on island picnics, or pick a spot on the endless shoreline and swim or play in the sand, our skins toasting to dark brown.

Until then, I had never spent so much time so close to a mountain I felt I could touch it. After two days, my favorite activity was to soak in the sea facing the great Halcon and just stare in awe at the peaks and the lushness of what the locals called their sacred mountain. Being mesmerized that way – that alone was well worth the tiring trip.

When school opened in June, Eric transferred to a teaching post at the UP School of Business. I began my MBA and Miguel started kindergarten. And to keep his word, Eric moved us into an apartment in the next district. I had earlier let the nanny go because she was ill, so we moved out without a maid. Even so, I relished reclaiming my own queendom.

Soon after, we began planning to build our own home.

One Saturday morning in June, Chona arrived at my place, frantic, saying Sonny was at Crame. Ever since martial law, it had become routine for the police to pick up anybody who broke some rule and detain him at Camp Crame, the national police headquarters.

"Sonny? Behind bars?" My mind raced. Sonny had been a bully as a kid. "Did he get into a fight?"

"No," Chona said. "Marijuana."

"He doesn't do marijuana," I said. "Maybe he was acting cocky and some cop simply didn't like it."

We rushed to Camp Crame. Along the way, she told me that Sonny hadn't come home the night before. She'd first assumed he'd had too much to drink and spent the night at a friend's house. But when he didn't show up at the usual early-morning time, Chona's husband went to the police precinct to check. There he was told that Sonny had been arrested after midnight.

At Crame, we were asked to wait in a small room with benches. My brother – my once-cuddly baby brother – came out and sat between Chona and me. His stark face was greasy. His long hair was gone; in its place were scraggly lumps.

"Why?" Chona said.

He shook his head and said, "Two men in a van picked me up."

"Were you drunk?" I said.

"I can't talk here," he said. "Try to get me a pass. They give day passes."

"I scrimp to give you spending money, and you use it to drink?" I said.

The officer on duty said passes were granted by only one person: the commanding general. Being a Saturday, however, the general might or might not show up. If we wanted, we could take a chance and wait.

Chona and I waited. After almost two hours, we agreed that she could go and do some errands while I stayed to wait for the general. I sat there for another two hours before the staff suddenly stiffened at their desks and all eyes were on the main door. The general had arrived.

The middle-aged man looked familiar. His nameplate: *Gamo, N.* I remembered a picture taken at my old crush Billy's military training graduation, back in high school. I had just hung a *sampaguita lei* around Billy's neck and was shaking his hand. The smiling man in the background was the guest speaker; his nameplate read *Gamo.* Of course! This was Noel Gamo, the father of Noel Junior, who was in Billy's class. My anxiety eased a bit, thinking this connection might improve my chances for a pass.

I waited my turn for half an hour. When I was at last called into the general's office, I walked in and said, "Good morning, sir."

"Take a seat," he said, waving at a visitor's chair in front of his desk.

"Thank you, sir," I said. "Sir, I would like to ask for a pass for my brother. If you will, sir."

He scribbled on a note pad. "Name?"

I gave Sonny's name and then said, "Sir, you once gave a speech at my high school."

"What school?" he said, rose from his seat and walked around his desk toward me.

"Philippine Science High School, sir. In fact, I know your son Noel. He was a year ahead of me." He was now standing to my left, very close.

"Hmm," he said and then put his right arm around my shoulders. Startled, I pulled away and looked at his face inches away from mine. He pulled me closer and put his right cheek next to my face. My heart beat faster. I wanted to push him and run, but he was holding me tight. Besides, I was afraid to upset him, knowing he could easily take it out on my brother. And I needed a pass! He looked and felt like a father coaxing his little girl for a kiss.

I gave him a quick peck on the cheek. He loosened his grip, walked back to his chair and gave me a twenty-four-hour pass.

I took Sonny home to Chona's apartment. Chona and Francis laid out a big lunch, but we hardly ate. "I headed for home past midnight," Sonny said. "Too drunk to walk on, I sat for a moment on the pavement in front of the store next door. When I got up to walk the few steps to our gate, a van pulled up. Two men took me away – *barangay tanod.*" These were volunteers deputized with police powers in every city district. They usually patrolled the streets at night, to watch out for criminals. "They took me to the police precinct and then the police brought me to Crame." He insisted that he didn't use marijuana, that the small amount they found on him was a friend's.

"Are you sure?" I said, recalling the time when he was small, and Mom found him on the floor next to a small bookshelf that had toppled over. Mom had admonished him, and he'd said he was simply walking by when the thing tumbled down. Although we all suspected that he'd been fiddling with the shelf, Sonny didn't get a spanking from Dad for that one. In fact, Dad loved to tease him about it afterwards, and all the while Sonny maintained his innocence. I was certain that if it had been me, Dad would have lectured me, if not whacked me on the butt. From then on, I'd seen Sonny fib his way around. This day though, my brother looked so miserable I chose to believe him.

Then I told them about the general, which added to the misery in his face. We all agreed not to tell our mother, so as not to compound her grief over Dad's death.

Chona and I took turns taking time off work to visit Sonny twice a week. One time, I had been waiting for three hours in the queue for a pass when General Gamo arrived. When I walked into his office, he was leafing through a booklet and patting his crotch. I caught a glimpse of the pages, shocked at what I saw: drawings of different sexual positions. He closed the booklet, looked intently at me and said, "Give me one good reason why your brother deserves a pass."

"Sir, he is very young, only eighteen," I said. "Our father just died."

"And how young are you?"

"Twenty-six, sir," I said, holding back my tears. "My mother is still mourning. If you could please help us."

He looked at me for a few moments; I sat unmoving, my eyes on his hands. Finally, he wrote a pass and handed it to me across his desk. I thanked him and hurried out.

"If I go there again, I'll be raped," I told Eric. "Can you please come with me?"

"I have two projects running, a trip coming up," he said. "Then exam papers to mark."

I didn't go to the camp alone again, but took along either Chona or Francis. Sonny felt remorseful but maintained that he didn't do drugs. He was scheduled to have a blood test soon, and if found to be a user, would be charged with both possession and use of marijuana and moved to another detention facility, in Bicutan, where security was much tighter and passes were not allowed.

It was time to tell Mommy. She came to Manila and went with Chona to Camp Crame. The general's aide wouldn't see them, saying his boss wanted to deal with 'Lorenzo's other sister.'

Mom stayed for a week and visited Sonny often. I stopped going. A few days after Mom left for Montaña, I got a phone call at work. It was Sonny. "I left the camp," he said.

"What do you mean?" I said.

"I left. I'm outside now."

"You mean you escaped? How?"

"I asked permission to go and buy cigarettes. Then I simply walked out the camp gate pretending I was with a group of people."

"So where are you?"

"I can't tell you. I have to go." Click.

Apart from being anxious about Sonny's safety, I worried about what the general might do upon learning of my brother's escape. "What if he has me kidnapped?" I told Eric. "And when he's done with me, gives me to his soldiers to gang rape? And then I'll be a statistic among those who've simply vanished." Although the press was severely controlled, there had been rumours about the military doing terrible things to families of detainees or escapees.

"No, he can't do that," he said, shaking his head.

"But I'm much easier to find than Sonny," I said. "He knows my name, where I work, everything! You sound as though you're new to martial law. Look at Ninoy."

"What about Ninoy? And you're not Ninoy."

Ninoy Aquino had been in the news lately. In spite of a death sentence, Marcos had allowed him and his family to travel to the US for medical treatment. He had been in prison for seven years and recently had a heart attack. I said, "Don't you wonder what those military men did to his family before they were allowed to see him? His daughters, his wife? And all those beauty queens who once marched the streets and are now in jail? You suppose the soldiers respect them as women?"

"Why don't you level with that jerk Gamo?"

I was taken aback. "What are you saying? You mean I shout to his face that he's being a jerk? I'm only asking you to drive me to and from work."

"I have no time," he said, and that was the end of it.

Why was he so mean one minute, nice the next? Sure, the issue concerned my brother who did a stupid thing, but if he couldn't regard Sonny as his own brother, shouldn't he have seen being safe as my issue? Like several times before, I tried to excuse him by telling myself he was stressed at work and that I could handle this matter alone.

I prayed hard each night for Sonny's safety, wherever he might be. And for mine. I prayed each moment on the commute to work every morning and on the way to my evening MBA classes after work, feeling safe only when Eric picked me up in his car after my class.

Several weeks later, I learned I was pregnant, but this didn't change anything. I still took the bus to work and to my evening classes, alone and afraid.

One night, I got home from school and did the usual. Washed the morning's breakfast dishes while dinner cooked. Hand-washed Miguel's soiled school uniform because he only had two sets. Ironed our clothes for the next day. Ate dinner with Eric and the boys. Tucked the little ones in bed and clipped their dirty fingernails. At last, at one a.m., I was ready for bed.

A few minutes after I said my night prayers, the doorbell rang, long, insistent buzzes. I groped for the light switch; Eric also got up and we ran downstairs. Peeking through the blinds, I made out the outline of a scrawny man clad in shorts, naked from the waist up. He yelled out my name. My brother's voice.

"Francis?" I scrambled to unlock the door and ran the few steps to the gate. "Oh God, what happened?"

"Ccuh...ccuh...." With each aborted syllable, he stomped his foot and thrust his upper body forward. "Ccould you...pay the taxi?"

Eric ran to get some cash and paid the cab driver.

"What happened?" I said. The three of us were now sitting in the couch.

"I wwas..." This time, Francis slapped his lap with each word that got stuck to his tongue. His face twitched, his dark eyes narrowed. "I was mugged."

I was shaking. "Where? Why? Did they hurt you? Who were you with?"

He was in Quiapo, the old downtown Manila. They took his bag, his clothes and shoes and gave him a dirty pair of shorts and rubber slippers, maybe so he wouldn't look like a lunatic walking home naked.

"What were you doing in that seedy part of town?" I said. "They could've killed you."

Francis looked down.

"What'd they want to do with your things?" I said, knowing he didn't have money. After all, I only gave him barely enough for his school needs. He lived with Chona and was working on a fine arts degree at UP, taking some music courses on the side.

In spite of his intelligence and musical talent, Francis grew up with a lot of ridicule – from peers, relatives, even a teacher or two – because he was effeminate and he stuttered. The church reinforced this bias by stressing that homosexuality was evil. The brave souls who didn't hide their sexual orientation – like Auntie Celina and Ninang Florie, or numerous younger men who even flaunted it – were taunted or gossiped about. When I entered UP, I saw that gay people there had more freedom to be themselves without being judged. Seeing how they flourished - mostly in the arts – I wished the same kind of freedom for my brother.

After high school, Francis topped the admission test for a zoology course at a Catholic university in Manila but hesitated to enrol, saying he didn't want to go into science. "Tell me the truth," I had said then. "Just between you and me, are you gay? Because I think you are, and if I'm correct, I suggest you go to UP instead. You'll be more accepted there." He nodded, welcomed my support and went to UP where his artistic talents were nurtured. Girls swooned over his dark good looks, but, of course, he wasn't interested in them. In fact, he started to be more daring in the way he dressed, choosing unconventional colors and styles. Perhaps the muggers chose him because he looked like an easy target.

Francis refused to eat. Eric lent him some clothes and he went to shower. When Eric and I got back in bed, it was almost three a.m. "Get some sleep," he said.

"Why do I have brothers who specialize in finding trouble?"

"Sleep."

I turned to God. Please, keep my brothers safe. Keep us all safe. And then to Dad. When you made me promise to look after Francis and Sonny, you didn't tell me it'd be this tough. You only said to send them to school. This is not fair at all.

As my pregnancy progressed, I felt safer walking around on my own, and my fear of being hunted by the general abated. In January 1981, Marcos lifted martial law, and although he actually kept all his powers, I was relieved. When I gave birth to our third son Rico in April, Sonny was still nowhere to be seen.

Eric soon finished his MBA at the top of his class. He bought a new and bigger car, a Toyota Corona, and I got to keep the old Corolla. To break in the new car, he suggested we go to Pagsanjan Falls, a couple of hours south of Manila. "Can we go alone?" I said, knowing he always preferred to take the boys along. "Just you and me. And we can't shoot the rapids with little boys." The majestic waterfalls could only be reached by a risky boat ride.

We left the kids with Eric's parents and drove off. Like the day we ran away and holed up in a cheap motel, I felt the thrill of escape, except that this time we rode in our own car and made reckless love in a clean, canopied bed in a decent tourist hotel. Three babies later, we finally had a real honeymoon in a secluded, rustic town. I thought of Prince Charles and Lady Diana who were also on their honeymoon and felt like a princess myself.

The next morning, we got into a *banca*, the Filipino canoe, with a boatman in front and another at the back. They steered the *banca* upstream, against the swift currents of the Pagsanjan River. Within minutes, we were at the bottom of a deep gorge with jungle growth amidst rocks and tiny waterfalls on either side. I heard a familiar bird call that brought my mind back home to Montaña. To steer the boat between boulders, the front boatman stuck his left leg out against a boulder and pushed to propel the boat forward, then brought his left leg in and stuck the right one out against the other boulder.

After half an hour, the main waterfalls, my first time seeing a big one this close. We were at a pool where the roaring, foamy deluge hit the surface from about ten storeys high. God is indeed smart, I thought, for making amazing things such as this.

The way back was a more intense kind of thrill. The boatmen rowed the *banca* between the same slippery boulders, but this time down the river to shoot some fifteen white rapids that made me shut my eyes tight a good part of the time. But they were skilled boatmen and brought us back in one piece. When we reached the hotel, I told Eric, "We should do more of this. Just you and me, alone."

The following year, Eric took me on another trip, and even if I was just a tag-along on his business trip, for me it was a treat. This time, it was to Zamboanga, a shopping haven nicknamed the City of Flowers, at the tip of a peninsula in the far south of the country, closer to Malaysia than to Manila. Because Eric was mostly at work, I went a little crazy with the shopping – Indonesian *batik* wraparound skirts and dresses, Spam, chocolates, and cigarettes. Yes, cigarettes, for I'd gone back to smoking once again, after weaning my baby Rico. Even if I didn't see many of the famous tourist spots – like the pink sand beach, for instance – to me it was another honeymoon. What else could I ask for? Two months earlier, my best friend Amanda offered me an exciting new job as actuarial manager at Pag-Ibig, which I took no time to accept. Eric and I were building our own house. I at last had a car to call my own. And here I was, alone with my man in an exotic place that was the farthest away from home I'd ever been.

CHAPTER 20

I worried about Sonny, who had told Chona that he was moving from place to place. Once, he'd told Chona where he was, and Chona had gone to visit him. She found herself in a squalid dwelling in a slum district, so she chose not to tell Mom about it. After over a year of hiding, Sonny finally went home to Chona's apartment. By then, Marcos had lifted martial law, and my brother hoped that the military had forgotten all about him. He went back to school and tried finding a job. Francis was also plodding along in his schoolwork, and so we could all live normal lives once again.

Eric and I focused on trying to be good parents, building our careers as well as our first house, a bungalow with a big yard in suburban San Jacinto. When we moved in, my heart was bursting with hope: This is it, we are fully committed now, our nine-year old marriage bond sturdier than our house's four thick concrete posts combined.

One early May morning, I had just fetched Mom and my two bigger boys from the bus station. For the third summer in a row, Mom had taken the boys to Montaña for three weeks. It worked for everybody. My city boys loved the interesting things they discovered in the country and also picked up some Ilocano. Mom spoiled them with her cooking, sewed them pajamas and gave them funny haircuts. And I got to have a little respite from child-minding.

Mom handed me a Kodak envelope, saying, "Look at these. I also brought *marunggay* cuttings." Since we'd moved to San Jacinto three months ago, she'd slowly turned my backyard into an Ilocano vegetable garden – mangoes, avocado, *chico, calamansi, saluyot.*

We sat down for breakfast but I wanted to see the pictures first. "Look at you!" I said, pointing at a picture of Miguel receiving his first Holy Communion. "Thank you, Mom, thank you."

She beamed. Apart from the usual simple prayers, I hadn't been teaching my children about God. When Miguel turned seven a year earlier, I realized that he should have been prepared for his first Holy Communion. This was routinely done in Catholic schools, but from the start he had been going to school at UP which taught nothing about faith. I'd asked my mother to prepare her grandson for it.

Over garlicky Ilocano sausages, scrambled eggs and fried rice, the boys recounted how delicious their grandma's banana cake was, and how thrilling to swim with the current in the river.

"What's new in Ilocos, Mom?" I said.

"It's still unnerving to see those strange faces in town," she said, referring to Communist rebels from the big cities, who had chosen to fight their war in the rural areas. "They're in the faraway mountain villages, but sometimes they come down to get supplies. I don't feel safe. I remember that Christmas when Marya and I were on our way to a dawn mass and found Matias and two other men sprawled on the town square."

Matias had been our neighbor. He and the two other men were the mayor's bodyguards, killed by rebels who tried to break into the town hall. I shook my head, wondering if any of Mom's 'strange faces' belonged to former classmates, for I knew of two who had fled to the hills after martial law and had later died in shootouts with the military. "Be sure to lock your doors," I said. "I don't think they intend to harm ordinary citizens like you. They're after corrupt people in government."

"Mommy, know what?" Miguel said. "Know what a hand suit is?" He and Mateo guffawed.

"You saw an old man wearing a hand suit? Or was it a woman?" I said, laughing along with them, for I knew then that they'd seen either a farmer or a fisherman swimming naked in the river after washing his clothes and laying them on the stony riverbank to dry. After his swim, the man would have gotten out of the water and, his hands covering his privates, walked to pick up his clothes, now dried stiff by the scorching sun.

The boys giggled on. I turned to my mother. "What else, Mom?"

"What else? Imelda is sprucing up the place like crazy for Irene's wedding is what else," she said.

"So I read in the papers," I said. "But tell me the inside story." Imelda Marcos was in a frenzy, preparing for the wedding of her second daughter Irene to the son of a business tycoon. The wedding was going to be at the centuries-old baroque Santa Monica church in Sarrat, the town where Marcos was born, ten minutes from Montaña. Two years back, there'd been rumours that Imelda was furious when her first daughter Imee ran away with a married man. She'd wanted to marry her off to Prince Charles. Shortly after, the man disappeared but surfaced after a few days. He told reporters he was snatched by Communists, but talk was that Imelda had had him kidnapped.

"Well, to begin with," Mom said, "all households along the main roads in Ilocos Norte are required to beautify their yards and gardens. Suddenly, there are full-grown bougainvilleas all along the highway. In full bloom. Different colors."

"So she means to make this grander than Lady Di's?" I chuckled.

"She just might," Mom said. "They're building a big hotel to house all her guests. Converting the family home into a museum of Marcos stuff. Rebuilding the church, even air-conditioning it. So much stress for all the mayors."

"Taxpayers' money, I'm sure."

What do you do when you hear about Imelda's penchant to show off? Watch, of course, besides fume. Which is what the entire country did on that sunny June day. Naturally, the big wedding was covered by all the TV networks.

A red carpet ran down the middle of the streets of Sarrat, and *sampaguitas* lined the sidewalks. Then came Irene in a gorgeous gown on an antique horse-drawn carriage. Huge tents around the majestic church. Guests dressed to the nines fanning themselves in the pews. Tulips along the church aisle and all over the altar. Tulips? Yes, imported from Holland, and not just tulips but many other fancy flowers besides, almost everywhere the TV camera panned.

The shy bride was resplendent; the groom looked like a prince. The bride's mother, as expected, dressed to wow the crowd like a real queen would. And then there was the bride's father who had not been seen in public for a while, amidst rumours that he was not well. There he was, the usually handsome and cocky Ferdinand, looking a bit weary, his eyes watery, his face bloated.

Two months later, a big earthquake struck the northern part of the country, hitting Ilocos Norte the hardest. It ravaged most of the churches built by the Spaniards during their four centuries of rule. After having lost a belfry here and a buttress there to previous earthquakes, our church in Montaña lost its main altar altogether, which made me sad. But the church that suffered the heaviest damage was Santa Monica, its bell tower and facade crumbling down, as though God was reminding the Marcoses who the real boss was.

After his first Holy Communion, Miguel wanted to go to mass every Sunday. I didn't want to, nor did I have any time. He usually went alone on his bike to the San Jacinto Chapel. After a while, I felt ashamed and took him and Mateo to mass every now and then.

August 21, 1983 was a hot and humid Sunday. I took the boys to UP for a late-afternoon mass. The sun had set and it was drizzling when we left the church, the damp earth pungent as it breathed out the hot sun. In minutes, the drizzle became blinding torrents, transforming the dimly-lit Marcos Highway into a blurry wading pool. I turned on the car radio to listen for news on where there might be flash floods. An agitated voice. Something about Ninoy Aquino being shot. What? The rain banged against my windshield so hard the wipers could barely catch up. I turned up the radio volume while reminding myself – lest I lose sense of where the paved surface ended – that somewhere to my right was a heavily-potholed shoulder. God, who shot Ninoy? Is he dead?

At home, confused news was all over television. Ninoy had been shot at the airport. A military van had taken his body away. The crowd that had waited for him with yellow ribbons at the terminal never saw him.

In the morning, the headlines screamed: *AQUINO SHOT DEAD – Assassin Killed by Military Men*. Amidst the sketchy details, a puffy-faced Marcos announced that the assassin was a Communist hit-man.

I drove to and from work glued to the radio, read all the newspapers, watched as much TV as I could. Marcos was still as powerful as he had been before officially lifting martial law, so the press, though no longer openly censored, remained muted as before. I stuck to Radio Veritas, which was run by the Catholic Church and gave the most daring reports.

The next few days brought some order to the chaos. A short video clip of Ninoy sitting in the plane as three soldiers approach him, Ninoy first smiling as a soldier grabs his arm and asking the soldier where they were going, the next moment his face turning eerily serious. Seconds later, a shot rings out, then more shots. Images of Ninoy's body clad in white, lying face down in a puddle of blood on the airport tarmac. A few feet away, another body, much less bloodied but just as dead – that of the alleged assassin, an ex-convict named Galman. Accounts of Imelda saying she'd warned Ninoy when visiting him in Boston not to go home because there were people who wanted him dead and the Marcoses couldn't protect him.

Ninoy's mother did not allow the morticians to disguise the bullet wounds on his face and had his body laid in a glass coffin, so the world could see what had been done to her precious son. The next day, Ninoy's widow Cory and their children arrived from Boston and were met by throngs of people lining up in the streets, to pay respects to the new martyr.

As each day passed, more details trickled out. Ninoy had become restless in Boston, seeing the Philippine economy declining, Communist insurgency continuing to rise and Marcos apparently very ill. He traveled home under an assumed name and by a circuitous route, to throw off whoever might be trailing him. On the trip, he wore a bullet-proof vest and clutched a rosary and invited some foreign journalists along. He told them that he had no more appetite for politics but wanted to help restore democracy. "In three to four minutes it could all be over," he had said, "but the Filipino is worth dying for."

It was quite clear that the military had done it and that Galman was just a scapegoat, but who gave the order?

One dreary mid-morning ten days after Ninoy was shot, my friends and I sneaked out from work, intending to be away for only an hour. We drove for ten minutes to Buendia Avenue, where we expected Ninoy's funeral procession to pass by around 10:30 a.m., knowing it had just left Santo Domingo church twelve kilometers away. The six-lane street was lined with people two- or three-deep, some in ragged clothing, some, like us, in business suits and nylons. People were out on balconies, peeking out of windows, perched atop vehicles. We stood and waited, listening to Radio Veritas from a transistor radio someone had brought. We heard that the cortege was inching its way along because of the immense turnout, with many folks joining in along the way. Veritas estimated the crowds at two million. Then it began to pour. We managed to climb the balcony of an apartment building under construction. Three hours.

Four. For lunch, we bought some Coke and crackers from a street vendor. The head of the procession finally came into view late in the afternoon. Inspired by the yellow ribbons waiting to welcome Ninoy at the airport that he never got to see, the crowd was a sea of yellow and black, the biggest crowd I'd ever seen. Section after section of people marching in the rain: nuns and priests praying the rosary or singing hymns, student activists and leftist organizations shouting slogans with raised fists, labor unions, politicians, common folk chanting Ninoy's name over and over. The marchers sang *Bayan Ko*, a plaintive love song to the motherland which I'd learned by heart at pre-martial law rallies in the seventies and which had been banned by Marcos during martial law. I sang along as did the others around me. At long last, after an hour of people marching by, the casket. The sight of the glass coffin lying on the bed of a ten-wheeler truck decked with yellow flowers sent goose bumps all over me, and tears to my eyes.

I had long arrived home and had dinner when the funeral procession reached Manila Memorial Park. It was nine p.m.

Two million people. Thirteen hours to cover a distance of barely thirty kilometers. If Marcos didn't get the message, he had to be terribly dense. Maybe there was hope.

Then began the quick plunge into a horrible recession. The stock market crashed and businesses started folding. Eric and I were fortunate to keep our jobs because we were both working in government, where the threat of lay-offs was minimal.

Marcos ordered a thorough investigation of the assassination, but most people believed it was all for show. Businessmen protested when inflation hit double digits. The church joined in; the archbishop issued pastoral letters that were read at Sunday masses, calling for justice. Ninoy's widow led yellow-clad women – politicians, rich matrons with their maids, housewives, artists, nuns, teachers, office workers – on a march along Ayala Avenue in the heart of the city's financial district, demanding that Marcos resign. As they passed, office workers from the high-rises along the avenue rained down confetti made of shredded Yellow Pages. The placards read: *God saw who shot Ninoy and knows who ordered it.* Alluding to a kidney ailment: *Marcos, where is your kidney? Mamaga sana ang mukha ng nagpapatay kay Ninoy.* May his face bloat who ordered Ninoy killed.

Marcos, to prove that he hadn't had any kind of surgery, went on TV raising his shirt to show his midsection and saying, "I don't intend to die." But his face remained puffy.

Amid the turbulence, I had to work even harder to keep a steady course. Several months later, I passed the sixth and last actuarial licensure exam and became a full-fledged actuary. I also finished my MBA. As a gift to myself, I decided to replace Eric's hand-me-down Corolla. Car prices were rising ridiculously, and I was happy to find a Ford dealer that offered a Laser hatchback for the reasonable price of seventy thousand pesos. I paid a deposit of ten thousand and signed the documents. The agent promised to deliver the car quickly.

But his face was sullen when he came to my office the next day. He handed me back my deposit check, saying the price had doubled. "How much?" I said.

"A hundred thirty."

One hundred thirty thousand pesos? Not quite double the original seventy, but this was a big joke. "But I signed your offer. You cannot..."

"The dealership is closing shortly." He pulled out a ten-peso bill from his pocket. "This is all I've got for my wife and baby. Tomorrow I'm out on the streets."

I realized he was serious. I had read a few days earlier that inflation had shot up to fifty percent and there wasn't a quick fix in sight. But the fifty percent was an average, so for luxury items like cars, it could be as high as a hundred or more. Prices could truly double, even triple. Well... I could live with my old car, but this poor guy.... I gave him the last twenty in my wallet and wished him luck.

Pag-Ibig, the agency where I worked as actuarial manager, was a government-mandated housing fund for workers. Imelda Marcos was Human Settlements Minister, so my boss reported to her. My boss had impressively novel ideas, and I loved being part of the team that translated these grand plans into numbers. Being out of the routine, it was exciting work for me. One little problem was that my boss sometimes expected us to come up with voluminous reports overnight. Literally.

One day, I stayed overnight at work with my team, rushing through a financial study for a billion-peso retirement village that the boss wanted to present to Imelda. The next morning, Amanda, Jun, and I went with him to Malacañang Palace. Our boss led us to a big hall with several round tables covered with white linen skirts and some guards walking about. Imelda sat at a table in front of a white board. The hall smelled of sweet perfume that I could not identify; it reminded me of when Imelda's daughter Imee came to school at UP in the seventies, and you could smell her perfume from a hundred feet away when she walked by with her guards. Looking at Imelda for the first time in person, I realized that her photos didn't lie: creamy, flawless skin, big eyes, high cheekbones, aquiline nose. Commandingly beautiful, with the Spanish *mestiza* features envied by three-fourths of Filipino women, who grew up believing that their own Malay features were ugly. Just like in her pictures, Imelda's hair was done like a giant black brioche. About fifteen men in business suits or *barong* Tagalog, the native formal men's shirt, sat at three tables in front of her. Our boss told us to sit at a far table, went up to Imelda to greet her, and then took a seat with the big men in front.

I sat there with my friends nibbling peanuts and sipping soda, ready to be asked to provide more information about our report. Everyone fell silent when Imelda started talking.

"If you're a little presentable, you're called frivolous," she said. "Beauty is frivolity, it seems, but beauty is love." She rose and drew a big heart on the board. Tall for a Filipina, she wasn't wearing a magnificent ankle-length *terno* as in her photos but an elegant blue dress that ran down to just below her knees and was accented with a long scarf. I thought her legs were a bit too thin for her body, but she stood so regally I couldn't help but gawk.

"You can never have an excess of what is democratic, just and beautiful," she continued and drew a circle. "It is against religiosity to be surrounded by ugliness."

She drew flowers and arrows, connecting them as she spoke. The bigwigs at the front tables looked at her, faintly nodding, like a row of schoolboys who had just been lectured on good manners. "Beauty is love made real, and the spirit of love is God. Peace and love is a state of beauty, love and God. That's peace."

I looked at our boss and the other men, wrote on my notepad and shoved it to Jun: Are they seriously listening?

He wrote back: They're mentally ripping off her dress.

I wrote: Ha ha. What if she has magical powers and has them all sucked into her hole in the sky?

We suppressed our laughter, straightened up in our seats and pretended to listen once more to the Madam, she who had once told a group of American scientists that there was a hole in the sky through which God sent cosmic forces to protect the Philippines, and that she could use these forces to protect America against Soviet missiles. I hastily scratched out what we'd written, remembering the guards in the room.

Around two p.m., Imelda finally said, "Okay, let's all have some nourishment," and immediately uniformed waiters came in with food trays.

"What a waste of time," Amanda whispered.

"Sshh," I said, smiling in agreement. "Mind where you are, what you're saying. You want us to be dragged out of here and chained to each other in the dungeon?" There were rumours that there was a torture chamber and a jail inside the palace compound, where some 'special' individuals were dealt with. "Let's just enjoy the food. After all, how many times can you dine with the queen?"

"I wouldn't want to be seen walking out of this place, or my reputation as an activist would be forever ruined," she said, although we all knew that times were hard and we needed our jobs, even if it meant being identified with the establishment.

The project we'd toiled over wasn't brought up. Our boss carried the report binder back to the office and said maybe next time he'd have a chance to bring it up with Madam.

After three or four similar visits to Malacañang, we suspected that our boss was just trying to make a good impression on Imelda to keep his post. Nevertheless, each time he had a brilliant new idea, we churned out pages of financial analyses and sophisticated reports, none of which even Imelda's staff ever got to see.

My team at Pag-Ibig worked hard and also partied hard. We'd spend weekends together with our young families at a beach resort out of town. Some Fridays after work, we'd buy peanuts and booze and bring them to the office, where we'd dance and sing and drink until we threw up. One evening, Amanda called Eric to fetch me home. When he arrived, I'd already had too much to drink and was crazily dancing with the others. He had a beer and chatted with the boys before taking me to his car.

"See that," he said, pointing to a totalled car being dragged by a tow truck. "That could have been you."

"No way," I said, "because you're nice and will always come pick me up."

"Jun tells me you're a booze guzzler, challenging him and Tony to bottoms-ups."

"Ha!" I said, pulled up my legs and curled up in the front seat. "Wimps, good for two beers, three."

I saw him shaking his head, and then I fell asleep.

The next morning, waking up with a big headache, I crawled out of bed, grabbed the Marlboro pack and lighter from my purse and went out to the garden. I sat on my favorite bench – the antique wooden one that had old cart wheels for arms – and lit a cigarette. I didn't notice Mateo come out a few minutes later. "Mommy," he said, "you told me you'd quit smoking." He started to cry.

I felt a wave of guilt, although I knew I wasn't willing to quit. Besides drinking with close friends, smoking was my only vice. Wasn't a hard-working woman entitled to one vice, especially one that could keep her from piling on the blubber? And one that gave her a little comfort from the crazy stress at work, and sometimes at home?

My headaches worsened. I had them even if I didn't drink. In spite of pain medication, I had them in the morning, mid-morning, noon, afternoon, evening. Every day now. Violent headaches. Doctor Pineda took me off the pill, saying my having been on it too long was causing the headaches. He was right, but very soon after, I craved green mangoes and *bangus* – milkfish cooked whichever way. I was pregnant again. This was good for Mateo, because once again I quit smoking and drinking and staying for the overnight sessions at work.

Late in 1985, two years after Ninoy's death, Marcos declared that there would be snap elections the following February. This was one year before the next scheduled elections, but apparently Marcos felt pressured to react to the mounting protests against his administration. He confidently declared that he knew he was well-accepted by the majority of Filipinos, but just to prove his critics wrong, he was calling for an early election. By then, most of us regular folk were fed up with the Marcos show that had been running for thirteen years. As for me, whoever dared run against this man, be it chimp or dog, would have my vote.

The opposition decided that the elections were winnable if they fielded Cory, Ninoy's widow, against Marcos. The problem was she had never held a paying job. However, she was educated and had been exposed to the world of politics as Ninoy's wife, and had a clean and honest heart.

Good enough for me.

One day at work, we were told to get ready because Imelda was coming to give a talk in an hour. We were required to fill up the auditorium as an entranced audience. While she did her truth-beauty-love diagrams and reminded us of the hole in the sky, I ached to be at Ayala Avenue, the protest center four blocks away, where I knew it was raining yellow confetti.

"Our opponent doesn't wear make-up," Imelda said. "She doesn't even have her fingernails manicured. But the Filipino is for beauty. Everyone who likes beauty, love and God is for Marcos."

Shit.

After Imelda left, I sneaked out with my friends to Ayala to catch the final hour of the big rally. "Cory, Cory!" we shouted with the crowd and bought yellow ribbons from the street vendors. The boss reprimanded us when we returned to work. I said we were out for a coffee break, even though we both knew I was lying. Afterward, I tied the yellow ribbon on my car antenna but was careful not to be at Cory rallies any more during work hours. I needed my job more than ever, now that the recession had become even worse. Nobody was hiring anywhere and my fourth baby was due in a couple of months.

CHAPTER 21

When I was in labor for my fourth child, the hospital staff expected the process to be over quickly and took me straight to a delivery room. After two hours, a nurse said the labor wasn't progressing, put out the lights and told me to get some sleep. I was disappointed, but I realized that in an hour, after midnight, it'd be January 25, Cory's birthday. Worth the impasse, I thought, to have my baby born on Cory's birthday.

With the elections barely two weeks away, the 'yellow fever' had become an epidemic. The once-complacent middle class had sprung up to show that Ninoy was right, that the Filipino was worth dying for. The task at hand was to make sure that Marcos could no longer easily manipulate election results, or at least to make it harder for him to do so. Big businessmen and the church rallied behind Cory and organized groups to guard the polls and to make independent tabulations of the votes. It was no longer just leftists who made their presence felt, but big and small businessmen, priests and nuns, students, teachers, artists, movie stars, journalists, laborers, employees, retirees, housewives. Everyone but one poor pregnant woman who lay abandoned in a delivery room.

The baby, whom we named Isabel, came out after twenty hours of labor. "She looks like Eric when he was a baby," Nanay said, for Isabel couldn't have gotten her big eyes, perfectly-arched eyebrows, fair skin and tiny black curls from me. What a lovely little doll. Eric adored her and called her his princess.

Three days before the elections, Cory held a final campaign rally at Luneta Park. With my nine-day-old infant at my breast, I listened to Radio Veritas. Oh, how I wanted to be there. The park was a sea of yellow, they reported. With a million people attending, it was the largest-ever campaign rally in Philippine history. Pigeons with yellow ribbons tied to their legs were set free to chase the yellow balloons floating above the crowd. In answer to Marcos's earlier comment that she was just a woman whose place was in the bedroom, Cory said, "Mr. Marcos, may the better woman win." Then fireworks exploded over Manila Bay, just behind the podium where Cory stood.

On Election Day, Eric and I went to the polls to vote for Cory. He dropped me at home right afterwards and then went to help at Namfrel, a volunteer group formed to watch every step of the election process. There was a lot of work to do, given a long list of cheating tricks that had been used in previous elections, from tampering with voters' registers, vote-buying, waylaying people before they could vote for the opponent, stuffing ballot boxes with fake ballots, all the way to doctoring the final tallies. A provincial governor had been murdered earlier that day, apparently by a Marcos supporter, heightening public outrage, and Eric's especially, because the governor was his relative.

Cory was consistently leading in Namfrel tallies. Government counting took longer and showed Marcos leading. A few days later, a group of computer technicians walked out of the government tabulation center after noticing that the numbers they entered into their computers didn't match the bigger ones being flashed on the big screens onstage.

After a few more days, Parliament proclaimed Marcos as

winner. In response, Cory held a protest rally at Luneta Park. An even bigger crowd turned up, a million and a half people. She called for non-violent resistance: a nationwide work and school stoppage on the day Marcos was to take his oath of office and a boycott of Marcos-controlled banks, media, and businesses that dominated the economy.

The following week saw bank runs and a marked dip in the sales of the businesses identified with Marcos – beer, Coke, newspapers, some food brands. A big department store lost its usual crowd of high-society clients. I watched anxiously from the sidelines, feeling that at any time now, this would have to come to a head.

Saturday, February 22, 1986. The breeze was cool and crisp and the garden glowed under a big moon. I had fed the boys their supper and they were playing board games in their room. I nursed Isabel while waiting to have supper with Eric, who was out on an errand. When Eric's car honked, the maid rushed to open the gate. Eric's voice was drowned by the slamming of the car door. What was he so excited about?

"Listen to Veritas!" Eric said and turned on the living room stereo. "Enrile and Ramos have turned against Marcos! They're now holed up in Camp Aguinaldo and have called the press over."

Enrile had been a true-blue Marcos boy, defense secretary before Marcos declared martial law. Afterwards, with the change to a parliamentary system, he became defense minister. Secretary, minister, what was the difference? Same dog, same master. General Ramos was a seasoned soldier, the chief of the constabulary and also a cousin of Marcos. He was reputed to be upright, a truly professional soldier. The two men were withdrawing their support for Marcos and were now at Enrile's office inside the military camp, waiting for Marcos's men to come and arrest them. They were protected only by a dozen armed soldiers plus a horde of media people mostly from the foreign press in the room and a couple of army tanks at the camp gates.

Eric turned up the radio, and we sat down for supper. "This is exciting," I said.

"Remember back in 1972," Eric said, "when Enrile was ambushed and almost got killed?"

"That was just a show, no?"

"We've always known that, but now Enrile has confirmed it. That he staged his own ambush. From the horse's mouth, at long last."

The defense secretary had staged his own ambush and blamed Communists, and this became the official trigger for his boss to declare martial law. "He knows too much," I said. "Marcos won't let him get away with it."

After supper, I turned on the TV but found only the usual Saturday night programs. Eric and I sat beside the radio. Then came the voice of Cardinal Sin, the Catholic Archbishop of Manila. "I'm calling all the faithful to support our two good friends. Leave your homes now, gather around the camp to protect them. Bring them food if you like. I'm also calling all the cloistered nuns to pray non-stop. Fast and pray for non-violence."

In the next minutes, Ninoy's brother Butz gave a similar call, followed by calls from other Cory supporters. Then Marcos came out on TV Channel 4, the government-owned network. "There's no truth to the rumours that there's trouble. I'm in control of the situation," he said. "I've told Ramos and Enrile to stop this stupidity and surrender so we may negotiate." He presented an army captain – Imelda's aide – who had confessed to being part of a *coup d'état* plot led by Enrile and Ramos. "They planned to kill the First Lady and me. I've instructed my men to surround Camp Aguinaldo," he continued. "If the two men refuse to surrender, they'll be annihilated with heavy artillery and tanks."

"God, he's gone mad," I said.

"I'm going," Eric said. "Let me use the Corolla."

Not a problem; my car was the older one, more run-down. But could it take heavy artillery? Or tanks? My heart smashing in my chest, I hugged my husband tight and said, "Be careful, okay?"

"I will," he said, kissed me and left.

As Eric drove away, I realized he hadn't said good-bye to the boys. What if he got hurt? But he had been seething in anger since that day in 1972 when Marcos declared martial law, and today, he wasn't one to be stopped. This was his chance to show his defiance. If I hadn't had a three-week-old baby, I'd have gone with him, the way I did when we were in university, marching toward Malacañang and shouting our hearts out against the establishment. Surely, I'd be terrified to death, but I wouldn't forgive myself if I'd just sat at home listening to the radio and sipping tea. I didn't tell the boys what was going on. After tucking them in bed, I turned off the stereo in the living room and went to the storage room to look for an old transistor radio. I dusted it off, took it to our bedroom and tuned in to Veritas.

Disillusioned with the politics within the armed forces, a group of young military officers had formed the Reform the Armed Forces Movement, or RAM, with Enrile as their mentor and Ramos as supporter. They had plotted a *coup d'état* and had planned to take over Malacañang the next day, but Marcos's men discovered their plan. Hearing they'd be arrested, they huddled together in the camp and called in reporters, so they could witness their end and tell the world about it.

There was Enrile admitting to election cheating in the Marcos camp, telling his boss that his time was up, enough was enough, no negotiations. Then Ninoy's brother Butz Aquino saying he'd gathered a huge crowd – ten, twenty thousand – and they were now marching on Epifanio de los Santos Avenue, or EDSA, on their way to Camp Aguinaldo to protect Ramos and Enrile with their bodies. Then the radio announcer said that Marcos was again on TV, so I ran to the living room to watch Channel 4. Marcos was presenting another alleged assassin from among the palace guards, a member of the RAM, and saying he was never going to budge.

Rabid dogs bite master. Master bites back.

Veritas announced more military defections as well as the

resignation of a Supreme Court justice and other government officials. Calls came in from all over the country giving support and promising prayers. I didn't have a phone at home, so all I could do was listen and worry. With both TV and radio blaring, I lay in bed, dozing off every now and then. Isabel was a calm baby and didn't fuss much, but that night, even if she had, I wouldn't have cared because I was awake, listening to history unfold on the airwaves and praying for the big crowd's safety, above all my husband's.

Sunday. Eric was back just before sunrise. "Thank God you're safe," I said. "Tell me, tell me."

Over breakfast, Eric said he didn't reach EDSA but only Santolan Avenue. Camp Aguinaldo, where Ramos and Enrile were expecting to be attacked, covers two square kilometers in the thick of the city – the busy EDSA in front, upscale residences to the south and east sides, old, cramped neighborhoods to the north, across Santolan Avenue. Across the ten-lane EDSA from the front gate of Aguinaldo is the main gate of a much-smaller military camp: Camp Crame, the constabulary headquarters, Ramos's territory.

"The streets were crammed with vehicles and people," Eric said. "I parked at the far end of Santolan and walked as close to EDSA as I could."

I said, "I listened to the radio all night. How about you, did you know what was going on?"

"Yeah, many people brought transistor radios, tuned in to Veritas, of course. A reporter had a short-wave radio, so he could pick up distant broadcasts from foreign media. BBC, VOA. More fearless reports."

"What did they say?"

"The crowd was noisy. Only got snippets. Looks like Reagan is starting to believe that his good friend really did cheat." Marcos had always been America's boy; he and Imelda were known to be close friends with Ronald and Nancy Reagan.

The newsboy threw the day's paper into the carport. When the maid came to hand it to us, I told her to run to a nearby newsstand and buy one copy each of the other alternative newspapers. "Where's Cory?" I said to Eric.

"In Cebu, they say," he said. "She had gone there to hold a rally. She spent the night in a convent."

"Good for her. How about tanks, did you see any tanks?"

"No, but the crowd was tense from two a.m. until daybreak. Many believed that if Marcos was to attack, he'd likely do it at that time. Cardinal Sin kept on pleading with Marcos troops not to use their weapons."

After Eric showered and went to bed, I turned my attention back to Veritas. The anchorman's voice was calm. "My brothers and sisters, a group of armed men has just blown up our main transmitter. Please know that we are all safe, no one is hurt, but we're broadcasting from a back-up transmitter that will not last us the day."

Damn. But surely, that's the first thing the enemy would do, cut off communications. The station continued its reports – of the EDSA crowds dwindling, of calls for more people, of more military defections – with apologetic reminders that they might go off the air at any time.

"What's happening, Mommy?" Miguel said.

I called Mateo over, hoping that his eight-year-old brain would grasp the idea as well. "Marcos cheated Cory in the elections," I said. "He's ruled for twenty-one years, has caused a lot of suffering, made himself and his friends rich. The people are tired of him; he has to go." My children – martial law babies all – knew no other president but Marcos, and they deserved to experience real democracy. I told them where their father had been the night before, adding that he was risking his life for our freedom, theirs especially. "Read these," I said, handing them the papers.

Around noon, Marcos was on TV, presenting four detained officers who were part of the *coup* plot. "My men have surrounded the camps. I've told them to move closer. I will not resign. If you're frightened by two thousand civilians, what's the use of running a government?"

"*Saan nga dua ribu, Apo. Dua gasut nga ribu,*" I said to the TV, mocking Marcos in Ilocano. Most Ilocanos – my people, my tribe, the chosen few – reverently called him Apo, or Lord. It's not two thousand, my Lord, but two hundred thousand. Much more, actually, for Veritas was now estimating the crowds at half a million. More frantic calls came in for non-violence, reminding Marcos's soldiers that their wives or daughters or aunts could be among the crowd. In the meantime, Enrile and Ramos had moved to the smaller Camp Crame across EDSA, shielded by their men and by nuns praying the rosary, carrying statues of the Virgin Mary.

Lunch had been ready for a while, but I didn't want to disturb Eric in his sleep. Now, because of what Marcos was saying, I had to wake him up. As we ate, Veritas reported that a convoy of tanks and Marine troops had just left Fort Bonifacio ten kilometers south of the camps and was headed toward EDSA. Other troops were also massing from the north and east of the camps.

"I'm going back," Eric said.

"Please take care, Daddy," Miguel said, worry on his face.

"I will," Eric said and rushed through his lunch. He hugged and kissed all of us and left.

I stuck to the radio: Four kilometers of EDSA were packed, as well as the traversing streets like Santolan and Ortigas. There were layers of barricades: buses, trucks, cars, vans, tree trunks, sandbags, burning tires. In between them, people and more people. Tents. Entire families on picnic mats sharing food from their baskets with the nameless crowd. Transistor radios blaring. Organizations holding up their banners and placards. Priests celebrating mass on makeshift altars with statues of the Virgin and the Infant Jesus. Fans cheering the movie stars in the crowd. Little old ladies giving out sandwiches. Professional singers perched atop jeepneys, leading in the singing of *Bayan Ko;* folk and pop songs, too, to ease the tension.

I held my rosary, mumbling prayer upon prayer that may not have made sense.

198

During lulls, the radio played *Onward, Christian Soldiers* and *Bayan Ko*, and I buried myself in the photos and stories in the newspapers.

The radio voices became agitated. Action on EDSA. Tanks rumbling, closing in from the south. Armored personnel carriers, army trucks approaching. Five? No, no, more. More than twenty huge vehicles. Jeeps, too. Soldiers with rounds of bullets on their chests. How many soldiers? "We can't tell." Fierce-looking ones, as Marines should be. Maybe a thousand? Two? A gentleman called to say that the general commanding the troops was his nephew. "Artemio, this is your Uncle Fred. Your Aunt Florence and all your cousins are here in Crame. Now, son, listen to me: Please think of the next generation."

Another anxious reporter's voice. "There's also a contingent of tanks in Cubao, from the north side; their guns are trained on Camp Crame."

Tanks from the north and south? Eric would be on the east side of the camps, so that was some relief. But tanks' guns can reach far and wide, can't they? God, please, I prayed. Please keep all those people safe. Please, Jesus, keep my husband safe. I'm not ready to be widow at thirty-two. What happens to our young boys, to our baby girl?

"From the south," said the report, "the tanks and trucks are fast approaching. They're now half a kilometer from the crowds. People are linking arms, building a thick human chain across the highway." Some of them were lying down on the road. The tanks rumbled on and on. Then stopped. The crowd was shouting. "We are your sisters, mothers, grandmothers, brothers. We are your children." They held up their rosaries. Soldiers alighted from the tanks. Everything froze.

No one breathed for what felt like a hundred years. Then the tanks rolled again and retreated.

After the tanks left, various reports and conjectures came in as well as calls for people to stay in EDSA, for the battle was not over. Then at sundown, Radio Veritas's transmitter finally gave out.

So, what next? On TV, it was just another Sunday evening. But who could care about *Dallas* and *The Golden Girls*? Knowing that Eric was safe, I calmed down and had supper with the kids, talking about EDSA. I left them watching TV in the living room and went to bed with the radio on, even if all it had was static, in case Veritas came back. I had just dozed off when Miguel came tapping me gently. "Mommy, come!"

I sprang up and rushed to the living room. There was breaking news over Channel 7: Marcos had fled, although it was yet to be confirmed. *Yehey*! I watched on, but that was all they had to say, stressing the word 'unconfirmed,' so I went back to bed and expected Eric to be home soon.

Monday. One a.m. and Eric was still not home. The radio was crackling. I turned it up and got a scratchy sound. *Onward, Christian soldiers, marching as to war*. Veritas was back! I sang along: *With the cross of Jesus, going on before*.... When the song was over, a familiar Veritas female voice came on: "We are broadcasting from a borrowed studio that technicians have set to the Veritas frequency. I cannot disclose the location, so this is *Radyo Bandido*, if you will. The reports that Marcos has fled are false. I repeat: Marcos is still in the country. In fact, there is word that he is going to attack anytime now."

The devil!

For the next two hours, *Radyo Bandido* went on in a frenzy of Veritas reporters' voices. Church bells were ringing, they said. Households were walking out around the camps. More defections. Another call from the archbishop: Don't leave our friends unprotected; pray more; to the nuns, don't stop praying and fasting until I tell you. Then armored personnel carriers were again rolling toward the camp.

Here we go again. Please, please, Jesus.

Enrile and Ramos once more asked the soldiers to lay down their guns and instructed the crowds on what to do when tear-gassed. "Our brothers are being tear-gassed in Santolan," the anchor said. Precisely where Eric would be! "Riot troopers are dispersing the crowd with truncheons."

She was interrupted by a screaming reporter: "Big helicopters are circling Camp Crame. Gunships, that's what they're called. One chopper is flying very low now. Looks like it's going to land on the campgrounds. The others are flying low too..."

Many tense minutes later, the anchor announced that seven Sikorsky helicopter gunships, fully loaded with cannons, had landed on the Camp Crame parade grounds – waving white flags. Good God, white flags! Goose bumps crawled all over my skin, and for the first time in two sleepless days, I wept.

"Nuns and young women walked up to the soldiers and gave them flowers," the anchor said. Hearing the tears in her voice, I wept some more. But before I could fully digest that, her voice rose. "Marcos and his son have taken off from the airport. Imelda and the daughters left last night. To our brother-soldiers who are loyal to Mr. Marcos, you're not fighting for anything anymore."

The EDSA crowd cheered and danced. At the camp gate, Ramos and Enrile stood on a makeshift stage and announced liberation. "*Yehey!*" I said, jumping up and down, Isabel in my arms. I called the boys to the living room. "It's freedom day!"

"What is freedom, Mommy?" Rico said.

How to explain freedom to a four-year-old? "It means no school!" Mateo said, for it was a Monday, but most schools had called Veritas to say they were closed that day.

"Liberty and justice for all," Miguel said in his wisdom of eleven years, jumping for joy with the rest of us.

Eric arrived shortly after. "It got really tense and scary when those gunships came," he said. "You should've been there when they landed. No one stirred in the huge crowd."

"So, these guys were sent to bomb the camp and defected, no?"

"Yeah. That was some air show."

"I wish I'd been with you, but God, I'd have died of fright. And what about the tear gas? Truncheons? Where were you?"

"Oh, that. I got some of it, not a big deal. Funny but the wind blew in the other direction. I mean, the tear gas made a U-turn toward the soldiers."

I loved it when he chuckled and his eyes shone like a little boy's, so I gave him a peck on the cheek. "Good for them," I said. "So, how did Marcos leave? Did his friend Reagan have him fetched?"

"I don't know. Conflicting reports. Let's wait and see."

I fed my handsome hero a big breakfast, gave him a nice rubdown and sent him to bed. He hadn't been in bed for a full three hours when Marcos came on TV again. His family was standing behind him, and to prove that this was a live telecast, he was holding the day's newspaper.

Shit, he's still here? Another false alarm? I hated to rouse Eric, but I did anyhow. I also called the boys to watch TV with us. Marcos gave his old, tired line. "Everything is under control. Don't listen to rumours. I am not resigning." In the middle of the press conference, his top general appeared on the screen and walked toward him.

On live national TV, the general said, "Mr. President, we must immediately conquer them. Immediately, Mr. President."

"Just wait, come here," Marcos said.

"Please, Your Honor, we have to immobilize their helicopters. We have two fighter planes flying now to strike at any time, Sir."

"My order is not to attack. No, no, no." Marcos held up his hand. "Hold on. My order is not to attack."

"We cannot keep on withdrawing, Your Honor," said the staid general. "Sir, you asked me to withdraw yesterday."

"Yes, but my order is to disperse without shooting them."

"We cannot withdraw all the time, Sir," the general said, saluted his boss and walked away.

Was that for real or just a show? What a crazy world. For a few moments, I admired Marcos once more, just like twenty-one years ago when he was promising to make the nation great again. Throughout his years of dictatorship, he'd always expressed hope that history would look kindly on him. If he was thinking straight, he'd easily see that attacking two million civilians would brand him as a butcher of men in the pages of history till the end of time.

After that intriguing interruption, Marcos went on with his pronouncements to the press. Suddenly, at mid-sentence, the TV screen went blank. We turned to *Radyo Bandido*. An hour later, they said that Marcos's Channel 4 had been taken by rebel soldiers, accompanied by priests and some civilians.

When Channel 4 came on again, past noon, it was no longer Marcos on the screen but a panel of broadcasters – the Veritas voices, now with faces. Haggard, unmade-up, unshaven but very lovely faces. "We're almost there," they said. "Please don't abandon EDSA."

And once more, off Eric went to EDSA.

That evening, Enrile and Ramos appeared on TV, announcing that most of the Armed Forces were already on their side. Then Washington DC endorsed Cory and called for a peaceful transition. In response, Marcos went on three other TV channels to say he was going to defend the palace to the last drop of his blood.

Standoff.

Tuesday. Eric was home at dawn. Mid-morning, at the historic Club Filipino, Cory was sworn in as President by a Supreme Court justice. She wore a simple yellow dress and yellow-rimmed eyeglasses. Ninoy's mother held the Bible. Ramos, Enrile and Cory's children stood behind them. The crowd cheered lustily after the brief ceremony. All the while, friendly gunships flew overhead.

Half an hour later, it was Marcos's turn. In a small room at the palace, he stood ready to be sworn in by the Chief Justice. A regally-clad but somber-faced Imelda held the Bible, her children behind her. Most of the audience were uniformed men. As Marcos raised his hand, the TV went dead.

Well! How could you not love those rebel Air Force pilots who knew just when to strike the TV transmitters? They and all the RAM boys, I could kiss them all.

A crowd that had gathered around Malacañang clashed with soldiers and civilians loyal to Marcos, but no one was seriously hurt. A part of the EDSA crowd marched toward Malacañang to lend support. In the meantime, gunships hovered over the palace and strafed it some. Late in the afternoon, after a few hours of sleep, Eric joined the two million in EDSA.

It was ten p.m. when the first sweet word came on Veritas. "We have just received confirmation that the Marcos family has left Malacañang, on board U.S. Air Force helicopters." Good God! I checked the TV and other radio stations. They were all saying the same thing! I yelled and leapt and laughed. "It's truly freedom day!" I said and hugged the boys. Isabel was oblivious to everything, sleeping in her cozy crib.

"*Yehey*! Freedom, freedom!" the boys cheered along with me.

Shortly afterwards, Eric arrived, playfully honking his horn. As soon as he opened the car door, he shouted, "We've won, we've won!" We all ran out to meet him; we couldn't stop jumping and cheering. A collective cheer boomed in the neighborhood. Cars honked to the "Co-ry, Co-ry!" rhythm and dogs barked along.

"Let's join the crowds," Eric said.

"Won't you eat first?" I said.

"No, no, let's go. Everyone! As you are, don't get dressed."

I collected the sleeping baby and wrapped her in a blanket. When I got to the car, the boys were bouncing in their seats, bombarding their father with questions. "I can't believe we made it," Eric kept on saying.

"You're my hero," I said over and over.

Eric drove out, meaning to head toward the camps, but we were met with traffic jams. Midnight, and all of Manila was out in the streets, dancing, honking, laughing, screaming, crying, singing, drinking, shooting fireworks into the stars. And even after four sleepless days, no one wanted to go home. I squeezed Isabel tight and kissed her. "Our good-luck baby," I said. "Our lucky charm."

The morning after a big rowdy party, you have to pinch yourself. The newspapers did it for me: *It's all over; Marcos flees!*

These five simple words came with photos of the ex-president and his family boarding helicopters.

Where did they go? Or where were they taken? Old buddy Ronald Reagan had sent his men to fetch the beleaguered Marcos camp. They spent the night in American territory, at the Clark Air Base in Pampanga province, an hour north of Manila. At dawn, a U.S. Air Force jet flew them to Guam, and then to Honolulu.

Mobs looted Malacañang after Marcos fled, and it took a couple of hours before rebel troops took control. Weeks later, parts of the palace were opened to the public. Although not all of our questions were answered, we saw enough to get us talking non-stop: a lavish but half-eaten meal, Marcos's bedroom with a hospital bed, dialysis machine, oxygen tanks and all sorts of medical equipment. Plus a separate operating room! Imelda's ornately-carved and canopied bed, shelves upon shelves of lingerie, rooms full of gowns and dresses, gallons and quarts of French perfume labelled *First Lady*. And shoes, shoes, shoes, shoes – size 8 ½ shoes.

"Look at that bed," Eric said. "What a pity she almost never slept." Imelda had said she had so much energy that she barely slept more than two hours a night.

"If you want to wear each shoe for at least an hour, you won't have time to sleep," I said, picturing the nameless barefoot children who routinely roamed the streets of Manila to beg for food. "What could drive a person to lust for so much?"

Reports varied as to how many pairs of shoes Imelda had to leave behind when they fled Malacañang, from two thousand to four. Analyzing the Marcoses quickly became a national pastime. Some people wanted them tried, and then hanged. For the moment, I was happy just having them out of the way, so the nation could start a new life. Justice could be served later, for if Reagan hadn't rescued Marcos and his cohorts, there'd likely have been bloodshed. Although I regretted not being part of the EDSA crowd that won our freedom, I was never prouder to be a Filipino and was eager to do my part in making our nation great again.

CHAPTER 22

Cory's honeymoon with the Filipino people was short-lived, if there was any honeymoon at all, for every other person had a better idea than hers on how to run the government. She had to face several *coup* attempts, from Marcos's men as well as Enrile's RAM boys. But even though reforms weren't happening fast enough, the majority of citizens wanted to give Cory a chance to succeed. I did. I wanted to do my part in making the country rise and be whole again, mostly for the sake of my children, even if Cory had replaced my Pag-Ibig boss with someone who didn't know what he was doing. I believed that with hard work, we as a nation could do it. Just like my little happy family, for didn't it also go through something similar?

First is the euphoria when, after rebelling, you finally get your way and fly free. Then you learn – the hard way – that you don't actually know how to handle that much freedom. That while you were in a cage, freedom to you meant endless nights of partying, but after getting drunk and partied out, the other side of the shiny freedom coin stares you in the face. Voilà: Responsibility, with a capital R, for yourself and the rest of your little world. When you're past the hangover, you realize that, just like that, you could blow it. And for a long time I thought that Eric and I had blown it, but look now, after thirteen years of fumbling, we had managed to make our marriage work.

When Isabel was four months old, Eric came home one night and sat on our bed for a long time, staring at the sleeping baby. "She's so pretty," he said. "Have you ever seen a lovelier baby?"

"Tell me about it. I spend hours just watching her, forgetting my to-do list."

He took me in his arms but his eyes remained on Isabel. "I don't want to leave."

"For where? Zamboanga? Take me with you."

"I have a fellowship offer from Wharton," he said, tightening his arms around me.

"The Wharton?" I knew that he'd been eyeing a doctorate at the Wharton Business School in Pennsylvania, but didn't know that he'd actually sent in an application. "Really? You didn't tell me."

"I first wanted to hear back from them. They're giving me a fellowship."

"And did you say you don't want to leave?" I said, trying to absorb what this meant. I thought of how he'd turned down a Ph.D. offer from an Australian university ten years earlier, on my account, and although he'd also considered doing it in UP, he didn't have the time given that he had to earn a living.

"I said I don't want to leave."

"Because..."

"Because of this lovely little princess here. I can't bear to be away from her."

"That's good," I said, "because I also want you around. For selfish reasons, of course, because obviously you can't bring us all with you to the States. But I know you've been putting off this Ph.D. dream of yours."

"It's fine," he said and squeezed me harder. "I might just accept the Glaxo offer instead."

"Thank you, from me and the kids, thank you," I said. "I love you, too."

A month later, Eric left his job as university professor and joined the multinational company Glaxo as a financial planning executive. It meant bigger career challenges and much better money. Because he didn't want to stop teaching altogether, he taught one course at UP in the evenings.

Meanwhile, at my workplace, I tried to give the new boss a chance to learn what our agency was all about. But he was making one stupid mistake after another, so after six months, I resigned. I had been dying to be a housewife anyhow – to devote all of my time and energy to my family and make up for all my previous years of bumbling motherhood and wifehood. Since Eric was earning enough to support the family, he indulged me and allowed me to just be a homemaker.

One day, he bought me a stunning gold bracelet, on impulse; another day, a piano, which he knew was my childhood wish. I took piano lessons, drove my kids to and from school and spent plenty of time with Isabel. I went on a cleaning spree, scrubbing the house until it gleamed and organizing the closets and bookshelves until not a hairpin was out of place. Wrote the maids' daily tasks on index cards, like full-blown job descriptions and action plans, and posted these on their bedroom wall. Devoured all the books that had lain unread for ages and tried out new recipes to everyone's delight.

I was loving it all.

Late that year, a university theater group invited Eric to appear in a play. He loved acting and had been in a university play a few years back. This time, offered a plum role in the Anton Chekhov play *Three Sisters*, he grabbed the chance and spent late nights and most weekends at rehearsals.

He got home past midnight that day. When he came to bed, I snuggled close and started kissing and caressing him. "I miss you," I said.

"Hmmm," he said and turned his back to me.

"Please?" I said and licked his ear.

"You know you can't get pregnant again." He patted my thigh.

"But I'm breastfeeding," I said, spooning him and kissing his back. "It's a proven fact, breastfeeding is a contraceptive."

"Not taking any chances. And I have to be up in four hours. Long day tomorrow."

"But I'm going mad; it's been almost a year," I said but he was already snoring. "Do I have to beg?" I cried myself to sleep.

Three Sisters opened shortly before Isabel's first birthday. Eric gave us tickets – for the two bigger boys and me, most of his family, as well as some friends. I drove the boys to the theater, bragging about how good an actor their father was.

I'd read a few Chekhov stories in high school but not any of his plays. Eric played the role of Vershinin, a lieutenant colonel who is assigned to a town where three unhappy sisters live. Masha, the middle sister, is bored with her husband Kulygin and falls for the gallant Vershinin.

"My wife decided to frighten me; she almost poisoned herself," Vershinin says. "If I had my life to live again, I would never get married."

Ouch! Is he talking about the Phenobarb I took when Miguel was a baby? No, he doesn't know about that. He regrets marrying? C'mon, he's only acting.

Vershinin and Masha have tender, flirty scenes. Later, Masha tells her sisters, "I love, love, love that man. I fell in love with his voice, his words… And he loves me. But is it wrong?"

I squirmed in my seat and clenched my jaw, especially since Masha's Kulygin knows about the affair but does nothing.

Toward the end of the play, Vershinin has to say goodbye to Masha because his regiment is moving elsewhere. "My love," Vershinin says, holding Masha.

She begins to cry and says, "My love." They lock in a long,

passionate kiss, the spotlight on them, the rest of the stage darkened. Violins.

Kulygin catches the end of this good-bye scene, and as Vershinin walks away, he tells Masha, "You're my wife. I'm happy no matter what. I'm not complaining. I won't say a word." Masha is disconsolate.

I wanted to bolt and scream but, of course, I didn't. Reminding myself it was just a play, I stayed till the end and clapped and stood with the crowd in ovation.

After the show, Eric took us out to dinner with his family members. "I didn't know you were a fine actor," one of his sisters said. "Or maybe you weren't acting." She winked at me. I had no energy to respond and tried to eat beside my quiet sons, even though my gut felt like it was flipping about. Stop it, I told myself; he was just acting. What are you, a country girl too unpolished to know art?

To hell with art. The next day, I took Eric's lipstick-stained shirts from the laundry basket, burned them in the backyard while guzzling a bottle of beer, hurled the empty bottle against a firewall, flew high with the sound of shattering glass, and then plopped back into my hot puddle of tears.

A few days later, my husband was at his closet picking what to wear to work. "Missing the white shirt with the red pinstripes?" I said, "And the light blue one? For your protection, sir, I've burned the evidence. I humbly suggest you cover your tracks more smartly next time. Just to remind you, sir, I'm no idiot."

Cold silence.

They ran the play three times each week for five weeks. One night, after tucking the kids in bed, I drove to the university theater. After locating Eric's car in the parking lot, I parked where I could see it, but in the dark. Curtain call was fifteen minutes away. In half an hour, there was Eric with Masha and her two sisters, hopping into his car and driving away. I tailed them for a couple of minutes and then wondered: What if he was just dropping the girls at a bus or taxi stop and he saw me? Feeling like a fool, I drove straight home

Eric got home past one a.m., a good four hours after I did. "Where were you?" I said.

"None of your business," he said and went to the bathroom.

Putang-ina!

The play was shown again two days later. After the children were all in bed, I stuffed a suitcase with Eric's clothes. "Here are your things," I said when he arrived, as usual past midnight.

He began to empty his pockets.

"Don't empty your pockets," I said. "You're leaving now!"

He slumped on our bed, looked down and sighed.

"I could leave, but won't," I said. "I'm staying in this house with your children. *My* children. Don't worry, I can feed them, in case you didn't know." I picked up a pencil from the desk and broke it in two. "Just go!" I said, pointing the jagged pencil halves at him.

He didn't say much besides ask for a couple of hours. He lay down on the couch, and before sunrise, he left while the kids were still in bed.

So he was gone. Why wasn't I relieved? I wept like a widow might weep. When it was time to rouse the three boys for school, I collected myself and ate breakfast with them. On the drive to school, I told them that their dad had gone on a business trip to Cebu.

I spent a good part of the day at a mall, trying on a hundred dresses and shoes that all looked awful on me and buying nothing. In the afternoon, I fetched the boys from school and tried to act like nothing was the matter. After supper, Miguel and Mateo washed up and changed into their pajamas and went about with their homework at the dining table. Exactly the way they should. I prided myself on raising well-behaved and disciplined children who did their homework without my help.

Still in his school uniform, Rico crawled under our bed to retrieve a toy car. "Hey," I said, "what are you doing in there? Go and change."

No response. I knelt down to peek under the bed. He was crawling further toward the corner. "Come out here!" I said. He wiggled out. "Look at all the dust you've collected. Thank you for cleaning my floor." I picked up my bedroom slipper, grabbed his thin arm and gave him a big whack on the butt. "How many times do I have to tell you to wash up and change?"

He looked at me with blank eyes.

"Do you have homework?"

"I don't know." His almost inaudible voice trembled.

"What do you mean you don't know?" I said and gave my five-year-old son, who was in kindergarten, a bigger whack, this time on his spindly leg. "Go, go before I hit you again."

The boy began to cry and ran out. I yelled for the maid who came running. "Yes, Manang?"

"Yes, Manang what? Do you ever clean this house at all? There's an inch of dust under the bed, on the furniture. How often do you scrub the bathroom? Know that what looks clean to you looks like shit to me. I'm not paying you good money to gossip with the neighbor's maids all day!"

"Sorry, Manang."

"Sorry, sorry? Right now! Get my floor truly clean. Under the bed especially!" She scurried to get her mop and broom.

I walked out to the garden, slumped on the cart-wheel chair and sobbed until my insides stung. Then I went to my poor Rico, hugged him and said, "I'm very sorry. I love you, please know I love you." I stroked his hair and kissed him, wiping his tears. When he said nothing and didn't hug me back, I returned to the garden.

"Mommy, can you help me with geography?" Mateo had followed me.

"Come back here, don't bother Mom," Miguel called out from the dining table. "What do you need? I'll help you."

I hung my head in shame at the kind of mother I was becoming and wept until the house was quiet.

The following days, I drove around town trying to choose which truck to ram my Corolla into, picturing the scene in slow motion, wondering if death was any more painful than my present pain.

A week later, Eric came home, asking for another chance. And like Kulygin, I took him back again. He insisted that there was nothing between him and Masha.

"But you left without a fight," I said. "It means you're guilty."

"I'm not guilty. But I was so stressed because I had to finish the remaining shows," he said. "I didn't want to fire up your anger any further. I thought it was simpler to get out of your way for a while."

"What's worse," I said, unable to hold back my tears, "what's most painful is how I found myself begging you for sex. And you refusing me."

He gathered me in his arms and began to make love to me, tenderly, furiously. My heart and body floated and throbbed, and then burst in a fiery kaleidoscope.

"Do you love me?" I said afterwards.

"I love you."

"I'm telling you, if you do it one more time, it'll be the end of us."

"I didn't do it," he said, but his eyes were on the ceiling, not on mine.

Eric brought up a notch, maybe two, his usual peace offering: not just any old trip to a local spot, but a trip for me to Singapore to visit Amanda, for he knew how much my best friend would help soothe my bruises. Two years earlier, she'd moved there with her husband, and I'd missed her terribly. I travelled with Beatriz, one of our common friends from UP. We toured the sights, shopped 'til we dropped, feasted on Singaporean food, went disco-dancing, and chatted until dawn. I told them how Eric had been unfaithful yet again, and they were both sympathetic with me. I truly enjoyed everything, but at bedtime when my girlfriends' bright smiles weren't in sight, I felt miserable.

213

One night, after supper in Amanda's high-rise apartment, we brought some cans of beer out to the balcony. We sat on the floor and chattered while Amanda tried a new mascara on Beatriz's lashes. On my fourth beer, I lit up another cigarette, walked to the railing and looked down. The neons of Orchard Road winked and chased each other far below.

"I wonder how much you'd hurt if you fell to the ground from this high," I said. "Do you think you'd feel any pain, or does it knock the lights out of you instantly?"

"Hey, come back here and sit," Amanda said. "Don't be crazy."

"You serious about wanting to die?" Beatriz said.

"I've had it!" I said. "I can't take anymore of this crap. Do I want to die? Yes and no. It's scary when I think of it; I wish I could simply vanish."

"Are you nuts?" Beatriz got up and held my wrist tight, her eyes widening. "If you die, then Eric will be free to marry whomever he chooses. Then your kids will have a brand-new mother."

"Indeed," Amanda said. "How about that?"

Suddenly, I felt the beer-wooziness leave my head. My poor kids with a bitch stepmother? I decided that very moment that I'd never attempt to end my life again, ever. "No, no way! I cannot die. I will not die," I said. "And then what? I can't flee, I can't fight. I will still have my marriage to deal with. Somebody help me! Maybe I need to see a shrink, the hell with what people might say."

"Do you go to mass?" Amanda said.

"Only on Christmas, Easter," I said. I'd not been going to mass regularly for thirteen years.

"Try going regularly."

When I returned to Manila three weeks later, a friend suggested going to the Cenacle, a retreat house in Quezon City, so I went there one day.

Inside the high walls, hedges of red and yellow jungle geraniums bordered a lawn, and butterfly palms graced the entrances to two small buildings. A nun left me alone in an empty chapel. I knelt down on a back pew and gazed at a crucifix on the wall above the bare altar. I began to pray: God, I'm tired and I don't know what to do, where else to go. Will you help me? Please.

Sunlight filtered through the frosted glass windows. I could hear birds chirping and the faint sound of the traffic outside. I closed my eyes and continued praying: God, I won't understand whatever you'd like to tell me, being hopelessly dumb – as you should know. Could you please show me instead?

Then I closed my eyes, determined not to open them until I received some kind of message from God. After what felt like an hour, I saw in my mind's eye a door and wondered what might be behind it. Moments later, the door was gone, and I saw a pedestal on top of which sat a dove. A white dove enveloped by a soft glow. Feeling a deep sense of peace, I kept my eyes shut. I wanted to simply stay there, there at God's feet.

With that powerful image fixed in my mind, I started to pray daily and attend mass every Sunday. Still uncertain of what to profess as my faith, I bought books about documented miracles. The most compelling book was one about the miracles of the Eucharist. It listed scientific tests on consecrated bread and wine that had reportedly turned into flesh and blood. The findings: These were human tissue, blood type AB. Similar tests were done on the Holy Shroud of Turin and they found that the stains were of human blood type AB. Each time I read about yet another miracle, my scientific mind became more convinced of a strong basis for Catholicism and decided I would believe.

I also read about the lives of saints, looking for a role model. Being men, San Judas Tadeo and San Jose, my good old novena patrons, wouldn't do. I needed a female saint, but I discovered that most female saints were virgins and nuns. I kept reading until at last I came upon the stories of Santa Monica and Santa Rita, wives and mothers.

Santa Monica's life reminded me of my mother. She had married a man with a violent temper. Of her three sons, she worried most about the wayward Agustin, who had a string of illicit relationships. After years of fasting, praying and weeping for them, Monica was rewarded with their conversion to Christianity. Agustin would later become a saint and one of the greatest Christian thinkers of all time.

Santa Rita, patroness of difficult marriages, was known as a very powerful intercessor. Wife to a violent man and mother, she handled these roles with prayer, patience and affection. After being widowed, she entered the convent and received a Stigma on her forehead, a wound resembling Christ's and a sign of God's favor. She died in the fifteenth century but remained incorruptible, meaning her remains have not decomposed. I picked her to be my role model.

Soon, I was going to mass almost daily. All my praying seemed to help, because Eric treated me better. He took the kids and me to fancy dinners. Sometimes, we drove to the beach for the weekend.

Around that time, Miguel was admitted to my high school alma mater, making Eric and me very proud. One afternoon, when I went to pick up my son from school, I saw a small boy hanging up a pay phone and wiping his eyes. He must have lived in the dorm and had probably been talking to his mother, surely aching for home. My mind flew back twenty-two years; once again, I was eleven and a freshman at that very school, thrown into the big city, with a strange language, strange people, strange food, and strange schoolwork. How different Miguel's circumstances were, because he was city-bred and had me around. I resolved to give my teenage son the right mix of love and guidance so he could grow like I did, but without having to feel so lost and alone. If I couldn't be a good wife, I was going to be a damn good mom.

In September, I was offered a job as vice president and actuary of Guerrero Financial Plans. Right up my alley and hard to refuse, the job paid well, offered exciting challenges, and made me feel that, even if only at work, I wasn't a nothing. In spite of its demands, I didn't allow it to take away my evenings and weekends, for those were strictly for my family. I also didn't neglect nurturing my new-found faith, the magic fix for my biggest troubles, so I went to mass during my lunch hour.

Soon it was Christmastime. In place of the daily noonday masses, I decided to go to the dawn masses for the nine days leading to Christmas, just like back in Montaña when I was little. The closest church that had dawn masses was the Chapel at UP, ten kilometers away. The first day, I got up at 3:30 a.m. and was off in half an hour to catch the 4:30 a.m. mass. It was refreshing to take part in this tradition once again. When I got back home, it wasn't sunrise yet, and Eric was still in bed. He stirred when I entered our room. "Where'd you go?" he mumbled.

"*Misa de Aguinaldo*," I said. "At UP."

"Who were you with?"

"Just me."

"You should have brought one of the maids along. Or Marya." My sister had moved in with us the year before to go to university.

I told him I was fine alone and thought nothing more of it.

After I did the same thing the next day, Eric and I had a similar conversation. In the evening, he asked if I was going to mass again at dawn.

"Yes, of course," I said. "I'm completing the nine days."

"So what's wrong with bringing someone along?"

"I told you I'm okay."

"But you're out there on the lonely highway with thugs and drunks. Why won't you listen to me?"

"God is good," I said defiantly. "I'm going to go visit Him so He'll have to protect me."

"Look," he said, louder. "We might not see eye to eye about your religious beliefs and practices, but am I trying to prevent you from doing them? No! I simply want you to be safe."

"Louder, I can't hear!"

"You're not only stubborn, you're irrational. Then you'll have that deathly scowl on your face all day."

"Damned if I do, damned if I don't! If I speak up, we get nowhere. If I keep silent, we get nowhere."

I completed all nine dawn masses on my own, unscathed. I couldn't see what Eric was so agitated about and took his advice as criticism. I merely wanted to show him that God was protecting me.

After only four months at my job, I got a promotion and a big raise. One night, Eric came home with a set of jewels that a friend was selling: a necklace and bracelet studded with seventeen diamonds as big as mustard seeds, all of them quite perfect. He thought it was a great buy, no cracks nor black carbon spots in the stones, and a fair price. My heart fluttered and I thought, At last, after fifteen years, he's buying me diamonds! He placed the necklace around my neck, the bracelet around my wrist. "They look nice on you," he said.

I wasn't impressed by the design, but trusting Eric's taste, I said nothing and grinned. Besides, I wasn't about to refuse an expensive present.

Then he said, "Why don't you buy it? Would be a great investment."

What did he just say? But I didn't have the courage to protest. I hesitantly reached for my purse and wrote a check for the equivalent of two thousand dollars, convincing myself that this made more sense than keeping my spare money in the bank.

I wore the jewelry to Glaxo formal parties, where I struggled to make nice with the other ladies whose faces often graced the society pages. They talked of plastic surgery on their noses and eyelids, thousand-peso hairstyles, paid male escorts, and central air-conditioning in their homes. Even with my diamonds, I felt sorely out of place.

One August evening after work, I rode with two girlfriends to the

Army and Navy Club to attend our first big high school reunion. The tables were arranged in a wide horseshoe and I sat next to my friends. We were just starting dinner when someone approached. "Can I sit here?" he said.

Oh my God, I know that voice, I thought, and looked up. David! I hadn't seen nor heard of him in eighteen years. "Oh!" I said. My voice sounded strange to me, tinny. "Hi, long time... Of course, of course." He sat down and dragged his chair closer to mine.

We tried small talk as I felt my knees shaking. After the soup, he said, "Why'd you cut your hair?" He obviously remembered my waist-long hair back in college, not the cut I'd had the past many years, just above the collar.

I was tempted to say, 'Because if I didn't, you might fall for me again and we'd both be in trouble.' Instead, I tucked my hair behind my ears and said, "It's easier to maintain for a working mom." I smiled and looked at him. Same lean brown body. No. More manly, sexier. Same curls crawling on the temples and nape. Same droopy eyes. Ssh, quiet, silly heart, please.

"Nice earrings, nice dress." he said. For the occasion, I'd worn the dress and the pair of fun costume earrings – not Eric's diamonds – that Amanda had insisted I buy in Singapore. "You look great," he continued, "as ever."

My heart danced a jig behind my tingly breasts. I cleared my throat and said, "Thank you. Tell me about your children."

"I have three boys," he said.

"I have three boys too," I said, "but I beat you because on top of that, I have one girl. My little one, turning three next year. How old are your kids?"

"Hmm... the oldest is twelve, and then..."

"Twelve?" I said. "My oldest boy is thirteen. Yours can't be younger."

"Why not?"

"Because you got married first," I said.

"Says who?" He looked into my eyes. I thought his eyes

suddenly turned sad. "I was in jail when I heard you'd gotten married."

"What?" I said, thinking he'd got to be kidding. "Didn't you get married in the Movement? Before martial law?" I looked closer at him. His jaw tightened.

"Not at all!"

All of a sudden, my heart stopped dancing. A chill began to grip me. I bit my lips and put down my fork. David was staring at me. I inhaled deeply, sighed and said, "I didn't know."

Just then, the emcee started the program and asked everyone to take turns telling the group what they'd been up to the past eighteen years. David and I didn't talk much after that, although we stayed close to each other. It was past midnight when Eric appeared at the door to fetch me. The party was just breaking up. I gave casual good-bye hugs to my girlfriends and then looked at David. "Bye," I said, my hands gripping the straps of my shoulder bag.

"Take care," he said, bowing slightly. "It was nice to see you again."

"Same here," I said and hurried for the door.

I slumped on the passenger seat. The rain poured in torrents. Many streets were flooded, forcing Eric to take a detour. I told him I was really tired, reclined my seat and closed my eyes. All the way home, I struggled to keep the tears from creeping out of the corners of my eyes, grateful for the dark.

Most of the night, while Eric snored beside me, David's somber voice and sad eyes tumbled in my head. I kept asking myself a thousand what ifs, feeling alternately angry and sad.

The following days and nights were no different. I could hardly eat nor sleep. After a month, I felt a grinding in my stomach. A few days later, the grinding stung and sent me reeling, curling up in bed. Diagnosis: stress-induced ulcer.

I tried to get well. One day, I decided that apologizing to David for the sheer rudeness of the way I'd dumped him eighteen years earlier would help quiet down my soul. I called him and asked if we could talk. My staff had gone home for the day when he arrived at my office.

"What's new?" he said and sat on a visitor's chair in front of my desk. I stayed glued to my swivel chair, afraid of what might happen if sat on the other visitor's chair and got too close.

"I didn't expect to be affected like this when I saw you again," I said "I've been so disturbed an ulcer has started to eat away my stomach."

"Oh," he said, furrowing his brows. "Is it bad?"

"I'm taking medication and mustn't go hungry."

"Take care of yourself, please," he said. Then after a while, "Okay, talk to me."

"Uh, I'm sorry. I'm deeply sorry."

"For what?"

"You know what. You know how rudely I dismissed you that afternoon eighteen years ago, at Ilang-Ilang dorm. You don't know how much I've regretted behaving so badly, especially because you'd treated me so well." My stupid tears were on the brink of falling.

"I have to say I was devastated," he said. "Because you are the first girl I ever loved. I was feeling so lucky having hit the jackpot, and then boom," he said, snapping his fingers.

"You know I cared for you too, don't you? I was simply dumb. Immature, like you said. I wanted to ask you back not long after that, but I couldn't get myself to do it. I was so ashamed." I collected the papers on top of my desk and piled them on one side. I wiggled my toes because they felt numb. "Can you please forgive me?"

He extended his hand across the desk. "Friends," he said, shaking my hand. His hands were clammy, just like that prom night ages ago when he first told me he loved me. He wiped my eyes with his handkerchief.

"Thank you, thank you," I said.

David didn't own a car and lived along my route home, so we left my office together in my car. I was surprisingly calm as I drove.

"You can drop me off after the Manggahan Bridge," he said. "It's only three blocks to my apartment from there."

When it was time for him to get off, I pulled over. "Thank you and good night," I said and offered my hand.

He took my hand and squeezed it as he opened the car door. His eyes lingered on me for several moments before he finally let go of my hand. "Good night," he said and got out.

As I drove away, I felt like I'd just downed a strange new cocktail that hit me in random ways. Like you're happy one instant and you can't stop giggling, and the next moment you feel like crying. Then you're tipsy and floating, and then suddenly you're scared. But you don't care. You abruptly get up and dance and sing even if you'd always been afraid to do those things in front of a crowd before.

Afterwards, I saw David every month, when our bunch met for dinner. He'd ride with me to and from the meeting. I was grateful to have him back, if only as a friend. If I'd wasted the chance to have him as my man, at least I could have him as a very good friend. He'd surfaced from the underground after Marcos lifted martial law and eventually managed to finish an engineering degree, although not from UP but from a university in his native Tacloban. He came to Manila after being offered the job of managing a big snack-food plant, but his wife and children stayed behind in Tacloban. I liked this arrangement, not that I wanted us to cheat on our spouses. It just made things much simpler.

He started to occupy my fantasies. He's taken good care of himself. I thought, See, no beer belly, still lean and muscular. Look at him now, at thirty-five, he must be at his sexiest. What a shame that I didn't even get to ruffle his hair back then, much less have a real kiss. And he's still as gentle as before. Maybe if I'd married him, he wouldn't yell at me, cheat on me. He'd treat me like a queen. I should never have dumped him, or at least should've humbly asked him back.

My spirit rebelled at the double standard that allowed men to follow the dictates of their hearts – or their groins – but condemned women for doing the same thing. Ages had passed since Jesus's time when they stoned adulterous women to death. It was now 1988, more than a century after Hester Prynne was made to wear a scarlet *A* on her dress to broadcast her shame to the townspeople of Boston. Still, in my part of the world, a man had no balls who took back an unfaithful wife although he himself might have been guilty of the same offence.

If I went with David, I'd have to wear an invisible *A* on my dress. Or maybe a *W* for whore. Could I live with that? Could my children? Was I willing to drag my family's honor down with me? How about Eric's name, his family's? And how about God, what will I say when He asks me how much I had loved those He'd sent me to love?

Then I'd remind myself of the unflinching way Santa Monica and Santa Rita suffered their difficult husbands. Although I'd forgotten when Eric had last shared his inner self with me, he and I had had no big fights for more than a year. Our marriage was on a plateau, which was probably as good as it could get, and I didn't want to jeopardize that.

One day, Miguel was mugged on his way home from school. It was his first year of commuting by public transport. In the middle of busy Cubao, a man put his arm around my fourteen-year-old's shoulder and greeted him like they were friends. Then he held my son closer and pointed a knife at his chest, demanding his money. Miguel gave the man all his money, after respectfully asking to keep just enough for his fare home. Angry and afraid, I told him I'd pick him up from school from then on. But it didn't work perfectly because I usually got stuck at work and in traffic, and when I reached Miguel's school, they'd have closed the gates and he'd have been waiting at the guardhouse for an hour or two.

"I'll be fine, Mommy," Miguel said. "Let me go home on my own."

And so I anxiously let my son fight his own battles. But a few weeks later, again on his way home from school, he was standing on a curb waiting for a ride when a jeepney backed out and hit him, and he fell on the ground. Onlookers pulled him from under the jeepney. Thank God that apart from a tear in his pants, he only had a few scratches. Then my brave boy simply took another jeepney and went home.

What was going on? Was God punishing me? But why not just hit me instead of my son? So it would hurt me more?

On my next birthday, my thirty-fifth, David gave me a dish garden – foot-high ornamentals artfully arranged in a shallow ceramic pot. "Treat this as my love for you," he said. "Keep it next to you, maybe in your office? If you take good care of it, it'll live forever."

"Thank you," I said, giggling. I took the dish garden home and put it on the coffee table, telling Eric it was a gift from my staff. I didn't pay much attention to the plants in our garden because that was Eric's department, but I tended to this one dish garden like it was gold.

Then guilt caught up with me and I started going to the Blessed Sacrament often. I asked God why He'd sent me David at a time when I was very vulnerable. Was this Satan at work, sending temptation my way to test my faith? Why did Miguel have two brushes with death? Was I a bad mother? A rotten wife?

One day, I went to confession, telling the old Dutch priest about a high school boyfriend who'd come back a-courting. He reprimanded me, almost yelling out his whisper: "Quit it. No phone calls, no meetings, nothing! No such thing as just friends."

At the Blessed Sacrament to pray my penance, I asked Jesus why He made things so hard. Jesus said nothing. He just sat there, a white round wafer enshrined in a golden monstrance, and kept on being the Son of God, as He'd always been and ever will be, amen. But I could imagine Him slowly taking human form with the gentle face and pleading eyes, putting His arm around my shoulder, challenging whoever was sinless among the crowd to cast the first stone, and then whispering to me, "Daniela, I do not condemn you. Now, go and sin no more."

The next day, I calmly phoned David and told him we should

stop whatever was going on between us. He protested, saying he didn't mean to cheat on his wife. "Neither do I," I said, "but I can't bear to think of what might happen to my children if I end up hurting them. Think of your children, too."

He didn't argue with that, but I could hear him sigh. We held the line for many minutes, listening for each other's breaths. "Let's hang up now," I finally said. "Please take care of yourself. Promise me."

"You take good care of yourself, too," he said. "For me."

Once I put the phone down, my heart flew out in little shreds to the far ends of the earth.

CHAPTER 23

The thought of David haunted me for weeks until I just needed to tell someone. Although Marya had been in university and living in my house for a few years, I still regarded her as my baby sister and therefore too young to be my confidante. One day, when Eric was away on a business trip in Singapore, I went to visit Chona at her apartment.

Our children were playing upstairs. Chona, in a housedress with two huge, bulging front pockets, was cooking her perfect *pinakbet* and *adobo* that she knew I loved. "You look like a fish market vendor in those," I teased her. She kept all her cash and jewelry in her pockets at all times, to make sure her husband didn't get to them. Rex had never been able to hold down a job longer than a month, and a year after they married, he stopped working altogether. He'd been selling things in the house, from my sister's jewelry to kitchen appliances to eaves waiting to be installed on their roof, and using the money to buy drugs.

The kids rushed down the stairs to buy candy from the store next door. Chona's six-year-old climbed the door jamb and took a coin from the top of the door.

"How did that get there, Chico?" I said.

"I put it there so Papa can't find it," he said and ran out to the store.

Shocked, I turned to Chona. "You mean it's that bad?"

She shook her head. "The other day he threw a chest of drawers down the stairs. He was high... angry."

"He has no right to be angry at anything!" I said, feeling heat rushing to my temples. "Are you going to sit here until he physically hurts you or your children? You must leave."

"If I do that, he'll come and find me, make a scene at my workplace," she said, giving a deep sigh.

In my mind I saw the scene: In her cashier's booth at the Metro Manila Development Authority, my sister is giving out pay envelopes to a queue of city workers – street sweepers and traffic aides, hundreds of them. Since she knows most of them by name, she chats a bit and puts smiles on their faces the way I'd seen her do several times. Then a drunk, stoned Rex barges in and yells at my sister, accusing her of running off with another man. Suddenly, my troubles seemed puny. "You know, you sound like Mom. You should leave him. You could die here."

"I don't know."

"There has to be a way! You've been suffering him for, what, eleven years?"

"I've been asking God to just... maybe take him."

I was annoyed that my sister was unruffled, but knowing her, I let the matter go. I promised myself to find a way out for her, and soon. After lunch and the kids were back at play, I took the bag of ripe tamarinds I'd bought and put it on the coffee table. "Try these," I said. "Really sweet."

We both loved tamarind, eating even the green and sour ones back in Montaña. They weren't that easy to find in Manila. I cracked a pod between my fingers and bit at the moist brown flesh inside, feeling like my sister and I were again little girls. Then I told her about David.

"Ah," she said, "your dream boy come to take you back?"

"It's killing me." I put my hand on my chest.

"How did we get ourselves buried in dung heaps?" she said, spitting out a seed and licking her fingers. "Now, now. Are you ready for this?"

"What?"

"I've seen your hunk of a husband," she said, "on two occasions."

"Where?"

"In his car, driving to Makati in the early morning."

"Big deal. He does that every day, even weekends. Good Friday, too, mind you."

"With a woman who slides down in the front seat and hides behind a newspaper?"

"He meets with a lot of clients," I said, trying to conceal my shock.

"I can't tell who's dumber," she said. "You or me."

"The creep. But I don't want to confront him and look paranoid. How do we get to the bottom of this?"

"You shouldn't have dumped David in the first place," Chona said. "He'd kiss the ground you walk on."

"Don't rub it in," I said. "Do you realize I've done it all? Loving my husband to death didn't work. Slapping his girlfriend didn't work. Sleuthing, trailing him, besides being demeaning, didn't work. I should just kill him."

"If I know you, you'll stand by your man."

"Why is it so hard to be a good Christian wife?" I said and sighed. "A good Filipina Christian wife?"

After a few days, Eric came back from Singapore and surprised me with a delicate gold pendant – a real orchid dipped in twenty-four carat gold. No-occasion presents thrilled me, made me feel I mattered. Afraid to ruin the moment, I kept quiet about what Chona had told me. Instead, I thanked Eric and tenderly kissed his mouth, but he didn't kiss me back, saying I smelled of cigarettes.

He had been a heavy smoker for many years but had successfully quit two years earlier. On the other hand, I'd quit whenever I was pregnant or nursing, but would pick up the habit again afterwards. Smoking soothed my raw nerves, eased the stress at work, and kept my weight down. I simply made sure I didn't do it in front of the children anymore, after Mateo cried, begging me to stop. I was surprised and embarrassed to hear that I smelled awful, for I showered morning and night, brushed my teeth after each meal, wore cologne to work and a lighter scent for bed. I tried to quit smoking over the next days but the worse I felt, the more I smoked. I had been feeling a vague kind of sadness for many weeks, and apart from the prayerful hope for a miracle, smoking was my most dependable and accessible source of comfort.

Was this another thing I absolutely *must* give up in order to keep the marriage intact? Since Eric first had an affair, I had had to give up a great deal of pride in order to focus on loving him and restoring the magic. Because if marriage was unto death and breaking up wasn't an option, I didn't want to stay and be miserable. I needed to keep the love – and the lust – going. I needed kindness, a listening ear, forgiveness for my own quirks and trespasses. I needed to feel safe to be myself. To sometimes be able to throw a tantrum without fearing a fiercer counter-tantrum. I did receive those, but in sporadic doses, and I rarely knew beforehand whether something would please or annoy him.

A few months later, I was with a group of Guerrero's top executives for a three-day training camp on rustic and balmy Tagaytay Ridge, expecting a regular conference.

At the gate of the camp, the bus carrying the twenty of us was met by five young people, twenty-somethings, almost young enough to be my children. They gave us numbers to wear on our chests and told us to forget that we had names because as far as they, our masters, were concerned, we were mere numbers.

Thus began three days of hell. Maybe this was what army bootcamp was like. Memorizing a long poem while jogging up and downhill and carrying all my belongings with me. Being given three minutes to put up my tent. Executing whistle signals pronto and with precision – as in: short-short-long meant 'lie down in neat rows on the ground,' or long-short-long meant 'run in circles while staring at the sun.' Washing a big pile of greasy plastic plates with a laundry bar, a pail of cold water, and my bare hands. Sleeping in a chilly tent and waking up at dawn with my hair moist with dew. Negotiating an obstacle course through wooded, steep, mud-slippery terrain I'd never before seen, while blindfolded and handcuffed to another person, and at certain points, yelling out slogans that we were earlier told to memorize. After getting all muddied, having only two minutes to wash up in a common bathroom where we all shared a barrel of very cold water. And then, negotiating the obstacle course once more, but this time, all twenty of us, our ankles tied together, and still blindfolded. And all the long while, forbidden to utter a word.

I silently questioned the objectives of the program, but I did everything I was ordered to do without flinching, constantly reminding myself that this was part of the job. I proved much tougher than the two other women in the group, which was no surprise, but I also learned that I was actually tougher – in spirit and even brawn – than most of the men. If I took away anything from those three days, it was a singular smugness from knowing that I was no wimp.

As I relished this knowledge on the bus ride home, my thoughts turned to a book I had read on making choices regarding one's marriage. The author had said that it took courage to divorce, and I thought, yes, true, especially if the woman needed financial security from her husband. But many things in that book ran counter to the Catholic Church's stand against divorce, so I didn't pay much attention to it. In fact, I leaned the other way and believed that it took courage to stay in a difficult marriage, and more so if the woman, like me, had the means to support herself. That God sent people custom-made crosses, and if He'd decided to send me a challenging marriage, it could only have meant that He knew I had what it took to make an astounding success out of it. I had actually wanted many times to ask Him for a lighter cross but didn't dare question His wisdom. The past three days was perhaps His way of patting my back for my strength in letting go of David and egging me on to keep on fighting the good fight.

When I got back home, I had a bad cough that wouldn't heal for weeks. The doctor ordered an X-ray and then flatly told me I had TB. She assured me I was in a non-contagious stage but emphasized proper nutrition, sufficient rest, some expensive medication, and absolutely not a puff of smoke.

What else could I do but obey? I didn't want to die. The expense didn't bother me, but I hated to part with my cigarettes. However, I learned that the fear of death was the most effective motivator. I quit cold turkey and never looked back. And now, as a neat bonus, Eric had one less excuse to find me less than desirable.

In October, Dad's remaining surviving sibling died in Manila. Mom traveled from Montaña for the funeral. We had just left the cemetery in my car – Mom, Chona, Sonny, Marya, and myself. "Mom, tell us how Ilocanos are mourning Apo Marcos's death," I said. "And what happens now to Doña Josefa?"

Marcos's mother Doña Josefa had been dead for over a year, but her embalmed body had not been buried. It had been her wish for her son to bury her, but Cory had been firm about not allowing Marcos back in the country. A mortician had been regularly injecting preservatives into the corpse, which lay on display in the Marcos house in Ilocos Norte, waiting for the beloved son to come home. But poor Doña Josefa's wait would now be in vain, for Marcos himself, the man who never intended to die, had died in a Honolulu hospital, a month ago – of the lupus that made his face puffy, of kidney and heart failure. Cory hadn't budged, saying that dead or alive, Marcos wasn't allowed back. Imelda maintained that Marcos belonged in the Heroes' Cemetery in Manila and vowed to bury him there. In the meantime, Marcos's embalmed remains lay in a freezer somewhere in Hawai'i.

"Did you go and see Doña Josefa, Mommy?" Marya said. "Isn't it creepy?"

"Last year, when she died, I went with my church friends," Mom said. "She looked just like her pictures."

Chona said, "Do you think Cory will eventually let the Apo's body home?"

Everyone started talking at once. I drove on and let them chatter for a few minutes, and then I said. "Okay, people, enough. Let's move on to the next item on the agenda." Once they'd all shut up, I said, "Mom, we have to rescue Chona and her kids." I went on to describe how bad the situation had become.

"Good God," Mom said. "I've always known. Before you got married, I warned you that you could never change him," she said to Chona. "You didn't listen. You can never ever change a man, remember that."

"Yes, Mom, we know," I said. "Let's just figure out how to help her now."

"Every time I try to leave him, he threatens me harm," Chona said.

"I have an idea," Sonny said. "We go and pull out Chona and her kids, commando-style. Then we take them to my house where Rex won't be able to locate them." Rex had been to my house several times, but Sonny had just moved to a new house with his wife and child, and Rex didn't know the address.

Although Mom subscribed to the convention of wifely suffering and sacrifice to keep a marriage unto death, she didn't need a lot of convincing when she realized that Chona and her kids risked being harmed. And so we hatched a rescue plan.

The following Sunday, Chona told Rex that her mother and siblings were coming over for lunch. She went to market and then started cooking. I drove to Chona's apartment with Mom and Marya. Rex was there when we arrived. A while later, Sonny arrived in his car with two boyhood friends. While Mom and I were helping Chona in the kitchen, Rex walked out the gate, just as Chona had predicted. "Good," Chona said and then called her maid. "Go see where he's going. If he sees you, say I sent you to the store."

"Are you sure he won't have lunch with us?" Mom said.

"A hundred percent," my sister said. "His guilty face can't stand facing you all."

"So where would he likely be?"

"At Pedro's, six blocks away – where he and his gang do their thing."

I'd once asked Chona's pre-school daughter who brought her to school, knowing that her mother had to be at work. The little girl had said her father did. And when I asked what he did while waiting to fetch her home, she casually said, "Get drunk." So today, I wondered what was on his menu. Was it booze, pot, drugs, or all of the above?

While we were rushing through lunch, the maid confirmed that Rex had indeed gone to Pedro's.

Then we set about our task. On the street outside, Sonny's friends stood as lookouts – and additional fistfight power if Rex should arrive and turn violent. Marya told the three kids she was treating them to a movie and took them away by public transport. Chona and the rest of us went upstairs with empty shopping bags. She showed us which drawers to empty onto the bags, which items to carry downstairs. She hadn't packed any suitcases or boxes beforehand so as not to alarm Rex, but she'd prioritized which things to haul out, only what could fit in two small cars. Among the first things she brought out were twenty-odd shoeboxes. I peeked in, expecting to find important things, but I only saw shoes of different colors. "All these?" I said.

"Yes, yes," she said. "I'll die without them."

I shook my head and carried as many boxes as I could. "Madam Imelda, how about your children's stuff? Important documents?"

"They're okay. Everything's under control."

I had long admired my sister for the way she coolly handled her troubles, but I didn't expect her to go about this operation as though she was directing a nursery school skit. If I were in her place, I'd be pulling out my hair and feeling sorry for myself.

As fast as we could – anxious that Rex might show up – we loaded the two cars and left only room for one passenger apart from the driver. In less than an hour, the cars could hold no more. Chona rode with me, Mom with Sonny. The maid and Sonny's friends left by public transport. My car groaned as I drove away, and my heart was pounding. "Whew!" I said when we reached the highway. "That was scary."

"But aren't we good?" Chona said. "Everything went according to plan."

"What will you tell your children?"

"That our place needs some repairs so we have to move out for a while."

"And if Rex shows up at your office and makes a scene?"

She shrugged. "*Bahala na.*" She literally said 'Come what may,' but I knew she meant she'd do her best and leave God to pick up the rest.

"You learned your lesson from Imelda, huh? No shoes left behind," I said, at last able to exhale. "All aboard on the choppers... Hawai'i, here we come!"

Sonny took in Chona and her brood for a few days. Then Mom brought the children to Montaña and sent them to school there, while Chona lived with Sonny in Manila for her job. Rex didn't show up until two months later, when we were all in Montaña for Christmas. He was sober and meekly asked Chona for another chance, weeping as he spoke. My wise, precious sister firmly said no.

"That's my girl," I said after Rex had left. "For a moment I was afraid you'd get back together again because I saw you crying."

"I can't go back to that hell," she said.

"Go back and we won't come rescue you again," I said. "But tell me, how are you handling this? You're mostly away from your kids, and your heart must still be aching from the breakup."

"I miss the kids. About the breakup, *tatlong sine lang iyan*," she said, managing a smile. All it takes is three movies, she was saying.

She loved her movies.

"Be serious."

"I'm serious. I don't dwell on stuff as much as you do. I pray. I used to ask God to just take Rex, but now that He's let me live away from him, I know that He won't abandon me."

"But you must be feeling awful about the bad hand you were dealt."

"The trick is I tell myself that all men were born lacking in smarts."

"I should remind myself of that too," I said, laughing hysterically. "Excellent mantra."

Wasn't my big sister clever? Why couldn't I be like her? What was wrong with me? But then, her husband was an outright jerk. Mine wasn't. There were many things about Eric that still made him a prize catch. Handsome, intelligent, dignified. Three academic degrees, an enviable job and salary. Nice and loving, at least some of the time. Yes, he had been unfaithful, but aren't all men at some point in their lives? He didn't do drugs. And most important of all, he didn't hurt me physically. I'd always known that no matter how far backward I had bent over, and was willing to bend over, I would stop if he physically attacked me.

Still, I could learn a thing or two from Chona, couldn't I?

CHAPTER 24

It had been a tough four years for Cory's government. In spite of the nine *coup* attempts, the economy had picked up. Eric and I were rising in our careers, at least in terms of job title and salary, and with progress came stress.

From being financial planning manager at Glaxo, Eric had become vice president for marketing. This new assignment meant more traveling. In addition to major Philippine cities, he traveled to London, Hong Kong and Singapore. And if he was in Manila, he worked even longer days than before, including most weekends. He also had to give up his teaching load at UP. He was good at his job – for he never allowed himself to perform below par at anything – but he hated it and it was draining him.

On the rare weekend days when he chose to stay home, he tended to his orchids and *bonsai*. Although I'd secretly wish I were an orchid or a *bonsai*, I'd tell myself at least he was home and not breaking his back over Glaxo work. He might spend most of the day at the garden and take the kids and me to a fancy dinner, although he might get impatient with the traffic and drive recklessly. Then I'd remind him to keep his cool and he'd bark at me to do the driving instead. Little incidents like this could spark a heated exchange or a cold war that might last for days, but I'd convince myself that he was just too stressed. At least he wasn't running around.

But whenever I yearned for attention, I'd think of David and the thriving dish garden he'd given me two years earlier. And when Eric and I made up, all would be well again.

But no. One day, I went out to lunch with my girlfriend Beatriz. "I'm so cheap," I said. "A surprise present here, a little sex there, and all's right with my world again. What's wrong with me?"

We were both thirty-seven now. Beatriz was still single, and I admired her for her straight thinking. "Nothing's wrong with you," she said. "But I suggest you use your head, too."

"That's what I'm saying. I forgave him for major offenses, deal-breakers, actually. Then he won't even allow room for my moods, to let me express any kind of negative emotion. When I tell him what I feel, he thinks I'm whining and pulls away. Half of the time, he gets me wrong, accusing me of being angry when actually, I'm not. He says I'm glum even if I'm just deep in thought. Okay, so I might transform into a she-devil when I start yakking, but all these sixteen years, I've never been unfaithful. Don't I get any credit for that? Isn't there a kind of point system here?"

"And David?"

"I know David complicates the plot, but didn't I cut it off before it developed into an affair?"

"How about you both go for some counseling? Eric and you."

"Ah, he'll never admit to anyone that he needs help. The thing is, I'm so cheap. Sex-cheap. Touch me tenderly and I feel treasured. Pull down my panties and my thinking brain instantly closes shop. I hate myself!"

"Eric is a rational man, very logical," Beatriz said, for we'd all known each other since college.

"But his *cum laude* doesn't translate to how he treats me. We never talk any more and when we do, it's mostly business. Like, where to send this kid to school, who's picking up that kid from a friend's party. Sometimes I feel like running away – to shock him, you know – but what if he doesn't come looking for me? I'm so lonely I could die."

"Tell me about loneliness," she said, her eyes turning sad, for she'd also had a few heartbreaks and had been mostly alone.

"I've given him my all," I said. "Love, honor, obey, for richer, for poorer blah blah blah. I know true love's not supposed to expect anything in return. But all those corny things, I want them too! The Philippine version of the marriage vows should have the wife say something like: And because you're a man, a Filipino macho man, I grant you unlimited philandering rights; and if I as much as look at another man, I grant you the right to banish me to Tala Leprosarium."

"Hahaha. Eat," she said. "You've hardly had a bite."

I dug into my *palabok* noodles. "What he does to fix me, besides sex, is splurge – an expensive present, a trip. But why won't he sit down and talk? He hacks at me then covers my wound with a damn Band-Aid."

"Maybe that's the best way he knows how," Beatriz said. "What's a woman to do?"

Eric's family planned a trip to Boracay over that Easter. "Let's all go," he said.

Boracay was paradise: a small island, palm trees, turquoise sea, bamboo huts, *puka* shell necklaces, grilled freshly-caught fish and shrimp, luscious young coconuts. Eric and I had been there with the kids, toasting in the sun, swimming, snorkeling, building castles in the dazzling-white, sugar-fine sand. "But it's Holy Week," I said, feeling sorry to have to refuse paradise. Now, between God and the beach, the clear choice for me was God. "We have a four-day weekend to allow for solemn observance. What do people do? They go to the beach."

"I thought you wanted me to slow down," he said. "You know this is the longest break I can ever have, and I'm sorry it has to run into those four holy days."

There was no tempting me, so Eric took five-year-old Isabel with him to join his family's holiday. The boys chose to stay home. I spent most of the four days in church, doing Stations of the Cross, last-supper mass, midnight vigil at Easter Eve, and then mass early the next morning.

Miguel soon finished high school, ranking third in the graduating class. I'd never been prouder, especially when I recalled how much I had slaved in the same school just to get passing marks and not be kicked out. A year earlier, Mateo had also been admitted to my high school alma mater, and as a treat to both boys, I took them on a trip to Hong Kong. I wanted Eric to come along, but he didn't because he was tied up at work.

How do we handle this? I endlessly nag my husband about his need to relax and spend time with the family, but the few occasions that he acquiesces are usually the wrong times.

During this time of confusion, my brother Sonny was my inspiration, his life an ideal that I strove to attain. Our father had doted on him right from the start. Dad had longed for a son as early as when Mom was expecting me. He was thrilled when Francis was born, and was even more pleased when Sonny came two years later. But before long, when it became clear that Francis preferred to play with Chona and me and our girlfriends, Sonny became the focus of Dad's passion for a son, a truly masculine son. Our father wasn't particularly harsh with Francis on account of his being effeminate. In fact, he had bought Francis an expensive violin when his musical talent became evident at an early age. He was strict with all of us, but he poured more attention on Sonny who eagerly absorbed everything he taught, like how to throw punches and defend himself from bullies. When Dad wanted to bring the two boys to cowboy or action movies, Francis refused, so Dad and Sonny had regular movie outings, just the two of them. Dad had taught Sonny to never start a fight, but whenever challenged, not to back down but finish the fight. Sonny first applied this lesson by punching the boys who teased Francis for being a sissy. But later on, he started fights as he fancied, giving headaches to Mom but putting smiles on Dad's face. Dad had a revolver and a hunting rifle, and when Sonny was in his teens, my father taught his favorite son about guns.

After escaping from detention and hiding for several months, Sonny had to drop out of university. A couple of years later, he pulled himself together and got a computer programming job but started drinking too much. He met and married Lani, a nice young lady at his workplace, and they started a family. Now, Lani introduced the Bible to Sonny, where he found spiritual nourishment. The couple soon joined a Catholic charismatic community. They went to prayer meetings and prayed to the Holy Spirit before doing anything: starting their day, eating meals, driving out, making big and small decisions.

If Lani had led my recalcitrant brother to make a 180-degree turn, I certainly could do the same for my husband, right? Wasn't this a more reliable approach than Chona's hang-loose *tatlong sine lang iyan*?

CHAPTER 25

When Eric suggested that we obtain US visitor visas for us all, I said, "There's six of us, we can't afford the fare. And what are our chances? The whole family leaving? They'll think we don't intend to return, especially because you have plenty of relatives there." The US Embassy had been wary of issuing visitor visas to Filipinos, because of the growing number of people admitted as tourists who had stayed in the US to look for jobs, especially after the Philippine recession.

"You and I, we don't have ordinary jobs here," Eric said. "We can easily convince them that we're not hungry for better careers in America."

My husband had a point but I wasn't convinced it was wise to spend a big part of our savings on a trip, so I made no move to do the tedious paperwork involved in applying for six visas. After a month, he surprised me with a US visitor visa issued to him and said, "Get yourself one so we can both go on a holiday in the summer."

That was all I needed to hear – a chance to spend time alone with him, and in America, too. I'd envied friends who had gone to the States and who returned with stories about the wonderful First World out there. After obtaining a visa, I got all worked up making travel arrangements for the trip.

A few weeks later, Eric filed his resignation from Glaxo. Relief was written all over his face when he showed me a letter from his boss accepting his resignation, and wishing him luck on his return to teaching at UP. He had given his boss more than two months' notice, so after the trip to the States, he was to go back to work for four more weeks until the end of July. Afterward, he'd return to UP.

"You did it," I said, hugging him. "And you do need a good, long break."

Soon, America! Eric's cousin was waiting for us at the Los Angeles airport. If the airport was a maze, the web of highways was a bigger maze. She showed us where the movie stars shopped and ate in Beverly Hills, how they shot scenes using make-believe sets at Universal Studios. As expected, Disneyland was bigger and more impressive than the one in Tokyo that I'd seen years before. I feared, but couldn't get enough of, the rides that sucked my guts out. Other cousins took us to a ski resort on Big Bear Mountain two hours from the city, my first encounter with snow as well as with American nature. Crowded, manicured Venice Beach near the city didn't count as nature for me.

We visited friends, ate out, cooked at home. No maids, as I'd known, but it was interesting to see how their daily routines went. Shove frozen packages in the microwave *et voilà!* You call that a meal? Efficient, leave-alone laundry machines, sure. But, what, no ironing? And can we open the windows for some fresh air? No, don't, the alarm will go off.

Jetlag, magic, thrills and bits of a new lifestyle crammed in five days in the City of Angels felt like a NASCAR race.

Then we flew to Chicago and spent a week with my best friend Amanda and her husband, who had moved there a few years back. The long girl talks and the laid-back sightseeing and shopping in a city that felt friendlier than LA were rejuvenating.

Later, we visited with Eric's cousins. Millie and Jacob groomed horses and gave riding lessons at their ranch in Beecher, fifty miles south of Chicago. We awoke at dawn with the moon shining on our faces through the big, airy windows. We took walks on the wide swath of grazing land in the soft May breeze. We petted the horses, trying to remember their names. Then we had lazy breakfasts on the patio as the birds chirped above. Not the America I had imagined; an interesting change from frenetic Los Angeles and Chicago.

One night, Millie threw a small party for her father's birthday. When the guests had left, I helped her tidy up while Jacob and Eric sat on the patio, still drinking. "I'm jealous," Eric said. "I like this."

"What do you mean?" Jacob said.

"Your place, it's fantastic. Nice house, fancy and comfortable, yet far from the crazy city. Laid-back lifestyle. You do what you love, actually playing while you work."

"Hey, honey," Millie called out to her husband. "Don't give my favorite cousin too much to drink."

"I'm not drunk, Millie dear," Eric said. "Come join us."

Millie and I joined the two men for drinks. We joked around. Then Eric said, "I love it here; I'd like to come back. I've quit my job as of the end of next month. After that, I want to come back here, to the States."

"You mean move here?" I said, surprised, because we'd never before talked about moving to America.

"Yes, why not?" he said, taking another sip of his brandy.

"I don't want to move here," I said. "Sure, it's pretty and progressive. But we're fine back home."

Eric was drunk, as was Jacob. Millie decided to hide the rest of the booze, and we left the two men still blabbering. I was already in bed when I heard them yell out a cheer downstairs. They'd found the booze. I couldn't sleep, thinking of what Eric had just said.

Marcos had now been dead for three years, and his body still lay in a freezer in Hawai'i. There had been many *coup* attempts against Cory, the biggest one leaving ninety-nine people dead. It had been frightening to hear cannons explode in the middle of the night and to hear the next morning that a friend's sixteen-year-old son had been shot dead for refusing to stop at a rebel's checkpoint. But overall, I thought the Philippines was a good place to live and raise my children. Cory didn't run for a second term, making good her promise that she was there only as a transition president. Imelda had run and lost to General Ramos, one of the key players in the EDSA Revolt. An action, take-charge guy, Ramos looked more promising than Cory. Eric and I and the children, we weren't wanting; in fact, we were comfortable. My job paid very well, and even if Eric was leaving Glaxo, he had good prospects in UP. And that orchid-*bonsai* business he was considering would surely prosper, with his passion and know-how. Our smart children went to the best schools, practically for free, mainly because they were bright. Also, America made people move away from God; I didn't like that, for I was close to God in the Philippines. I saw no compelling reason to uproot us all and move to a place of uncertainty.

And whatever happened to our nationalism? Our resolve as young graduates to stay and help build the country? Our frowns on those who used their brains to enrich America? Had my husband forgotten all that?

Eric didn't bring up the topic again. I dismissed the conversation as drunk-talk as we proceeded with the rest of our travels. We spent the next ten days in Philadelphia, New York, Maryland, Washington DC and Toronto, soaking in the sights and the company of relatives and friends. Those four weeks were one of the greatest times of my marriage. We didn't talk heart-to-heart as I had long yearned for, but we did spend a lot of time alone together, which to me was a priceless treat.

CHAPTER 26

Back in Manila, when at noon Eric called me at work to say he was taking me to the Mongolian Grill for lunch, I told my secretary to move the staff meeting to two p.m. My motto had always been to drop everything for my husband, and thank God I had the power to disrupt other people's schedules, just like that.

I lined my bowl with bean sprouts, sweet red peppers and lettuce, going easy on the onions. "I thought you were at UP," I said. His last day of work at Glaxo was the week before, and he'd earlier told me he was meeting with the dean of the UP Business School to arrange for his return to teaching.

"Yes, but we finished early," he said.

Although Mongolian Grill was crowded and hummed like a hawker's market, I loved it because I could make my own healthy meal. I did the sauce a little sweet, a bit of sesame oil, no *chili*, and topped my bowl with limp squid tentacles. Eric poured two scoops of spicy sauce onto his. We queued up our bowls for the griddle.

We sat at a table to wait for our bowls. "I actually met with someone who bought the old Galant," Eric said.

"Good," I said. "For how much?" We'd owned three vehicles

for more than a year, which I thought was a waste, because there were only the two of us driving.

"A hundred twenty," he said. "I'll use it to pay down my car loan with Glaxo."

"Good idea," I said. A waiter laid our steaming bowls on the table. I poked mine with my chopsticks to cool it off a bit.

"There'll be a hundred-plus loan remaining," he said. "Are you able to get a loan from your bank to pay it off, since for now I don't have income?"

"Hmm," I said, wondering where to source the money for that. I was paying instalments on a pickup truck and didn't have much to spare after covering my share of the bills. "Let me see what I can do."

Eric dug into his bowl. "I just got my ticket," he said.

"Ticket? To where?"

"Try my concoction." With his chopsticks, he put a chunk of beef in my mouth.

"You always make it too hot," I said and downed the beef with water.

"Hot and spicy is cool," he said. "Philadelphia."

"But we just got back," I said, furrowing my brows.

"I like Philly," he said. "I need more time to unwind."

Although it was a couple of months before the second semester opened in UP, I hadn't imagined Eric spending those two idle months abroad. "Why spend that much money in between jobs? Wasn't one month enough for you to unwind?"

"I'm all burned out," he said. "Just six weeks."

Puzzled, I dug for the squid. I loved squid, especially tentacles. We ate quietly for several minutes. When he finished his bowl, he went back for another while I sat at our table, watching the people scurrying in the sudden downpour outside.

When Eric returned, he said, "We'll also need health insurance," pointing at me and then himself with his chopsticks. "The kids, too. Because, of course, our coverage with Glaxo is gone." He paused and then continued, "And would you please pay for my life insurance premiums while I'm gone? It's you and the kids who are the beneficiaries, as you know."

I just looked at him.

"I leave one week from Sunday," he said. "I'm back in late September."

Utterly bewildered, I crossed the street in the rain and went back to work. It hit me that I was simply being told about his decision, not consulted. But I told myself that my poor husband must have been thoroughly burned out at a job he hated. Soon he'd be back to teaching, his real love, his calling, and he'd be a much happier man. I went to my meeting in a daze, trying in vain to focus on the agenda.

When the workday was over, I drove out of the Guerrero compound and joined the rush-hour traffic. Amidst gray sheets of rain, white jagged blades of lightning flashed on my face. The roaring claps that followed reminded me of how I'd snuggle with Lola during thunderstorms, back when I was five and she and I were home alone. I'd cling to her long skirt and she'd shush me and say it was okay, for the thunderstorm would bring lots of mushrooms. In the morning, the mushrooms would magically be there in the backyard, on the ground, on tree trunks. But my grandma had been dead for five years now. My mother hadn't stopped taking care of her until she had died in her arms. Mom looked after everyone, didn't she? I suddenly yearned for mushrooms, the sweet and juicy kind we had back home.

The next day, I went to the bank and took out a loan to pay for Eric's car, even if I knew that I would have to scrape bottom to pay it back. I'd also have to cover what used to be his share of the household bills. Half the income, double the expenses. But it was only for a couple of months before he started earning money again. Six weeks, only six weeks. I could manage that.

It rained almost daily the following week, soaking the ground and cheering up Eric's *bonsai* and orchid garden. The day before he left, he inspected his plants and reminded me to make sure the maids watered them properly. Then he took the kids and me out to a big dinner. Back home, as we packed his bag, the children made a list of things they wanted their father to bring home: Disney movie tapes, the latest Super Mario video games, Superman comics, books, Barbie dolls.

On the second Sunday, in the rain, Eric drove the pickup to the airport. The children chattered in the back seat, making last-minute changes to their lists. At the airport, they kissed him good-bye the way they always had when he left for business trips, very casually, knowing he would soon be back, but I was queasy, with an unnameable fear nibbling at my gut.

My father-in-law had given us an open invitation every Sunday, when he cooked big pots of delicious food, and two Sundays after Eric left, the kids and I were there for lunch. We phoned Eric who was staying with an aunt in Philadelphia. He spoke with each of the kids, his parents and me, saying he'd been to Vancouver and New York, visiting relatives. I asked him if he'd had his fill of galleries and museums yet and told him how much I already missed him.

"I don't understand," Tatay said afterwards, "why he's throwing money out that way. Traveling to the States twice in two months? He even threw in Canada."

"He needs to rest and relax," I said. "He was badly burned out at Glaxo."

"And leave you alone to look after the children? That's not right."

"It's okay, Tay," I said. "It's only a few weeks."

He shook his head. "Here, eat more," he said, pushing the steaming bowl of *bulalo* toward me.

Several days later, a notice came in the mail about a Post Office Box in Eric's name. When I went to the Post Office, I was told that Eric had opened a PO Box account three months earlier, and that they needed to know if he was continuing the subscription. Oh? Why did he need a PO Box? When I told them to close the account, they gave me two pieces of mail from the box.

Well, I'd never been in the habit of opening other people's mail, but this time, I felt entitled to. The first envelope contained a rejection letter from the World Bank; the other from the United Nations. Eric had secretly been applying for jobs abroad! I kept quiet and prayed. God seemed to be saying: Be patient, persevere, understand – in the way the bewildered Mary, the mother of Jesus, 'kept all these things and pondered them in her heart.' So I did as Mary did and kept this to myself.

Toward the end of the six weeks, in late September, the children and I were eager to have Eric back. As the kids wondered what gifts he might surprise them with, I simply ached to snuggle up and sleep with him. And afterward have a serious talk about his plans, about us. Although we didn't have long talks anymore, I hoped that his time away might get him talking this time.

One afternoon, two days before The Day, my secretary pulled me out of a meeting. Eric was on the phone. "So, I'll pick you up at the airport," I said, almost jumping up in excitement. "Of course, you'll want the kids there too, right?" He was silent. "Hello?" I said, anxious about wasting precious long-distance time. "Are you there?"

He cleared his throat and then said, "I need more time."

"What? You're not coming home Saturday?"

"Only for a month," he said. "I'm looking at job possibilities here, and I'd like to explore more."

Outside my door, my secretary was preparing to mail a parcel; the roll of packaging tape screeched as she tugged it around the box. I covered my other ear with my hand and let out a deep sigh. "I got letters from the World Bank and the UN," I said. "From your PO Box. You didn't tell me you'd applied for jobs in the States before you left. And that you had a PO Box…"

"Let's talk about it later," he said. "I just called to tell you I'm staying here another month. Something might come up."

"Talk to me now!" I said. "How about us, the kids, me?"

"If I find something… Later, we'll talk later."

Besides wanting to grab the roll of packaging tape and throw it out the window – or perhaps at Eric's face – I didn't know what to do or say. Which didn't matter, because my husband quickly said he had to hang up since the call was expensive.

"Please," I said to my secretary. "Your tape, the sound, it drives me nuts."

I ran things over in my mind that evening and began to see that Eric hadn't been joking at his cousin's ranch in Beecher three months earlier, when he said he wanted a lifestyle just like theirs. But why didn't he tell me? Although I had been clear about not wanting to live in the States, I certainly wasn't going to kill him if he had sat down and told me his serious reasons for wanting to move there. Was he afraid I'd object and he would never make first base? Maybe he wanted to quietly find something and present me with a hard-to-refuse offer when he had put it all together? Or had he walked out on me the easy way?

When I told Eric's parents the news, his father said, "Why did you let him go?"

"Tay, he didn't ask me," I said. "He told me."

"You should tell him to return."

Did my father-in-law know he was asking me the impossible? I didn't tell him what I thought, that maybe God wanted Eric to be in the wilderness for some time so he could figure out what he truly wanted. I didn't tell him that I was willing to give Eric space to search inside himself. Anyway, I was doing just fine. Apart from the physical strain of doing more driving, the sleepless nights, the tight budget, the loneliness and the confusion, I was doing just fine.

"It's all right, Tay," I said. "I'm fine."

PART III

1992 – 2000

CHAPTER 27

Three months after Eric left, I was dumbfounded one day when Mateo showed me his report card. He had failing marks in English and chemistry. I had never fully learned chemistry, and I knew how tough it was in his school, being my alma mater. But English? My son was a voracious reader and dreamed of becoming a writer someday. "What's the matter?" I said. "Why didn't you ask me or Miguel for help? I know your school can be daunting, but why English?"

"I don't know, Mommy," he said, clenched his fists and looked down.

Mateo promised to work harder to prepare for the exams that were three weeks away. Miguel also helped him. The next days, Mateo had bouts of asthma. He'd be fine in the evening as he studied his lessons, but in the morning he'd wake up wheezing, hardly able to breathe.

A month later, Mateo handed me his report card, shamefaced. His English had gone up to just-passing, but his math went down. And he had failing marks in all the sciences – biology, chemistry and physics.

I told the guidance counsellor of the timing of the asthma attacks. "The change in his behavior is so drastic from the first two years," she said. "He writes cryptic answers on his test papers, or fills them with question marks. Sometimes he leaves them blank altogether."

"I'm surprised to hear that," I said. "He's always wanted to do everything perfectly."

"Sometimes he stands by a shelf in the library and stares blankly for several minutes, clenching his fists."

Another big surprise. What was going on? This was not normal behavior. After a few moments, I said, "His father has been away for a couple of months; maybe that has something to do with it."

"I suggest you have him seen by a psychologist," she said and gave me a few names.

I took Mateo to one of the psychologists on the list. She evaluated him and handed me a report that was so technical, I couldn't fully understand it. In any case, she didn't recommend further follow-up, which I took to mean that there was nothing seriously wrong with my son.

Knowing the standards of PSHS, I figured it would be almost impossible for Mateo to turn his failing marks around during the rest of the school year. I certainly didn't want him to be kicked out. I took him to his doctor; she gave a certificate that Mateo had severe asthma and needed a few months of rest. Based on this and the psychologist's report, the school allowed my son a medical leave of absence.

I wrote Eric all the details of Mateo's crisis, hoping he'd hastily fly home. And for spiritual strength, on top of the daily masses, I rose at half past four in the morning to read the Bible and pray, more intensely than when I started five years back, taking to heart the poem from Proverbs 31 that speaks of the virtuous wife looking after her family and helping, not hindering, her husband all her life.

The extra month that Eric said he'd need passed without any sign of his coming home. In mid-November, during one of our three-minute phone conversations, I asked him to be home for the Christmas holidays.

"I need a little more time," he said, his voice breaking.

"But we all miss you," I said. "Forget those American employers. If they won't consider your Philippine experience, it's their loss. Besides, I still prefer for us to raise the kids here in Manila."

"I miss you, too," he said, sniffling. "But I can't come home just yet. I don't want to have to explain to everyone why I quit Glaxo. You're the only person in the world who understands me."

"I'll always stand by you, you know that," I said. "Just come home. Please."

He didn't. In my prayers, I felt God saying that more than needing to find a job, Eric needed to find himself. That although he was now lost in the wilderness, he'd eventually arrive in the Promised Land. That if he were left without a job, money, power, prestige, and his family – his loving wife, his adorable children – he'd more easily identify his priorities in life, and at the end of this search, discover that his family was the one thing he could not afford to lose. In reply, I told God that whenever the moment of my husband's epiphany came, I'd be there waiting for him.

But half of the time, I would wonder what Eric was truly up to. We were now both thirty-eight. Wasn't it a bit too late to find oneself and too early for a mid-life crisis? How could he abandon us? Wasn't it outright irresponsibility to walk out on young children who didn't ask to be born? If he had indeed walked out, what a coward to not tell me straight. I would fume and rack my brains for hours and still end up more confused than when I started. And so I'd go back to praying, for it was much less painful to just let God take over.

I took the children to Montaña for Christmas, extending our stay beyond New Year's, happy to be with Mom and my siblings and to have time to stroll in my childhood hangouts by the rice paddies. Unfortunately, Mateo got sick and spent most of Christmas Day in a clinic.

Besides praying over Mateo, Sonny spent time talking to him. Hungry for a father figure, Mateo took to his uncle easily. But Sonny was moving to Canada in four months. Many Filipinos had become disillusioned with Cory's government and considered moving out of the country for a better life. Canada had recently begun welcoming more skilled and professional immigrants, and it was a good alternative to the States, which had become more restrictive. Although Ramos had shown over the past year that changes were possible, times were still tough. Electricity was rationed, water service was erratic, garbage littered the streets, traffic was unbearable. Several of my colleagues and friends had left or had applied for entry to Canada.

"Are you losing hope in the Philippines, too?" I asked Sonny.

"Looks like a hard hill to climb," he said. "I want to make a fresh start while the two kids are still young."

"Just like a real Benito," Mom said, recounting how Daddy's family couldn't stay put in one place, first going as sugar farmers to Hawai'i – where Dad was born – and then returning to Montaña but later moving to Davao to homestead.

"Why did Daddy and Uncle Badong stay here in Montaña?" Chona said.

"I don't know why your uncle decided to stay here. Your dad and I fell in love, and when he asked your *lola* for my hand in marriage, she made him promise to never take me away from this town."

I'd heard that before but didn't think much of it. But this time, I wondered if Dad's gypsy spirit had rebelled at this restriction. Sometime during my high school, he was applying for jobs in Manila. I had never known the outcome; all I knew was that he stayed in Montaña until he died.

Come to think of it, I had done the same to Eric with respect to his attempts to do a doctorate abroad. Was he rebelling, too?

Sonny and Lani were trained in computers, so they had good

prospects in North America, but I had mixed feelings about their plan. What a waste to spend Philippine talent and brains building already-developed countries. But I, of course, had no business dissuading them. After all, Eric himself had decided it was time to give up on the Philippines. And I had also gradually become frustrated, tired of being a productive, law-abiding citizen, paying the correct taxes, only to see even post-Marcos politicians using my taxes to enrich themselves. Though shanty areas were mushrooming around the city, the Catholic Church kept insisting that it was a sin to use condoms and contraceptive pills. As I drove, I saw many half-naked toddlers running around, and I wondered how many of them would end up living in the streets, and how soon.

So the entitled class kept, if not piled up, its riches. The poor, uneducated mass base grew in number and poverty. And we, the honest, educated working men and women who poured their time and skills into their jobs and their families, as well as into helping the less-fortunate, were left out in the cold.

I continued to write Eric long letters, updating him about the children, especially Mateo, and reminding him that for me, the simpler way was for him to just come home. He wrote back to say that although he was terribly homesick, he was going to stick it out in the States for the twelve months allowed by his visitor visa.

His job search wasn't going anywhere. The consulting firms politely turned him down; the teaching jobs required a doctorate. Which was a pity, he said, because unlike in the Philippines, the salary of a university professor in the States could comfortably support a family such as ours. Knowing it was teaching he loved, I suggested that he get himself a doctorate if it was going to take only a couple of years. After all, it was one of his great unfulfilled dreams.

From that point on, he focused on looking for a school that would give him financial support to see him through a Ph.D. I kept the letters going and sent him money for his application fees. Then I was promoted at work, which I took as God's partial answer to my prayers. It meant much more responsibility and a greater workload, but the money that came with it eased a lot of my financial worries. After all, what was more stress at work to the virtuous wife who was supposed to be energetic and strong, a hard worker, and whose light burned into the night?

In the meantime, I attended a high school reunion and saw David again for the first time after asking him to stop calling three years before. I was cordial to him but didn't encourage anything more than the kind of casual conversation I had with the rest – because it wasn't something that the virtuous wife would do. He was also friendly without paying me special attention, and although that hurt, I convinced myself it was better that way.

I read a book about the Virgin Mary's apparitions to three teenagers in Medjugorje in Yugoslavia. Intrigued, I picked up every available bit of material on the subject. The apparitions that had started several years earlier were still happening regularly. Throngs of pilgrims visited the site and experienced miracles, like their rosaries turning to gold or the sun spinning in dazzling colors. Church groups organized pilgrimages from Manila. Since I didn't have the money, I could only envy a friend who went on such a pilgrimage and came back feeling so pure, so blessed.

Just like at Fatima in Portugal, the Blessed Virgin told some secrets to the teens. And to save the world from tragedy, she urged them to go to frequent mass and confession and to pray the rosary. I could do all those right where I was, without traveling to Medjugorje. With a stronger resolve, I continued with the daily masses and started going to confession once a week. Before then, I went to confession only when I had a fresh sin that I wanted to be absolved for. After a few weekly confessions, it became harder to name sins to accuse myself of, and I worried that Father Gervasi might think I was a hopeless case after hearing the same sins from me over and over: I had very little faith in God; I didn't pray enough; I was distracted at mass; I was impatient with my children; I envied co-workers who made more money than I did but who had very little by way of brains.

Each morning, I prayed the rosary on the long drive to work – all fifteen mysteries, even if the church prescribed only five per day – not so much to save the world, but to save my family from ruin. After a few weeks, I noticed that my metal rosary beads were changing in color, becoming yellowish. I kept the excitement to myself until one day, when I couldn't hold it any longer, I excitedly told my confessor my rosary had turned to gold. That maybe, like in Medjugorje, the Blessed Mother was telling me she had heard my pleas. When I showed him the rosary, he examined it briefly and said, "It's just tarnished."

That night, I took my guitar and softly sang praise songs beside my sleeping daughter, letting go of all the tears I'd held down the past few days- about everything, everything in my world that had become tarnished.

When Sonny and his family left for Toronto in April, Mateo and I were sad to see him go. Now my crutch was gone.

In May, nine months after Eric left, I joined the *Bukas Loob sa Diyos,* or BLD, a Catholic charismatic community similar to the group that Sonny and his wife had joined. I attended prayer meetings where people sang their prayers. They also chanted words I couldn't understand, calling it praying in tongues, a gift of the Holy Spirit. With eyes closed and hands up in the air, they sang, "God will make a way where there seems to be no way." I sang with them and wept.

BLD assigned me a shepherd, someone who would hold my hand through the process of my renewal. She was a lawyer named Ellie, five years older than I, married with children and also an Ilocana. "I came to the community deeply wounded," she said. "My world is not perfect but I've been healed, renewed."

I warmed up to her quickly. We spent many hours together – with me, the lamb, baring my soul and Ellie, the shepherd, praying and crying, too. She affirmed what I had earlier read and heard about the foundation of charismatic renewal: You want to be baptized in the Holy Spirit, to allow it to bestow its gifts on you, so you can let Jesus walk with you in your daily life. Now, there are evil spirits that inhabit a person to sabotage his efforts at living a Christian life – spirits of lust, hatred, lack of forgiveness, despair, and so on. There are also spirits passed down through generations. Finally, there are spirits attached to physical locations that influence the behavior of humans in the vicinity. These spirits – in your person and around you – enslave you and prevent you from living as you should. For you to be freed from this bondage, the spirits should be rendered powerless through a prayer of deliverance. Only then can the Holy Spirit freely work to renew your life.

Ellie gave many examples of broken marriages miraculously mended after a Marriage Encounter, a weekend retreat for couples seeking to strengthen their fractured relationships. For starters, the leaders of the community were a happy couple, very devoted to each other, but did I know that they had previously been separated for eighteen years? I had hope!

How to get there needed some work. First, I was in spiritual bondage rooted in some deep spiritual wounds. To have these wounds healed, I had to forgive everyone who had hurt me and ask forgiveness of everyone I had hurt. Next, I needed to identify objects in my home that carried the devil's emblems, like dragons, snakes, vampires, ram's horns and pagan symbols. Or harmful books, music, movies, video games and toys. Total healing wouldn't be possible in my family as long as those objects were around. And because I had submitted myself to shepherding, the devil was now working twice as hard to keep me in his hold.

Ellie believed that Mateo was in deep trouble because he, too, was in spiritual bondage. "What does he have?" she said.

"He loves to read," I said. "He spends a lot of his savings on books. There's a series that he collects - *Choose Your Own Adventure*.

260

He'd like to be able to write something like it someday."

"Let me come to your house to see what objects might be inhabited by demons. After my initial visit, I'll ask Gabriel and Liza to come and pray over you and your children and do spiritual warfare in your home."

Gabriel and Liza – I felt at home with this couple who were elders of the community. In their fifties, they had wise, gentle faces and welcoming smiles. I couldn't wait.

The moment she entered my home, Ellie said she could feel negative, heavy energy, like an unseen force pushing her back. She identified half of Eric's collection of antiques and knick-knacks as likely abodes of demons: vases and jars with dragon designs and all sorts of icons gathered from his travels. There was a wooden sculpture of an indigenous Igorot hunter woman that Eric had bought from Baguio and which the children and I found creepy; it'd be nice to get rid of that one. I pulled out books that I believed were not in line with Christian teaching. I asked the maids to carry all these objects out to the back patio. Among my jewelry, I found two gold pendants with forbidden designs: an Egyptian ankh with a small diamond and one that looked like a ram's horn. I thought of the cost and hesitated a bit, then wrapped them in tissue and set them aside.

Now, to the children's rooms. Toys that looked like grotesque creatures had to go. *Ghost Buster* stuff, too, because they suggested reliance on the paranormal and not on God. Monsters and superheroes – Superman, Batman - because their powers are not of God and can mislead children. All of Mateo's *Choose Your Own Adventure* books that he'd bought with five years' savings – Ellie and I saw snakes and dragons and vampires in them. I put them aside; because I wanted to talk to the children first, I didn't have them brought out of the house.

After Ellie left, I told the children why some of their toys and books had to be destroyed and promised to replace them with good ones. They didn't argue. Then I took Mateo aside. "I know these past months have been tough for you," I said. "And you know how much I've tried to make things better. I've found the answer to your troubles, to our family's troubles."

In the *Adventure* books, the reader is the protagonist, and at certain points, he is free to choose the outcome of the story from several options. I picked up one of these books and opened them to a page I'd marked earlier. "Look at this one," I said, pointing to a picture of a boy eating a live snake. "When you read, you assume you are this boy. You are eating a wiggling snake here – isn't that gross? The devil disguises himself and sneaks into the minds of young people. Do you want him to do that to you?"

"No," he said, fear in his eyes.

"I know you spent a lot of money on these," I said. "But they have to go so you can get well. I'm going to pay you back double so you can buy safer reading material."

We sat together in silence for a while. Then I offered to pray with him. We were both in tears at the end.

"You're going to get well now," I said.

"My books... I saved up a lot for those books," he said.

"God will take care of you," I said, but my son didn't stop crying.

The following Saturday, Ellie arrived with Gabriel and Liza. It was only mid-morning, but the April sun had dried up the lawn that the maid had watered only two hours earlier. We sipped iced Coke and chatted, then Gabriel said, "Let's get to work."

I took them first to my bedroom. Gabriel told me to bring down two paintings of nude women from the walls. As I took the paintings and brought them outside to the patio, I thought: Oh my, Eric paid a fortune for those. When I returned to the room, Gabriel asked me to stand in front of him. Liza and Ellie stood behind me. Gabriel took out a bottle of holy oil from his pocket, put some on his thumb and with it made the sign of the cross on my forehead. Then he began to pray with his hands over my bowed head. The women behind me prayed in tongues. A short while later, I felt a strong force push me backward, but certainly not Gabriel's hands because they weren't touching my head at all. My knees buckled down and I started falling. I was floating, floating. Powerless to resist the force, I expected to hit my head somewhere. I didn't, because Liza and Ellie caught me and gently lay me down on the floor. I closed my eyes while the three prayed in tongues. I felt very peaceful and safe, as if I were in a loving embrace.

I did not lose consciousness but was in a daze and lay there, merely wanting to rest in that warm hug. When at last I opened my eyes and rose to my feet, Gabriel, Liza and Ellie were praying over Mateo. A short while later, Mateo also fell on the floor. Then I joined them when they prayed over the other kids, although none of them fell.

"That was very powerful," I said after we finished praying.

"It wasn't me," Gabriel said. "It was the Holy Spirit."

I must matter, after all, I thought, for the Holy Spirit to bother coming down for me. I kept quiet, trying to probe the depth of what had just happened, but after a few moments Gabriel signalled for me to follow him and the others.

We went out to the backyard now, to destroy the harmful objects. I asked Gabriel if they could spare the paintings, afraid of Eric's ire. I was willing to risk the consequences of destroying most of his things without his knowledge, but I drew the line on the paintings. Gabriel agreed but told me to keep them out of sight, outside the house if possible. We all prayed Psalm 91:

If you make the Lord your refuge,
If you make the Most High your shelter,
No evil will conquer you;
No plague will come near your dwelling.
For he orders his angels to protect you wherever you go.

The three spiritual warriors sprinkled holy water and prayed the prayer of deliverance over the pile of curios, books, and other things, ordering the devil to depart. We smashed the ceramics, metalware, and toys. Set fire to the wooden sculptures. Under the noonday sun, we made a big bonfire of the books. With a hammer,

I pounded my gold pendants flat and threw them into the fire.

Four hours later, as I watched the fire consume the last of the harmful items, I felt hopeful but anxious. We went back to the house drenched in sweat. Over a late lunch, Gabriel encouraged my children to join me for prayer meetings, Mateo especially. Then he said, "This is not to scare you, but the devil isn't pleased with what we did. He's going to put up a fight. Better to be forewarned."

Greatly relieved that the devil had departed, I profusely thanked the three good people and walked them outside to their car. Though exhausted, I rearranged what remained of the ornaments and books, delighted with the liberating feeling of a roomier house. Thinking of Gabriel's warning, I read Psalm 91 and left the Bible open to that page on my night table, reminding myself that the Holy Spirit was in me and I could face whatever danger lay ahead.

Two days later, I was preparing to go to work when a stale-fish odor began to permeate my room. Strange, because everything around me was clean. Then I saw two small, white, roundish worms below the window air-conditioning unit. Maggots? All the windows were screened, and the only way any small creatures could enter was through the narrow slot below the air conditioner. I peered in there. Nothing. The stench intensified, and more worms wriggled down the wall and on the floor. What was this, the devil come to claim me back? After I threw holy water on them and said the prayer of deliverance, the worms still wiggled about. Then I bombarded them with bug spray until they all went stiff. Later, I went around the house and the yard, sprinkling holy water and asking Jesus to cover my home with His blood.

That same day, I bought crucifixes and pictures of the Sacred Heart of Jesus and hung them in each of the rooms at home. I prayed with all my might and thankfully, the ominous stench and the worms did not return.

I was now ready for a general confession. Because it was going to take longer, this was done face-to-face instead of in a confessional box. I entered the room and greeted Father Frank, one of the community's spiritual directors. He gave me the wide smile that made him so popular. Filipino and my age, known for funny, self-deprecating but profound homilies, he was a refreshing change from the old, foreign priests I usually went to for confession.

He asked me to take the seat in front of him. I pulled out my list and said, "Bless me, Father, for I have sinned. My last confession was a week ago." Then I began reading. He looked at my four-page list and bowed his head. He seemed to be bracing for boredom, but I didn't care; I needed to go through each item on my list. I was going to name the biggest and smallest things I had done to offend God, from the time I was falling for David, down to the times I took staples and envelopes from the office for my use at home. Maybe if I came out scrupulously honest and remorseful, He'd glue my life back in place. When it was over, I felt thoroughly cleansed.

In addition to the weekly prayer meetings, I attended a series of teaching sessions conducted by community elders. Two months after I first started as a lamb, on Pentecost Sunday, I was baptized in the Holy Spirit. I walked out of the ceremony feeling like a brand-new person, bleached spotless, ready to take on the sinful world.

I wrote Eric a long letter describing my charismatic renewal journey and why I'd decided to destroy parts of his collection. I assured him that while the nude paintings had to go down, I hadn't burned them; they were in the storage room. That although I knew how much these things meant to him, they had to go to clear the way for Mateo's healing, as well as everyone else's.

For weeks, I waited for Eric's reply. When none came, I assumed he was angry. I wrote again, begging him to come home. By then, he had received three viable offers but hadn't made his choice of a school. Still, he refused to say when he'd come home.

Meanwhile, Mateo's health had improved. His guidance counselor said they could admit him the following year, but he'd have to repeat the third year, and she was concerned that if my son found himself a year behind his old classmates, he might feel defeated.

She had a point, especially because of the school's overly competitive environment. I also began to wonder whether it was wrong to send Mateo there in the first place. After all, it was a science high school, and while being its alumna carried enormous snob appeal, was it the right school for a child who wanted to be a writer or an artist? So I sat my son down and said, "I know that when you passed the admission test, your dad and I got all excited. Miguel, too. And we all assumed that you were just as excited. But let me ask you now, did you really want to go there? Did we ever ask you if you wanted to go?"

"No, you didn't ask me," he said. "But I wanted to, because you said it was the best school, and because you and Miguel had gone there."

"And then?"

"Then I found out that there were too many science courses. Very tough."

That decided it. I regretted having imposed the school on Mateo and started looking for a school to transfer him to. His old school, the UP Integrated School, turned me down, saying they'd given Mateo's slot to someone else. The Jesuit-run Ateneo de Manila was my second choice; they told me they admitted transfers to the second year at the latest, never the third. The other private Catholic schools said the same thing. Because I refused to even try the public schools, knowing the inferior quality of their teaching, I was running out of options. I prayed hard for a way.

One day, after dropping off the kids at school, I was driving to work when I thought of trying the Ateneo one more time. Sure, they'd turned me down earlier, but perhaps I could ask a friend who was the school librarian for help. Before I finished the thought, I swerved to the left to catch the turn toward the Ateneo. I sought my friend in the library. She made some calls and said, "It's true that they don't admit at the third year. But just yesterday, someone dropped out and now they have one available slot. Only one."

I ran to the admission office and pleaded my son's case. And a few days later, he was admitted. Stroke of luck? I called it a miracle.

CHAPTER 28

Eric finally agreed to come home after making a decision on where to do his Ph.D. – at the Louisiana State University in Baton Rouge. I drove to the airport with four giddy children. "Don't expect too many treats," I said. "Your dad doesn't have much money. Don't you miss him? Don't you want to just see him, even if he isn't bringing any surprises for you?"

Of course they did. Oh how much I did.

Eric's skin had grown even fairer, more *mestizo* than when he left ten months earlier. He looked more casual and had lost a bit of weight. When he saw us, he couldn't decide whom to kiss and hug first as we crowded around him. I drove us home amidst the prattle while Eric pulled little gifts for the kids out of his shoulder bag.

At last in bed, I couldn't hold back my tears while we made glorious, glorious love. "What took you so long?" I said afterward. He let his weight collapse on top of me and silently cried. I embraced him as tightly as I could and said nothing more.

I couldn't easily put a finger on why, in spite of the many things my husband had done that hurt me, I still craved physical intimacy with him. I stuck to what I'd learned from BLD: that love is a decision, a commitment, not a mere tingly feeling. A high-speed cable seemed to run between my privates and my heart, that one heart chamber I had reserved for the man I'd vowed to die loving. Whenever I opened that chamber, a signal ran through the cable that quickly opened the other end, my legs... and blurred all the hurts I'd felt. The tingly feeling came with the firm decision to love. And each instance of lovemaking sent a signal in the opposite direction, refreshing my heart and replenishing the hope that had eroded during times of distress.

The next few days, Eric didn't say much as he surveyed his antiques and paintings to see what had survived the spiritual cleansing. I watched him rearrange what remained, remembering the many times in the past when I'd dust the precious pieces – because he didn't want the maids touching them – and I'd carefully put them back the way I found them. When he saw what I'd done, he'd usually reposition an item a teeny bit, perhaps half an inch to the left. Or push a corner of a painting a tad upward, because it wasn't hanging squarely on the wall. I used to tease him about how he seemed to have a surveyor's level built in his head. But this day, I was anxious that he might get angry at what I'd done. Look, your garden is intact, just needs some pruning, I almost said but didn't, for it might annoy him even more.

It was two weeks before Philippine schools opened, and as one happy family, we packed the time with thrilling days at the beach and visits to relatives. Back in Manila, Eric refused to attend a Marriage Encounter retreat with me, but I was pleasantly surprised when he agreed to come with the children to a BLD mass. I thought, The Lord has started working on him. It won't be long now.

One afternoon shortly after school had begun, I was at work when I got a frantic call from my maid. "You know," she said. "Rico... you know."

"What?"

"He fell. A teacher called. He fell from his school bus."

"Why? What happened?"

"They took him to the infirmary. He was unconscious."

I rushed out of the office and took a cab. I hadn't driven to work that day because Eric was going to fetch all the children from their schools, then they would pick me up from work and we'd all go out for dinner. I asked the cab driver to hurry because my son had been in an accident, but he could only speed so much in the traffic. For one long hour, I drove myself crazy, wondering if the maid hadn't been told the whole truth. Is my son alive? If he's alive but seriously hurt, will he still function normally? Why was he in the school bus when his father was supposed to pick him up? How could he fall from the bus? My son cannot die, he's only twelve. I cannot have a dead child, I would die too. Please, dear God, please.

At last, the infirmary. Eric's sister Gina was waiting at the curb for me. "They transferred Rico to Saint Luke's," she said.

I thought, if they took him to a hospital, he must be alive. "He's alive then?" I said.

"Yes, yes," she said, and that calmed me down.

"Thank God," I said. "But was he badly hurt?"

I asked the same cab to take us to the hospital. During the drive, Gina told me what had happened. Eric had first fetched Isabel and together they went to Rico's school. When they got there, they learned that Rico had playfully stood at the door of the school bus after the rest of the students had boarded. Then the bus moved and about a block later, Rico jumped off. Obviously, he didn't mean to ride all the way because he was expecting Eric to fetch him. He fell on the asphalt road and was unconscious when bystanders picked him up and rushed him to the university infirmary. When Eric and Isabel arrived at the infirmary, Rico had come to, and Eric decided to move him to a hospital for more thorough checks.

I walked into the hospital room, my heart banging on my ribs. There was my son, lying on a bed, his eyes open, looking at me. My son was alive! Jesus, thank you, thank you, thank you. I stroked his hair and kissed him. "How are you, my little boy?" I said. "Where does it hurt?"

He looked relieved to see me but said nothing. There was a bruise on his forehead and some scratches on his arms. After three days, we took him home when the doctors found no fractures or internal injuries. The only restriction was that he was to stay in bed for a week and to make sure his head was not jarred. It was not easy to keep him in bed because ever since he could walk, he'd always needed to be moving about, climbing trees and even door jambs, which was why I fondly called him my little monkey.

Eric stayed with Rico at home while I was at work. He bought whatever food the boy wanted and watched TV with him. Although I shuddered at the idea that my son could have died in that fall, I suspected it was God's way of making Eric stay and protect his family. Among our three boys, Eric had a special fondness for Rico. He'd sometimes taken the boy along on business trips before he was in pre-school, so he could have airplane rides. Now that his little boy was nearing his teens, wouldn't he love to be around to guide him, to make sure he grew into a fine young man? And how about Isabel, his little princess? She was a very tender seven and she'd ached for her father all those ten months. I couldn't see why Eric would punish himself – and his children – with the pain of separation. And how about the wife? Didn't he ever pine for his poor wife?

Two months later, however, Eric again left for the States, this time to start his Ph.D. Every night, I prayed for God to help my husband settle in a new place, to send angels to cheer him up and keep him safe. I pushed back the thought of the three years ahead – for Eric had said the Ph.D. was going to take at least three years, not two. Three long years of raising and supporting four children by myself. Three more long, loveless, lonely years.

After being baptized in the Holy Spirit, I became a full-fledged member of the BLD community. I now rose earlier at dawn, at half past three, to pray and read the Bible more intensely than ever before. Then I prepared for work and got the children ready for school. We were out the door at six a.m. to beat the traffic. I drove the kids to school, then on to work, thumbing my rosary beads, with praise songs on my car stereo. I went to mass during my lunch hour. Most nights after work, I attended BLD activities like teaching sessions, prayer meetings, bible-sharing groups – all to advance in holiness. I now also spent a good part of many weekends with the community.

Eric wrote that he had found a small apartment within his budget. It was quite a distance from school and since he didn't have a car, he had to walk both ways. After working long hours at the computer lab, he'd walk home tired and hungry in the chilly autumn night. There was no way he could eat out, it was too expensive. "Very tough life," he wrote. I felt sorry for him, thinking of how he'd never had to do housework in our home, and how he'd gotten used to driving himself everywhere, even if it was only a kilometer away. How he never had to think twice about eating out. And how, after my own long day at work, I used to give him a massage almost every night.

I wrote him long, encouraging letters each week, careful not to sound like I wasn't weary myself. Sometimes I mailed him cassette tapes of the children's voices and mine – with perhaps the dog barking or silverware tinkling in the background – to give him sounds of home. He wrote back, too, but not as often and not as long. Every now and then, he sent things for the children, like VHS tapes of Disney movies, books and toys, and once in a while, a voice tape that I'd listen to over and over until I memorized each word. The sound of his voice lulled me into feeling that he was around and all was well.

After four months, he wrote to say he'd found a Catholic church in the area, a pleasant surprise for me because he hadn't gone to church in maybe twenty years. The miracle was underway!

For Christmas, I got together with Beatriz and Verna and her husband Bong, the only ones of the old group from university remaining in Manila. Verna, who kept up with the latest in fashion, had her hair in little wet-looking curls playfully dangling over her eyes and wore a skirt just above her knee. She was forty – we all were – but her legs were still lean and smooth while mine had started to show some varicose veins. "I love your hair," I said, touching her curls.

She tilted her head provocatively and said, "Thank you. Let's get yours done like this, too. That ponytail makes you look like a *manang*."

I fixed the black bow that held my hair in a bundle. "But aren't I a *manang*?" I said. Apart from meaning older sister, *manang* was also used to refer to the old women who served at the church, typically wearing veils, long dresses and sullen faces to match. "Besides, I once tried curls and looked like an idiot."

"Well, at least let's get your hair styled. And please, your dresses. Show off a bit of the pretty little thing hiding under them."

"For your information, my dear friends," I said, "my latest calling is to be a nun."

Laughter.

"I'm not kidding," I said, for it was true. My saint model, Santa Rita, became a nun after she was widowed and I'd sometimes wished I could escape my stressful life and enter the convent instead, and spend the rest of my days praying and serving the poor. It sounded much simpler that way.

"You go to mass daily?" Beatriz said. "Why?"

"I love Jesus," I said. "If you love someone dearly, wouldn't you want to spend as much time as you could with that person?"

"Okay," Verna said. "But you also need to let your hair down a bit. You're too uptight. Go out and socialize, for God's sake."

"No time to socialize. And I don't want to give Eric any reason to think I might be running around. Besides, the kids have only me now, so I choose to spend every spare minute with them. I don't go on business trips anymore, I send my staff instead." I started to cry. "It's hell, well, almost, so I'd like to cling to heaven."

I told them how I was praying and working for a miracle. How I knew it was coming soon. As ever, the safety of their welcoming ears soothed my frayed nerves. "And you know what?" I said. "I, of course, make the day-to-day decisions regarding the children, but I do consult him on bigger issues of discipline. What does he do? He gives me his opinion but refuses to talk to the child about it, saying it's better if I do it. Freaks me out."

Bong shook his head and said, "He abdicated, so he doesn't feel like he has a right to impose anything on the children."

"You're right," I said. "But why abdicate in the first place?"

"I can't imagine how a serious husband and father can do that," he said. "Knowing him, he'd not have done it on impulse."

"You mean I should take it as a clear sign that he wants out?" I said.

"Maybe he's intimidated by you. You've got everything, you can do everything. Maybe he doesn't feel needed."

Eric wants out? No, not possible.

After a year in Baton Rouge, Eric came home for the summer, and we filled the month with trips to Montaña, to beaches, to Baguio. I invited him once more to a BLD Marriage Encounter weekend, but again he refused. I didn't insist and simply enjoyed his presence.

Once Eric was back in Baton Rouge, although overseas calls were expensive, I made sure the children and I spoke with him at least once a week. On one phone call a couple of months later, Eric sounded distressed. "I miss you," he said. "Can you come and visit?"

If I only had the power of bi-location like some saints, I'd have appeared in front of him in a snap, so even if I had to empty my bank account, I went. I arrived in Baton Rouge on Thanksgiving weekend and stayed for two weeks. Eric couldn't get his hands off me, and we both felt like honeymooners. I cleaned up his place, shopped and cooked his favorite food, did his laundry, and ironed his clothes.

"You're spoiling me," he said. "And when you leave, I'll have a hard time getting used to normal life again."

"There's an easy fix to that," I said. "How about I move in with you, be your full-time homemaker? I can throw in some hard-core sex, too, for free."

"You know it's not possible at this time," he said.

"Would you like an instant brood with that? I can bring four."

He turned serious. "I do miss the children. And you. But…"

"Can't you bring us as your dependents? Aren't you allowed?"

"Technically, I am. But I have to show proof that I can financially support all of you, because you won't be allowed to work here."

That killed me. He was earning barely enough for himself. And although I was making enough to comfortably support the rest of us in Manila, I didn't have the savings to allow me to quit my job and move to the States with the children, and then sit there unemployed for an indefinite period of time.

Still, I needed to find a way for us to be together, for wasn't a family supposed to be together? I had read enough accounts of teen-agers acting up because of absentee fathers and I wanted to prevent that from happening to my own kids. "You know this, but I'll say it again," I said. "All you have to do is say when, and I'll drop everything in Manila, pack up the children and be by your side in a heartbeat. Wherever on this planet you may be at that time."

"But I thought you didn't want to move here. What changed?"

"The children miss you, they need you. I do, too. We have to be together as a family, no other way. And if you prefer to settle here in the States, then we're all going to move in here with you. As soon as it's feasible, that is. The kids are all excited with the idea of living here. At least Isabel and Mateo are. Rico doesn't seem keen."

"I'm working my ass off, can't you see?"

"I know, I know. But I'm just saying I can't wait to be full-time wife and mom. Oh, how I'll pamper you. I'll give you a massage every night…"

"You're just saying that," he said. "But you cannot not work. You're cross when you're not working."

He had a point – I could get bored without a job after a long while – but I took offense. What I heard was rejection, that he didn't want me to join him in the States.

"Happy birthday!" Eric sounded cheerful.

"Thank you, thank you," I said. "Know what? I was promoted to senior vice president. A nice raise, but a ton more responsibility."

"Your boss should pay you double for the kind of work he squeezes out of you."

"I know," I said. "It's crazy at work. And here at home. I'm drained, exhausted. Lonely. How I miss you."

He was silent for a while, then said, "I'm sorry to hear that. Life is tough here, too. I have to check crappy test papers daily. Students here are lazy, a far cry from the hardworking ones at UP. Then there's my own coursework to do. I have no one to do household chores for me. Good for you, you're not alone. You can't be lonely the way I am."

"I just need someone to talk to," I said, feeling like he was belittling my issues. "And being my husband, you are the most logical choice."

"It's all my fault," he said.

He had used this line before to end similar conversations. I took the cue, shut up and called each of the kids to talk to him. Afterwards, I opened the children's birthday cards and small presents. Rico, my quietest child, wrote: *Every time you go to a prayer meeting, I miss you because they take so long, but I think it's good for you because you can spend more time praying.*

I put my arm around his shoulders and said, "Sorry for the late nights and weekends. I'm doing it for you, for all of us." A fierce pang of guilt gripped me as I thought of the BLD couple who were earnestly serving the community and one day found that their teenage son had hanged himself at home. Of other couples whose children were deep into drugs. Were they overdoing the community bit? Was I? But how could I, why should I, turn back when the miracle was already within smelling distance?

I sought other ways of speeding up the miracle without having to be away from home so much. I had read that spiritual dryness – where God seems to be nowhere and one feels no consolation in the spiritual life – can actually lead to a greater love of God. The great saints like Ignatius and Teresa de Avila suffered long periods of spiritual dryness, but they conquered these by doing spiritual exercises. How to do them? My shepherd Ellie said that just like the saints, she had a spiritual director who helped her along.

I wanted one, too, my own spiritual director. Father Frank would have been perfect, but he was very popular and therefore too busy. So I set my eyes on a young priest who sang the blessings at the end of his masses and who gave not the fire-and-brimstone kind of homilies but funny, down-to-earth ones that struck me in the core.

Before long, I was choosing Father Tim's masses, even if it meant leaving the house an hour earlier in the morning or staying later after work. These became the highlight of my day. One day, I approached him after mass and asked to have a copy of his homily. He said he didn't write it down, but I didn't mind; I was glad to have broken the ice. After a few more short after-mass chats, I found enough courage to ask if he could be my spiritual director. His eyes widened, his brows furrowed. Sensing his impending refusal, I begged him to hear my story first before saying no.

Father Tim had very little time to spare. The first time I went to see him, I told him my story in ten minutes, to save the remaining five for whatever he was going to say. "I'm falling apart," I said.

"No, you're not," he said. "You're doing all the right things."

I walked away thinking, You don't get it at all; I'm going crazy and I need help. Somebody, anybody, please listen to me!

When the school year ended, Mateo graduated from high school at the Ateneo de Manila, and Miguel finished his physics degree at UP, heavily decorated. Two more children's milestones without their father. I posed for pictures with my beaming boys, feeling sad about the missing face. How many big moments had

Eric missed by now? Isabel's first communion and ballet recitals, Rico's puppet show, father-and-son camps with only the sons showing up, big and small school programs, three Christmases, fifteen birthdays if you included mine. Memories crowded my mind of my kids on a stage, their eyes anxiously scanning the audience until they found me grinning, giving them an eager wave.

For a summer treat, I took the children to Hong Kong. Flying from Baton Rouge, Eric met us there and we all had a fabulous time for a few days. Eric stayed for a couple more weeks in Manila.

One Saturday morning, Eric and I were lingering at the table after breakfast, reading the papers, when the doorbell rang. "Manang, it's that woman again." The maid sounded annoyed.

I rose for the door. "Ma'am, good morning, it's Petra," the woman at the gate called out. I talked to her for a few minutes, then I went to our bedroom and returned with a hundred pesos. After taking the money, she thanked me and hurried away.

"Who was that?" Eric said, a curious look on his face.

"Petra. I found her crying at our gate one afternoon. She said her husband had just left her and five small children, and they were being evicted from their rented room. She wanted to go back to her family in Pangasinan and needed money for bus fare. I gave her eight hundred, old clothes, canned sardines, rice."

He looked at me, big eyes popping out, and said, "And?"

"She was happy, and I was happy to have helped. A few weeks ago, she was at our gate again. She'd left her children with her mother and had come back to Manila to start a small fish stall at the market and could I lend her some money. I gave her three thousand; she promised to pay me back in installments soon. Today she said she needed just a little bit more."

"So you gave her again? How much?"

"Not much. Only a hundred."

Eric shook his head slightly and smirked. "She's bilking you, can't you see?"

"She may or she may not, but my conscience won't let me turn away someone in need."

"Ever gullible," he said. "Remember Edna, your high school friend? The one who conned you into co-signing a loan and vanishing with the money. How much was that?"

"Thirty thousand," I said. "God will take care of her. I actually give a tenth of my earnings back to God now. So, when I help the likes of Petra, the money comes from the ten per cent for God."

"Gross or net?"

It was my turn to be incredulous. "If we pay taxes to our corrupt government based on gross income, why should we cheat God and use net?"

"Are you serious?" His tone was sober now. "Even if you use net, that's seventeen thousand each month. That's what... six, seven hundred dollars."

"God gives back a hundredfold to those who tithe in full faith. And it doesn't have to be material wealth."

He stood and walked quietly to the garden. He didn't look angry, just uneasy. Why would he fret? It was my money I was giving away. Although I knew that six hundred dollars a month could make his life in the States much more comfortable, hadn't he been refusing my help lately? Hadn't he said no to my offers to buy him plane tickets so he could spend all these past three Christmases with us? Was it my fault if he was scraping bottom?

For the third time, I had arranged for Eric and me to attend a Marriage Encounter retreat with BLD. For the third time, he refused. "How about a private retreat?" I said. "Just you and me and a priest."

"No," he said, more bluntly this time.

"Well, no priest then. Just you and me in a sacred place."

The way Eric looked at me reminded me of how Daddy glared at me when he was fed up, his eyes telling me to shut up or else a whack in the butt was on its way. So shut up I did.

After Eric left once more for Baton Rouge, my shepherd Ellie invited me to a weekend retreat in Don Bosco Batulao, in nearby Batangas province. I grabbed the chance because I had never done a spiritual retreat before, and I wanted a taste of what I'd heard was a very enlightening experience. It was just Ellie and me for two days of quiet with the Lord. I picked her up in my car and drove south toward the green countryside. Barely two hours later, as we approached the retreat center, Mount Batulao loomed to our left. I'd never paid much attention to that mountain before, but this day, when I glanced at its jagged peaks, it reminded me of Good Fridays back in Montaña when, as a child, I'd stand along the road with Chona to watch the evening procession. Old women holding lighted candles and singing church hymns walked alongside statues of saints on carriages. I'd be proud of myself for knowing all their names, but one thing scared me: a glass box trimmed with flowers – the *Santo Entierro*, Jesus Christ in a glass casket wearing a scarlet robe and a crown of thorns on His bloodied head.

Today, the jagged peaks of Mount Batulao looked like the profile of the *Santo Entierro* of my childhood: the crown of thorns, a broken nose, jutting jaw, bony chest.

The retreat center stood on top of a hill at the foot of the mountain. The moment I stepped out of the car and into the whistling breeze, I felt an intense kind of peace. The gentle Irish rector welcomed us and spoke kindly about God's love, then he mostly left us alone. I headed for the chapel and started weeping at its door. Everywhere I went, the silence rocked me in its embrace. I roamed in the wild garden that looked out into the foggy, rain-soaked side of Mount Batulao and wept all weekend, wondering if anybody fully understood why all those tears were gushing out. Did Christ? Not the dead one but the resurrected one?

If Jesus was alive and within earshot, I wanted Him to tell me why my husband was still physically and emotionally distant after the demons in my urns and books and other household things were gone, after all my intensive prayers and masses and confessions and rosaries, after transforming myself into the virtuous wife described in the psalm, after blindly giving away a tenth of what I broke my back to earn. What was so wrong with wanting a family intact? What else had I not done to deserve it?

Reading the Bible, something struck me, a passage where Jesus is asked by his apostles why they couldn't drive away some demons, and He replies, "This kind is driven away only by prayer and fasting." Was I up against some headstrong demon? I decided to fast.

After the retreat, I began to deny myself food. One day each week, I ate nothing but plain bread and water, ignoring the headaches and weakness that accompanied the hunger.

There was a consistent theme in the things I heard and read: forgiveness. Forgive seventy times seven. Four hundred ninety times? The priests said it's not a literal seventy times seven but a symbol of a continuing process. Like an onion, you go deeper each time until there's nothing left. What, until your guts spill out?

In full faith, I examined my past once more. There was Daddy, whose sleeping around had greatly angered me, but he'd long been dead so all I could do was pray for the salvation of his soul, begging God not to throw him into the eternal fire. Then there was my cousin Zenay who wailed like a widow when my father died. I forgave her deeply before my baptism in the Holy Spirit but had to admit that some bitterness still lingered in my heart. I decided to speak to Marya about it one night when the house was already quiet. She was now twenty-six, done with university, had a job but still living with me.

"I need you to listen to me," I said. "There's something you need to know."

She said, "Did I do anything wrong?"

I said no and started telling her about the day Chona saw Daddy sleeping with our cousin Zenay. As I went on, her face froze, her eyes aglow with fear. Then she began to sob.

"You must be angry at Dad," I said, rubbing her back. "It's okay to be angry. You must feel sorry for Mom, too."

"You don't understand," she said, shaking her head violently.

I assured her I did.

"No!" She sobbed even harder. "I've been keeping this to myself since I was three."

"What?"

"Manang Aning…" She tried to catch her breath. Manang Aning had been her nanny, Zenay's younger sister, the one who'd run away twice.

"I was very small. Dad would give me a box of raisins and tell me to play in one corner of the room."

"What do you mean?" I said, holding my breath.

"I'd sit there quietly with my raisins and my doll and play… until Daddy and Manang Aning stood up from the bed."

"What the fucking hell?" I said. "Her too?"

My kid sister kept on sobbing while I sat stiff. Just who was this man I called Daddy? The son of the devil? Instead of going a few little steps forward in holiness, I slid a hundred steps back as I held not just another onion to peel to the core, but a huge, freshly-uprooted one, all covered in sod and flakes of dung.

I wrote one long letter to my mother and siblings, saying I needed to forgive everyone who had ever hurt me and be forgiven in return, and I might as well begin with them. I listed everything I was forgiving them for. The times I fought with my siblings, as many as I could recall. The fact that Mom had wished I'd been a boy, with the result that I felt unwanted and unloved, even ugly. Her inaction and seeming indifference when I told her about Daddy's affair with Zenay long, long ago, making me feel that we, her children, weren't important enough to fight for. I told her I'd thought her dull-witted, a coward. At the end of the twenty-odd pages, I humbly asked for their forgiveness for the countless times that I had also hurt them.

And then I wrote Eric a similar letter, just as long, but more pained. I said I was forgiving him for being unfaithful, for abandoning me and the children, and for sometimes being unkind. I didn't as yet know how to approach my two cousins, so I prayed more about them and Dad.

I heard from my siblings first. Chona spoke to me amidst a waterfall of tears but didn't explain why she had chosen to keep quiet about Dad's sleeping with Zenay. The two boys Francis and Sonny had had no clue about Dad's secrets until they read my letter. Marya said she felt much better, after releasing the heavy load she'd borne alone for so long.

Then I received a letter from Mom – seven typewritten pages. No, she never wished I'd been a boy, it was Dad who did. On the contrary, she'd always treasured and was immensely proud of me. She was deeply grateful for my taking over Dad's duties as family provider, for the checks I was sending her each month. If she had chosen not to confront Dad about his affairs, it was because she didn't want us to grow up shamed. She admitted that she was never happy with Dad, that he gambled away all his salary even before he received it, and that she had solely supported us on her own meager earnings. No, she had never told any of this to anyone except God. And yes, the deepest of her wounds were those that had to do with the string of women, beginning with Chona's nanny when Mom was away teaching in a distant village. Then came Zenay, then Aning, then Rosita. And God knows who else outside the home.

Rosita?

Dad routinely had sex with all three sisters? I've lived for forty-one years without knowing this? Any more dirty secrets out there?

After more inner raging and praying, I sat down to write each of the three sisters. It dawned on me that perhaps Daddy had forced them, and they were mere victims instead of temptresses. It was I who needed forgiving, for the hatred and contempt I'd held onto for so long. But then I'd remember the private jokes and giggles between Dad and Zenay, and I'd flinch and get mixed up all over again. Yet I forged on and wrote in the most civil manner I could manage. Wanting to end the silent war for all our sakes, I offered forgiveness and sincerely asked them to forgive me as well.

I expected to receive letters afterwards, hoping to read about their relief and understanding. None came, except one from Eric replying to my long one – two or three lines to say I'd make a good writer of spiritual books and that he'd write me longer when he found the time. Convinced that it would indeed take him time to bare his soul, I waited patiently.

Besides my mother and siblings, did any living creature take me seriously? Father Tim didn't have enough time to listen to what was bothering me, so I decided to write him, too, about my struggles and why I was desperate for someone to help me see the way. One morning, I brought the letter to mass, planning to hand it to him afterwards. He wasn't there. Two more days passed and he wasn't at any of the masses. I asked the parish priest about Father Tim and was told that he had left the priesthood!

How was that possible? I felt the familiar big hand squeeze my head and chest, the mighty hand declaring that I was abandoned yet again.

Because I also personally knew the parish priest, I showed him the letter. After reading it, he said that one thing he did when overwhelmed was to go to a cemetery and just sit there for a while, to be reminded that all things shall pass.

I thanked him and went to work. At mid-day, I left the office and drove to a memorial park near my home. It was a new cemetery built on a hillside dotted with ancient mango trees. There were but a few tombstones, all toasting in the unforgiving August sun. Besides a handful of people visiting gravesites, I was alone in the wide expanse of green and brown. With, of course, the souls that lay still under the dry earth.

I parked at the farthest end, close to a lonely grave. I read the epitaph: Berto, sixteen years old. What did this boy die of? Hit by a car? *Dengue?* Drugs? I read the loving words from his parents and started to cry. I sat on the grass, sweating in my business suit and pantyhose. I cried for Berto's parents whose hearts must have been shattered and for the poor boy whose life ended before he could figure out what he wanted to become. Wept for envy of everyone in the grave who was now free of life's unjust blows. I cried and cried, not knowing any more what I was crying about.

Apart from the risk of Berto's family finding me weeping at his grave, I found the spot a good place to let my tears go. At least it wouldn't bother my children. Or the people at work who surely were curious when I showed up at meetings with swollen eyes. Safer too, than crying in my car while driving.

I headed for home totally drained and slept very little. The next morning, I decided to go on a serious fast. Coffee in the morning. A throbbing headache for lunch. A floating sensation most of the afternoon. After work, on the way to a prayer meeting or a BLD teaching session, burger and fries with Coke from a McDonald's drive-through. My new routine became: early hours at prayer, a harrowing workday, one hurried junk meal, late night, and at most four hours in bed – barely asleep.

I called Eric in Baton Rouge, offering to visit him. "Not now," he said. "I'm too busy."

With no one else to talk to, I went back to my self-talk: If I fasted and prayed hard enough, all this shall pass.

That Saturday was just another bright October morning. It was Mateo's turn to go to the supermarket with me. We were there early, so we'd have enough time to get to Chona's place for her birthday lunch. I was loading the shopping cart with cans of Spam when I tripped on Mateo's foot. I gripped the cart to keep from slipping, ignored a feeling of lightheadedness, and went on with the shopping.

Once we got home and the maids had unloaded the trunk, Rico and Isabel hopped in the back seat – Miguel had left to be with friends – and we headed for the birthday lunch. Halfway up the mountain to Antipolo, on the narrow winding road, I felt like the car was floating on air. Then the road began to tilt and slowly spin. I pulled over.

"Why, Mommy?" Mateo said.

"I'm dizzy. It's bad. Let's go back home."

None of my boys was old enough to be licensed to drive, so I had no choice but to drive home myself. I sat still for a few minutes until the spinning subsided, then carefully turned around for home.

"Pray. No, let's sing." I said and began, "I am the Lord that healeth thee, I am the Lord your Healer…"

Thank God we made it safely home. But three hours later, an ambulance wailed in the Saturday afternoon gridlock. Inside, I lay dazed, looking blankly at Mateo who sat beside me, anxiously stroking my arm.

CHAPTER 29

Although I didn't pass out, I lay dizzy and trembling in the ambulance. When we reached the hospital, they wheeled me out, and I could see my poor Mateo trying to catch up, his face crumpled with fear. They set my gurney along a wall, and a nurse came to ask me questions.

"Does anyone in your family suffer from heart disease?" the nurse was saying.

"My father," I said. "Died at fifty-four." Then I heard a frantic shuffle of feet and an insistent 'Code blue, code blue, emergency!' on the intercom.

"Would you know what ailed his heart?" she said.

The shuffle came nearer, and a group of workers wheeled a gurney to the spot next to mine. "What does code blue mean?" I said, looking at the burly man lying stiff on the stretcher. A plump fifty-ish woman in a threadbare duster and rubber flip-flops clutched the man's hand. As more hospital workers rushed to attend to the man, my nurse drew the green curtain around me. She ignored my question and repeated hers. Once she was satisfied with my answers, she said that someone would be with me shortly and left. Some of the frantic voices behind the curtain were saying 'DOA' and a woman started screaming. For all my envy of the dead, I was gripped with the basest instinct to cling to life. I kept mumbling strings of Our Fathers and Hail Marys until a resident came to ask me the same set of questions. I patiently answered them all and was told that Doctor Quizon was on his way.

Guerrero, my workplace, was a fast-growing conglomerate. In my eight years with the company, I had helped establish a life insurance company and a health maintenance organization. By now, I was in charge of client services for four companies, the HMO among them, so the company's medical team – led by the gentle, no-nonsense Doctor Jay Quizon – reported to me. We respected each other's professional expertise, and I had asked him to be my primary physician.

When at last, Doctor Jay arrived and held my hand, I said, "I thought you'd never come."

"What are you doing to yourself?" he said, shaking his head. "Your blood pressure is high."

"Don't give me bad news," I said. "I can't take bad news."

"We have to run some tests," he said. "We're admitting you, can't say how long. You're my boss at Guerrero, but here, I order you what to do. One word: rest."

"Then drug me but make sure I wake up," I muttered.

"*Ako ang bahala*," he said, squeezing my hand. That was his standard response to problems at work, meaning he was going to take charge. I calmed down.

"Don't worry, son," I said to Mateo, who had been standing by my side all along. "I'll be okay."

Technicians came to draw blood. I was given an intravenous drip. Miguel came rushing. Chona and Marya spent the night in my room. "You're too uptight, silly girl," Chona said. "Look at you. You really need to have some fun, loosen up."

"*Tatlong sine lang yan, 'di ba?*" Marya said. She usually went with Chona to the movies while I excused myself saying I had to go to BLD or do something for the children. Since Chona left her husband six years earlier, her three-movie formula of dealing with heartbreak had become a classic in our family.

In the morning, Jay returned. "Your cholesterol is up there," he said, pointing to the ceiling.

"How high?" I said, surprised. "I hardly eat."

"Incredibly high. That's the problem – you cannot not eat. You need to eat. Three things: enough rest, exercise, the right foods. That's all."

"You make it sound simple. You see how I slave at work, don't you? And the driving alone…"

"I do. And I know as well that you hardly sleep. Now you tell me you hardly eat. That's slow-motion suicide, my friend. You have to de-stress."

Later that day, I was paged for a phone call at the nurses' station. Chona helped me up. My knees felt like jelly, the room swayed. Chona held my Dextrose bottle above my head and supported me as I walked the few steps to the nurses' station.

It was Eric. "What happened?" he said.

"I got dizzy while driving up Antipolo," I said. "Hypertension, high cholesterol. Mateo saved me."

"Who's looking after you?"

"Jay," I said, holding back my tears. "He won't let me die."

"Please take care and keep me posted," he said.

A cardiologist came to see me, and then a neurologist. I had X-rays and ultrasounds. After three days, Jay discharged me and ordered two weeks' rest at home, with a supply of sleeping pills.

The children looked relieved to have me back home. We hugged each other tight without voicing the fears in our minds. I didn't tell them I was lucky I didn't have a quick, treacherous heart attack. That I could very well be my father's daughter and go the way he did, succumbing at fifty-four to extreme hypertension and a heart attack, perhaps even outdo him and drop dead at forty-one. A picture of my four beautiful kids wailing over my casket played over and over in my mind.

My mother came to San Jacinto and made sure that all the

doctor's orders were followed – the right foods, medication, rest. I had just woken from my nap one afternoon when she came to sit on my bed to watch TV with me. My mother, now sixty-seven and retired, still looked beautiful even with her gray roots showing. Her jowls had started to sag and her eyelids drooped over her gentle eyes.

I said, "Mommy, how come you don't have as many wrinkles as your friends?"

She smiled her wise smile and said, "They smear all kinds of creams on their faces. You know me, just plain soap and water."

"And Johnson's baby powder," I said, picturing the pink crystal powder case that had sat on her dresser for as long as I could remember, with the fawn that stood on its lid that I called Bambi.

"Plus a bit of lipstick," she said.

"Red lipstick. You're so serene, mother dear. How do you do it? Can you tell me more about the long letter you sent me? I mean, Daddy and the women. Who was Chona's nanny? Was it Mona? The bow-legged woman in the picture?" I was referring to a photo in my album: Mommy, me, Chona and her nanny, seated on a sofa. Tall, large-boned, stark-looking woman.

"Yes," she said. "That's her. I hate to remember it, too painful. It went so far that it could not be hidden."

"I have a sibling somewhere?"

"No, they had it aborted."

"What? How could you stand that?"

"As my nature is, I kept silent. If I raised hell, the whole world would know. My only consolation was that your Dad admitted it and asked for forgiveness. From then on, it was a closed book."

"Just like that? Didn't you slap his face even once?"

She gave me a look that said: Are you crazy?

"Mom, I'd have kicked him in the groin, God bless his soul. Hang him upside down by the balls…"

Swallow all the pain to keep the goddamn almighty dignity. I'm sorry, darling, it was hot so I took off my clothes, tripped over the nanny and accidentally fucked her. It's alright, my love, I forgive you in the name of God; now go and fuck some more.

Same plot, different scripts, my mother's life and mine.

After a few moments, my mother wiped a tear and said, "I've cried an ocean – by myself, naturally – and have long forgiven your dad. Your cousins, too. Maybe they were helpless."

"But they're your nieces, Mom. So essentially, that's incest."

"I believe there was also at least one abortion among them. Help me pray, will you? I need the grace to thoroughly forgive."

"Mommy, your life is one high-intensity forgiveness exercise. What more do you need to do? You were never mean to your nieces, and you treat them as close family even now."

Mom never threw out any of my cousins. Aning ran away twice. Rosita got married. After Dad died, Zenay stayed with Mom at home and they got along well, which drove me nuts. Together, they looked after Marya, who had a hard time dealing with Dad's death. A few years later, Francis went home to Montaña after he finished university in UP and couldn't find a suitable job in Manila. He settled in with the two women and Marya, and all was well until one day, he and Zenay had a big fight. When I heard the news, I wrote Zenay to say that I'd known all along how she'd cheated on Mom for years, and if she had any trace of shame left in her body, she should leave my mother's home. She did, but afterwards she and Francis made up. Also, she and Mom continued to be good to each other, so I eventually gave up and let them all be.

"I have no problem with your cousins. They're my kin and they're the ones I can easily run to when I need help. My problem is Mona. After more than forty years, I still carry some resentment."

"I think you've done all you could. More than you should."

My mother nodded and looked at the TV while my mind remained on Francis. After returning to Montaña, my brother managed a store that Auntie Celina had started with her retirement money. He quit after a couple of years, frustrated with how he wasn't free to implement his own ideas. Which was no surprise, because he clearly detested authority. He did private violin tutoring for a few years, and a year ago, with some financial help from Mom and me, opened his own art and music school in Laoag.

By now, my mother and brother had been in a love-hate relationship for eight years. Mom would tell me on the phone, "Can you talk to your brother? He's such a headache, hangs out too much with his gay friends. See, he's not home yet." And I would say, "But, Mother, it's only seven p.m. and your son is past thirty." And she'd say, "But they drink!"

On the other hand, Francis would complain of how Mom wanted him to do things just so, like buy bread only from one particular store, or how she found a lot of his ideas for the school quirky and therefore too risky. "Live apart from her and do things your way," I would say. And he'd say, "But each time I bring up the idea, she develops a fever."

Mom sat there focused on her favorite TV soap. I waited for a commercial break and then said, "By the way, how's Francis doing? He should be happy being his own boss now."

"Thank God he's getting more and more students. He's very busy, but I try to guide him. I'm afraid that boy will squander the money because he doesn't pay attention to his costs."

"Mom, *that boy* is thirty-six. Why don't you give him a free hand and let him fail if he has to? He cannot thrive under someone else's control."

"He comes home drunk, won't put out the lights, even leaves the front door unlocked. How can I leave him alone?"

I hoped Eric would come running home. Instead, he wrote to scold me.

I think that now is finally a good time for me to do a little nagging myself. I have refrained over the past so many months from admonishing you about your not taking care of your physical well-being. You've just kept on going and going with hardly enough sleep each day, and I guess that that tough grind has finally caught up with you.

If I have refrained from doing this, it's probably in part because I learned some years back how you resent being 'prevented' from performing your religious obligations. You remember those early morning trips to UP for the misa de Aguinaldo which we fought about? Since then, and, more so, ever since you became deeply involved with the charismatic movement, I have made a conscious effort not to get in your way. As I told you in my previous letter, we do not exactly see eye to eye on some (that could be an understatement) of your beliefs and practices, but I owe it to you to at least respect your choices and to leave you be. Clearly, you have found a great deal of inner peace and happiness, in spite of all the turmoil you've been through in life – and I have, after all, been a significant source of that turmoil – because of your faith and hope and charity, three virtues that the Scriptures preach and which you have learned to embrace and practice so well. And I do respect you for those virtues.

But your body can only take so much punishment from the hectic schedule that you impose upon yourself. The traffic situation and your heavy workload at the office are certainly not of your own choice. But you do get up so early every morning, notwithstanding the late hour you are able to get to bed especially when you come from your prayer meetings and other BLD activities. And even your weekends haven't been decent weekends at all. I do appreciate how much you value prayer and bible reading, and I cannot fault you for that. But please learn to slow down. At almost 42 and with no cardiovascular exercise, your body isn't as fit as it was 5 years ago. Sorry to have to nag you. I love you.

I thought: Yes, it's my fault that I ended up in Emergency. Jay has lectured me enough on that. But aren't you rushing home to look after me? Remember how I'd skip work to nurse you when you had the slightest hint of the flu? How you'd never go to the dentist without me? How I'd give you a rubdown almost each night? Remember, my love?

After a week on sleeping pills, the doctor told me to stop. The first night, I was awakened by a nightmare and couldn't easily get back to sleep. It happened again the following night, as well as the next. Each night, I had the same bad dream followed by a struggle to move my numb limbs. Not unlike the horrible times long ago when frequent nightmares and sleep paralysis made me dread going to bed.

I roused my mother one night when the terror became unbearable. "Please keep me company for a while. Tell me stories. Anything. I miss you, Mom."

She rubbed her eyes and got up. "I miss you too, *balasang ko*," she said. "You were very young when you left home."

"Very young, terribly homesick," I said. "I can't forget those very tough days."

"It was tough for me as well. I used to cry every night, could barely bear the separation from you. In fact, I sometimes wished you hadn't passed the admission test at all so you wouldn't have to leave. But that chance at your high school was too big to pass up. Even if it hurt me, I let you go, for your future. Your dad had a hard time, too. One day, he arrived from Manila saying you had begged him to take you home and that he almost did. It broke his heart to see you so homesick. You were just too young. But it was all worth it – see where you are now."

I remembered that day. Dad and I had just seen a sad movie, and when he took me back to the dorm, I didn't want to leave the safety of his warm embrace. I had wanted to drop Philippine Science High School altogether and simply go home with him to Montaña. "I can't forget that day," I said. "But I didn't know that Dad almost took me home." My father's chubby face swam before my eyes, a face that could be tender one moment and stern the next. Then his favorite checkered polo shirts, his Rudolph Valentino hair, his spotless leather shoes. I remembered how, without saying so, he made me feel that I was his favorite daughter. How he'd cried when I wanted to get married and how he'd later come to take me back when my husband had an affair. "I miss Daddy," I said. "You don't know how much I longed for your visits. You came every two weeks – that must have cost a lot of money for you."

Mom turned pensive. "What I didn't tell you then, *anak ko*, was how big a financial sacrifice it was for us to do that. You had three other siblings then, and I only had my meager salary…"

"How about Dad's? Wasn't he a college dean?"

"He was a dean, but I never saw his paycheck. He always got advance payments on his salary, all to gamble away at *mah jong*."

I knew he played a lot of *maj jong* but I didn't realize it was that bad. "You mean you raised all of us on your salary alone?"

"Mostly. Yes."

"Oh, Mommy, you're an even bigger saint than I thought."

"By the way," she said, "did I ever tell you what happened to Abogado Blas? He was shot dead in Bacarra in the house of one of his mistresses."

"When? By whom?"

"A few months ago. Who knows? The police are still working on it."

Because she was not one who spoke much about herself, I relished these conversations with Mom. One time, I asked her to tell me more about her childhood.

My mother was fourteen years old when the Second World War broke out. Her family constantly moved from village to mountain village, away from the *población* – the urban part of town – where the Japanese had camped. One morning, a group of Japanese soldiers stormed the village, checking out the girls, taking those they fancied away to rape. The grownups shoved her into a granary. She stood among sheaves of rice, sweating and holding her breath, until her mother, my *lola*, went in at dusk to tell her it was now safe to go out.

Soon afterward, her father fell ill with tuberculosis, and each time they had to move yet again, they bore him on a hammock. He died before the war was over, and Lola carried on with her eight children, my mother the youngest.

As if this weren't enough for a young girl, Mom, with the rest of the town, was made to watch public executions at the town square. The Japanese soldiers poked bayonets into the eyes of those who refused to look. After seeing the Japanese torch Montaña, she developed an acute fear of fire, explosions and gunshots. Many years later, in the eighties, there was a skirmish between government soldiers and Communist rebels close to her home. When she heard gunshots, she scrambled under the dining table. My beautiful, tender mother, alone at home, froze there, and peed in her pants.

But I didn't always want to disturb Mom as she slept. Many nights, I stared at the ceiling thinking, thinking, seeing images in my mind. Of me clinging to my mother each Sunday when she had to go to faraway Daniw or when I was afraid of Dad's punishment. Clinging to my father when he had to leave me at my high school dorm. Relentlessly clinging to Eric – when early on he said he didn't love me, the times he'd wanted to study abroad, as well as now after he's probably walked out.

But I need to cling to Eric! For hadn't we vowed to be together 'til the end of time? Isn't it but proper for me to put in my own bit of effort to make that so? In fact, it's my Christian duty to make that so. Besides, the one time I had tried to be strong and not cling – to David, after I dumped him in college – caused me nothing but pain and regret.

Who would know better than I how terrrifying it is to be abandoned?

Reluctantly, I went back to work when my two weeks were up. I felt a bit stronger and tried to drive, but after a couple of kilometers I felt dizzy, so I turned back home and took a cab to work. I hated having to work again, having to catch up with two weeks' worth of decisions that had waited to be made. Why did everyone lean on me?

A few days later, I was devastated to see Mom go back home to Montaña, realizing that for the first time in my forty-one years, I'd had my mother to myself for a full two weeks. She'd come to help me out whenever I had a baby, but those visits were more about the baby than me.

The nightmares came almost like clockwork now. Many nights, I arose with my legs feeling numb, my heart rapidly beating, and I'd be afraid to go back to sleep and never wake up.

Eric wrote again soon after. During this time, Miguel was busy looking for a graduate school in the States. Helping our firstborn find the best opportunities to foster his genius became a new endeavour that united Eric and me, and we both did what we could to help him with his applications.

I'm still in the office working on some homework problems that are due this week. Hope everything went well with your day and you didn't get dizzy at all. I realize that – if you had your way – you'd rather just stay home and be away from your dreaded work at the office. If only I could just tell you to do that...

I just opened my e-mail mailbox about half an hour ago when I switched on the computer to solve the equation $e^x (1+x) = \frac{1}{2}$, which by the way is solvable using the Excel solver function – but I don't think you'd be interested in that right now, so let me get back on track. I just got an e-mail from Miguel saying that he was going to go ahead with his applications! In particular, the MIT application is due Dec 1st. I'll call you to discuss this new development.

Will have to close for now. Take care. Love again, and miss –

Back in the seventies, Eric and I solved mathematical formulas longhand, sometimes with the aid of a slide rule or of numerical tables at the back of textbooks. When the scientific calculator came about, we retired our slide rules and learned how to program the magical new gadget. In the eighties, we had our first personal computer, and together we taught ourselves how to use the spreadsheet software *Lotus 1-2-3* to do tedious math more conveniently. Now, Eric was sharing the great news that the latest software, *Excel*, was making spoiled children of us mathematicians by solving complex math equations with the touch of even fewer buttons.

This was exciting news alright, but *Excel* and e^x be damned. Had our marital communication come to mere business correspondence?

CHAPTER 30

Eric came home eight months after I fell ill, long after I had gotten back on my feet. By then, I had reluctantly quit BLD.

Gabriel and Liza, the BLD elders who had done spiritual warfare at my home, had advised me to set priorities and were clear about family first, followed by work, and then church and BLD. In the past, most of the members subtly heaped guilt on those who begged off from some activity by saying, "Can't you give just a bit of your time for the Lord?" Because I had wanted to be the perfect handmaid of the Lord, I attended all activities and volunteered where help was needed. It was now a pleasant surprise to hear this suggestion from the leaders themselves.

Even Father Gervasi was firm about the importance of balance. "What you've been doing is fanatical. You cannot go for months without enough sleep or enough food. God is not stupid to expect you to kill yourself praying or helping others."

I then realized that in my desire to be perfect at whatever I had set my mind to, I had approached things in extremes, usually taking my physical limitations for granted. When I was a year away from finishing my math degree, I had been tempted to go into medicine

– which had been my first dream – but I didn't because I couldn't abandon what I had started. When my children were small and I was working to be a licensed actuary, I'd study far into the night after a day at work and get up at dawn to study some more. The moment I committed to something, I didn't allow myself to be mediocre about it, let alone give up.

But because I was now afraid to die, I capitulated and slowed down. I had to acknowledge that the twenty-four hours in a day were not even enough to properly do the now-required exercise, nutrition and rest apart from being a mother and a corporate officer. This meant I had to leave BLD. I had become a hopeless insomniac, though, so sleeping didn't come easily, but I did well in following a strict exercise regimen. I also made sure that I ate regularly, for if I was even a bit hungry, I'd have a dizzy spell. These dizzy spells made me afraid to drive, so I took public transportation to work. Feeble as I was, I did my best to make Eric's two weeks fun for everyone, especially because Miguel was about to leave home as well.

Down to three choices, Miguel had picked the Massachusetts Institute of Technology in Cambridge, which was offering him financial support for a doctorate in biophysics. When I took him to the airport, I felt sad but put on a brave face. I reminded myself that my mother went through the same kind of pain when, at eleven, I left home for boarding school. At least Miguel was ten years older.

"Mommy," he said, hugging me, "I feel that I should stay. Daddy said to take care of you."

"No, son," I said. "There's a big world out there waiting for your hungry brain. Go for it."

As expected, Miguel took to graduate school like a natural. Soon, we started to make grand plans for the following summer. Because Eric was busy with his doctoral dissertation, the children and I would go and visit him in the States instead.

Miguel helped me plan our six-week grand vacation – coordinating schedules, booking air tickets, rental cars, and hotel rooms, and calling the people we'd see. The first three weeks, the children and I would visit Los Angeles, Toronto, Philadelphia, New York, and Washington D.C. The next three precious weeks, we would be with Eric, in Chicago, Baton Rouge and Disney World in Orlando.

It was going to be the three younger children's first trip to North America, and they were all excited, especially about Disney World. But I was most excited about the prospect of being housewife and mother for the almost three weeks that we'd all be together by ourselves, not crashing in other people's homes. This was going to be practice time for us on how to live in America, for when Eric eventually brought us to be with him, and I'd be a simple housewife and mom, free from corporate-world stress. I daydreamed about all these things, and of the long talks I'd have with my husband to plan our new life.

The children and I had a great time the first three weeks. The day we flew to Chicago, we all couldn't wait to reunite with Eric after many months. On our first night in Chicago, after everyone else had gone to bed in Eric's uncle's house, Eric sat in the living room couch watching TV. I curled up close to him and then lay my head on his lap, my skin tingling in anticipation of furious lovemaking. "I missed you," I said, stroking his thigh.

His eyes fixed on the TV, he said nothing. I looked: a SWAT team was on its way to the house where a pretty woman was being held at gunpoint. "It's late," I said. "Let's go to bed."

The SWAT arrived. One of them shouted through a megaphone.

"*May kasalanan ako sa iyo*," Eric said, the red lights from the TV swirling on his face.

Stunned, I braced myself. What was this new confession about, yet another woman? He sired a child? I got up and sat beside him, moving a few inches away to be able to see his face. "What?" I said, tugging at his arm.

301

"I gave up my apartment," he said, looking at me for a moment, then casting his eyes down.

"When?" I said and turned off the TV. "But weren't you there yesterday when I called?"

"Yesterday was my last day."

"What? Where will you have all six of us stay?"

"My lease was up yesterday. I don't have any income until I can find a job. Couldn't afford to keep the place any longer."

He explained that his teaching assistantship was over, and he had no more source of income. That he needed another four months to finish his doctorate. Before then, he'd have no time for a job and planned to move to a cheaper place during that time, maybe just a room. But actually, his friend Anding had offered to put him up in his house.

"Why didn't you even mention it to me?"

No answer.

"How much is four months' rent?" I said. "You know I could've helped you. All you needed to do was ask."

He shrugged.

"Where will we all stay these next two weeks? Apart from the three hotel nights that Miguel has booked in Orlando, where do we stay?"

"I've arranged with Anding and Dely," he said. "I've moved my things to their place and will stay there until I find a room to rent. They have two spare rooms. We're all welcome there."

Anding was from my hometown Montaña, but I'd met him only once before. The couple had become Eric's 'family' in Baton Rouge. But still, to impose on them this way wasn't right. And there went my eighteen days of privacy with the five people who meant the world to me. "We can't do that. I won't," I said. "I want privacy, a hotel."

"We're driving to Charleston – Fred and Winnie's – to stay there a few days before Orlando," he said. "I've made arrangements."

"Why didn't I know?" I said, clenching the remote control. "I

302

don't want that. That wasn't the plan. Miguel and I consulted you. Sure, Fred and Winnie are nice people, but I want only us. Just us!"

I wanted to smash the remote on his head, but he'd surely raise his voice and rouse the household and perhaps hit me back. So I sat there gritting my teeth. Many long minutes later, knowing that it was the only way to end the impasse, I apologized for my outburst. In bed, I expected some make-up sex. When he did nothing, I initiated it, but he turned away.

Was I too sex-starved? Why wasn't he? I couldn't see that he was overworked and broke pursuing a dream that had eluded him for so long – and recoiled at how I had been rejected, taking it as the biggest of insults. If he couldn't even pretend to desire me, what was I doing there clinging to him?

The next days, we acted like nothing was the matter and took the children around Chicago. When we flew to Louisiana, Anding was waiting for us at the Baton Rouge airport. He took the three boys with him in his van. Eric had Isabel and me in his white Toyota Tercel. Along the way, he said, "So, what should we do? I mean, where do you want to stay?"

I bit my lips and then said, "You created the problem, you fix it!"

"I'm trying to work with you, not start another fight!" His voice booming, he stepped on the gas. The evergreens lining the highway whizzed by in a blur.

"Didn't I say we should stay in a hotel?"

"What do we tell Anding?" he said.

"What do I know?"

"The problem with you is your pride. You always insist on your way!"

"Drop me off!" I said. "Right here." We were in the middle of a lonely interstate. He sped on, but if he had as much as slowed down the car, I'd have jumped right out.

We were quiet the rest of the way, but I decided that once I got hold of a phone, I'd call the airline and arrange to go back to Manila on the first plane out. I'd leave the children with their father and let him take care of them. I glanced at Isabel in the backseat. She looked horrified. Eric drove to two or three hotels so I could ask if they had room for six. They all did, but, alas, I couldn't afford their rates.

At Anding and Dely's, I worked hard to look happy and pleasant, helping in the kitchen and making nice, even if all I wanted was to disappear. I cried my eyes out at night and worried about facing them with swollen eyes in the morning.

After a couple of days at Anding's, we set out on a long road trip in a rented Buick Le Sabre, first to Atlanta and then on to Charleston. We did have new and fun experiences and visited with good friends and kin, but the children could hardly wait for Disney World. A week later, at long last, Orlando. Our first night alone as a complete family, like old times. The kids horsed around the roomy hotel suite – two bedrooms, living room and separate kitchen. I stuffed the groceries we had brought in the fridge.

"This is great," Eric said and brought out his papers. "I can work here."

"Won't you rest?" I said, rubbing his back. "You did a lot of driving today."

"Why don't you all go and I stay here and work tomorrow? I won't go on those rides anyway." he said.

"But we want you with us. We've missed you."

He thumbed his manuscript. "I've lost almost three weeks. I could make better use of tomorrow than sitting under the hot sun and gawking."

Trying not to lose my cool, I said, "Please? It won't be the same without you."

He relented and came with us to Disney World. As we pulled into the huge parking lot, a billboard about a new attraction stared down at us. "Alien Encounter!" the children chimed, saying that it was a high-tech horror ride, and that if they had to pick only one ride, this was the one.

Because he wasn't interested in most of the attractions, Eric stood by while the children and I were either queuing up for or screaming our heads off on the rides. He said at lunch, "Let's plan the rest of the day well so we don't miss the electrical parade at seven and the fireworks at ten."

Expecting shorter lines at dusk, the kids decided to do Alien Encounter during the two hours between the end of the parade and the fireworks. We watched the parade along a sidewalk close to Alien Encounter. Once the last of the glittering floats drove past, we rushed to Alien Encounter. The queue looked manageable, maybe thirty minutes. The five of us lined up while Eric stood by. After twenty minutes of inching along, we stepped inside the door and were shocked to see that inside the building, the line went much longer. A sign read: *90 minutes from this point.* It meant we were going to miss the fireworks.

"You have to choose," I told the children. "This ride or the fireworks?"

"This ride!" was unanimous.

"I should tell your father," I said but quickly changed my mind, thinking I'd be too shy to cut my way back in line, to have to negotiate a long snake of people and explain why I deserved to go ahead of them.

At last, The Ride. The kids were thrilled. I wasn't that crazy about it, but I loved hearing their shrieks. When it was over, we walked out of the building, dazed and chuckling. And there was Eric, standing where we'd left him, arms across his chest.

"My best ride ever!" Isabel said.

"It's over!" Eric said. "The fireworks – you missed them."

"It's fine," I said. "I asked them if…"

"I stood here looking like a fool!" he said.

"Very long line," I said. "Inside…"

"Just because I have no money, no one listens to me!"

I was too shocked to say anything. The boys looked at each other and then looked down. We all walked to the parking lot in silence, Isabel gripping my arm. We drove to the hotel in silence. We were all starved; my stomach turned, not from hunger but from indignation. At the hotel, Eric slumped on the living room couch. I

305

herded the children to the kitchen, laid food on the table and told them to eat.

Back in the living room, I glowered at Eric. "Why is it an issue, your not having money? Why shout about it?"

Silence.

"I worked hard to make this vacation happen," I continued. "To get the children to spend time with you. To give them great memories of their first trip to America, of Disney most of all. And you treat us like shit!"

Miguel walked in from the kitchen. "Daddy, don't do this," he said. "After all, Mommy and I did most of the work. We tried not to bother you."

"*Putang-ina!*" Eric said.

"Talk to me," Miguel said, "instead of calling my mother a whore!"

Eric made a fist at Miguel. I jumped between them before the father could hit his son. Eric grabbed the briefcase that held his paperwork and headed for the door. I pulled him back and begged him to stay. Eric froze at the door and after a few moments came back inside. I signaled for Miguel to leave the room, and he went to the kitchen.

Not uttering a word, Eric sat on the couch. I left him there and walked to the kitchen. Most of the food sat on the table untouched. I found the kids in their room, Isabel crying in bed, Mateo comforting her. Rico sat staring at the floor. "Did you eat?" I said. The boys nodded.

"Thank you for standing up for me," I told Miguel, who was in tears. "But we are treading on very shaky ground here. Your dad is stressed from his work, and we don't want to aggravate him any further. If I argue with him, we'll get nowhere."

"But he can't keep on treating you badly," he said. "And us, too. I worked so hard to put this vacation together. Why does he bark at us? And how could he have looked like an idiot watching the fireworks alone? Was anybody even looking at him?"

"I know, I know," I said, choking on my own tears. "I'm sorry."

I spent the next hour convincing the children to apologize to their father. I tried to explain that we were all to blame for not honoring our agreement to watch the fireworks together, although deep inside me, I didn't believe it. They didn't say much but merely shook their heads and gave me blank looks.

It was past midnight when we filed into the living room and sat around Eric. I started by apologizing for not letting him know – once we realized that the queue would take much longer than we'd first expected – that the children were giving up the fireworks in favor of the ride. Eric sighed every now and then, in between giving us impatient looks.

The next hour, the four children took turns saying sorry to their father, that they didn't mean to take him for granted. I spent another hour begging Eric to forgive us all. "Please," I said. "Let's all go to bed in peace. Let's not grind the already-sore spot that will surely be part of their Disney memories."

My husband didn't offer any explanation for his outburst. He didn't apologize either, and I had to be content with what looked like peace: no more angry words. It was close to daybreak when we went to bed. I lay there beside Eric, wondering if I'd ever get out of the quicksand I'd fallen into.

At Epcot Center the next day, the children clustered together, always asking me how much time they were allowed at each attraction they fancied. We took pictures with forced smiles pasted on our faces.

Eric warmed up to everyone a few days later, so when we left him in Baton Rouge, all seemed well again. Miguel flew back to Cambridge and the rest of us to Manila, each back to a quieter life.

I didn't sleep much during the long trip back home, repeatedly asking myself why I'd spent all that money only to be humiliated. The situation had clearly gone past toxic. How idiotic of me to ignore the signs. Eric hadn't wanted to come home, and yet I insisted on bringing all the kids to him. And he not only terrorized me but the children as well. Was he worth all the trouble, all the sacrifice? Was I obstinately fighting a long-lost battle?

Since I'd left BLD more than a year earlier, I had relaxed my tendency toward religious excess. I kept my belief in God, went to mass and prayed but without neglecting my health. I taught myself to separate God from preachers, who are human and therefore prone to making mistakes. Still, I remained fiercely committed to my marriage vows.

I had promised God I'd die fighting, and surely, I'd have tucked in loads of reward points by now for I knew He never slept.

CHAPTER 31

The first night back home in Manila, I pulled out a small book from the shelf: Ed Wheat's *How to Save Your Marriage Alone.* Jetlagged, I stayed up all night to re-read all sixty-odd pages, to check what I might not have done right. Written by a marriage counselor, the book teaches that the only mature choice in a turbulent marriage is to love one's spouse with *agape* love, the way God loves humankind, no matter – or especially – if the spouse doesn't show much interest in saving the relationship. Just the book for me, I had thought when I first saw it in a Christian bookstore. I'd taken it to heart and tried to follow its advice to love and keep on loving my spouse even 'in the depths of his waywardness.' Now, as I read it for the third time, I marked the areas that I thought I should learn deeper, until almost all of the pages gleamed in fluorescent yellow.

Armed with a renewed passion to love as Christ did, I volunteered to teach math at Tahanan ni Santo Domingo, a center that took in children who lived on the streets, and housed, counseled and educated them. The center was right next door to the church where I went for daily mass, so after the 6:30 a.m. mass,

I'd teach for an hour at Tahanan and then walk the three blocks to Guerrero to begin my workday. This was a good substitute for involvement with BLD, which had mostly required my evenings and weekends.

I taught fourth grade math to teen-aged boys who had been abandoned or orphaned or had run away from an abusive home. I wasn't rewarded with students who quickly learned long division, if they learned it at all, but with smiles from otherwise toughened faces the moment I entered the room. For once, I felt needed and appreciated, and the class became the high point of my day. I found it a good training ground for loving without expecting anything in return, for putting *agape* love into action.

But, of course, the days, the nights, had low points. Lonely points filled with doubt. One day, I phoned Dely, Eric's friend who had welcomed us to her home in Baton Rouge, and dared ask if Eric was seeing someone.

"I don't notice anything," she said, sounding concerned.

"Please don't tell him I asked," I said and thanked her.

Was that helpful? How can you be sure your husband is not being unfaithful unless you stuff him in a burlap sack that you drag around all day?

Later that year, Eric finished his doctorate and found a temporary teaching job at the University of Colorado in Boulder. Excited, I offered to attend his graduation and help him move, but he said it wasn't necessary. I had to content myself with photos he later mailed, of him in a black toga and tasseled cap, the resplendent colors of his hood telling the world that he was now a doctor. I daydreamed some more, about joining him soon, perhaps within the next year, and what better way to mark our new life together than to celebrate our twenty-fifth wedding anniversary in June, a few months away? I would ask Father Frank to officiate at a special mass where Eric and I would renew our wedding vows, with all our children behind us at the altar. And then we'd throw a simple party for family and friends at the Tahanan Center, with the street children as our special guests. Eric should be able to make it home because the school year would be over in Boulder by then.

Miguel would be the best man, Isabel the maid of honor, Mateo the ring bearer, and Rico the coin bearer. Should I wear the same wedding dress? I was sure it still fitted. Miguel would sing the Song of Ruth with Francis on the violin: *Wherever you go, I shall go; wherever you live, so shall I live*...This time around, I'd say my vows with full understanding and conviction.

Once Eric moved to Colorado, he told me what a beautiful place it was, that maybe I wanted to visit. Without thinking twice, I flew there to celebrate his birthday and mine and to travel with him to visit Miguel in Cambridge.

My husband's apartment was more comfortable than the one in Baton Rouge, which was only proper, because he was now earning more. As before, he spent weekdays at school while I kept house and waited for him in the evening with a warm meal. We spent the first weekend driving to the mountains, taking in the breathtaking sights, and gorging on mountain pie, which gave me a thrill, except that I didn't travel for the tours and treats. I traveled to be with him.

Always, always, Eric would turn in at night too exhausted to talk or touch, leaving me wondering why I'd been spending a fortune on long-haul flights only to be ignored this way. After dinner one night, we lay in bed watching TV, the TV that I wanted to smash for being more important to Eric than the things I wanted to say. During a commercial break, I said, "When do you think we can all come and move in with you?"

"I can't tell," Eric said. "My job is temporary. When the nine months are up, I don't know where I'll be."

"But can't you show them what a great teacher you are so they'll keep you?"

"It's not that simple, getting tenured here," he said.

"If they don't hire you afterwards, I'm sure you'll find something else."

"America is different. Competition is stiff, especially if you're not a native here."

I thought: So why not just come home? Why complicate things when a deanship is waiting for you at UP? "So, have you found what you came to look for in America?" I said instead.

"I don't know," he said.

I didn't want to push him further so I changed the subject. "I know what we'll do," I said. "June is coming up soon. We're turning twenty-five!"

"Hmm."

"I'm thinking of celebrating it back home," I said.

"I don't have time to come home."

What's a wedding without a groom? But I wasn't fazed. "Then the kids and I will come to you," I said, mentally saying good-bye to my meticulously-planned event in Manila. "Maybe you can ask the priest here if they do silver wedding ceremonies like back home. If not, if he can at least give us a special blessing after mass."

He turned away from me and said, "Let's sleep; busy day tomorrow."

After we'd spent a weekend with Miguel in Cambridge, I flew back to Manila, revising my silver wedding anniversary plans. It'd be a much simpler celebration in Boulder. What would I wear? The kids and Eric? I waited for word from Eric, who was to make an enquiry with the Boulder priest. Nothing. Three months later, when it was time to start packing, I e-mailed him to ask what was happening. His reply was quick and curt, asking why I had to impose on him my religious beliefs and practices. Why couldn't I just let him be?

Stunned and angry, I cried for a few days. Why didn't he just say no the first time? But because I wanted to save our forthcoming visit from disaster, I e-mailed back to apologize, explaining that because I had asked him much earlier and had gotten no reply, I only wanted to know the priest's answer so I'd know what clothes to pack. That if he didn't want any hoopla, I'd just bring all the kids over so we could spend time together.

As had become the norm, nothing much was said about the matter afterwards. In May, I flew to Colorado with the three children, without any big plans besides just being there. And as also had become the norm, Eric had planned road trips to fill most of our days, finding it a big waste of time and money if we flew halfway around the globe and did not see new places. Miguel flew in from Cambridge. While Eric worked on weekdays, I drove the children to nearby mountain parks and to picnic in campgrounds.

Once, when we got back too late to pick him up, Eric yelled at us because he had to walk the two miles home from school. When the boys took the initiative to clean his car, he admonished them for leaving scratches on it.

On the final weekend, Eric drove us toward the Flatiron Mountains. We had planned to explore as much of the area as possible, and to stay the night wherever we found ourselves at nightfall. We ended up at a Holiday Inn in a small town. In the morning, we went to mass at the closest Catholic church. Before his homily, the priest said, "Any couples celebrating their wedding anniversaries in the next few weeks? Please come forward for a blessing."

My heart jumped. Eric looked at me, his eyes asking if I wanted to. What a foolish question, I thought as I rose and headed for the altar. He followed me. Among the five couples, I felt proud that we'd been married the longest. The priest didn't ask us to say our vows but simply said a short blessing. As the congregation clapped their hands, I thought: See, if you don't like to do it, God finds a way. After the mass, we went on with the road trip, and I was smug all day, secretly savoring my victory.

On the way home, it was my turn to drive. All out of steam, the kids were asleep in their seats after a few minutes. Eric sat beside me to navigate. "Go to sleep. I'll wake you when I've gotten us lost," I said, poking fun at my addled sense of direction.

I'd enjoyed the times I'd driven the American highways before, because I could speed more safely, and for much longer stretches, than back in the Philippines. But I soon realized that tonight would be different, because most of the hundred miles zigged and zagged down the mountains, and with barely any streetlights to compensate for my night blindness. So I did the best I could to bring us safely down the unfamiliar terrain. Eric didn't sleep and tried to help with his constant terse reminders: You're holding up traffic, get on the turnout; you're going too fast; you're too close to the shoulder; dim your lights.

Trying not to be rattled, I told myself he was only concerned for our safety. I drove on, tightly grasping the wheel, my heart racing all the way. When we were all finally home safely, I again berated myself for making an expensive trip, for being the hopeless idiot that I was, for believing that I could love my husband into changing.

The next day, I was sad to say good-bye to Miguel, but I couldn't wait to get on the plane home to Manila.

One evening, I was on the phone with Miguel when he mentioned something about his father's new teaching job. "Are you sure?" I said. "How come I don't know? Maybe you misunderstood him."

"I'm sure it's what I heard him say," my son said.

"Oh," was all I could say.

I called Eric soon after. "Any news about your job search?" I said.

"I accepted the offer from UI-UC," he said.

"You had offers?" I said, because he hadn't mentioned any before. I only knew he was looking. "Where's that?"

"Illinois. Champaign is the name of the city. Urbana-Champaign."

"Hmm... when was this?"

"Last week."

"Why didn't you tell me?"

"I was busy... I forgot."

Without whining about why I hadn't been told of the big piece of news I'd long been praying for, I said good-bye and hung up.

It was drizzling on my drive to Don Bosco Batulao that mid-September morning. Soon, Mount Batulao loomed to my left. Shrouded in mist, the *Santo Entierro* silhouette looked deader than before. Did Christ truly rise on the third day? If so, where the hell was He?

Father Frank guided me through the weekend individual retreat. We'd meet twice each day, and then he'd send me off to think about things in the hilly garden. "Why are you here?" he said at the first meeting.

"I'd like to hear what God has to say about my marriage," I said. "I've hung on for twenty-five years, doing what I believed He wanted me to do. The first few years, I stayed because I needed a man. Then the children came, and whenever I felt like walking away, I'd tell myself that they needed a father. Now, over the last six years – which have been torture – it's become very doubtful that my husband can be a good husband and father. I mean, my first two reasons for holding on are totally shot. And I'm left with only one reason: I promised God I'd stay until death. But Father..."

"Go on," the priest said.

"I'm holding on to that vow by the tips of my fingernails," I said, showing him my nails. "If I decide to clip them..."

"Look here," he said, walking to the whiteboard. "There are three C's in a relationship..." He began to write as he explained to me the three C's: commitment, communication, and conflict resolution. Once he was certain I had understood the concepts, he asked me to grade each C on a scale of 1 to 100.

"I'm fully committed," I said, "so I'd give myself a hundred."

"No, you're not grading yourself alone. You're grading the

relationship. You can be a hundred and he a 70. You average it and get 85. Okay?"

Father Frank gave me a few minutes to put values on the three C's. When I was done, he wrote the numbers on the board – all dismal marks. "You see," he said, "this is a dead relationship. You have to face it. You can stay in it without changing anything, at status quo, but how long can you last?"

I recounted to him the countless times I had wanted to escape the marriage. When I first took Phenobarbital as a young mother, the times I was driving and trying to choose which truck to ram my car into when I could no longer bear the pain of the repeated infidelities. And on and on. "Sometimes, Father," I said. "I'd wanted to run away but I was afraid he wouldn't come looking for me. How embarrassing that would've been. So he'd hurt me and butter me up with sex, gifts, trips, and I was that easy to fix because I wanted us to be like when we first started. But now, I have nothing more to give. If I stay at status quo, I'll go crazy."

He motioned with his hands for me to keep talking.

"But God said to carry His cross, and that marriage is unto death."

"He meant carry the cross joyfully. Are you still joyful? Or do you need anaesthesia?"

"You mean I can have a way out of this?"

"When you get back to Manila, I'd like you to go to the Marriage Tribunal at the Archdiocese and inquire about a declaration of nullity."

"But I thought there are only two or three grounds. We were sane when we got married, no one forced us…You mean I have a case?"

"I'm not a canon lawyer. Just go and ask, so at least you're aware of your options."

I stayed up most of that night trying to absorb this new bit of information. I could actually be set free of my vows? Based on what I'd heard and read, I had always assumed that what God had put together, no man or mistress could put asunder. That the church made it almost impossible to obtain a nullity declaration. But would Father Frank suggest it if he was certain I had no case?

Commit all you want, but the relationship is dead, he was saying. It became crystal clear that my life now depended on my willingness to face reality, to go for broke, now or never, or altogether lose the last bit of self-respect I still had. The old church hymn based on the Biblical prophet Isaiah echoed inside me, giving me strength:

He shall feed His flock like a shepherd
He shall gather the lambs in His arms
And carry them in His bosom
And shall gently lead those that are with young.

By Sunday afternoon, I had written a long letter to Eric, my bravest ever. I first thanked him for the things that I sincerely appreciated about him. Then I said all the things I'd rehearsed in my mind for many years, or written in my prayer journal, or cried out while driving alone, but had kept to myself just to keep the peace. Like how I had to put up with his temper, his infidelity, how he never apologized. How deceitful of him to pretend he was leaving for a holiday in the States when in fact he intended to move there. How he never really talked! In the end, I made it clear that if we were to proceed as a family, we needed to be physically together wherever it would be most feasible for everyone. That if this reunion wasn't going to happen by the end of the school year – that is, in ten months – I'd separate from him, but I needed him to send financial support for the children. I demanded that he make a clear stand and let me know about it in two months.

I sent the letter by Federal Express the next day and then began to pray ever so fervently that Eric would say yes, he wanted to keep his family. When I was sure he'd received the letter, I waited for him to call. He didn't. I phoned him a few times but he didn't pick up. My insomnia got worse. I became more anxious and withdrawn.

A month later, Supertyphoon Iliang struck the country, leaving a hundred dead, as well as close to a billion pesos in property damage. The howling wind woke me in the pitch-dark night, and I groped my way to the children's rooms to make sure they were all right. No electric power meant no access to news. The phone was dead. I waited out the storm, praying until daylight, all the while listening for one of the trees in the backyard to topple over and crush the roof.

At daybreak, I went out to survey the damage. My roof was intact, thank God, and all the backyard trees, though wobbly, were still standing. Debris littered the streets: twigs, garbage bins, iron roofing sheets, snapped power cables. My neighbor's majestic mango tree lay on its side blocking the road, its gigantic roots up in the air. The front yard was a big mess: driftwood tree trunks holding Eric's precious orchids had toppled over plant pots, the orchids entangled with weeds, *bonsai* pots and trunks broken, a snake slithering in a puddle, the concrete pathway and carport all muddied. I had a handyman come over to prune the trees to a safe height. I told the maids to put the *bonsai* and orchids back in their places and wash down the carport, and then I drove through the flooded streets to bring used clothing and canned food to a nearby relief center.

A few days later came Loleng, an even more furious typhoon, killing a couple of hundred more in landslides and floods. My house and my family, thank God yet again, survived the fury unhurt. But the garden looked more hopelessly chaotic this time. When all was quiet once more, I sat on my favorite garden chair watching the maids clean up. Marya came to sit beside me. "Look," I said. "Is this all we do, fear for our lives, then help the dead or dying and pick up debris?"

"Why don't you and I redo the house and the garden?" she said. "Your style, your way." Save for the crucifixes and a couple of religious paintings that I'd added, Eric's collection of antiques and paintings – what had survived the spiritual cleansing – still adorned the house in the same way he'd left them six years before. And the only thing I'd done with his garden was to make sure the *bonsai* and orchids had enough sun and water so that they didn't die. Even when I thought they needed some pruning, I didn't mess with the *bonsai* for fear of ruining them. Eric had books on how to train and prune an already-stunted tree's roots and branches in the Japanese tradition. He used only expensive pots and tools and went to forests with other enthusiasts to hunt for trees of just the right maturity and aesthetic value. I found it too complicated and expensive a hobby. Too much work. Why not just let the poor tree grow to its full glory?

Same thing with the orchids. I didn't dare use the hormone sprays that Eric had left among his gardening supplies, because I didn't know how. And why pamper a wild plant with all sorts of artificial sprays when it has thrived unattended in the jungle for centuries?

"I think," Marya said, "it will do you good to have his stuff out of sight. Tell me what to do and I'll be your slave."

"No, he's coming home soon," I said. "Let's leave the house and garden as they are, the way he wants them."

The FedEx envelope arrived on a late Friday afternoon in November, just when I was winding down at work. I closed my office door, sat down and slowly opened the cardboard envelope. My husband's letter was a bit shorter than mine. He began by saying that he could hardly concentrate on his work after receiving my letter, and that he'd actually been afraid I'd one day give him an ultimatum. He said that I had shown the world how to love and thanked me for all my love despite his shortcomings. That he had never been a good father and perhaps would never be one. So far, the letter looked hopeful to me. My hands shaking, I tripped over the words, skimming through to find what I wanted to see.

But what I wanted to see wasn't there. Somewhere in the middle were the words I'd dreaded. He wasn't ready to ask me to give up my stable job in Manila and join him in the States. In answer to my standing question about why he wouldn't just come home, he wrote that after all the sacrifices he'd gone through, he couldn't abandon the life he had started in the States. And although he intended for us to be together as a family in the future, because I was giving him an ultimatum, he had to choose his life in America. *After all the pain I have given you, it's time you set out to find elsewhere the happiness you deserve.* Nevertheless, he still wanted to be part of the children's lives and earnestly asked me not to vilify him in their eyes.

A few close friends at work took me out drinking. "It's his loss," they said.

"But I love him," I said, in between sobs. "I love him. I can't possibly find happiness with someone else."

"Listen," one of them said, "you're one of the most intelligent, wisest women I know. And you still turn a lot of heads. So why won't you stop chasing a moron who's chosen to throw his gold away?"

"But he's my husband."

"More beer, you need more beer!" He pushed a new mug toward me. I picked it up, clinked it against his, and downed it in one big gulp.

Around four a.m, they took me home dead drunk. I lay in bed feeling nothing, watching the ghoulish shadows from the garden until sunlight began to stream through the jalousies.

Two weeks later, when some of the numbness wore off, I went to Father Frank. "Well, at least he's clear about where he stands," he said.

"But what about miracles, Father? I still believe in miracles. I'm willing to do whatever it takes to save this. I've invested all of my being and cannot turn back."

He gave a deep sigh. "Of course God works miracles. That's what we priests preach. But sometimes, the more prudent way is to recognize – and acknowledge – something that is not humanly possible and work from there… instead of spending all your energies waiting for a miracle. *Nemo dat quod non habet.* You cannot give what you do not have. Sometimes a man is simply not capable of loving in a certain kind of way, most likely because he's been wounded, too. Look on it as his handicap."

"You mean, it's like I'm ordering gourmet food from the school cafeteria," I said, "and upset when they don't have it?"

"Exactly. You're very smart but hopelessly dumb," he said, pressing on my temple with his forefinger. "We nag God to answer our prayers and refuse to hear it when He says no."

"You're saying I should give up."

"I'm saying go to the Marriage Tribunal to inquire. And knowing you, don't keep on looking back. Just look straight ahead, will you?" He thrust his face forward and widened his eyes at me, looking like a grownup playfully making a scary face to a little kid.

I smiled weakly.

He gave me a name and a phone number, that of a priest who conducted some kind of retreat. "This should do you good," he said.

A couple of weekends later, I was back at the Don Bosco retreat house in Batulao. With a small group of strangers, I sat for a few talks, like a workshop, about the stages of a man's emotional development. Very enlightening. The part I loved most was when, under the night sky, we were each given an old mattress and told to do whatever the hell we wanted. My mind flew some forty years back when I was small and would take out my frustration on Auntie Celina's mattress. Mom had always said that I was her angriest child. Eric had often complained of how my 'eyes could kill' when I chose to be silent to keep the peace, and I had faulted him for it. I didn't realize then that anger and hurt, like smoke, could never be swallowed, that they would always find a way out. Tonight, I couldn't believe that I'd just been given my very own legit tantrum instrument. Wasting no time, I battered my mattress with punches – I would have stabbed it to bits if I'd had a knife – all the while yelling curses at the black dead-Christ mountain. I stopped every now and then to listen to what the sixteen-year-old suicidal kid next to me was shouting, feeling sorrier for him than for myself. When my knuckles and my throat were all spent, I lay down and allowed the stars to rock me to sleep.

At the Tribunal, they gave me a thick packet of documents and forms that I skimmed through and put away. It's Christmastime, I told myself. Instead, I went through the motions of Christmas like a zombie – buying countless presents, sending cards, partying and getting quite drunk and managing to be at mass early the next morning, and then traveling to Montaña with the kids to be with Mom and my siblings.

I told my mother about my plan to file for an annulment. "Maybe he walked out six years ago hoping I'd take a hint," I said. "Maybe I was simply too dense, too stupid, to understand."

Mom was intently looking at me, then looking away, her hands clasped under her chin – small brown hands with bulging veins and fingers bent by arthritis. A few moments later, she turned to me and said, "I don't know."

When my mother said that, it meant she didn't agree but didn't want to be offensive.

"See, Christmas Day came and went, and he didn't even call," I said. "Not even to greet his children. I went to the Marriage Tribunal. It's a tedious process getting an annulment – many forms to fill out, endless questions to answer. They told me that a church annulment doesn't take care of the legal issues of property and child custody and support. That it only declares the sacrament of marriage as not having been valid from the start. And if I want the legal things resolved, I also need to file for an annulment with the civil court, which is another long story."

"What about the children?"

322

"I will have to speak to them one by one, to make them see..." I didn't finish my sentence because my mother's somber face made me doubt that I was on the right track.

"God is kind," Mom was saying.

On New Year's Eve, after the midnight meal, while firecrackers rattled outside, Eric called. "Did you get my letter?" he said, sounding so far away. It had been more than three months since I'd last heard the deep masculine voice that had always sent my heart fluttering, as it did now.

"More than a month ago," I said. "Are you sure you meant what you wrote?"

"I'm confused," he said. "I need some space. I've tons of work to do, too."

"Take care of yourself," I said, a glimmer of hope warming my weary heart. "I love you."

"Bye."

And so I waited some more. Two months later, seeing that I was waiting in vain, I thought of how best to tell my children about the annulment. But each time I attempted to do it, I'd buckle under the fear of hurting them. After all, it isn't just every child's wish to have a happy family; it's every child's need. Who was I to rob mine of their chance for one?

Once more, I picked up the Marriage Tribunal packet and started writing the required case history. I wrote and wept and wrote and wept. After three harrowing months, reading what I'd written, I decided that growing old with Eric would be too much work. That the author Ed Wheat was dead wrong; no one could save a marriage alone.

One day, six months after receiving Eric's devastating letter, I told myself: Move now or lose your sanity. I phoned Mom. "I've decided to push through with the church annulment," I said.

"But why, *anak ko*?" Her voice was soft. "Your children…"

"Mom, I've been thinking and praying," I said. "I'm grateful that you endured all that pain and humiliation from Dad and kept quiet about it, for our sakes, to spare us from shame. But by doing that, you were showing me that it's okay for a woman to be treated like a dirty rag. So what did I do? What did Chona do? Exactly as you did. And I'm afraid she and I have been unwittingly teaching our children the same thing."

My mother was silent, but I could hear her sigh. "You've managed to take care of your family alone all this time," she finally said. "Can't you just go on that way? Why, are you planning to marry again?"

"It's not that, Mom. Marriage is the farthest thing on my mind now, for who wants to be burned again? But I'd like to know what God thinks, because I made a vow to Him. If He sets me free, then I can do things that a single woman does with a clear conscience, without worrying about my soul and what people might say. You taught me that, you know – what will people say. And if … what if I find someone who might be good to me, good for me? I don't want to be restrained by my married status and rush to get an annulment."

"*Balasang ko*," my mother said, "*no adda mangdungdungngo kenka a ket nasayaat.*"

The Ilocano word *dungngo* doesn't easily lend itself to translation, the closest English words being *treasure* and *cherish*. The word transported me back to my childhood, to the old love song and lullaby that every Ilocano knew by heart, *Dungdungnguenkanto Unay-unay: I will deeply cherish you, tenderly rock you to sleep in a hammock....* On rare mornings, my parents would cuddle on the floor mat while I folded the blankets, and I'd catch Dad calling Mom his *dungngo,* or the *love of his life.* When my young siblings napped in the back patio hammock, Dad required the nanny to keep close watch, always ready to swat bugs away, and if he later found the toddler with a mosquito bite, he'd reprimand the nanny. Whenever I was sick, he bought me expensive *sangkís* oranges, peeled them and put them in my mouth, one wedge at a time, stroking my hair afterward. My father tried, I could see, with his own brand of *dungngo* for his wife and kids. As did Eric, who, for a year or so at the start, had smothered me with *dungngo*, said he'd die without me, doted on our babies. What had happened? Why did they – my father and my husband – give their *dungngo* elsewhere? Wasn't my mother good enough? Wasn't I? Weren't my siblings and my kids?

Of course, by now, my *brain* knew better than to simply fix the blame on myself for not being good enough, for Father Frank was quite clear about Eric himself having a handicap. Although I had suspected that there was something grossly wrong with my husband, I had believed that whatever it was could be fixed by prayerful love and sacrifice, the kind that comes close to unconditional love. Mom must have thought the same thing of Dad. Still, my *heart* couldn't easily shake off the most convenient escape of blaming myself, especially after having tried to keep on loving for so long and nevertheless seeing no big changes.

My mother was saying, *My young lady, wouldn't it be wonderful to have someone who would cherish you?* Her words punctured my bag of tears, for not only did they tell me how much she longed for me to be happy, but also that she might as well have been speaking for herself.

"Someone who won't turn me into a *bonsai*?" I said, wiping my eyes and giving a faint chuckle. "Are you sure it's okay with you?"

"If God says so," she said.

"Thank you, thank you, Mommy!"

I gathered all my strength to tell my children one by one. Miguel wasn't surprised and said not to worry about him, he was now emotionally independent. Mateo was anxious that Eric's family might stop being our family, and I assured him they won't. Rico shrugged and said we'd been alone for a long time anyhow so what was the difference. It was Isabel who was totally blindsided and had the hardest time with the news, letting out a wolf wail and breathlessly sobbing for a long, long time. It broke my heart and I wanted to die.

I gave the orchids and *bonsai* to Eric's father, who was also an enthusiast.

The following weeks, I had the garden landscaped into something much easier to maintain and had a major facelift done on the house, repainting the exterior, changing the windows, bathrooms, kitchen, walls, and blinds. Bought myself a new bed. Cleared Eric's closet and bookshelves and carted everything, including his antiques and knick-knacks, to the storage room. Finally, I planted a hedge of *sampaguita* close to my bedroom, so their sweet perfume would waft in in the morning and perhaps bring back the freshness of the *sampaguita*-perfumed days of my youth.

I took a deep breath and looked straight at the long road ahead.

CHAPTER 32

At last, I filed for a declaration of nullity with the Catholic Church. Shortly after I told Eric of my decision, he filed for divorce in Illinois, explaining that he just wanted to be clear about his status with U.S. Immigration. Since the Philippines would not recognize the U.S. divorce, I decided to also file for a civil annulment in Manila, in order to take care of the legal issues of child support, custody and property. If I was going to end the marriage, I might as well do it thoroughly.

Then I faltered yet again. Especially for the sake of my daughter whose mournful cries haunted me, I wanted to take everything back. I told Eric I was willing to do whatever it took to have us all together again, that I didn't mind forfeiting all the fees I had paid for the annulment cases I had filed. But he said that although he could easily say yes to please me, he knew in his heart that he'd never be able to be the kind of husband and father I needed him to be.

One afternoon three months later, a FedEx envelope sat at my office desk. Inside was a divorce decree from a court in Illinois.

This was it. Stung, my heart flew back ages ago to Dad's sudden death. I had cried all night during the long drive to Montaña. At the sight of the *atong* log smoldering in front of our house to announce the death, I had wanted to run away, telling myself my father could not be dead. Now, I asked myself: What's the reason for the *atong* tradition in Montaña, in all of Ilocos? Is it to burn away your final bits of hope and denial and force you to do the dirty work of moving on?

One crisp February morning, I went to see Father McGuire, an Irish priest and psychotherapist assigned by the Tribunal to review my case. "It's clear from what you've written that this was a lost cause from the start. Didn't you see?" he said, thumbing my fifty-page case history.

Lost cause from the start? Did I hear right? "No, Father," I said. "I was under his spell. I can't explain. I felt that I would die without him."

"But now that you've decided to ask for nullity, do you regret marrying and hanging on for how many years, twenty-five?"

"Twenty-six, Father. If I look at my children and see how they've turned out in spite of our problems, it was all worth it. They're my biggest blessings. I cannot say I regret having married. No, not at all. I love them dearly, they love me back. Dearly too, if I may add."

"So now that you've begun to see reality, do you think you'll manage life without a man?"

"Why yes, Father, of course. After all, I've been a single mother for seven-plus years now."

"What if you meet someone who somehow fits your idea of the right man for you, but not a hundred percent? Let's say, one who has seventy percent of the things you need in a man, would you consider having a relationship with him?"

"Seventy? I'm coming from maybe twenty-five..."

"You're coming from zero!" His smile was kind.

"Oh," I said, "then seventy should be more than great. But

Father, I don't want to go into anything serious until my youngest child turns eighteen. I want to show my children that they're my priority at this time."

"Okay, but once your kids are all grown, you should focus on taking care of you," he said, pointing the case history binder at me.

It was strange to hear those words from a priest. Where had Father McGuire been all this time? I grew up hearing about selfless love, charity, patience, and a long list of other virtues. I had brought my case to several priests and had been told to persevere in loving, that marriage was unto death, and I had kept to my straitjacket until Father Frank gave me wide wiggle room by hinting it might be possible to be set free of my vows. Then suddenly, here was a blast of fresh air, a priest telling me it was okay to focus on myself.

Father McGuire did not promise I'd win my case. He said that his job was to submit his assessment to the Tribunal, and the judges would decide. Church annulments normally took three to five years, and civil annulments two or three. It was now mostly a waiting game.

One *atong* in, two to go.

CHAPTER 33

In Montaña the next Christmas, after a picnic lunch, I sat at the table next to Manang Aning as she held her sleeping grandchild. The heat of the noonday sun pierced through our shed's thatch roof, and, in the next shed, youngsters giggled and gyrated to Ricky Martin's blaring *La Vida Loca*. Our children were splashing each other in the surf.

"How's Hong Kong?" I said. She'd been a domestic there for fifteen years.

"Same," she said. "Job pays well, but I miss my family. Where's Eric?"

"He's been in the States since 1992," I said, "eight years now. It's a long story." I didn't volunteer the information about the annulments and the divorce to people in Montaña, thinking it was too much work to have them see my point. Besides, their most likely reactions would be disdain, pity or blame for the poor abandoned wife, none of which I needed. I decided to change the subject. "Remember my conference in Hong Kong, when you came to my hotel?"

"Oh that," she said and chuckled. "You'd said your room was

823 but I knocked on 832. The door opens and here's this bald man in a bathrobe."

"Who happens to be my boss," I said.

We laughed. Then we fell silent. I looked out to the sea. The breakers, gentle an hour ago, hit the shore more fiercely with the rising tide. I itched to join our families in the water but didn't want to waste this rare chance to be alone with Manang Aning. I'd written her the letter shortly after seeing her in Hong Kong and had not been with her since.

On the sand, Mom and Manang Zenay played with the smaller kids, chattering and laughing like the best of friends, making me wonder if I should bring up the long-buried subject of Daddy at all.

I thought of the time when I was nine and discovered that Dad was sleeping with Manang Zenay. And how, as our family grew over the years, two of Manang Zenay's sisters – Manang Aning and Rosita – moved in, too. Manang Aning was thirteen when she first arrived. After three years, she ran away with a boy, but Dad went to bring her back. Five years later, she ran away again and got married.

"Did you receive my letter?" I said after a few moments.

My cousin's brows furrowed. She tinkered with the Tupperware that held our lunch leftovers. Her hair had gray streaks, but her dimpled face was still charming. In the water, our children shrieked as a wave approached, then hurled their bodies against the crest. I dug my toes into the warm sand.

"Been waiting for this chance," she said. "I got your letter, but you know I can't write."

I put my hands under my thighs and gripped the bench. "Tell me," I said, my chest pounding. "Did Dad force you?"

She let out a heavy sigh and whispered, "He put a gun in my mouth."

"He what?" My temples throbbed, and I began to tremble. "What? Say that again!"

She looked at me with blank eyes. "The first time," she said, "everyone else had left for the day. Your father was getting dressed for work. I was doing laundry when he called me into his room.

'Come get my dirty clothes,' he said. I went in. He pushed me down on the bed." She began to sob.

"He put a gun in my mouth," she continued. "He said, 'Tell anyone and I'll kill you.' Then he forced himself on me." I saw terror and grief in her eyes.

Was I hearing this right? How could my dignified father do that? He kept a revolver only for self-defense. His hunting rifle, the one I'd kept after he died, was for shooting birds in the mountains.

"His friend Blas, he was evil," Manang Aning went on. "I heard him tell your father, 'Use a gun, it never fails.' They'd sit in the patio and drink and laugh a lot. Did you hear what happened to him? The bastard."

"Abogado Blas?" I said. "Wasn't he gunned down in the house of one of his mistresses?"

"God catches up with evil men sometimes. The case remains unsolved, but who cares?"

Stunned, I couldn't fully grasp what my cousin was saying. Dad was violent? He was fearsome, yes, but he spoke very softly when he was angry, didn't he? Trying to ignore the buzzing in my head, I sat still and stared at Manang Aning, not knowing what to say.

"Your father came at me every chance he got," she continued.

"Did you tell anyone? Your parents?"

"How could I? He made me watch him shoot one of his dogs when it went rabid."

"And your two sisters… I wrote them too, but they didn't reply."

She was shaking her head, her face now with a stoic look.

"No wonder you ran away," I said. "You were only sixteen, right?"

"The first time, yes, I was sixteen, with Jacinto. Your father came with his gun to bring me back home…" Her voice trailed off. "You can ask your mom or Sonny. I saw him peeking through the door then, just a small boy. We all sat in the living room of your house, the old house. Your dad had Jacinto and his parents come over. He asked Jacinto what he'd done to me and when he refused to answer, your dad beat him with the butt of his gun, right there in your living room. I don't want to remember it... He was down on the floor, bleeding. I had no choice. I didn't want to go back but I had no choice."

"I thought Dad used his gun only for hunting," I said.

"Ah, but you were always away in Manila," she said. "The whole town knows how much your father loved his gun. Ask your brothers, your mom. One time, someone threw stones at the roof of your house. He went out and fired shots into the air. The police came, but even they were afraid to confront him."

My head felt swollen and hot. When I finally blinked, the tears rushed down my cheeks. Up ahead, the waves roared.

The next day, I got up before sunrise and found Mom puttering in the kitchen as usual. I took a candle and a box of matches from a cupboard. "I'm going to Dad's grave, Mom," I said and headed for the door.

"Won't you eat first?" she said. "Why don't you wait for your sisters and Francis?"

"They're still in dreamland; I won't be long." Before I could reach the front door, I turned back and stood by the kitchen island. "I spoke to Manang Aning yesterday. Know what she told me?"

She turned off the faucet and looked at me. "Well?"

"Dad used his gun to force her."

She said nothing for a few moments, just stood there wiping her hands. "What a shameless, shameless man..."

"Tell me, Mommy, did Daddy use his gun a lot? Manang Aning says he got mad when someone threw stones at our roof."

"He went out to the street and then fired shots into the air," Mom said.

"What did you do?"

"Who could stop him? I cringed in fear upstairs, praying."

"And he beat up Jacinto in front of his parents?"

Mom bit her lips and nodded.

"Did Dad ever use his gun on you, say, in an argument?"

Her reply was quick. "No. If you recall, he didn't even yell at me."

"I'm glad. At least he gave you that much respect. Or that little."

My mother looked out the window by the sink. "He had his pants tailored in such a way that the right front pocket was bigger than the left to hold his gun. Big enough so he could fire the gun from inside the pocket if he had to. He carried it when he felt there might be trouble and he'd be forced to defend himself. And when you were…"

She abruptly stopped and picked up a sponge.

I moved closer to her. "When what? Mommy, please."

"When he came to take you back long ago. Remember when Miguel was a baby and your husband fell for a student?"

"Of course."

"Your dad was furious, naturally. When he came to talk to Eric and his family, he had the gun with him."

Silenced, I ran out the door and crossed the small bridge over the ditch. Our farmer neighbor and his son squatted before a bonfire of dead leaves, warming their hands. I walked the two kilometers to the cemetery on Rizal Street under the faint street lights. Some early jeepneys were on the way to Laoag. Newly-planted rice soaked in the mud paddies, filling the cool air with the fragrance of moist soil and fresh grass. I could hear Daddy's long-ago voice: Don't go out the gate; don't walk into the paddies; don't ride a bike; don't play in the ditch. And then his later commandment: Don't fall in love too early or you'll end up eating your tears.

Dad's grave hadn't changed much since we'd buried him twenty-one years ago. The statue of the Crucified Christ still stood there, keeping watch over him. Mom's lilies had grown lush, and pink *cadena de amor* had crept around them. Fingers shaking, I lit the candle, let it drip onto the base of the tombstone and stuck it on the wax pool. I sat on the wall staring at Dad's epitaph: *Loving memories never die as years roll on and days pass by.*

Stinging heat burst from my chest and then crawled up and down my entire body. A wrecking ball was banging at my ribs. "Why?" I said and wiped my eyes and nose with the neck of my T-shirt.

Why? You loved to say you were always right. So tell me what's right about raping women in your family. Are you down there? Why did you die before I could tell you what a loathsome beast you were? You loved to call people beasts who had bad manners. Well, how about you?

It took me a long time to forgive your sleeping around, your gambling. And treating Mom like trash while making the world think you were the perfect married couple. But this? How much time will I need to be able to forgive this new horror, that you drew most of your power from a gun? How could you have fooled me into believing you could never go wrong? I hate you!

I wonder if Mommy kept silent because you also threatened her with your almighty gun. I hated her and you for being slaves to what people might think or say, for obsessing about a good reputation. But maybe Mom simply didn't want her children to be orphaned on account of your rage. Did you threaten to kill her if she told anyone about you?

What's wrong with me? Why did God give me a pervert for a father? Should I be grateful that you touched only my cousins and not me or Chona? Or did you? Is that why I'm hopelessly screwed up?

Do you know how many heartaches I've had with the man I chose to love? Where were you when he failed me over and over? Why did you die?

You should've seen me make you really, really proud. Executive vice president and actuary, commanding five hundred people. Big-league enough for you? Four beautiful and brilliant children. How about that for a daughter, huh? Except that she's now a lonely single mother. Like Mommy was, even when you were alive. Just like I promised you, I looked after Mom and my siblings, and I'm helping Chona raise her children. She has her own load of heartaches too, did you know that? And Marya can't seem to find the right man. Look, your three daughters, all cursed!

At least Sonny had the good sense to mend his ways. But Francis? He grew up in fear, confused about his identity, knowing you were ashamed to have a sissy for a son.

For the longest time I was afraid of many things. Of you, for one. But no longer. You should've lived to see me end an impossible marriage, something your wife should've done too. Do you realize how much she sacrificed for you? Did you ever thank her?

Why did you die? Why do you refuse to die? Did you ever have a clue how much I loved you? And still love you!

I'm tired of hating you, Daddy. Can we just have peace?

The candle had long burned out when I could say and cry no more. I looked up at Jesus and then bowed my head and closed my eyes. I told Him it was draining to hate someone I badly needed to love. In reply, I could hear Him say that forgiveness is the only way out. So I prayed for the grace to forgive. Who knew how long it would take, but I was going to do it. When I rose to leave, my legs tingled, but my heart had slowed its violent pounding.

On the walk home, sunlight streamed through the acacias lining the road. To the east, the fields stretched out to the foot of the mountains, punctuated only by mango and banana groves and a scattering of small houses. Mount Pecho stood tall and proud, a deep jungle green. Behind it, the distant layers of the Cordilleras looked like a herd of pale blue doe chasing their fawns. The horizon bloomed into bands of tangerine above bands of yellow, as though God on his morning walk was strewing peeled *sangkis* oranges on the mountaintops, while right behind Him, an angel threw out the rinds.

I picked up my pace until the edge of the rice paddies. As I had wanted to do ever since childhood, I stepped onto a *tambak*, balancing myself on the doughy wall of earth between the muddy pools, hundreds of rice shoots shimmering at my feet.

ACKNOWLEDGMENTS

Special Thanks To...

- Beth Kaplan and Christine Pountney, my writing coaches, for showing me how to tell a story and for gently but firmly squeezing the best stories out of me.

- Aimee Alcantara, Kathy Coleman, and Gemma Nemenzo, for their helpful insights and suggestions on the early versions of the manuscript.

- My early writing teachers – Mom, Agnes Vea, and Helen Ladera – as well as the later ones – Joyce White, Alexandra Leggat, Christy Ann Conlin, Ronna Bloom, Lee Gowan, Ken McGoogan, and Kent Nussey – for generously lighting my candle with theirs.

- Amy DeMoulin and L'Arche Toronto, for supporting my writing.

- Emile Sanchez, for creating the perfect cover.

- My parents and siblings. Whenever I'm utterly lost, I think of home, *back home*, to get my bearings and then take my best guess at where north might be.

ABOUT THE AUTHOR

Dorotea F. Romero is a mother of four and a grandmother of two and eagerly awaits more grandchildren. She devotes a lot of energy to L'Arche, a charity that looks after people with developmental disabilities. Based in Toronto, she frequently travels to the Philippines where she is deeply rooted.

Made in United States
Troutdale, OR
01/22/2025